# XOXO, Summer

*New York Times* Bestselling Author

S.L. SCOTT

 Published in the United States of America. ISBN: 978-1-962626-62-0

*To those who fall too fast and love too much, that squishy, beautiful heart of yours is perfect just the way it is. XOXO* 🩶

# FOLLOW ME

To keep up to date with her writing and more, visit S.L. Scott's website: <u>www.slscottauthor.com</u>

To receive the newsletter about all of her publishing adventures, free books, giveaways, steals and more:

https://geni.us/SLScottNL

Follow on IG: https://geni.us/IGSLS
Follow me on TikTok: https://geni.us/SLTikTok
Follow on Bookbub: https://geni.us/SLScottBB

## ALSO BY S.L. SCOTT

Called **"The Most Romantic Book Ever,"** We Were Once, is available and FREE in Kindle Unlimited.

We Were Once

The international sensation, **Best I Ever Had**, has won readers over and is available in ebook, audio, and paperback, and Free in Kindle Unlimited.

Best I Ever Had

**Audiobooks on Audible - CLICK HERE**

**Peachtree Pass Series (Stand-alones)**

Long Time Coming /Lead Me Knot /Small Town Frenzy

**The Westcott Series (Stand-alones)**

*Swear on My Life / Never Saw You Coming*

*Forgot to Say Goodbye / When I Had You*

*Never Have I Ever / Speak of the Devil - Faris Family*

**Hard to Resist Series (Stand-Alones)**

*The Resistance / The Reckoning*

*The Redemption / The Revolution / The Rebellion*

**The Crow Brothers (Stand-Alones)**

*Spark / Tulsa / Rivers / Ridge*

*The Crow Brothers Box Set*

**DARE - A Rock Star Hero (Stand-Alone)**

**New York Love Stories (Stand-Alones)**

*Never Got Over You / The One I Want / Crazy in Love*

*Head Over Feels / It Started with a Kiss*

**The Everest Brothers (Stand-Alones)**

*Everest / Bad Reputation / Force of Nature*

*The Everest Brothers Box Set*

**The Kingwood Series**

*SAVAGE / SAVIOR / SACRED / FINDING SOLACE*

*The Kingwood Series Box Set*

**Playboy in Paradise Series**

*Falling for the Playboy / Redeeming the Playboy*

*Loving the Playboy*

*Playboy in Paradise Box Set*

**Stand-Alone Books**

*Then There Was You*

*Best I Ever Had*

*We Were Once*

*Love and Warner*

*Along Came Charlie*

*Missing Grace*

*Finding Solace*

*Until I Met You*

*Lessons on Love*

*Lost in Translation*

*Sleeping with Mr. Sexy*

*Morning Glory*

# XOXO, SUMMER

S.L. SCOTT

slscott

# PROLOGUE

FAITH SEASON

## *TWELVE SUMMERS AGO . . .*

"Shh," I whisper, pressing my finger to my lips. I'm met with an array of giggles—my favorite sound in the world. *My four girls.*

The quilt topples over my forehead until I push up with my hands to see their beaming smiles and eyes bright from the glow of the battery-operated lantern in the middle of our little circle. "You'll wake your dad."

Charlie's wide awake and will want the full rundown when I return to bed, but the girls like to feel like they're getting away with something, even if it is innocent fun.

Autumn's red hair trails over her shoulders as she anchors the blanket on the bedpost again to support the fort.

My littlest's laughter bursts as if it's too much to contain when Spring scores a match in Go Fish. She's eight, so it probably is. She's a lightning strike of a personality, commanding attention even when she's not demanding it from her sisters. Winter clamps her hand over Spring's mouth quicker than she gives up the card. “Be quiet, Spring.”

“It’s okay, Winter,” I whisper. “We can still have fun. We just need to keep the volume lowered so Daddy can sleep. He has an early meeting in the morning.”

Spring sticks her tongue out at her older sister and then giggles, quieter this time.

“Do you have a peacock, Mom?” Summer asks. I glance from my cards to my oldest. My sweet Summer with eyes that match the blue skies to her golden sunshine hair. Reaching over, I caress her cheek and laugh. “Go fish.” My kindhearted child smiles, bringing one to my face as well. She’s been my buddy, my sweet girl, and a great helper over the years. She gives up too much of her time, so I hope one day she can find the joy in living life for herself.

I’ve lived my whole life trying to walk a straight line that was never there, trying to blend in since my mom always stood out in this small town. Once I realized I didn’t need to live up to other people’s expectations, I found my own happiness and never looked back.

Looking at my daughter, I’m not sure when my Summer girl started growing up on me, but here she is, all of fourteen and carrying the world on her shoulders. “Hey, you,” I whisper, contorting my face. It takes a nudge of an elbow to finally win a laugh out of her. I wrap my arm around her, pulling her close. Teenagers are tough to amuse, so I count this as a victory. “I love you.”

“Love you, Mom.”

I whisper, “I want you to always remember that you’re strong in mind and resilient, but that doesn’t mean you have to walk life’s path alone.”

“Who will I walk with?” So sweet and innocent.

“That’s in the hands of destiny. You’ll know when you

meet them." I turn to meet her eyes. "They'll be the one who is there when you need someone most."

When I release her, she smiles, and my heart clenches. Time is a fleeting traitor. They're all growing so fast, faster than the blink of an eye. But I see the young woman she's trying so hard to become that these moments of frivolous fun feel more precious.

I take my necklace off, the little gold chain with the tiny butterfly, and hold it out. "I want you to have this."

Her eyes widen as she stares at the small pendant. "But that's your favorite necklace."

"That's why I want you to have it, Summer." She angles her back to me and sweeps her hair to the side. I clasp it around her neck, and when she turns back, the butterfly lying against her skin, I know I made the right decision. It wasn't planned, but seeing the genuine smile it brings to her face and the way her eyes turn brighter under a layer of tears makes me glad I did. "Looks beautiful on you."

She throws her arms around me, burying her forehead into the crook of my neck and causing our fort to topple over. "Thank you, Mama."

*Mama.* It fills my heart to hear her say it once more—like she did when she was younger. With the blankets fallen over us, I hug her back. "Take care of it just like you take care of your sisters, okay? Promise?"

"I promise."

The unexpected moment is broken by another round of giggles from the other girls, who are calling dibs on everything from my measuring spoons to my pearls.

They might not realize it yet, but I'd give them anything they wanted. Family is everything to me, and these four girls are my heart and soul.

# CHAPTER 1

SUMMER SKY SEASON

***TWELVE SUMMERS LATER . . .***

"Are you going to finish your breakfast, Summer?" Two more sausage links roll off Dolly's red spatula onto my plate before she holds it up with pride. The kitschy café-inspired kitchen is my grandma's arena. Silicone, metal, and wood cooking utensils are her weapon of choice. If she had her way, like she did having us call her Dolly, I'd be rolling out of here like those links just did.

"I can't if you keep putting more food on the plate." Hugging my stomach, I wince at the thought of taking another bite. "I'm so stuffed I can't eat anymore." I take one more bite, though, just to make sure. *Yeah, I'm done.*

"But sausage is your favorite." I love how she acts so surprised that I can't eat two pancakes, scrambled eggs, fruit, two links, and then two more.

I've been known to be a breakfast-food fanatic, but this is too much. "Even I have my limits, Dolly. Save some for the others."

"Muffins are coming out of the oven for Fall, bacon is ready for Winter, and biscuits are rising for Spring since we all know she won't be up for another hour."

The urgency of my morning whips through my veins, so I stand, tug the hem of my blue dress down to where it's supposed to hit mid-thigh, and collect my plate. "And she'll need another hour to get ready." I transport the links to a napkin to take with me because these won't go to waste. I'll eat them later. We're not part of the clean-plate club around here, but if I finish anything, it's going to be those.

I move to the sink to rinse my plate.

Wiping her hands on a dish towel, she asks, "Why are you rushing off so early on a Saturday morning anyway? Weekends are for rest, walks of shame, and causing a little chaos. Not work."

I choke out a laugh, wishing she wouldn't say things like that when I have an overfull stomach. My grandmother has always staggered through life as an unabashed black sheep, with a reputation that my sisters and I can't quite determine was rightfully earned or pinned on her by Mountain Laurel Cove's long history with my family. She's been raising us in her carefree spirit ways since our parents passed away ten years ago. The town only turned toward us instead of away, accepting us with open arms they didn't always hold for Dolly.

Give her a little attention and power, and she's either going to be a total menace or a legend around the Cove. Depends on the day, I suppose.

Sometimes I wonder if she's disappointed that I turned out so straitlaced. Sure, there was a little fun over the years, but being the oldest of four orphaned girls came with responsibilities I wasn't prepared for, even if I wasn't responsible for the bills. So, I haven't done any walks of shame, but it doesn't mean I don't wish I'd had the opportunity. Maybe I didn't fall so far from my grandmother's tree after all.

I grin. "I'm happy to have the steady income. After I recommended that Mrs. Dover raise the cottages' rates last winter—quite significantly, I might add—we haven't had a shortage of renters. So that paid off."

"When is she going to let you have those cottages? You've been running that business for four years now, increased her profits, and taken care of every renter to come through there. Seems the old coot would be ready to retire." Mrs. Dover and Dolly never really saw eye to eye, but again, who has with Dolly? She knows everyone's buttons to push and has jammed them her entire life.

"She's been retired for years. She just owns those properties to keep money coming in. And I don't want both. I'm not greedy. I only want the Cove Cottage."

Her eyes level with mine. "She and that cheating husband of hers made plenty of money in this lifetime. They need to sell you the property next door so you can make some too, especially since you're the reason those properties are bringing in money anyhow."

"We shouldn't speak ill of the—"

"MacKenny Dover died in Mistress Annie's barn loft. Underneath Annie, I might add." I try not to cackle at her calling Annie Dumplin, Mistress Annie, but fail, and a giggle escapes. There's never been a grudge Dolly didn't hold on to, and Annie did her dirty when they were cheerleaders back in high school. No way am I sticking around for that story again, though. She'll talk about it until the tides go out tonight if I let her.

"Dragging up ancient history isn't going to get my name on the titles of those properties. But you know what will?" I glance up through the window in front of me to watch the waves sweep onto the edge of our land and then back to deeper waters again.

"Begging?"

Glancing at Dolly, I smile. "Yes, begging. I'm going to try that since I'll have more free time and a bonus for renting out Cove Cottage for the summer. I don't have to check different people in and out every week for the next three months. There will be no new welcome baskets to deliver to guests. I won't have to deal with all the things that come with managing a hospitality business, other than occasionally checking on them. This is going to be a breeze. I'll have to find new ways to spend my spare time. One will be the presentation for Mrs. Dover, I know that much. I can put the bonus money down as collateral for my intent to keep the property in the family. The Mountain Laurel Cove Family, that is." I scrape the food scraps into the trash. "And in the meantime, you'll get sick of seeing my face."

"Impossible, honey." She swoops in to retrieve the plate just as I finish rinsing it and set it in the dishwasher. When she stands back up, her eyes are shining as she takes me with a gentle smile. "You look so much like your mother in the morning light. I can still picture her eating breakfast right where you just did."

I waffle my head on my neck and laugh. "I look like my dad, and you know it."

I don't kid myself anymore. Before I was ten, I was told how much I resembled my mom, but the preteens set me squarely on track to inherit the Season family's traits. Not unattractive by any means, but not as delicate or glowy as our maternal side. Dolly Loving is still beautiful and looks younger than her age. Despite her wild and youthful ways, she always had her choice of suitors. Maybe more so because she never needed a man to make her feel whole. She thrives in her independence. Gotta love that about her.

I can't say the same. Standing tall on my own is fine and dandy, but it would be nice to have someone help carry the load of the world instead of it all weighing on my shoulders. So I don't think a companion of the male species would be so bad, would it?

"Your dad was an attractive man, Summer. Your mom fell head over heels the moment she laid eyes on him."

She's never been shy about sharing our parents' love story. We've heard it a million times and still hang onto every word, like we cling to our memories of them. I stand next to her at the sink, resting my hip against the counter, and drag the gold butterfly along my mom's delicate chain wrapped around my neck. Silence comes over her so quickly that I'm worried she's gotten lost in her own memories of my mother, her only child. With the sponge in one hand and a plate in the other, she looks at me with a fresh glassiness to her eyes and smiles. "Faith and Charlie were a beautiful couple."

Yes, they were—notably so by anyone who met them.

I move closer to wrap my arm around her. Dolly's shorter than I am by a few inches these days, but we're as bonded as we were when I was little. We stare out the window as the wind picks up, causing the water to lap the rocky shoreline at our little part of the cove, and let the feelings feel, as she likes to say. After taking a deep breath that she releases, she adds, "You should be getting on before the morning slips away from ya. You don't want to keep your gentleman from New York waiting."

The eye roll comes automatically as I release her and cut through the kitchen. I knew I shouldn't have shared any details. She has a knack for letting her imagination run away with the smallest of details. "He's not *my* gentleman from New York. He's a guest, a tenant at most, and he's brought his son with him. So don't let the ideas I know you're already concocting hatch into plans."

"Sounds like he's single if it's only him and his son all summer."

I catch my fingertips on the doorframe to stop and turn back. When I meet her gaze, I level her with a flat look of my own. "I don't know if he's single, but he's here to get away from life, not get caught up in mine. So please, Dolly, don't make this into something it's not before I've even met him."

"Can I make it into something once you meet?"

Shaking my head, I want to laugh, but I can't relent, or she'll play matchmaker all summer long. "No." Total menace, but she still makes me grin like an idiot because I wouldn't have her any other way.

"You act like we get a new selection of men around these parts all the time. A missed opportunity can turn into regret."

"I'm not going to regret not jumping the man." I walk out knowing this conversation is heading toward the gutter if I let it. "See you later."

"You're twenty-six, sweet girl. Go have the kind of fun that leaves the town gossiping." Her voice follows me into the front of the house, but I don't reply. I haven't been a girl in some time, but the name still fills me with the warmth she's always given my sisters and me. She wholeheartedly loves us as her own, through the ache she carries inside over the loss of her own daughter and son-in-law.

I return to the kitchen and kiss her on the cheek. "Love you, Dolly."

"Stop getting sappy on me and take care of your business."

"On it." I make my way toward the front room when I hear the creak of that third step that's never been fixed. My gaze pulls up the staircase.

My sister's sunset-hued hair bounces around her shoulders as she comes trotting down the stairs. "Do I smell blueberry muffins?"

"Good to know your sense of smell isn't broken like your sense of time. It's almost ten, Fall." She couldn't have been named more appropriately for a season with her gingery hair color and vibrant green eyes. I may have inherited my dad's more defined features and oval-shaped face, but she gets her coloring after our dad, the only one of us to have that particular connection to him. And in stark contrast to my blond hair and blue eyes.

"It's Saturday." The skirt of her sundress swishes around her legs as her bare feet pad against the wood. "Saturdays are for sleeping in and daydreaming."

Quirking an eyebrow, I shake my head. "You sound like Dolly."

Stopping on the landing, she remains two steps up from where I'm standing with a solid grip on the baluster. "There are worse ways to be than marching to your own beat, dearest sister. You should try it." The wobble of the wood causes her to straighten her spine and release it. "One of us could get hurt. What if this broke on Dolly?"

I start for the front room. "Add it to the never-ending list of things we need to fix in this old Victorian. We need to start tackling one issue at a time. Surely, five women can figure it out." I prop the bag of mini cookies up in the back of the basket behind the scones, and ask, "Are you going to be around later?" A glance back is shared. "We need to plan for a sister meeting soon. It's been too long." Meeting means hang out and catch up. With all of us running in different directions lately, I miss them.

"Want me to schedule a Google meetup?"

"No. We're not scheduling sister time through an app."

She laughs. "Time to embrace technology, big sis. It's the easiest way these days."

Grabbing hold of the basket, I turn around. "I prefer the shouting down the hall method. It's been effective thus far." I laugh. "You're busier than I am these days. Add me to your calendar when you can fit me in."

Tucking her hair behind her ear, she says, "I'll take care of it."

"Thanks. I'm heading to the cottage next door to welcome the new summer guests."

"If he's cute, call me." Her smile is too familiar to all of us. This small town feels even smaller when you know everyone in it, and there's not a man over eighteen or under sixty in a twenty-mile vicinity who's the least bit interesting. "And I'll be right over."

"If he's cute, I'm not calling anyone. I may be blond, but I'm no fool." I walk to the door, unable to stop the girlish giggle from erupting. A girl can only dream he's as cute as they hope. With the basket balanced on my lifted leg, I scrounge my fingers through the bowl on the entry table for my keys. Taking hold of the hard shell of the enamel bee keychain, I nod toward the door. "Make sure the honey stand is replenished."

"I always do." The second-oldest sister opens the door and then leans against it after I walk outside. Turning back, I say, "If I'm not back by four, send help."

She laughs. "The only help you're going to need is resisting your own guest."

"Wait, why would I have trouble resisting—" The door

closes before I can interrogate her for more details. Maybe I should have done some online research on him. *Has she?* What am I walking into? Paying in full for the entire summer six months ago didn't have me questioning anything. It made me celebrate the profit I'd just made for Mrs. Dover and the bonus I had just earned, so how he looks is the least of my concerns.

Since the basket is too heavy to carry the half mile down the road, I slip it into the trunk of my car and start the short drive to the rental property.

A quick wave to Mr. Taylor mowing his lawn across the street is a Saturday ritual. I catch sight of Mrs. Browley, who lives next to him, weeding her side beds at her house. Slowing the car, I roll down the window. "Your hydrangeas are competition-ready," I holler through the opening.

She looks up, narrowing her eyes as she swipes the back of her glove across her forehead before she realizes it's me and smiles. "I'm thinking about entering this year. Blooms this beautiful in June deserve a blue ribbon."

"They sure do. Have a great day."

"You too, Summer."

I cruise on, reaching the dirt driveway of the waterfront property. It's beautiful, like our large lot next door, but there's something different here. Maybe it's the arrangement of the trees as they scatter across the grounds without blocking the view from the house. Or the lack of flowers around. We all love flowers. There's only a small patch of grass, enough to play around on but not enough to mow. A weed eater does a fine job of keeping it trimmed.

The blue siding and creamy trim complement the rustic backdrop. The wooden front deck my sisters and I built two winters ago extends far enough to accommodate lounge chairs for watching the sun set over the water. Dinner would be divine under the awning of the trees. And when the breeze blows just right, seeing the stars beyond them is a dream. Excitement still bubbles up every time I pull into the driveway. "Heaven."

My smile comes easy, along with my breath, when I'm here. This is my own little piece of paradise, entrusted to me to take care of and protect.

It's not a secret that I want this property as my own, but Mrs. Dover isn't quite ready to make a deal for it yet. I just hope we can reach an agreement before the vultures snap up this land in their venture capitalist greed.

The ache returns when thinking about the threat invading our coastline. I run my tightened grip around the steering wheel, starting to feel desperate to make sure nothing happens to it before I have my chance to save it. I glance at the time on my dashboard like it's an oven timer about to go off.

*Take a breath.*

*Do your job.*

*Greet the guests.*

A spot of sun beams off a black convertible—parked next to the house with the top down—striking my eyes. I squint, realizing the guests are early. I peek over at the car once more, the custom black-and-white license plate catching my attention this time. **HATTRICK.** *That's peculiar.*

My gaze veers to the sign in front of the car. *No Parking.* It's one I hung up several summers ago for the safety of the wood-sided house. *Why'd he have to park there?* I sigh under the weight of the forthcoming confrontation, but the rules are not meant to be broken.

I cut the engine after parking in one of the allotted, clearly marked spaces in the yard, away from the house. I gather my gumption and slip into my manager lady pants, ready to not only greet the guests but also tackle this issue head-on.

I grab the basket from the trunk and start toward the house. Small sticks crunch under my freshly washed white sneakers. But when my feet stop unwillingly, I just about topple over my toes when I lay eyes on him the first time.

*Oh my, my.* "Wow."

Tan skin like the sun kissed it itself. Sexy, muscular arms with tantalizing prominent veins in thick forearms that branch across the tops of his hands. Those are the kind of hands that only come with people who use them in their daily work.

I didn't realize I found such details a turn-on until now.

Slick hair wet from the water tempts me to finger through it to loosen the strands . . . *wait, what?* I blink several times to snap myself out of whatever daze I've fallen under and hold my chin up to shake off the ridiculous places my mind wants to take me with him.

He looks back, sunglasses covering his eyes, while nothing hides the rest of his body other than the swimsuit. A touch of hair on his chest leads my eyes lower to the foray of abs on display. *Good Lord.*

Moving his sunglasses to his head, he sits up from the lounger and sets his feet on the wood decking. Tilting his head and eyeing me, he maintains his neutral expression, maybe a bit curious, from this distance. And from the straight line of his lips, you'd think I was the one intruding. Maybe I am, like a Peeping Tom. *Oh God.* Embarrassment zips up my spine at the thought, heating my cheeks and making them pinken. But before I can fan myself back to reality or even turn away, he stands, and the basket slips from my hands.

*Swim trunks hanging so low around his hips that an old tan line is revealed.*

*Water trails over biceps built over time, not overnight.*

*Four. Six. Eight abs so hard and defined that the word perfection isn't accurate enough to describe them.*

The water god comes toward me just as I drop my bare knees into the dirt, needing any excuse not to stare—and this basket is a darn good one. I'm not even sure he's real, much less human. Where would someone like him have come from?

My hand stills on a jar of my sister's honey when it dawns on me. *New York City.*

Bending down in front of me, he hands me the baggie of Dolly's homemade scones that escaped during the incident. When I dare to peek at him, I'm met with brown eyes that hold both tetchiness and compassion so equally, I'm not sure how to react. *So I don't.* I just stare instead, gobsmacked that a man who looks like this exists in real life, much less on my big deck. I'm fairly certain my mouth is hanging wide open, but that's not confirmed until he lifts my jaw off the ground and smirks.

"You must be Summer."

*Oh my, my indeed.*

## CHAPTER 2

SUMMER

"Yes." My response comes out breathier than it should, like I've run around the block. Definitely not because he just stole it. I clear my throat. "Summer Season."

"Summer Season?" His pinched glare knocks me back into reality like I'm a freshman who made the social hierarchical mistake of running smack dab into the senior star quarterback. The memory rushes fresh through my veins, and I'm back in high school all over again. Embarrassment fills my chest at the new tenant and his main-character energy taking center stage on this property. Attractive. Deep voice. Brown eyes that seem to hide more secrets than they reveal. The hardened line between his eyes doesn't disappear. "Unique."

"It is," I say through a half-hearted laugh. It's not the first time someone has said that. My sisters' and my names are different, but so were our parents, who were more carefree than I am, less so than Dolly, and loved so big it was too much for the world to handle. We're not just their legacy. We're the reminders of what once was. So I'll take their uniqueness and carry my name with pride. "I'm grateful it wasn't dill or oregano." That joke always goes over well with the community center crowd when I'm volunteering, which is mostly made up of the elderly of our small town. It doesn't with him so much, though.

His tongue dips out to massage his lower lip before an eyebrow anchors itself in curiosity. "Rosemary was my grandmother's name."

I don't know why that makes me smile. Is it because he's relating? Or that he's stopped staring at me like I grew a third eye? *Both.* "I can't say I'd be upset over that name. It's quite pretty."

"And you're upset over Summer?" The curiosity in his tone reaches his gaze as if the world hinges on my answer.

"No." I laugh. "I love the name Summer at least one-fourth of the year."

"Clever."

"I try." I'd take a bow, but I'm still in the dirt before him. "I can't say being on my knees in front of you is the way I imagined us meeting, Mr. Sutton, but—"

"You won't hear any complaints from me."

My cheeks heat from the insinuation as my thoughts go where they shouldn't—straight to hell in a handbasket with Mr. Sutton. I grab the large plastic-wrapped double chocolate honey cookie that fell out of the basket, and say, "You might if you find my cookie dirty." *Wait . . .* My stomach drops faster than an anchor to the bottom of the ocean. I glance up at the tops of the tall trees, watching the leaves sway in the gentle breeze as I ponder what the hell I'm saying and why everything sounds like I'm offering myself up on a platter.

"I'm sure your cookie will be delicious either way."

*Oh my Lord.* My eyes dart to his, and as our gazes latch,

I'm left wondering if he thinks I'm coming onto him. An unsubtle clearing of my throat again causes me to cough as it dries out. I turn and hack a few more times before daring to return my eyes to his and whisper, "I think I've given you the wrong impression—"

"That's too bad. I was quite enjoying the *impression* you were giving." One swap of a word and that sentence has a whole new meaning.

He turns to check on his son, giving me the briefest of opportunities to study him. His confidence speaks of someone comfortable in their own skin. I'm not sure what the male equivalent of pretty privilege is, but he has it.

I feign a laugh, but I'm the worst actress, so I try to clean this mess up instead. "We've gotten off track, Mr. Sutton."

"Daniel."

"Mr. Daniel?"

He chuckles. "No, it's Daniel Sutton. My friends call me Daniel."

"Ah. Um." The straps of my dress leave plenty of exposed skin to keep me cool on this warm day, but a drip of sweat slides down my back. I have a strong suspicion it's not from the heat of summer but from the hot man before me.

As if it hadn't already been confirmed, he is real despite my initial disbelief when I first saw him. And almost too handsome to stare at for any extended period of time. He should come with a warning like what we're taught in school about the sun. Risking my retinas, I'm willing to let them burn to stare at his hotness a few seconds longer. I glance down and grab the Go Fish deck of cards that tried to bury itself in the leaves. Then I drop the box back into the basket as I riddle through what exactly is happening right now.

I'm the responsible one. The one everyone comes to

when they have a problem to solve—the listener, the advice giver, good ole reliable Summer that can be counted on. Just because I'm in the presence of the most gorgeous man I've ever laid eyes on, I'm now suddenly rendered both horny and ridiculous in equal measure?

*Snap out of it. Stop acting like you've never seen a man before.* "Man" doesn't seem appropriate to classify this specimen into such a generic category.

Adonis?

*Check.*

Apollo?

*Check. Check.*

Human rival to the statue of *David*?

*Check. Check. Check.*

When I peek up, his eyes crinkle at the sides with an air of confidence residing inside that I assume comes with knowing who he is. I really shouldn't find that as sexy as I do, but it's just stacking the deck in his favor at this point.

No ring is wrapped around his finger. Not even a tan line or the remnant of an indentation from wearing something that would tell me he's off-limits. Even the scent of him, the outdoors coating his skin like the water recently did, has my hormones going haywire. *This is a business, Summer.* As if I have a chance of turning this back around, I say, "You're here early."

"Traffic was lighter than expected."

"That's good."

He stands, his shadow engulfing me whole. When I swim my gaze all the way to the top of him, he offers me a hand. I've made a fool of myself several times over in the span of no more than five minutes, the sweet gesture wringing through my ill-equipped-edness of dealing with a man like him. I'm pretty sure that's not a word, but it fits the indescribable reaction I'm having, one I didn't think existed before meeting him.

Vicariously balancing between wanting to fasten onto him like a spider monkey and reminding myself I shouldn't entangle myself with a renter, I know that even considering anything with this man is pointless. He's temporary at best. A fun time at worst.

*Summer*... I blink several times in hopes of clearing my eyes as well as retrieving my brain from the gutter. *Who am I?* Flirting and winning over hearts comes so naturally to my sisters, but it's never been something I find natural. My mom always said we each have our own talents. I'm thinking anything to do with men is not one of mine after this catastrophe of a greeting.

There might not be any witnesses to my ludicrous behavior, but in my head, I can almost hear Dolly cheering from down the road. I'm sure my sisters would be reacting the same if they saw their trustworthy older sis as caught off guard as I am by Daniel Sutton.

"Anyway . . ." Angling the basket awkwardly under my arm, I accept his offer. Regret fills my knees, betraying me the moment his calloused hand presses against the softness of mine. The simple touch sends electricity zipping through me, and I weaken under the sturdy grasp that keeps me upright.

Our eyes connect as the bond remains strong. But as I steady on my feet, he lets go, and the magic is gone. Looking down, I rub my palm down the side of my cotton dress to ease the shock. "Well, that was—"

"Interesting," he says, glancing at his palm before tucking it into the pocket of his swim trunks. His expression shifts into indifference as if he'd been exposed too long without his mask in place. Or maybe it's a hint for me to get moving again.

Reaching down to dust my knees free from dirt and ground debris, I say, "We should get you and your son settled in, Mr. Sutton."

"That's not necessary. We're settled." His gaze tracks down the path to the small beach of rocks and sand mingling at the water's edge. "Roman has already made himself at home by the looks of it." His son skips a rock, then searches for another to toss. When his father's eyes land back on me, he says, "And you can call me Daniel."

"You've known me all of five minutes. Are we already friends, Mr. Sutton?"

He laughs. "We should be after filling out your guest profile. Seems you know everything about me from how I take my coffee in the morning to what I drink for a nightcap."

"Fair trade Death Wish coffee beans. Black, no creamer." I shrug as if I just nailed a quiz without studying.

"No creamer needed with good coffee." The click of his tongue is an unsubtle back pat to his ego. Fortunately, I'm not too bothered by it.

Licking my lips, I hold his steady gaze. "And you like to cap off your night with an old-fashioned without the twist of orange."

"I don't need accessories to make my bourbon more palatable. I'm not complicated like that."

I tilt my head and then shake it. Peering back up at him, all six-foot, wild guess, four of him, I find my body easing into the conversation. "You know, I had to drive over an hour to Stonehill to retrieve two bottles of the requested Blanton's Single Barrel Bourbon."

"It was worth it."

"I wouldn't know." I shrug, feeling a wryness come over me as my footing with him steadies. "I'm not complicated like that."

His eyebrows lift, not much, but noticeable. His attention loses its measured approach, and he smirks. "I beg to differ."

"You can beg all you want," I smart back with a scoff. "But I'm just fine with good old well drinks."

"Come over sometime, and I'll show you it was worth the drive."

It's tempting to pinch myself to make sure this is real, and I'm not dreaming.

My breathing quickens as I scramble for a reply. *Did he just ask me out?* I replay our banter quickly. *I think so.* That invitation was as straightforward as they come.

I attempt to calm my pitter-pattering heart. "To Stonehill or down the road to the cottage?"

"Both. One taste and you'll never go back to the ordinary."

Using a nightcap as an excuse to get a woman to visit is as old-fashioned as his drink itself. And I'm not upset over it. Apparently, neither are my heating cheeks as they put on a display for him. I fan myself to try to keep from heating all over for this man.

But there's such a charm to this version of flirting versus a booty call. I don't need to read about him on paper to know this guy prefers a steak to a burger and a one-night stand to forever. It's written all over him, carved into those hard muscles, and that jaw that ticks with impatience every time he thinks I'm not paying attention.

No one this hot walks around without some history. It's shaping his whole aura. And I know better than to tangle with a player. Especially when I can tell this player gets what he wants, which won't be me this summer.

I take a step back, needing the space and clarity, escaping the pull of my bee to his honey, and breathe a bit freer. It's only in my best interest to stick to business by backing away from this banter about being friends. We're not friends, so I need to stick to a formal-name basis and protect myself.

Wrapping my arms around the basket, I say, "I'm glad I got what you want."

His eyebrow cocks.

"I mean, the service I provide is what I hope sets me apart from others." When his lips part, I realize what I've said. "What I mean to say is that I want to provide the best service to my clients. Yes, the profile is long, but it really helps me curate the stay to your needs."

"Oh, really?" His dulcet tone could lure me anywhere.

*Oh, geez.* I smile sheepishly. It's time for me to stop, just stop everything—talking, ogling, mentally throwing my willpower away—and collect myself. I need to keep my mouth shut. *Close it. Zip it.*

A grin teases the corners of his mouth. "Does everyone get the best of you?"

"Pretty much." My brain can't keep up with these mind games. *Are we flirting? Are we talking? Is this business?* "I'll continue this level of service if I ever take ownership."

"You don't own the cottage?"

"No. Long story. Technically, it's a short story, but not one we need to get into."

"I have time," he says as if the day won't slip through our fingers when we're not looking.

"I don't." We stand in an unannounced staring contest as the seconds tick by in my head. I cave first to be polite. But losing to him feels worse under the circumstances—him, me, and this weird energy between us—draining my hostess battery. I shove the basket forward. "Here. This is for you."

He reaches forward, taking hold of one of the handles as his eyes graze over the goodies I packed for them. Should I be studying the dimple in his chin, or the lightest dusting of scruff clinging to the drift of his sharp jawline? No, but he's put both on brazen display, so it's hard not to.

When his eyes return to mine, his gaze travels the length of me like he's not sure where he wants to start first, while daring to drag his tongue over the flow of his bottom lip. "Looks good."

I exhale, trying to calm the butterflies he's awakened. If I don't, I won't survive this man if he keeps looking at me like that. "It's just something special we wanted to give to say thank you for being our guests for the summer."

Holding the basket, he replies, "You're welcome."

A laugh bursts from me like a clucking chicken upon hearing the response.

The little glimpses into who this guy thinks he is lead me to realize that looks apparently aren't everything. His personality comes with a sculpted body and face that could grace the pages of magazines. But I'm not foolish enough to fall for such superficial features. Doesn't mean I can't appreciate him, though. *Silently. To myself.*

I laugh under my breath. "Alrighty then." Though not an official meeting, I still need to visit with Mrs. Dover about the property. Talking to her is still hanging around the recesses of my mind, which doesn't allow me to invest as much time as I'd like bantering with him, so I start the obligatory tour of the house to hurry this along. I don't want to chicken out and put off talking to her for however long it takes to gather the courage again. It's time to be direct so there's no misunderstanding where I stand. Currently, standing next to his handsome giant isn't getting me anywhere, so I clap my hands once. "I should get you settled, Mr. Sutton."

"Daniel."

I turn back to catch his languid gaze over my shoulder, though I have the sneakiest suspicion his eyes were aimed lower before I caught him. "What was that?"

"You can call me Daniel, remember?"

*Get in. Get out. Pretend I didn't hang on every word that came from his mouth and move on with life.* "Yes, I remember, Mr. Sutton. But I think it's best if we keep things professional." I stop to face him again. "And you're parked in a no-parking zone."

"How is that area designated no parking when it's perfect for parking?"

Our gazes travel to the side of the house at the same time. "It's for safety purposes. No one can park there like the sign says."

"I'm partial to that spot."

"How are you partial to a spot you just started parking in?" My eyes flick to him. "Anyway, it's a hazard." He somehow manages to make me feel judged for caring about this. *So what if I don't have much to focus on?* It's a current life setback, is all. Not everything has panned out the way I'd like, but it will. I can feel it. "And rules are rules."

He shifts, though his gaze narrows like a hawk who's spotted his next prey. "Rules are meant to be broken."

I gasp before I can contain it. My fingers tap to my chest, and I hold back the offense from encroaching on my voice. "Not in Mountain Laurel Cove. Word of warning, it's best to stay on the right side of this town. The locals aren't shy and very vocal about troublemakers and rule breakers."

"Small town gossip, huh?" He chuckles again even though I was only giving him fair warning after seeing how disrespect gets handled here. "Everybody knows everybody—"

"And they are more than happy to give advice on how to live your life."

"Sounds personal."

I snort, involuntarily, of course, but that doesn't stop a taste of embarrassment from wedging its way into my psyche. Rocking my head back and forth, I grin. "Trust me. *It is.*" I start for the house. "Let me show you around, and then I can get out of your hair." I take a few steps across the deck. "I've stocked the fridge as requested, and—"

"That's not necessary."

Stopping, I look back to see his sunglasses set back on the bridge of his nose while holding the basket in the spot where I left him. "What's not? I already stocked it—"

"The tour." He summons me back to him with a wave of his hand.

*Excuse me?* The gesture raises my hackles. He hasn't really put off complete jerk vibes up until this point. I sure as heck hope he doesn't start now.

I stay in my spot. "I want to point out the tricky—"

"I'm sure I can figure it out." The arrogance pulls a smirk into place like it's in its natural habitat.

I find myself blinking slower as my eyes narrow in reflex. His reaction is rude, quite frankly, and as much as he thinks he can do everything on his own—he can't.

But if Mr. Know-It-All wants to figure out the quirks of this old place, I'll let him. *Why fight him?* One attempt at the shower will have him calling me to fix the hot water. He'll need my tips on unplugging the kitchen drain, and he'll be begging me to reset the box when streaming's not working every other time he tries, thanks to the tree coverage. And when that happens, I can drink my cheap wine with my sisters and have a good laugh. Pure entertainment. Until he has to take a cold shower, and then he'll be begging me to return.

I smile so sweetly I could rot a tooth. "I just bet you can, Mr. Sutton." Literally. The sister betting pool is back in play. "Have a good day."

I return to my car, leaving him to enjoy his day without me in it. This whole interaction was hot and cold, cold and hot. It was unpredictable at best just like the shower here at the cottage. I get into the driver's seat and start the engine.

Mr. Sutton is an anomaly that is probably best accepted as-is. Spikey. Moody. And the most tragic of them all, ridiculously handsome.

Good thing I won't need to be out here very often. I don't think my eyes can handle the hotness—or his attitude—all summer long. As I hold the button to raise the window and block him like the sun is blinding me by visoring my eyes, he says, "Thanks for stopping by, Ms. Season."

Glancing back at him, I can't help but wonder how I'm supposed to survive the summer with not much to do and this guy as a next-door neighbor.

*Yes, I do. I need to focus on the prize.*

And although he'd be considered one to most women, my prize is not a six-foot-four man with movie-star looks and a smile that is as deadly to my willpower as tequila is to me.

At least not this summer.

If I had the property in my name, I might be tempted to break a few rules with this man. But, right now, I have bigger fish to fry than Mr. Sutton.

"You're welcome," I say. "And oh! Don't forget to move

your car. Thanks." Keeping a smile plastered on my face, I feel better getting in the last word. I can't control if he'll listen, but I've done my job.

I catch that earlier smirk across his face before I even shift into reverse. I knew I shouldn't have looked back, but there was something about him that made me want to.

As soon as I reach the street, I let my mind flow back to what just happened. Who is he? Or more importantly, who does he think he is?

"Rules are for breaking," I quietly repeat and then laugh. I may be almost five-six in my highest heels and take after my mom in demeanor, but I got my grandmother's sass when pushed. Mr. Sutton has met his match. He just doesn't know it yet.

I'm absolutely positive about one thing regarding the infamous Mr. New York Sutton. He's either going to be the best tenant ever or the worst I've encountered.

Whichever way it turns out, it's going to be one long, hot summer.

# CHAPTER 3

SUMMER

Braking at the stop sign, I rattle my hands to shake off the growing nerves before taking a right and heading up to the farmlands of Mountain Laurel. The urgency I felt earlier, racing through my veins, has dissipated and been replaced by dread.

I'd been so busy pumping myself up to talk to Mrs. Dover all morning, ready to share my idea, that I forgot to strategize. So I take the leisurely drive to plot out my sales points.

1. She's known my family longer than I've been alive. Keeping the property in the Mountain Laurel Family and out of real estate moguls' hands is essential to preserving the land and our history.
2. The property is next door to my family and me. Taking care of tenants is easier due to proximity.
3. It could be my own home one day, continuing the legacy of generations of the Seasons and Lovings growing up here.

I turn onto her private drive and park next to her Cadillac. I take my time, building the gumption to lay out an offer as I trek across the lawn to the front door of the farmhouse. This place would be a dream to raise a family. I can imagine sitting in the rockers on the front porch with a glass of tea when it's too hot or sipping wine when the sun's setting. Even with those beautiful images, my heart clenches thinking of Mrs. Dover here all alone.

There's no sneaking onto this front porch. Boards creak under my feet. Pulling the screen door open, I knock on the solid wood door that needs painting and gently close the other before stepping back to wait.

Mrs. Dover peeks through the sidelight and answers. Her smile is as welcoming as her arms when they wrap around me. "This is such a nice visit." It's only been a few weeks, but when I think about her being on this big farm, that's a lot of time to spend without seeing anyone. "Is it social or business?"

"Both." I hate to lie, but it's not like I don't have the time to chat.

"Let me grab some sweet tea, and we can talk out here on the front porch." She swooshes me toward the rocking chairs. "Make yourself at home."

"You don't have to go to any trouble."

"No trouble, Summer Season." The screen door is already closing before the words leave her mouth.

She has never made me feel I can't come to her, but that doesn't stop the twinge of guilt rippling through me. This is her income. This could go well or extremely bad. I'm praying for good. I'd hate for her to think poorly of me, like I'm another hawk preying on her, or like I'm trying to take advantage of her. I would never. Fingers crossed she'll see the benefits of me owning the Cottage Cove property.

Sitting down, I look out where herds of cows used to roam. Now she has Bessie, the lone survivor, to keep her company. I rock back and take in a deep breath. We're spoiled with fresh air in these parts, but June thickens the air with the heat of summer as well. Or maybe that's my nerves kicking in. I swipe my palms down the tops of my thighs.

"Here we are." She sets the glasses on a wicker table between us and sits in the other rocking chair. Taking hold of a glass, she sips and then smiles at me. "What brings you by this Saturday?"

I pick up the other glass, condensation already building and causing drips to land on the cotton of my dress and spread through the woven fabric. "I checked in the summer tenant. His son was busy playing, but I spent a few minutes chatting with him."

"Is he nice?"

His smile comes to mind, along with that look in his eyes that had me mentally undressing. I swallow harder than I should before taking a quick sip to cool down. Unexpected comes to mind when thinking about Daniel Sutton. "He's . . . I don't think there will be any trouble."

"That's good." The boards cry for reprieve under the weight of the chairs while we rock, the distraction causing me to regret the last two sausages I ate. "I have a sense this isn't about the rental. What's on your mind, Summer?"

"I've heard about the interest on the upper shores." She sips, not revealing any indication of her thoughts about outsiders coming in to snatch up properties. She'd be the only one not thinking about it or gossiping, more accurately. "They're making offers."

"I need to be honest with you, honey," she starts. I was already unnerved by all the scenarios of the way this conversation could potentially play out, but now with my heart stalled in my throat, I need to keep breathing. Resting my hand on my chest, I check. "A gentleman from Seattle wants to have a call."

My throat tightens. I thought I had more time to talk to her, but it seems I'm the one who's behind. I clear my throat and straighten my spine. "Regarding Cove Cottage?"

"Regarding both properties."

I set the glass down and angle toward her. "And you're taking the call?"

Although she had been rocking, she stills, and takes another sip. "I'm old, but I'm no fool."

"Can I ask a favor?"

"I can't promise you'll get the answer you want, but you can ask."

Releasing a long-held breath, I say, "I want a shot."

The corners of her mouth soften upward. "I know you have a strong interest. You've treated them like your own, which I'm grateful for, but I'm not sure you're going to have the money—"

"I have some money." I stop myself from saying more. My inheritance is limited after I paid for college and helped with the house. There's a reason the list of issues is growing daily. They take money or time to figure out how to DIY it. I've been short on both the past couple of months. She knows my backstory, but not so much about my budget.

With a tilt of her head, a curl that's gone gray among the remaining blond falls over one eye. With a puff of breath, it floats to its rightful place on her temple. Her eyes steady on mine with the type of soft smile I've seen too much for one lifetime. *Sympathetic.* "Summer . . ." There's that damn pause I used to hear before every condolence. Though said in kindness, I hate the tone that accompanies it. "I'm not sure if you're aware of the value—"

"I've done my research. I won't be able to outbid a big company's banking power, but I'd like to have the opportunity to present my own offer."

"The letter I received already mentioned possibilities." She reaches over, and her hand covers my forearm with a gentleness that matches the shape of her eyes. "It's not going to be in a range you can afford. I'm sorry—"

"Give me a chance, Mrs. Dover. Please." She sits back and starts rocking again as if the words landed with impact. "If you decide to go with someone else after that, I'll understand."

Her gaze shifts to the large acreage before us and then to Bessie, who stands at the fence as if she's part of the conversation. When Mrs. Dover looks at me, she says, "You'll get your fair shot, but please remember business is business."

"Business in Mountain Laurel Cove is personal, and I'll fight the best I can to keep it that way. The last thing any of us wants is for the Cove to become a rich person's playground like they did over in Ocean's Bay."

"They have a good funnel cake, though."

Excitement bubbles up, causing me to giggle. "They sure do." Leaning back, I watch the black cow chew the tall grass in the pasture, content like I am in our pocket of heaven. "You won't regret this. I promise."

"I look forward to the pitch." The conversation veers into maintenance at the mountain cottage while we finish our glasses of sweet tea. When I stand to leave, we hug, and I dash to the car. Tucked inside, I exhale a huge sigh of relief. It's only step one in what I assume will be a long process, but I'll take it and run with it to make her not only proud but happy she's selling to me.

I leave the farm with renewed energy. It's good to have something to focus on, to have a goal that benefits all of us who live here. I look around as I drive past pastures and continue to the only stop sign we have in town.

How lucky am I to live in this beautiful town where the ocean meets the forests and the fields meet the trees? I have my grandmother and my sisters, a job that pays some basic bills, and friends around every corner and in each shop. What more could I ask for?

*The property.*

*A comfortable life.*

*Love?*

I take a long, shaky breath.

*Is love even real?*

I'm not sure anymore. Unless it smacks me upside the head or gives me what my parents had, I don't want it. Thinking love exists after the last time I got burned is a fool's errand. It's been a long time since I had someone tell me I'm beautiful. It's been longer since I've been kissed. I can't even remember the last time I—*get out of your head, Summer*. This train of thought leads to a dead end.

Sex aside, would it be greedy to ask for just a little more in life? I don't need hearts and flowers. I'd settle for companionship or someone who makes me smile at this point.

My chest burns with a loneliness that's been creeping up on me lately. It grows a little deeper each day. I've taken care of my sisters and grandmother since my parents passed. They don't need me anymore, not in any significant way. So maybe having this new project—an amazing opportunity—will help. Directing my energies toward saving our town from ending up like Ocean's Bay is really a godsend.

I'm startled out of my thoughts by the vibration of my phone against the console. I glance down, ready to let the unfamiliar number go to voicemail. But I pick it up just in case it's not spam. "Hello?"

"Summer Season?"

The warmth of the voice wraps around me like a cozy blanket on a chilly day. But I still don't recognize it. "Yes? Who is this?"

The sound of air sucked in pervades the call. "Daniel."

"Daniel who?" I ask, smiling at myself in the rearview mirror. I knew we'd get here—him calling me for help—but it came even faster than I anticipated.

"Daniel Sutton. Your summer tenant." His tone holds equal parts annoyance and surliness, which is both entertaining and satisfying. He's already becoming so predictable.

"Ohhh, *that* Daniel."

"Do you know a lot of Daniels, Ms. Season?" Impatience gets the best of him. It's glorious. I want to tell him that this is why we let people do their jobs and follow the rules, but I bite my tongue. Knowing he's squirming on the other end is satisfying enough.

For now, at least.

I shrug despite him or anyone else being able to see me. "It's not an uncommon name."

"That's not what I asked."

His tone is rough and raw, and I imagine his jaw flexing with irritation. There's something ridiculously hot about that.

I gulp, hoping he can't hear it, though it's so loud in my ears that I'm now worried they can hear me swallowing in Half Moon Bay. "I'm sure you didn't call to chat about the commonalities of your name, Mr. Sutton. How can I help you?"

"Despite what you might think, *Ms. Season*, I'm not so arrogant that I can't admit when I'm wrong."

I look around like there might be a camera hidden somewhere. There are miles and thousands of trees between us, but it sure feels like his eyes are on me. "Is this a setup?"

He chuckles, the edge of his annoyance dissolving. "It's not a setup."

"Oh. *Okay*. This is a good start." I start driving toward home.

"I was wrong." A man who can own up to his errors in life? I approve. "It's the shower."

I burst out laughing before he finishes speaking. *I knew it*. As my inner champion does another victory lap, I say, "Fine. I'll be right over."

Sure, I might be as smug as a bear that just got away with the honey, but at least I didn't say I told you so. *Yet.*

# CHAPTER 4

DANIEL SUTTON

"I told you so," Summer says as soon as I open the door. You'd think she'd won the Stanley Cup after shit-talking all season with that self-righteous smirk in place. It's something I'm personally familiar with since that was me in the third season of my career.

*And fourth.*

*Ninth.*

*Eleventh* . . . fuck it. It's every season.

Attitude shapes her body, her hand planted firmly on a kicked-out hip, giving those curves a nice S in the same fitted pale-blue dress she was wearing earlier. It's short, how I like them, showing off her great legs and shoulders, fantastic tits, and hips to hold.

The swim trunks I'm stuck wearing until I can shower don't exactly hide anything, so it's not wise for me to continue thinking about my new landlord's body or imagining holding her in certain positions. I drag my eyes back up to catch her staring at me.

Parted plush pink lips send my thoughts right to how they'd look wrapped around me. Blue eyes, brighter than the dress but softer than the sky, are fixed on my bare abs, inspiring me to run my hand over all eight of them.

Her bottom lip pinkens even deeper as she digs her teeth into it.

It's not the first time a woman has stared at me like that, and I'd be willing to wager my penthouse in Manhattan it won't be the last. Comes with the territory. Pro athlete. Celebrity, which I fucking hate. More money than I can spend in two lifetimes. Other than me being an athlete with enough to give my kid the life I didn't have, the rest is meaningless.

The goal wasn't to become famous. It was to become *a legend*. I want my name carved into the Hockey Hall of Fame next to the best that ever played the sport. Gretzky. Lemieux, Gordie Howe, Orr—and Sutton. Most valuable player seven times in my career has put me on track, and I won't accept anything less.

Hitting a genetic goldmine as *GQ* and *People's* "Sexiest Man Alive"—three different years—is a bonus.

Her gaze lingers, making me think she's not as innocent as she portrays. "Not sure if you knew, Ms. Season, but my eyes aren't down there."

I'm hit with a glare, though I have a feeling it's not as hard as she probably thinks it is. With a tilt of her head that leaves her ponytail swinging to the right, she blinks twice. "I'm well aware of where your eyes are located, Mr. Sutton."

"You sure about that?"

"Absolutely, thank you very much." By the hoity-toity tone, the lady doesn't like to be called out. I don't blame her, but I'm enjoying this little kitten trying to work herself into a panther. And failing. She'll need sharper claws for that.

"You're welcome."

The slightest of eyerolls is given before she asks, "Why do you say that?"

I feign innocence. "Do I say it that much?"

"Yes, you do. I wasn't really thanking you, and you claimed it like I was."

"Does that bother you?" I tease. She's too much fun to play with, and I can't help myself.

She scoffs, but I catch the smile burgeoning at the corners of her mouth. "It bothers me that you answer with questions redirected at me like we're in therapy." She pokes my chest as she enters the place like she owns it. "News flash, we're not."

We may not be, but now watching the sway of her ass, it was worth irritating her. She walks with such purpose that following her inside is the only option. Stopping shy of the kitchen, she turns around fast like there's something she needs to confront. Or someone.

*Me?* I grin in anticipation, but instead of words hitting me, her eyes land solidly on my hardest muscles and take in the view. *Definitely me.*

"If my being shirtless is too big a distraction—"

"What?" she stammers as her gaze tries to find a safe place to travel that's not on my body. The lamp, the window, the couch, the rug, her sneakers. "I hadn't even noticed." Her shoulders pop the slightest of shrugs, confirming she doesn't believe her own words.

"It was pointless to get dressed—"

"You're fine." She sighs as if she's caught in a reprimand. "Not *you're* fine. Though you are, but I mean, it's fine that you are . . ." Her hand flies out toward me, and she shakes it like I'm summed up easily that way. "Not dressed."

"Thanks." I grin, appreciating this version of Summer

Season best. She's cute when she's flustered. "Since I couldn't shower, I stayed in my trunks—"

"You really don't owe me the details, Mr. Sutton."

*Ah. Guess this is how it's going to be . . .*

But that's fine. I can play along. "I wasn't expecting you to come so fast."

Her jaw hits the floor, my words lingering in the air. The innuendos are coming to me quicker than usual today. But like in every other part of my life, I peak at just the right time.

She swallows like a lump is stuck in her throat. "I . . ." She usually snaps back without missing a beat, but she seems to struggle to find the words she wants this time. After searching the ceiling and the floor, she finally replies, "It sounded like an emergency."

"So you walked over?" She didn't have a car parked out front. Chuckling, I cross my arms over my chest. "Anyway, I wouldn't call it an emergency."

"You sure about that? I wanted fresh air. It's a beautiful day." Her tone is lighter, her smile natural as she finds her stride again. "It gave me extra time to imagine you in that cold water—"

"You've been thinking about me?" I walk to the kitchen but stop and whisper in her ear, "Naked?" Catching the scent of honey and flowers has me stealing a deep inhale before I move on.

"*Oh my God*. No." She staggers for a breath with her hand gripping the base of her throat. I have a feeling she'd be clutching her pearls if she were wearing them. "I would never—"

"That's too bad." Behind the peninsula, I ask, "Water? Soda? Something stiff?"

A heavy exhale leaves her chest as she turns and starts tracking me. "I'll pass. Where's your son?"

"Napping. We were on the road early. After spending time in the sun, he's wiped."

"I love napping on sunny days. Rainy days even more, though. The sound of the raindrops hitting the house, tapping against my window, or lying on a hammock on the front porch as a rainstorm rolls through." Her eyes have softened, giving up whatever internal fight she was having. "I don't know, it's relaxing like nature is forcing us to take some time to slow down."

Summer is adorable when flustered, but right now, with her armor down and revealing a part of herself that feels almost intimate, she's beautiful.

"I don't remember what it's like to nap, much less on a rainy day," I say.

Her smile is softer this time. "You should try it while you're here. We get storms rolling in out of nowhere, and then it's bright and sunny again an hour later."

"I'll have to do that."

She looks so at ease here that it's hard to imagine it's not where she lives. That same smile falters as she shifts her weight to the other side of her body. Our gazes are still locked together as if we'd lost the key. She clears her throat, breaking our gaze and glancing at the floor. "I think it's best if I take care of what I came here for and let you get on with your vacation."

"I take it you know your way around."

She quirks a smile like the words themselves are ludicrous. "I do."

In the span of three minutes, I've watched this woman go from looking like a bunny with a crush to flustered and ready to be done with me, but that peek into the real side of her . . . that was the best yet. Can't wait to see what comes next. "Since we're not drinking, what can I do?"

The smirk that splits those sexy lips is captivating. "You're already doing it. Stay out of the way and look pretty." She raises her finger in the air, "Oh, and watch and learn. You're going to need to do this on your own." The initial punch to my ego was swift enough to catch me off guard. But it was the follow-up I should have seen coming.

Chuckling, I reply, "You mean you're not going to come over and do this for us every day, sometimes twice a day or even three times?" I follow her into the bathroom, stopping in the doorway to give her room to work and to watch this magic that's apparently about to happen.

She steps into the shower but leans to look back at me. "Three showers a day? Lordy, that's a lot. Why in the world would you need to take three showers a day?" I don't have a chance to say anything before she adds, "Don't tell me. I have a feeling I don't want to know."

I like that she takes the swing and hits it out of the ballpark. "Funny." Crossing my arms over my chest, I add, "I work out a lot."

"I just bet you do." I can't see her in the tub due to the wall, but her tone tells me all I need to know. *She's on to me.*

I move to the side where she's standing under the showerhead with her hand on the faucet. "Tell me something—"

"Raccoons have the dexterity of humans and can open jars. Ask me how I know . . ."

"What the—" Laughter bellows from my gut. "How do you know?" I lean back, resting my palms on the bathroom counter.

She's messing with the faucet, but stops to glance at me. "It was a mess of a honey story, and better suited for another time."

"Sounds like we'll have more time together."

"Only if you're lucky," she replies with her eyes back on the job at hand and a smile set on her face.

From what I've seen, I'm not sure she's doing anything special other than fucking with the faucet. "Is this the trick to making it work?"

"No. This is," she starts. "Okay, here's what you do—"

"Wait."

Her eyes widen as she turns to look at me again. "What?"

"Since my job is to look good, how am I doing?" Tightening my abs, I prepare for her to ogle.

After a quick swipe of her tongue against her bottom lip, she laughs. "I'll leave you a full review later."

I release the muscles and blow out a breath. "I look forward to reading it."

She yanks the faucet that should only turn left or right away from the pipe. "Pull hard." And when she jams it back in, she adds, "Then slam it back again." *Does she hear herself?* Because I sure the fuck do, and need to rearrange for more room in these trunks. With a satisfactory smile firmly in place, she steps to the back of the tub and motions me in. "Now you try it." I'd be happy to . . . with her. "The faucet," she adds as if I needed the reminder.

I sure as fuck did.

*Pipe.*

*Pull.*

*Slam in.*

*Try it.*

*Fuck me.* This shouldn't turn me on as much as it does.

Eyeing the small space she's left for me, I balk, perplexed how this mathematically works. "You want me in there?" Not going to happen. I smirk, crossing my arms over my chest again.

She grins. "Well, you kind of need to be for it to work." She takes a final step back before she reaches the tiled wall surrounding the basin.

I angle the showerhead up so I can fit in without it jabbing me in the head. "I already miss my shower at my penthouse."

"Not sure what kind of shower a penthouse has, but this one has good water pressure. I've tested it myself." Her showering in here isn't an image I mind. "What's your shower like?"

"Well, for one . . ." I reach up and hold the pipe jutting from the wall. "I can fit under it. But there are jets on the walls as well. The high pressure of the spray eases my muscles after practice."

"Maybe you're practicing too hard."

My gaze whips back over my shoulder so fast that my neck twinges. Now I'm the one staring. "Impossible."

She shrugs. "Okay. Suit yourself."

"I will." Not sure why that felt personal, but she struck a raw nerve. I turn away from her again, mumbling, "Practice less? What the fuck? No one who is worthy of playing practices less."

"Alright." I can hear the teasing in her tone. I glance back again. Her smile was already wiped away, but now she's looking at me like I need to speak to a professional.

I *am* a professional. A pro hockey player, who at thirty-five is at the top of my game. That's all anyone needs to know to be the best. *Watch me and practice.*

"As fun as it is to discuss the worst approach I've ever heard to winning, are we fixing this or rigging it to work?" I ask.

"We've tried to fix it." She leans against the tile wall to see what I'm doing. "Now we rig it. It's really just a trick that seems to work. It's not necessary if you prefer cold showers—"

"I do not." I pull out the faucet.

"Quick learner," she whispers, pressed up so close that she's almost beside me.

"It's not really rocket science." When I jam it back just like she did, I hear a crack. "That didn't sound good."

Grabbing my arm, she leverages her weight to peer around me. "No, it didn't."

I jolt when water hits my face, her scream right after. "ACK!" I'm grabbed by the middle and pulled backward just as her sneakers slip out from under her. Strong in my stance, like I am on the ice, I reach around, catching Summer before she falls and takes me with her. "Oh my God," she says, relief sinking through her muscles. "I thought I was doneso."

"I'm known for my fast reflexes."

She snorts as the water spews all over us. "I don't even know what to say to that other than if you let go of me, I won't get entirely drenched." She looks down as I turn around with my hands still on her waist. "Too late."

Her wet dress gives me a sneak peek of the lace bra she's wearing under it. Her hair is soaked, too. But it's from the briefest of our gazes uniting that my heart begins thundering in my chest. And then she's gone, free from me and the water, standing on the bathroom mat dripping like a wet cat.

"Oh noooo." She's eyeing the faucet and then jumps forward to try to turn it off with no luck. The strength she carried in her body has all but escaped. "Great," she deadpans, staring at the fractures in the tile that lead to the cracked base of the showerhead. She looks me over, and defeat wins, dragging down not only the sides of her mouth but the outer corners of her eyes. "Are you okay?"

"With all this happening, you're worried about me?"

"You're from the city."

I burst out laughing. "I'm from the city, so I've never seen a broken pipe? We used to play in the water from fire hydrants. You don't need to worry about me."

"At least you're dressed for it in your swimsuit." She grabs a towel from the rack and hands it to me even though she somehow managed to get more wet than I am.

"You go ahead. I need to see if there's any hope of salvaging this pipe to stop the water from leaking out." I pull the faucet back out, but I'm gentler this time when I push it back in. Unsuccessful, I can admit my own defeat. "We need to cut off the water to the house. Do you know where that valve is located?"

She finishes patting her face and wraps the towel around her. "It's on the other side of the house. I'll go do it." I take the other towel on display and dry off as I follow her through the house, leaving a trail of water in my wake.

We walk outside opposite where I parked. I've never seen a chick so confident in the mechanics of plumbing. Not that I've been around many plumbers. When she pulls the lid up from the yard, she grabs a metal tool lodged inside the hollowed space. Turning once, and then angling to turn it again, the valve stalls. "That should do it. Can you check through the window and tell me if it's off?"

I look through the bathroom window and call back, "All good."

When I turn around, she's wiping her hands on the towel. "You won't be able to stay here if the water is off."

"Then let's get it fixed."

She balls the towel in her hands and grins, but it's

lacking joy. "It's Saturday. There's no way we'll be able to get a plumber out here until sometime next week."

"Huh." My gaze lands on the deck where Roman and I played and ate lunch. It's only been a few hours, but we've already bonded again just from being here. "That's not good."

She's already marching back to the house when she replies, "Not good at all. I'm going to see if I can get Rodgers out here to help since it's an emergency."

"Who's Rodgers?"

"A cousin twice removed."

Following her, I ask, "Maybe I'm not connecting the dots, but how does your cousin twice removed help the situation?"

She stops and looks back. With a big grin on her face, she laughs. "He's studying to be a plumber, silly."

"Silly me." Studying doesn't sound good, but I have a feeling we're taking what we can get.

I stay on the deck, reclining in the Adirondack chair as she takes her phone and starts pacing along the side of the house while making calls. Occasionally, she ventures into my vantage point, giving me time to check her out again. She uses her hands a lot when she talks. Everything from a tornado swirl to rolling out the red carpet makes its way into her conversations. Returning my gaze to the water, I find the calmness of the ocean helps relax my typically tense muscles. It's an incredible place. I'll owe Coach Spears's wife a thank-you for finding it.

Closing my eyes, I dance around the edges of sleep when fast-approaching steps drag me back to reality. When I'm shadowed, I open my eyes to see her standing over me, blocking the sun.

"I have good news and bad news. Which do you want first?" she asks.

I push to sit upright. "Bad news."

She plops into the chair next to me like she's not going anywhere anytime soon. "No plumber can come out until next week, at the earliest."

"What happened to the second cousin twice removed who's studying plumbing?"

Leaning the back of her head against the chair, she takes in the beauty of the water, and replies, "Visiting his girlfriend in Gainesville for the week. So he's a no-go as well."

"Shit, what happens now?"

She rolls her head to the side to face me. "There's more bad news."

"Can't wait," I reply, letting sarcasm drip through my tone. "Hit me with it."

"I called around to all my hospitality contacts in a thirty-mile radius. There's nothing else available, and Mrs. Dover's other rental is rented every week this summer."

"So there are no other places to go while we wait for the cottage to be fixed? Is that what you're saying?"

Nodding, she doesn't seem the least bit stressed. "The boiled-down version? Yes."

"Fuck," I mutter under my breath, carrying all the stress for both of us. Directing my attention fully on her, I ask, "What's the good news?"

"Well, the good news is I came up with two options for you."

Resting my arms forward on my legs, I look over at her. "Two's good. What are they?"

"One," she starts with hope resonating in her voice. She taps her finger on her other hand's palm and grins. "You head back to the city and return once the pipes are fixed.

We'd obviously comp the week, and I can talk to Mrs. Dover about—"

"That's the last place I want to be right now. Coming here was about getting my son and me out of the city and taking a break from that chaos. So I'm not interested in going back. What's the second option?"

A gleam of sunshine hits her eyes as she replies, "You stay with me until it's fixed."

"So there's no good news?"

Closing her eyes, she looks ready to take her own nap. After adjusting against the wood seat, she says, "Guess it depends on how you look at it."

"I'm looking at it like I'm shit out of luck."

"Or in luck if you ask me." With her eyes on me again, she adds, "Treat it like an adventure with Roman, and it will be fixed before you know it."

I can't figure her out. The woman who had no patience for my antics earlier is starting to sound like she wants us to stay. *With her.* I also can't deny that I'm intrigued by the proposition. "How would it work?"

"There needs to be rules."

*I expect no less from her.*

# CHAPTER 5

## SUMMER

"Avoid my sisters at all costs," I slip in quietly.

"That's the rule?" He chuckles just as a breeze blows through. And starts texting and mumbling like I need to know his plans, "RSVP no to the event."

"What event?" I'm nosy and shrug.

"Nothing I'm interested in."

"Fine." Closing my eyes, I take in the gentle wind. The cotton fabric still sticks to my body in some places where it hasn't dried, but the breeze sneaks through the openings to help the process along.

"Avoiding my sisters. That's the *first* rule." There's rarely much traffic on this road between the houses, so our pace has been steady since we left the cottage with Roman running up ahead of us.

"Naturally."

I'm afraid he already knows me too well. Am I that predictable? *That* boring? To someone like him, living life in the busy city, being able to afford to vacation the entire summer with his son, I probably am. "I do love rules," I blurt out like some weird defense mechanism.

"You do, and I love breaking them." A wry grin slides across his lips. "Both rules and records." Rules I understand. They curb fun from turning into chaos. Records, though? What does he have against albums? "Guess we'd never make a good match."

I'm not sure if I take offense to that or not. "Yeah, I suppose not. I like music too much."

Under a creased brow, his gaze glides over to me. He opens his mouth and closes it again. After a quick shake of his head, he chuckles under his breath. "Okay." We keep walking, but then he asks, "Why are we avoiding your sisters at all costs?"

"Because . . ." I can't tell him that we don't see many men, much less men who look like him, roaming around these parts. If his picture gets out or gossip spreads that a gorgeous man is staying here for the summer, he'll have an influx of visitors wanting to welcome him. I wouldn't put stalking past some of them either. It's my job to provide the privacy my guests want and deserve. As for my sisters, though . . . "I won't hear the end of it if they get wind of you."

"So they don't know I'm here?"

"They know, but it's more for me than you."

"I'm not following." His brow furrows as he stares at me. "How so?"

I take a deep breath, not really interested in laying bare my stale love life to this man who can probably get any woman to say yes to anything he asks of them. It's not much of an ego booster for me in comparison. I exhale, and reply, "Don't laugh." When he doesn't respond, I look at him, raising my brows. "*Okay*?"

He laughs. Not a good start. "Okay."

Why do I feel like I'm going to regret this? Ugh. It's the truth, though, so I'll own it. "It's been a bit of a dry spell."

"How dry?"

"D4 levels."

"I assume we're talking about a drought scale?" He had been keeping watch on Roman, but his eyes are locked on me like I might escape if he doesn't.

I cross my arms over my chest. "Yes."

"And a D4 means?"

I need my hands too much to keep them restrained. I free my right one and wave it in the air. "Exceptionally drought-y."

His mouth drops open, but it's the eyes widening like saucers that really secures my embarrassment. "Exceptionally?"

"I knew I shouldn't have said anything." I pick up my pace to give myself some room to get through the humiliation. Even if we're the only ones on this road, it doesn't feel big enough for the three of us. I offered them a foldout couch in the living room, but he wants to think about it. I don't blame him. But now they'll know the way and can come and go as they need.

He easily makes up ground to walk next to me again. "I didn't laugh."

"You didn't have to." I glance at him. "I could feel the—"

"I wasn't judging. I'm genuinely surprised." He looks me over from head to toe and doesn't shy away from taking the scenic tour back up to meet my eyes. "Look at you."

I look down at my water-spotted dress and my sneakers, sullied with dirt from walking around in them. The ends of my hair are straight and hanging over my shoulder, and my thighs have been rubbing since I was soaked in the shower. "What am I looking at?"

"Come on, Summer. You're not serious."

It's the first time I've heard him call me by only my first name. I've heard him call me Summer Season and Ms. Season, but the way my name sounds like a warm cuddle rolling off his tongue makes my heart clench. "I am serious, Daniel," I reply, trying his name on for size. I like it better. I like him better, too. Though liking someone who is not only temporarily in Mountain Laurel Cove but also someone I'm supposed to maintain a professional relationship with is one road I can't travel down.

He's grinning like he just won the county pie-eating contest. "So all it took was showering together to get us on a first-name basis? If I'd known that, I would have had you stay earlier."

I laugh, but keep it light. Don't want to feed that already satiated ego of his. Again. "Stay and do what?" It shouldn't be this fun to flirt with him. I've been thrown from the ballooning presence of Daniel Sutton. One day. Not even a full day and he's not just invading my thoughts but now my house. Granted, it's for the bathroom, but he's suddenly in every part of my life. I wish I knew if that presence is full of hot air, like most guys, or I'm making something from nothing. Maybe a little of both.

His silence draws my attention back, but his eyes remain relegated ahead of us. Shoving his hands in his pockets, the cocky grin I'm thinking is his standard issue reappears. Looking at me, he says, "Shower together. What else would I mean?"

"What else indeed," I reply more to myself than him.

Roman stops ahead and turns back with a stamp of his foot. "Why didn't we take the car?"

"Because it's only a two-seater," Daniel replies. "And Summer walked over because she lives close by." Daniel is already feeling second nature. That's what happens after what we've been through so early in our relationship. Not that we have a relationship, but ugh. I stop the hamster wheel from spinning my thoughts and tangling them even more.

"It's not that far," I add with a good five feet between Daniel and me, who's staying closer to the center of the road while I turn around and hug the side.

Roman scans the vicinity as he starts walking again. "I don't see any houses."

There are too many trees to see the house from here, but it won't be long until it makes a grand appearance. It's been the talk of the town for years. We refuse to change it. "It will be up on the left, same side as the cottage."

"But—"

"Roman." His dad cuts him off. "Patience, buddy. We'll be there soon."

Despite helping me out there, the only thing that really sticks in my head is he is a dad. Before Roman was napping, I was given a peek inside their lives when I stopped by earlier. But I wasn't there long enough to get a sense of what kind of parent he is. Heck, I don't even know if he's married. Sure, I can assume he's not by his ringless finger, but some guys don't wear bands. "Are you married?" I ask to confirm one way or the other.

If he's married, I'm going to feel like the dirt on my shoes for flirting with him. If he's not, does that make this an opportunity?

*No. Summer. Stop.* Why did I even open that door when I had already firmly closed it? Superficially, he's just so handsome. Otherwise, he's entertaining. Seems only natural to be attracted to him. We've survived a water incident together, so it's only normal to grow closer. Whether that's mutual or not remains to be seen.

"I was surprised it wasn't asked on your form." He veers a little closer.

There's still enough distance safely between us to keep me from jumping his bones as if he's onto me. . . I cringe at myself. If I can't keep control of my thoughts, the rest might be already too far lost. It's tempting to giggle. One thing he's awoken, other than my libido, is my sense of humor. Why is it so fun to flirt again? Or is it fun to flirt with him?

"It wasn't information I needed to serve your needs." I'm kind of proud of my innuendo-riddled reply. Two can play that game, and look at me go.

"You sure about that?" I catch the wink he sends me.

I grin. "Positive."

"It's pink!" Roman shouts with a jump as he looks back. "Your house is pink."

"It sure is," I say, cupping my hand to the side of my mouth for him to hear. "We love the color pink."

He says, "I like orange like my dad's colors."

I look at his dad, who's not wearing any orange whatsoever, but I'm not going to argue with the kid. Daniel says, "It's the jersey."

"Oh." I roll my neck, loosening a knot and remembering all the times I've been stuck on weekends watching football game after football game instead of out having fun. "Guys love sports."

"You don't?"

With a shrug, I reply, "Some."

"Which ones?"

Why does it suddenly feel like an interrogation? This is the most interest he's shown, and as usual, it's centered around sports. *Men* . . . "I don't—"

"A swing!" Roman starts running toward the tire hanging from the large oak at the front of the house.

"Are the ropes reinforced?"

My heart skips a beat at the concern in his voice. He starts jogging after Roman, and I run after him. "There's never been an issue." I slow on approach. Daniel is running his fingers along the rope even though his son has already climbed on. "It's the same ropes they use at the marina. Should last almost as long as this oak tree."

The tension eases from his tightened jaw, and he releases a heavy breath. "You ready?" he asks, pulling the tire back, ready to send him flying.

Roman giggles. "Ready, Daddy."

Daniel releases him, but is right there to catch the tire when it comes barreling back to him. "Hold on tight, Roman." He spins the black rubber and stands back, his watchful gaze full of both joy and caution. I'm so stuck on staring at this man, amazed to see how he shifted into daddy-mode with such ease from the flirtatious playboy he's been with me.

Daddy-mode. Daddy . . . *Good Lord, do me in right now, why don't ya?* I didn't know I had a kink until I met this man and watched those broad shoulders flex under the thin material of the T-shirt, his biceps pop out when catching the tire, and lengthen when pushing it into the air. He is fit, more in shape than most businessmen who rent the cottage for their families. They sit around on laptops pretending to participate in the family activities. Daniel is digging in right now and being present. There wasn't a laptop in sight earlier on the deck or inside the house when I come to think about it.

I stand back, watching them. Listening to the laughter is

sweeter than birds singing the first of spring after a long winter.

When he steps back, he crosses his arms over his chest with attentive eyes on Roman. "Pink is a bold choice. Unique like your names."

"It is. It had needed to be painted for years. We all chose pink and painted it ourselves. It was therapeutic, something we had together that kept our minds off . . ." My heart beats hard in my chest as the pain returns, still so eagerly it feels fresh all over again. I take a steadying breath before I add, "It was what we needed at the time. It felt like ours, like a new beginning."

I glance over at Daniel to find his eyes already on me. His eyebrows are knitted, and brown eyes hold questions that aren't asked. I've already shared more than I should have with a practical stranger, so I'm glad. I'm good leaving the past out of the present.

His gaze pivots over my shoulder, and he says, "Convenient."

The word tumbles around my brain as I try to figure out what he's referring to but comes up empty. Ah, we're back to the games again. I'm grateful for the change in subject. "Convenient for you?"

A laugh launches out of him as he moves in to catch the tire. "I meant it was convenient for managing the other house. You know, with it being so close to your own."

"Right." I don't have it in me to even feign I caught that. Thinking about the past always weighs me down, and it takes time to shake it off again. "I thought you were implying something else."

"What would that be?"

"I'm not falling for it this time, Sutton."

He laughs again. "Close proximity is good, too," he

concedes. Daniel Sutton is too handsome for his own good. He drops innuendos like bombs at my feet and seems to know just how to rile me up and make me smile. The last time someone was able to do even half of those, I got my heart broken. I need to be careful with him. He's dangerous in more ways than just my willpower. "For emergencies, of course."

My smile returns so easily that it's there before I realize my mood has shifted again. "Of course."

Holding the ropes, he helps Roman jump off into the grass. His son is cute with the same hair and eye color as his dad. But freckles sprinkle across his nose, and his smile must favor his mom more. It's not smirky like his dad's. I sneak a peek at Daniel to confirm.

Yep, the smirkiest of the smirky.

It's even worse when he busts me looking. "You okay?"

"Fine," I reply as nonchalantly as I can, which sounds suspiciously chalant to my ears. "You?" I squeak, wishing I would have kept my mouth shut.

His grin splits his smile wide open for me. It's the most genuine I've seen out of him. And does quite a doozy of a job of weakening my knees. I don't fall for him—literally and figuratively. Though it's darn tempting, almost like he was put in my path by Aphrodite herself.

"I'm doing good. Considering."

We follow Roman toward the house, and he asks, "What are we considering?"

"The broken pipes."

Fell right into that trap. "Ah. Right. That."

That wide smile of his is gentler like it's just the two of us. "I'm not married."

I stumble forward when my toe catches a lump in the yard, and his words catch me off balance. Just before I fall on my face, strong arms wrap around my middle, keeping me suspended in the air. *Still . . . just floating here . . .* "I think I'm good."

"You sure?"

Laughing, I reply, "I'm sure." When I land on solid ground again, I look at him. "Thanks for saving me."

He almost looks shy, like the spotlight is too much for him. Unexpected. Charming. "You're welcome."

My heart is racing to a finish line that he's waiting on like knowing he's single changes things. Does it? I know I can't be the only one feeling this connection. Can I?

It's a beautiful day, with temperatures in the lower eighties. A little hot when stuck in the sun for too long but cool enough in the shade. But standing under his gaze is bright, hot, and making me sweat. I pluck the front of my dress, and say, "We should go in. I need to change."

"Not one thing."

"Huh?"

"Nothing."

Roman's already waiting on the front porch when we walk up the steps. Grabbing hold of the doorknob, I don't twist. I turn back and say, "Remember what I said earlier about my sisters?"

He shifts until his feet are planted on the porch as if bracing himself. "Yes."

"They're nosy. Not nosier than I am, but as a collective, we're all pretty nosy, and they will ask you a million questions if they even get a hint of fresh meat."

"What's fresh meat?" Roman asks with worry in his tone.

Daniel reaches down to gently squeeze his shoulder. "There's someone new to talk to. That's all."

Roman looks up at his dad. "That's us. We're the new people?"

"Yes. It means they'll be interested in learning more about you."

I open the door. "The bathroom is the first door on the left." Roman runs in, and as soon as I hear the door close, I catch Daniel's gaze again. "Just a word of warning about what you might be walking into."

"A warning, huh?" He peers into the house and then glances back at me. "Should I be nervous?"

I shouldn't laugh, but I know what he's walking into. He was a hot topic before he even arrived, so when my sisters and Dolly see him, they'll eat him right up. "We don't have many guests, so you might be overwhelmed by the attention. That's all I'm saying."

"I'm used to an inordinate amount of attention, from women especially, though, guys have been known to crowd them out to get to me."

My head jerks. "What are we talking about?"

"I don't get overwhelmed easily is all I'm saying."

Patting his shoulder, I say, "That's good because I forgot to mention Dolly."

The corners of his eyes crinkle, giving me a glimpse into the one thing that apparently strikes fear into the giant of a man. "What's a Dolly?"

"Who's here?" a voice from the family room reaches us.

I smile. "That's a Dolly." Coming closer to him, I whisper, "My grandmother." I can only assume he wasn't prepared to meet my entire family, but here we are. "It will be okay."

"Promise?"

"Cross my heart."

## CHAPTER 6

DANIEL

"It's Summer," she calls through the house, letting the sound carry to the back of it. "I brought a friend."

That shouldn't leave me smiling, but there's something sweet about this girl. I lower my head, and whisper, "Friends, huh?"

She rolls her pretty eyes and pokes me in the arm. "Be good."

"Trust me. I'm always good." I give her a wink.

"Oh my, my," she mutters under her breath as she leaves me standing in the foyer of this old house. "I tried to warn you. They're going to make you pay the toll for use of the bathroom."

"What's the fee?"

"Your time."

Roman comes out of the bathroom, and says, "Nice throne."

"No." I bend down and whisper, "Manners, please."

"You taught me that."

"It's a guy thing, buddy. Not for the ladies."

Turning back, she signals behind her. "Come on."

I take his hand, which wasn't properly dried, adding something else we need to work on to the list, and head to Summer, who's waiting for us. Dark wood panels line the walls with an eclectic array of rugs and knick-knacks around. We entered near a small table with a ceramic bowl that looks like something made in elementary school and walked past a dining room with a long wooden table in the front that seats ten, while paralleling a large set of stairs with a floral runner beneath our feet. Summer said it was her sisters and her grandmother here, and by the looks of it, they've made the place their own, as evidenced by the pink paint and blue shutters outside. Unique seems to be an understatement when it comes to her and her family.

Waiting on us, she stands there in her beauty that I'm not sure she's fully aware of. She wavers between an innocence that peeks through like sunshine on a cloudy day, and on the flip side, she's proficient and even eager to please to get her job done. But it's the third wild element that's most captivating. Her shoulders ease, and a smile comes without warning when we dance around the suggestion of anything sexual. I'm so used to women being forward and telling me exactly what they want in the bedroom. Plenty are happy to hide their motives for fame, even the adjacent ones, and access to money. Mine, specifically.

*It's uninteresting.*

Summer Season is anything but boring. There's not been an ounce of wanting anything from me other than to make sure we're taken care of and having a good time. She treats me so normal like I'm not me, I'm not Daniel Sutton, super star right wing for the Brooklyn Breakaways, not famous or even known. It's refreshing. I appreciate her efforts not to make a big deal out of me. That's all I get in the city. It's a nice change here in the Cove.

When I reach her, she enters the back room. "Dolly, this is our Cove Cottage tenant for the summer, Daniel—"

"Sutton," her grandmother fills in as if it's been waiting on the tip of her tongue. Rushing past her granddaughter, she swoops right into me, wrapping her arms around my body like a vise grip.

"Yes." That is practically gut punched out of me when her Dolly clings to me when a handshake would have sufficed. "We're hugging. Okay. Alright." I pat her gently as the short woman buries her head against my abs. "You got a good hold on me there, Dolly."

Summer takes her arm with a laugh that's bordering on awkwardness as her eyes dart from me to Dolly again. "She sure does. Let's wrap this up and let Mr. Sutton breathe again, Grandma."

Dolly releases me as soon as "Grandma" comes out of her mouth. "Mind your manners, ma'am," she snaps at Summer.

Summer wraps her arms around Dolly from behind, and I can't determine if it's a hug or a restraint tactic. "You too," she teases right back. "This is Daniel's son, Roman."

Dolly leans down and taps his nose. "Do you like cookies?"

"I like cookies a lot."

"How do you feel about chocolate chip?"

If captured, the excitement on Roman's face could light up an arena. "They're my favorite."

She says, "You're in luck. I was just about to bake some." That's all it takes for Dolly to win over my son. Though, I'm weak to a good cookie too, so I don't blame him. Roman gets wrapped under her arm, leading him to the kitchen. "Summer, show our guest around."

"My mom likes snickerdoodles." I can hear him telling

her about his mom when I didn't even know that about Mia. Why would I, though? We didn't make it past a second date before we were trying to figure out the logistics of raising a son when we weren't together.

It's all worked out, but I'm glad Roman knows that kind of stuff.

"She forgets we're grown sometimes," Summer says, tapping the toe of her shoe on the floor.

She's all grown, alright. "I'm sure it's still great to have her close."

Straightening her posture and standing on two feet again, she has a shine in her eyes that's brightened since we arrived. "It is." Presenting the room in front of us, she says, "The family room." Looking at the corner, she waffles. "The kitchen is back there. The dining room up front and the bathroom. We came here so you could use it, so don't be shy."

"I'm good." I glance at the stairs. "What's upstairs?"

She laughs, pressing her hand to her chest and rubbing gently. "We're not going upstairs." Grabbing hold of a baluster that wobbles, she stills it and takes two steps up. Incredibly, she's still shorter than me. "We got wet together. That was all."

"Getting wet together justifies a tour up there, if you ask me."

"That's why I'm not asking." Eyeing her lips as she licks them and then sucks the bottom under her top teeth, I realize that resisting her is going to be a challenge. "But can I ask you something personal?"

"I like when we get personal."

Her hold on the wood tightens, whitening her fingertips. Nervous? "Are you always this flirtatious?"

"Is that what this is? Flirting?" I tilt my head to study the minutest of reactions she's willing to reveal—the quick gnaw on the inside of her cheek, the sway of her body, her gaze distancing when she's deep in thought.

"If it walks like a duck and talks like a duck—"

"I think it's safe to call this a duck. But to answer your question, no, I'm not."

That pretty smile of hers reaches her eyes, and when she looks down, a spray of her lashes kisses the tops of her cheeks. "I should change my clothes."

I look at the dress that's dried and stretched out more than it was, and ask, "Should I wait here for you?"

She nods with a growing grin. "Sounds like a good option since you're not coming upstairs with me." *She winks.* She winks at me, and my whole chest tightens as I grin like a fucking fool. "Or you could spend time with Dolly and make cookies."

"It's not a bad option."

"Why do I get the distinct impression you're up to no good, Mr. Sutton?"

"I prefer it when you call me Daniel." Moving closer, I rest my hand over hers and lower my voice. "It feels less like we're strangers."

She leans in, and whispers, "We practically *are* strangers, though, so acting like we're not doesn't change the facts."

"We can change—"

"I didn't know we had company."

My eyes dash to the girl at the top of the stairs as I move away from Summer. Summer's gaze whips over her shoulder as she tucks strands of hair behind her ear. She's breathless before she even speaks, and when she does, she asks, "Spring? Um . . ." Returning her attention to me, she says, "This is the summer tenant next door."

The girl's hair is a shade or two darker than Summer's,

and her eyes are just as blue as she studies us like we just got busted. “Didn’t mean to interrupt.” Apparently, that smirk runs in the family. Thumbing over her shoulder, she adds, “I can go back upst—”

“No, you didn’t interrupt.” Summer peeks at me before angling toward who I assume is a sister who’s starting down the stairs again. “This is Daniel Sutton.”

Embracing Summer’s words, she bops down the stairs with an energy I haven’t felt in years, only stopping when she reaches the same step her sister is already occupying. Holding her hand out, she says, “Spring Season.”

I shoot a look straight at Summer and then back before shaking her hand. “Spring?” Releasing her, I look at Summer, and ask, “As in the four seasons?”

“The Season Sisters,” Spring says, bobbling her head. “That’s what we’re known as. It’s annoying but kind of grows on you.”

“It’s not annoying,” Summer says, and then looks at me. “Our mom gave us those names.”

“Unique.” I don’t know what else to say. Summer Season was different, to put it kindly. But all four. “So there’s also—”

“Fall and Winter.” Spring steps to the landing beside me. “Well, technically it’s Autumn but that just doesn’t work as well. I read you have a son?”

If looks could kill, Spring would be dead and Summer convicted of the murder. “That’s proprietary information, dear sister.”

“You left the file on your bed.”

“In my locked room.”

She laughs. “I didn’t notice. Anywho, I’m sure he doesn’t mind talking about his son, big sis.” Turning her attention back to me, Spring adds, “Right, Daniel or do you go by Danny?”

“Daniel, never Danny, and yeah, I have an eight-year-old named Roman. He’s in with Dolly making cookies.”

Moving around us, she starts in their direction. “Great. I’ll see if I can help and leave you two to enjoy some time alone—”

“We don’t need alone time,” Summer says in a panic. The door is already swinging closed behind her when she turns to me. “We don’t need alone time.”

“Speak for yourself.” I grin. “So, the four seasons, huh?” I rock back on my heels, tucking my hands into my pockets. “I feel dumb.”

“I’m sure it will pass. It always does for me.”

Besides chuckling, I say, “When we met, you mentioned your names being different. You even mentioned Dolly, but this isn’t what I expected.”

“No one ever does. You can imagine how fun it is for us to meet new people,” she deadpans as she takes a seat on the stairs. “Spoiler, it isn’t. It’s always a topic of conversation.”

“I can imagine.”

“We get it,” she drolls like she’s bored. “Our names are different. Spring even hated hers for a few of her teen years and made us call her Ava. She thought Spring was too grounding, too earthy and hippie, and Ava was glamorous.”

Coming to sit next to her, I lean against the opposite baluster. “She seems to have come back around.”

“I’d say in the past two years. As the youngest, I think she struggled more to find her own identity. We’re all so similar. Makes sense because we’re close, but it was good for her to spread her wings instead of settling on being part of a group. She came around when she was ready.” She scrunches her nose. “I’m sure none of this makes sense—”

“It does. But what about you?”

"I didn't have a choice." It would have been easy to throw something out, to deflect, but she doesn't take that route. She goes with honesty. "As the oldest, I had three girls to raise."

"What do you mean? Why did you raise them?"

"Because Dolly was grieving her only child and struggled to get up in the morning, or any time of day, for that matter. If I had done the same . . ." Her pause has her looking away from me. She clenches her eyes and then reopens them with a raise of her chin. "You know what? We should get you what you need and—"

"Daddy, come taste." Our gazes are pulled to the kitchen door that's been swung open. My cute kid looks like the sugar is already taking effect by the wild look in his eyes and a smile that's giving a full view of his molars.

"We'll be right—"

"It's okay," Summer says with a quick tug on the hem of my shirt. "That's enough about me. You came here on vacation, not to listen to my tragedy." The sweetest smile shines as she stands again and dusts the back of her skirt with a sweep of her hands.

"I want to hear more about you."

"Well, you're going to be stuck with me more than you bargained for since you're out of water and we're the closest bathroom."

I don't remember the last time I've been interested in a woman, but Summer is the most fascinating woman I've met in some time. No water is a real bitch of an inconvenience. Silver lining, an excuse to get to know her better. "We'll muddle through somehow."

# CHAPTER 7

## SUMMER

"He sure is cute." Shifting her can of soda to the other side of her on the butcher block island, my sister leans in closer, and whispers, "How long has it been?"

"How long has it been for what?" I straighten the V-neck of the T-shirt I threw on with a pair of shorts, aligning the drop point with my cleavage. Not that Daniel's noticed. There are cookies, so the competition is stiff in this kitchen.

Turning her back to Dolly, Daniel, and Roman, who are crowded around the oven, Spring grins at me with a glint in her eyes. I know that devious look. "You can't play dumb with me, Sum. How long has it been since your last date? A year? Two?"

"Why does it matter?" There's no rush to correct her. I get enough lecturing from Dolly and Winter. I don't need my twenty-year-old sister's opinion added into the mix. "I'm doing fine."

Bending down, she messes with the loose threads of her cutoff denim skirt. So easily distracted, and I'm grateful for it. She pops up again, and says, "All I'm saying is he's cute. If you don't claim him, someone else will."

"What? I'm supposed to rush and pee on him to mark him as mine so the single ladies stay away?" I laugh. "So ridiculous."

Turning around again, she watches them like I do and then grabs her soda. "You don't have to pee, but a hickey would do the trick." She smacks me on the ass, and says, "Now go get 'em, tiger."

"Spring," I gripe quietly at her between pursed lips as I watch her flee the kitchen.

"Laters, Dolly. Nice meeting you, neighbors."

She's gone before Dolly can turn around. "That girl. She's faster than an F1 driver."

Daniel glances at me with a grin. "Are you into Formula 1, Dolly?"

"Who isn't?" she replies, slipping her oven mitts back on.

Roman steps back to the side of the island and out of the way from the heat of the oven. "I like hockey." Looking at me, he asks, "Do you watch hockey, Summer?"

"I don't. I know there are a lot of fans in Mountain Laurel Cove. There's always a game showing on TV at Bixby's down on the water." Resting on my forearms, I say, "Maybe we can watch a game together while you're here this summer."

He laughs and looks at his dad. When he turns back, he says, "It's the offseason."

"Oh." I stand upright. "Guess that makes sense, being a cold-weather sport. Who's your favorite team?"

Giggles get the best of him. When I hear Daniel chuckle as well, I'm not sure what's so funny, but I laugh lightly, not wanting to be left out. Roman finally says, "The Brooklyn Breakaways are the best in the league."

"Your hometown team. That makes sense. Do you get to go to games?"

"Sometimes, but only if it's on a weekend. I have too much homework, so Mom won't let me go."

Daniel comes behind him, mussing up his hair. "School is important, buddy. Your mom and I agree that it comes first. There are plenty of matches in the season for you to watch. And you can always watch one on TV."

"It's not the same. I don't get to see you in person."

Kneeling next to Roman, Daniel takes his hand. It's so small against his—protective but gentle. My heart clings to the moment I'm witnessing between father and son and remembering how I felt the same when my dad was alive. He loved us with his entire being and made it known. There wasn't a time that I didn't feel the full wealth of being my parents' kid. As the oldest, I know I was the most fortunate to have the extra years with them that I did. I could only wish my sisters had the same.

Daniel says, "I know it's hard with me on the road most of the time, but we have the summer to make up for it. Okay?" Roman nods, his expression not convinced, but he hugs his dad anyway. "I love you, buddy."

"Love you, too."

When Daniel stands, he continues holding Roman's hand. "I think we'll stay at the cottage tonight. It will be like camping but with nice beds."

"In case you change your mind, I'll keep my phone on."

He looks down as if a shyness comes over him. "Thanks."

Dolly turns with a tin in her hands. "Cookies for the road?"

"We won't say no," Daniel replies. "Thanks, Dolly." When his eyes land on me again, he grins. It's not smirky in the least, but it is endearing. "We'll get out of your hair for the night."

"I'll walk you out."

Roman gives Dolly a hug. She gives Daniel another vise-gripper right after. They use the facilities once more before I lead them out the front again. I stop on the top step of the porch just as Roman takes off for the tire swing again. Daniel stops in the grass and turns back. "Thanks for the bathroom."

"Anytime." I lean against a column and cross my arms over my chest. "Sorry about the water situation. What a nightmare."

"It will give Roman a good story to tell his friends. How he roughed it over the summer without indoor plumbing." He laughs, but I'm not sure he found it that funny by the tone. After checking on Roman over his shoulder, he turns back to me with a foot parked on the bottom step. "Tell me something."

"I'm an open book."

That has him grinning with his eyes locked on mine like he might change his mind and stay. I've been on the fence since the cottage. This feels fast. Not that we can control broken pipes. That part feels more kismet if I believed in such things. It's okay to want nice things, and Daniel Sutton is a very nice thing.

"Who chose the pink?"

I burst out laughing and gallop down the stairs to take in the same view as he is. "Truth? Spring. It was her ninth birthday, the first after . . ." I don't say it and pretend I didn't stumble into the story that still hurts just thinking about it. "All she wanted was a pink Barbie house." I glance at him while he studies the architecture of the house. Our Victorian has some interesting features that I've not seen in others locally—a turret and trim that others removed long ago to modernize their homes. Holding my arms out wide, I say, "We surprised her with a Barbie pink house she could live in." I point toward the roof. "Winter chose the green gingerbread trim, and Fall wanted blue shutters."

"What did you choose?"

I stare up at the circular third-floor window tucked into the roof. I still feel closer to my parents when I see it, which isn't as often these days since I don't hang out on the top floor much anymore. "The stained glass design in the window. It's two lovebirds. My parents used to call each other "lovebird," so it felt like a way to hold on to the memory and honor them."

Glancing up at it again, he says, "It's beautiful. I think it completes it."

I nod, unable to speak words with the lump in my throat blocking them. Daniel wraps his arm around me, and though it's only a side hug, I feel safe in his arms.

"Dad?"

"One minute, bud," he calls back to Roman.

I swipe under my eyes and slip out from his arm. "No, it's okay. He needs you." The time to part feels heavy between us. I take a breath that feels freeing from being around him. "You're sure about tonight?"

"I'm sure. Thanks, though." He walks backward with a rogue grin lifting his expression. "You have a good night, Summer, okay?"

It's only evening, but I nod as if it wasn't rhetorical. "You, too, Daniel." Daniel . . . my summer tenant, my short-term neighbor, my friend. And if you asked me how much I'd bet that there will be more with the handsome Mr. Sutton, I'm going all in.

As soon as I shut the front door behind me, I lean

against it, closing my eyes while imagining him in my head, and smile.

"You're in so much trouble."

I pop open my eyes to see Spring standing on the stairs. I push off the door and start toward her. "I'm in no such thing."

She laughs. "Keep lying to yourself, but I'll bet dishes for a month that you sleep with him before the Fourth of July."

I take four steps past her and turn around with my mouth hanging open. "That's in . . ." I calculate from today's date, and my jaw hits the floor. "That's three and a half weeks, Spring."

"And the problem is?" she asks, batting her wide eyes.

"There's no problem, but—"

"Exactly. There *is* no problem. Don't overthink it. He's hot, and you can't ask for anyone more convenient."

There's that "convenient" again. I don't know when convenient meant automatic sex with someone, but I'm feeling out of touch with how things work nowadays. You'd think I was decades older than twenty-six. "Why is my little sister all up in my business?"

"Because your business is going to cobweb over if you don't get out there again." She trots down the stairs but stops at the bottom to look back at me. "It's time, Summer. Don't let something good slip away because you're worried about what others will think." She turns the corner, leaving me on the staircase, and calls, "Dolly?"

I trudge up the remaining steps and down the hall to my bedroom. It's cracked open because my sister was obviously "borrowing" something I told her I wouldn't loan out. I close it and sit on the edge of the bed. Falling backward, I let my arms fall wide open and stare up at the ceiling. I never find any answers there, but it doesn't stop me from trying.

My sister did a good job of making me question what I should do about my sexy neighbor. It wouldn't be professional to sleep with him. But I have no doubt it would be fun.

The man is pure sex appeal. Add in that smile of his and a sense of humor, and I'm surprised I'm not already naked. But I know as well as he does that having sex with each other would be a terrible idea. Not only is his son staying with him but I'm sure there's something in my contract for this job about behavior.

*I should check just in case.*

## CHAPTER 8

DANIEL

"It's two in the morning, Roman." I scrub a hand over my face. Opening one, I rub the inside corner of the other.

"I have to go, and I don't want to go outside alone."

"I don't blame you, kid." New place to get used to, unfamiliar landscape, and it's pitch-black inside this house and out. I flip the covers off and set my feet on the wood floors. "You sure this can't wait?"

"I'm sure."

"When you gotta go, you gotta go, so let's go." I stand, taking his hand and leading him from my bedroom down the hall through the living room to the front door. Unlocking it, we step out onto the large deck and walk to the corner. I release his hand. "Aim for the dirt." I give him privacy by turning my back.

The moon reflects off the water, providing plenty of light out from under the trees, but it's dark where we are due to the coverage. My eyes have adjusted, but I don't hear anything coming from my son. I look back over my shoulder and see him standing there. "What's up?"

He looks from the ground to me with a grimace. "I can't do number two off the deck, Daddy."

"You need to do number two?" I try to pull back my shock so I don't shame him, but this is an issue.

"Yeah."

I look in the direction of Summer's house, but it's too far to see from here. "Is it an emergency or can it wait until morning?" There was a Buc-ee's fifteen, twenty minutes off the highway. Give another ten to fifteen minutes to get to the highway. Doing that would be better than bothering Summer and her family at this hour.

"I need to go."

If it did take thirty-five minutes to get there, we'd probably be twenty minutes too late. No way is he going to make it that long in the car. "Let me get dressed, and you put some shoes on."

Three minutes later, we're loading into the car, and I'm backing out. I say, "Everyone is sleeping, so be very quiet when we get there, Roman."

"I will."

Other than my headlights, there are no lights to guide our way. Until their porch light pulls us toward the house like a beacon in the night. I park in the distance so the engine or tires on the gravel don't wake anyone. Pulling my phone from my pocket, I hate doing it, but when nature calls, so do I.

*One ring.*

*Two rings.*

*Three.*

*Four...*

"Hello?"

"Summer, it's Daniel." It's two in the morning, so when there's no reply, I add, "The tenant from next door."

"Oh. Um. Hi." Her voice is rusty as her breathing lightens from when she first answered. "What's going on?"

I latch my seat belt. Roman does the same as we prepare to dash inside to take care of business. "I hate waking you, but my son needs the bathroom. He says he can't wait for morning."

There's a longer pause this time. "You're guys."

Logic would reason we had options at the cottage, but not this time. "It's number two."

"Meet me at the front door." She hangs up so fast that I'm left still holding my phone to my ear.

I pop the door. "Hurry, buddy."

The screen door is already opening when we approach the porch, and she greets us with a welcoming smile like we didn't just wake her in the middle of the night to use her bathroom. "Not sure if I should say good morning or good night."

Grinning, I walk up behind Roman. "We seem to be caught in between."

Dressed in a loose pajama top that hits her midsection with straps over her shoulders and shorts with a blue bow in the front, Summer smiles at him and nods toward the inside of the house. "You know where it is."

He runs past her while I remain on the porch. "Sorry about this."

"It's okay."

Running my hand over the back of my neck, I'm disappointed I didn't figure out a better situation for my son. "It's really not. Not to you or him. We can't stay at the cottage. I'll make different arrangements in the morning."

She quietly closes the screen door behind her and moves to the railing to look out into the dark. "You know what they . . ."

"No, what do they say?" I move across the large porch to a wicker loveseat parked there and sit. Since I'm not sure how long this is going to take, I might as well make myself at home.

"It's all fun and games until someone needs to go number two." She laughs too loud for this hour before she clamps a hand over her mouth.

Not sure if she's goofy from being woken up or delirious, but I chuckle. "I'm pretty sure that's not a saying."

"You're probably right." Her smile is softer in the moonlight. Not surprised, since she was sleeping five minutes ago, but there's something different about not only that but also her body language. She's relaxed with her hair hanging down from the elastic earlier, a thin strap straying toward the edge of her shoulder, and her ankles crossed as she rests against the railing. It's her tipped nipples pressing against the lightweight fabric that draws my eyes. I'm such a bastard. I didn't wake her up to ogle her, but here I am.

I look away, though it's hard to do. She's relaxed, and it's good to see. No rules or things she needs to get off her chest. Now I'm thinking about her nipples again, and I know I did the right thing by looking away. For her, not myself.

And I'm really starting to think she might not know who I am, that I play pro hockey, or even that I'm famous. I shouldn't find that as appealing as I do, but to know she's treating me how she is because of me being me instead of the league MVP is so fucking attractive.

Scraping my fingers through my hair, I look over at my car, needing somewhere for my eyes to land other than on her. "Sorry he's taking so long."

"It's okay." She pushes off and comes to sit next to me. Tugging on a loose thread at the bottom of her pajama shorts, she says, "The offer still stands." Her tone is as casual as we are, but I know there's a lot behind the words. She may be more at ease at 2 a.m., but I have a feeling her mind is still always spinning.

Glancing at the house, I say, "You have a full house. We would only be in the way."

She brings her legs to her chest and loops her arms around them. "We have a guest room downstairs. It will only be for a few nights." When her eyes find mine, what little light is out here is captured inside. "It really wouldn't be any trouble at all."

I could say no, take the burden off her and out of the mix, but I promised Roman time away from the city and fans barging in anytime we go somewhere together. "I don't think I've ever been anywhere that's as quiet as it is here."

"When I return from the city, my ears ring for a day or two after."

"Yeah, I get that. This is nice, and Roman is having a good time." I rest my arms on my knees and look at her out of the corner of my eye. "You sure about that offer?"

"One hundred percent."

I nod. "We'll accept."

Standing, she says, "How about you stay the rest of tonight? The guest room is ready, and we can make a pallet for Roman to sleep on." Stopping shy of the door, she thumbs over her shoulder. "I can head in ahead to make sure you have everything you'll need."

"You don't have to do anything special." I stand, tucking my hands in my pockets. "We can just dive in and fall asleep fast. It's a skill Roman inherited from me."

"All done." Roman pushes the screen door open and is about to let it slam behind him when he walks out.

I fly forward and catch it before it startles the whole house awake. Summer's hand is over her chest like she's trying to keep her heart from leaping out of her chest. "All good," I say, almost grinning as much as I do when I score a goal. Nothing touches that high. Other than holding my son for the first time, but that's a matter of the heart.

"Thank goodness. That would not have been good." She lowers her hand and comes closer, not enough to touch but to stand together as if we're suddenly a united front.

I look at Roman. "We're going to stay here tonight." The joy in his smile is a good sign. He likes Summer. *He's not the only one.*

"Do we get to sleep in Summer's room?"

My eyes go wide and dart to Summer as I chuckle under my breath. "That *would* be fun." She seems unfazed until a laugh escapes. Indifference isn't something she can pull off. Scooting him inside, I whisper, "We're going to share a room downstairs tonight."

Toeing the floor, he huffs. "Oh, man."

"Are you already sick of me, kid?"

"No, but Summer has a tire swing."

She shrugs. "It's true. That automatically gives me bonus fun points."

Ruffling his hair, I say, "Well, I can't compete with that, but I can promise that swing will be out there in the morning. But right now, we need sleep."

Summer leads us to a room off the entry and opens the door. We all walk into the bright white room with yellow trim and curtains featuring suns. Colorful pillows cover the top half of the bed and catch Roman when he dives in. He giggles as they fall on top of him. I pull his shoes off and then return to Summer's side. "I have a feeling I'm not getting him out of there tonight."

"Do you want me to make a pallet for you?" She nudges me with her elbow. "Happy to."

I angle my mouth closer to her ear, and whisper, "I'm still thinking about how fun it would be in your room."

"That's not happening."

Watching Roman get off the bed only to jump back on it again, I laugh. "Never say never."

Leveling me with a look that wobbles between amused and believing she can resist me, she replies, "It's never happening, Sutton."

I take my shirt off and toss it on a puffy chair in the corner. Why can I imagine her curled up in it reading? It would fit her just right.

"What are you doing?" she asks with her eyes glued to me when I walk to the side of the bed.

"Getting ready so you can tuck me in."

"I want to be tucked in," Roman says, freeing himself from the pillows, some of which go flying off the bed.

"I think your dad can tuck both of you in."

"Boo." Roman gives her two thumbs down. This kid is harsh.

She tilts her head, shooting me a dirty look, and then smiles when she comes to his side of the bed. "Fine. Tuck your legs under the covers." He does so lightning fast with a smile on his face. Who is this guy? The little charmer. She tugs the covers to his shoulders and then leans over him with her own smile in place to whisper, "Sweet dreams."

Turning around, she heads for the door. "See you in the morning."

"What about me?" I ask, lying on top of the covers with my hands behind my head, ready to be tucked in.

She stops, pausing before she finally looks back.

Roman says, "Daddy needs tucking in, too."

I owe him a snow cone for doing me the favor. "Thanks, buddy."

Summer's hands anchor on her hips as she stares at me with a wild debate in her eyes. She gives in and comes to my side of the bed. "Legs under the covers."

I scramble to tuck them under. She tugs the blanket to my chest, and says, "Good night."

Catching her arm before she leaves, I keep her close, and whisper, "Sweet dreams, Summer."

There's a spark in her eyes that tells me everything I need to know. She wants me. She just doesn't know what to think about me or what to do with me. I'm happy not to be shoved in some dumb jock box, called a millionaire playboy, or judged by my actions on the ice rather than who I am on solid ground. She probably hasn't ever met a celebrity before. Look where she lives—in the middle of nowhere. She's kind because of who she is, not because she feels obligated to impress the famous guy.

She taps me on the nose. "Get some rest, and I'll see you in the morning." I roll my head to the side to watch that ass as she walks out and shuts the door behind her. She gives good fucking exit.

My feet hang off the end, and my shoulders take up most of the mattress. It's got to be a queen-sized bed at best, but there's a bathroom across the hall, so I guess this is what we get for the next few days.

Roman's head falls against my arm when he rolls to his side, facing me. "Night," he says, already sounding like he's on the edge of sleep.

I lean down and kiss the top of his head. "Good night. I love you."

His arm flops onto me when I lie back again. "Love you."

He probably fell asleep before Summer could make it back to bed. I'm stuck lying here wide awake, though, thinking about her and this mess we've found ourselves in with the cottage.

Getting out of the city meant getting rid of distractions and thinking about the ultimatum on the table. The offseason will give me the clarity I need to decide which direction I'm heading—retirement or another season or more. Coach swore to keep it under wraps and supported my decision either way, but I can't keep him waiting much longer.

But Summer is a whole next-level distraction I didn't see coming. *Yet* . . . I smirk. I need to focus on salvaging my career, not fucking the landlord. She's not making it easy. Nothing worth the effort ever was.

I thought this would be a good break, but here I am, stuck in a small bed with my son kicking in his sleep, in a pink house with five women in a small town without so much as a stoplight.

There's a lot on the line with my future, but all I can think about is how this summer just got a whole lot hotter.

## CHAPTER 9

SUMMER

"That's the tenant?" Winter asks, peering over my shoulder out the kitchen window. Basically, she's spying like me.

Steam wafts from my coffee as I shamelessly stare at a shirtless Daniel. Every muscle coordinates to push Roman on the swing and sends my thoughts somewhere inappropriate considering he's a guest in our home.

"Yep." I take a gulp of coffee this time, feeling particularly thirsty this morning.

"Wow."

"I know. It's a problem."

I turn when she opens a cabinet to get a coffee mug and try not to stare at the half-naked man in the yard. "A good one to have," she says, pouring herself a cup of coffee. "Why don't I get those kinds of problems? I get delayed shipments and the bees being moody and not producing properly, so I need to plant more flowers."

"Back up. What do you mean, the bees are moody?"

She sits at a table with her mug in front of her, holding on to it like life itself is held inside. "Jeremy, the kid who does the yard work, mowed down the flowers near the hives. Now the bees are protesting."

"By not producing honey?"

"Wouldn't you if your favorite thing in the world, other than the queen bee herself, was gone in an instant?" I blink once and then again, not sure how to respond to that. "I owe the candlemaker eight gallons, or I'm not getting my next two shipments."

"That is a problem."

Taking a sip of her drink, she sets it down and looks at me. "The shop needs more products. I have a new honey mustard coming in and a lotion I'm dying to try, but if I don't have the honey, I can't keep the products coming."

Having a honey hive on part of the property wasn't something I encouraged. Dolly had bees before we moved in, but it was Winter who spent the time and made the effort to learn everything she could. I'm convinced it helped her through the death of our parents by giving her something to focus on, but I never thought she'd be returning after college to her hometown to open a shop. The income isn't much, but she's growing it month by month.

"What can I do to help?"

"Nothing. Jeremy felt bad, so he's helping me plant the flowers when they come in this week. I'll give him some honey-vanilla ice cream to take home. It's his favorite."

"Mine too." I finish my coffee and rinse my mug, watching through the window again. "Daniel and Roman are still in full swing outside."

"Pun intended," she says, and laughs.

I walk over and wrap my arms around her to hug her. "You'll figure this out. You always do, and if you can't, we're here for you."

Patting my arms, she takes a breath of relief. "I know. I'll keep you posted."

"I'm going to check on our guests."

"So, tell me. What's the situation with the hot guy and his son again?"

My youngest sister pushes through the kitchen door. "Oh, they're here again?" The two of them together remind me so much of our mom. Their delicate features and heart-shaped faces. Their coloring couldn't be more different yet fitting for their season—Winter's dark hair to Spring's blond. Winter's brown eyes to her opposite's blue. None of that matters, though, when you see them together. The resemblance is striking.

"Spring will fill you in." I cut through the house and walk outside. They don't see me before I start across the lawn. "Good morning. How'd we sleep?"

With his grip tight around the ropes, Roman leans back as far as he can as he soars through the air. "Like a baby."

Daniel laughs. "*He* slept like a baby. A baby who kicks all night, keeping me up most of it." As if he hadn't taken the time prior, he drinks me in like his morning coffee, savoring parts of me more than others. "Good morning to you. How'd you sleep?"

"Like a baby." I grin, allowing my good mood to dictate my expression.

He catches wind of it and smiles before he leans in to push Roman again. Once the tire is off and spinning, he says, "Glad to hear it." His tone shifts, as if he wanted to say something more. The smile that felt so casual slips, and he opens his mouth. But he just thinks better of it because he closes it again and turns back to the swing. "Hey, Roman, I'm going to talk to Summer for a minute."

"K."

"Walk with me?" We walk out from under the oak tree and toward the house.

Not sure I've seen him serious before. Strangely enough, he's still just as attractive when I feel like I'm in trouble. "Sure, what's up?"

He stops and looks at me. "I'm grateful for all you've done for us, but I think we're going to need to leave."

"No." I hate myself for letting the desperation seep out. "I mean, why?"

Guilt coasts across his expression, dragging down his brow and the corners of his mouth. "The room is great, but . . ." Waving a hand up and down in front of him, he adds, "It's made for someone more your size, not mine. My feet hang off the end, my kid sleeps hot and there was his kicking. I'm exhausted. The lack of sleep has me thinking it will be best if we go somewhere else. And since you said there's nothing available in the area—"

"Take my bed." Tilting his head, he narrows his eyes on me as if he didn't hear me correctly. Desperate times call for desperate measures. I haven't felt anything for anyone in so long, and now, like the bees, it's going to be ripped away from me. I want to ride this high as long as I can. I repeat, "You can sleep in my bed. It's bigger."

"Now, why would you go and offer up your bed?"

His question has me digging deeper than my desire for him to stay. I need him to stay so I can keep my bonus. That extra money is the only thing making an offer to Mrs. Dover possible. I can't lose my shot at buying the cottage from her. "Because I'm responsible for the situation at the cottage. This was supposed to be a summer getaway for you and Roman, and he looks so happy here. It's a temporary solution until we can get the two of you safely back in the cottage."

"At the cost of your own comfort?" He shifts back a step, giving us room to consider this option. Maybe he thinks I'll back out and change my mind. "Where will you sleep?"

The words flow from my mouth like a waterfall. "We can put Roman in the guest room, you in my room, and I can sleep on the couch."

"I can't let you sleep on the couch."

Sharing a bed would lead to so much more, more than I'm ready for. I had no intention of being in that room with him, but the sudden inclination to be close to him has me replying, "The couch in my room."

His gaze steadies on mine as he drags his tongue over his bottom lip twice before he takes a breath, releasing the tension building between us. "That's generous."

"It's called hospitality. It's what I went to school for."

"So you're a trained professional people pleaser?"

I hate that he's hit the bull's-eye with that characterization, but I won't deny it. "Unfortunately for me—"

"Lucky for me."

I should hate how happy he makes me. It feels good to laugh about ridiculous stuff like this. It feels better to flirt with someone who I'm insanely attracted to, who seems just as attracted to me. But it's the best feeling in the world when everything comes together like destiny had a hand. I'm not sure why I believe in that stuff—though not nearly as much as Fall does—but this feels like something bigger than us creating a problem to solve. And we're doing just that.

Bonus, we get to spend more time together.

We start back toward Roman at a leisurely pace. "Tell me, Ms. Season, what are the rules? Number one was to avoid your sisters at all costs. That's been broken."

"I never expected it to last. We're way too involved in each other's lives not to know everything going on."

"I wanted Roman to have siblings." I glance up at him when I hear the change in his tone. His chest inflates with the deepest breath before he slowly deflates. "That didn't work out."

Before I have a chance to ask any burning questions, he looks back at me and says, "His mother, Mia, and I were never a couple."

I don't know why I look at Roman when my heart pangs. "Oh." I usually have plenty to say, but what would I say to that? Was the sex at least good? No. No. No. Do not say anything.

When I look at him again, he's stopped a few steps back. I turn to face him. Maybe it's the light that hasn't broken through the cloud cover, or that the arrogance he wears like a second skin seems to be missing this morning, or perhaps he's just tired like he said, but it's the most connected I've felt to him. He's strong in muscle and quick-witted, but he's still just a man looking for approval from the world around him. I've been there.

"It doesn't matter if you and her worked out. You got Roman. And it sounds like you guys are great parents. She takes him to see you when you're not traveling, you have him for the summer, and he's polite and as cute as a button. He's a great kid." I take a step toward him, wanting to leave room for the conversation. "Anyway, it's not too late. You're like what, forty?"

"Forty? Fuck me." His head rolls back on his neck. When he pops it up again, he asks, "Are you serious right now?"

Laughing, I do a little tap dance to the side and curtsy. "No. But I had you going." I close the gap and poke him in the stomach. Hard as a rock. "I know your age from your profile."

It's cute seeing him annoyed as he shakes his head.

"Right." Bumping playfully against me, he asks, "How old are you? It's only fair."

"I'd have you guess, but I'm way too sensitive for that game. I'm twenty-six." The nod feels like the approval I needed. "A little age gap thing is happening." The smile is wiped from my face. Really, Summer? Ugh. "Not that we're together. I didn't mean to infer you'd date me or any—"

"I would date you."

That shouldn't be as sexy as it is, but hearing him say that makes me wish I'd chosen a different outfit than denim cutoffs and a striped crop top. A little more makeup wouldn't have done any harm, but it's too late now. Blush, a thin line of eyeliner, and a swipe of mascara will have to do. It's tempting to pull my hair from the ponytail at the crown of my head, but I raise my chin and look at him instead. "You're good with the comebacks, but I have to say your sweet lines are my favorite."

"They're not lines if they're true."

"Come watch, Summer," Roman calls as he turns the tire and jumps on, entertaining himself. Even with a gaggle of siblings, I've done that myself.

Smiling, I reply, "Coming."

Daniel's steps slow to fit my stride. *So sweet.* "About those rules?"

"Ah. Right. Number two: Don't go in the woods past the shed."

With a furrowed brow, he glares at me. "That's ominous."

I laugh, pushing back on the tire when it comes swinging in my direction. "It's not meant to be. It's just an area of the property we like to protect."

He nods. "Okay, easy enough. Any other rules?"

"Only one more."

It's his turn to push the swing. "My mind is going wild."

Watching his muscles work under the pressure has me staring at him. "My mind already did." He flexes his bicep for me and sends a wink along with it. I want to die inside. Instead, I wait for the tire to be away from us, and say, "Rule three: we can't sleep together."

His eyes practically bug out of the sockets. Covering his heart, he leans back as if the pain is too much to bear. "Wow, straight for the kill." When he finishes the Academy Award-winning performance, he says, "I tell you I'd date you, and you pull sex from the table. I'm losing my touch."

I cackle, holding my arms out. "Easy come. Easy go."

"Except we never had the easy coming part." He's not wrong, but we're not going there.

Glaring at him, I frantically nod toward Roman. "Little ears."

He chuckles. "Don't worry. He was out of earshot."

"Out of earshot for what?" Roman asks, swinging by. "What'd I miss?"

As he whips through the air in the other direction, I say, "It's time for breakfast. Do you like eggs?"

"I like pancakes more," he replies, hanging upside down with a cheeky grin on his face.

"You're a stinker, you know that?" I start for the house.

"What's a stinker?"

"Your dad will explain." I look back at Daniel, and he's already got his eyes on me. That gorgeous face sends a shiver up my spine, and his body is so hot it about knocks me dead. "What happened to your shirt, Sutton?"

He throws his arms out wide. "I couldn't find it this morning. I thought you stole it."

"Nope. But I'll help you look for it." Now, how in the world would his shirt go missing? I step onto the porch just as my phone buzzes in my back pocket. I pull it free to see Mrs. Dover calling. "Good morning," I answer.

"Morning, Summer. What's this I'm hearing about a plumbing issue at the Cove Cottage?" Word travels too fast in these parts.

I start pacing the porch. "I was waiting until a decent hour to call you. The shower we have been getting hot water from using a trick decided it was going to bust on us. It soaked the tenant and me. Water was spraying everywhere and wouldn't turn off. I got the water turned off outside, though, but that means no water to the house until the pipe is fixed."

"No toilets or sinks? No water in the kitchen?"

"No water at all. It would have flooded the whole house if I'd left it on."

She asks, "Where are the tenants?"

Stopping, I look at Daniel chasing Roman around the tree, then the reverse. The giggles drift all the way over here. "They stayed in our guest room last night."

The silence is louder than my confession. I look down, waiting for her to say something, anything. When she finally speaks, she says, "What would I do without you? That was generous to take them in. I know you have a full house over there, *and Dolly*."

Some things never change. Sounds like the feeling is still mutual between them.

"It worked fine." I peek back up at them as they start heading this way. "They're content to stay until it's fixed this week."

"This week won't do. I'm getting someone in today. We can't have good-paying guests staying with you all summer."

There are worse things I could imagine than Daniel and

Roman staying with us. With me . . . "Do you need me to meet the plumber to let them in?"

"Yes, if you could be there by ten, they should be arriving by then. We'll get this sorted today. Thanks, dear."

"You're welcome."

When I hang up, I stuff the phone in my pocket again and look up to see concern wrinkling Daniel's forehead. "Everything okay?"

I shift into pro mode like I always fall back on and plaster a smile on my face. It's not that I don't want him in the cottage so he can enjoy the rest of his stay. It's only been a day and one night, but it's already brought an energy back to my life that's been missing. Once the pipes are fixed, I'll have to make up reasons to see him since I won't have business to tend to.

Worst of all, I made up rule three just so we could break it. What excuse will I have now? I finally cut loose, and look what happens. Every time. I think my sex life is doomed. And the drought continues.

# CHAPTER 10

## SUMMER

"Dolly?"

"In here," she replies, sending me spinning in the hallway to figure out where the voice came from.

"Here where?"

She barges out of the laundry room by the kitchen, holding a gray shirt that looks awfully familiar. "I washed your gentleman's shirt." My stomach drops, worried her meddling will send Daniel running. He already has one foot out the door, and if he leaves, I lose the bonus that came along with his stay. Does she not realize what's on the line for me? I'm undecided if that's sweet or stalkerish. Either way, she sure has taken to Daniel. I don't blame her.

"I wondered if you'd seen it." Studying it, I see it looks brand new. Any potential crease has been steamed right out. "Do I want to know when you got this from the guest room?"

"No, you don't." At least she's honest. But my heart races in my chest. A mixture of panic from the situation and a bit of pride that Dolly ensured a great view this morning wars within me.

*This is exhausting.*

"Is that my shirt?" Daniel comes into the hall after searching for his shirt again in the bedroom. I gasp, but he walks right up to her. "You washed it for me?" Bending down, he kisses her on the cheek. "You're the best, Dolly. Thank you."

I blink. And again. The interaction was so sweet, like he was part of the family. Are they besties now? Did I just panic for nothing? Seems so.

But more importantly, why do I find it so cute that in the short span of him being here, he's weaseled his way into the family dynamics? At this rate, I'm going to be hanging his and Roman's stockings next to mine come December.

Oh God. My knees don't stand a chance against this scene playing out. I flatten my hand to the wall to keep me upright before I swoon to the floor.

Dolly isn't holding up much better. If she were wearing red, I'd say the bright color is reflecting on her cheeks, but even I can't make up an excuse for the blushing and girlish giggle she releases. I'm thinking someone has a crush on Daniel Sutton, along with me. It's easy to do.

She says, "We make sure to dress for breakfast, but we'll make an exception for you, Mr. Sutton." *Shameless.*

He's already pulling it over his head. "No need to treat me special. Happy to oblige by the rules." *These* are the rules he has no problem following? It's only mine that are challenged. Got it. I roll my eyes as I lower my hand to my side again.

Ushering him toward the kitchen, she says, "I've made some breakfast. Let's get you and Roman fed."

"What am I?" I ask, holding my arms out. "Old news around here?"

Dolly looks back, and her smile softens. "Don't worry, honey, I never forget about my girls."

Not fifteen minutes later, I hear, "Save some sausage for Summer." I cringe. "She loves her meat." Dying would be less painful than this.

Reaching over to point out the eggs left on his son's plate, Daniel adds, "It's good to know she has a healthy appetite for meat."

Roman adds, "I like meat."

Dolly sets a basket of biscuits fresh from the oven in the center of the table. "She was always my good eater."

We all reach for one at the same time. I let Roman get one first, then Daniel, but he hands his to me. *She always was my good eater.* Ugh. He's using my love language against me. I ignore the fluttering in my chest as I accept it, noting how careful I need to be with him. He's smooth. Maybe too smooth. "I think that's more information than he needs, Dolly. Daniel doesn't want to hear about my eating habits."

"Sure, I do." He takes a bite of the fluffy biscuit, releasing some steam from inside. I can relate to the same need for a steamy release.

Dolly comes to stand behind me, a spatula in one hand and a dishcloth in the other. "Nothing wrong with your appetite, Summer. Look at her figure, Mr. Sutton. I don't know how she packs it all in."

He's not even trying to hold back the laughter. "It's a fine figure. And you can call me Daniel."

She swats my shoulder with a dishcloth. "See, even Daniel agrees." *Kill me now.*

"As fun as this is, I need to get over to the cottage. Mrs.

Dover somehow got a plumber to come out today to look at the situation and hopefully fix it."

"On a Sunday, the Lord's Day?" It's surprising to hear the disgrace in her tone when she doesn't even go to church. She used to say no one had to be in a particular building to talk to God, and it was safer for her if she didn't enter.

"Yes, on a Sunday." I push up from the chair. Giving Dolly a hug, I add, "I need to get going. Thanks for breakfast."

She wraps her arms around me. "You be good, okay?"

"Always am."

"Too good if you ask me," she smarts like it's an inside joke with Daniel. He already knows I'm hard up. My grandmother confirming that to the world, a.k.a. the guy I'm interested in, is plain humiliating.

A chair grinding against the tile has me looking back. Daniel stands with his plate in his hand. "I'll go with you." The butterflies in my stomach flutter, or it's the sausage not agreeing with me today. I'm hoping for the former.

Dolly clasps her hands together loud enough to startle me. "That's perfect. You two run along while I take Roman to the dock to fish." She collects Daniel's plate and then mine. "What do you say?"

He pops up from his chair. "Can I stay and fish, Dad?"

Coming to stand beside me, Daniel asks, "Promise to listen to Dolly?"

Roman's gaze volleys from his dad to Dolly, and he nods. "I promise."

As I head for the door, Daniel moves around the table to bring him to his side. "I won't be too long, buddy. But Dolly has Summer's number if you need anything. You can reach me that way." He places a kiss on his head.

"Okay." The look Roman gives him causes my heart to

clench and has me wishing I could capture the moment for them in a photo keepsake. He's his hero, as it should be.

I grab my phone and keys on our way out the door. Stepping off the porch, I spy his car parked in the distance, also how it should be, and glance back. "Want to walk?"

"We can walk."

There's no rush in our steps, nerves making it awkward, or a pull to fill the silence. It's notable, if not unusual, that we can be this comfortable together when we barely know each other.

The clouds have burned off, leaving us with blue skies, singing birds, and the ocean waves in the distance, if we listen.

We get past the lot the house sits on and walk next to the woods where we keep our secrets. At least some secrets. Others are becoming better known as Winter grows the honey business.

I peek over at Daniel when his gaze hooks on the houses across the street. It's easy for anyone to be physically attracted to the man. From his face to his body, he's practically otherworldly. But it's the other parts of him, not the ones that are visible but who he is, that tug at my attention. Make me see *him*. He's a good father, willing to wake the world for his kid to use the bathroom. I smile, never actually upset to be woken for a good cause or desperate need. He'd do anything for his son, including pausing on giving him a sibling until a valued relationship comes along. That's sweet in such an unexpected way.

Our dreams aren't so different from each other's. A significant other is the missing piece to making that dream a reality for me as well. But this is temporary. The whole reason rule three came into play. I can't have him and the cottage. He'll be back in New York City, and I'll have my heart broken.

But he's so flirty that my cheeks are in a constant state of blushing flux. It just feels good to be around him. The universe put the most perfect man right in my path, and I can only see a setup for heartbreak.

"It's nice here," he says from a few feet away from me with a kind smile that seems to be easy for him to summon when we're together. "Peaceful. Was it a good place to grow up?"

"The best. It hasn't changed much. We get shoddy internet, so more time was spent outside than indoors. Friends from school are scattered all over the county, so my sisters were my best friends. My parents, too. They always had something fun planned for us. My mom would sneak in and help us make a blanket tent so we could hide under it and tell stories. S'mores on a warm night down at the shore. We used to have a picket fence around the front of the house that my dad had us paint. Every picket was a random color. Didn't matter how 'girly' it was, my dad loved to see us happy." Swinging my arms, I step over the cracks in the concrete. "Dolly used to paint in the nude." I laugh at the memory. "Don't ask me why, but I remember walking in on her in the middle of what she called her 'Cove Series.' Each was an abstract portrait of a man she dated."

"She's quite the character." The midmorning sunlight cuts through the trees to shine in his brown eyes, revealing a few stories of his own hidden inside.

"She is. She taught us never to be ashamed of being exactly who we are."

"How'd that work out?" I can feel his gaze hot on me as if he sees through the front I portray.

Keeping my eyes ahead, I reply, "It's a work in progress."

"What others think doesn't matter, Summer. Live life how you want. Do what makes you happy. We only get one shot at this. Might as well go for it."

How does he manage to make me smile so effortlessly? I'm starting to think it's going to be a permanent fixture on my face. "In other words, you miss every shot you don't take?"

"Something like that."

"What about you?" I ask. "Where'd you grow up?"

His gaze drops to the road beneath his feet. "Jersey City, but I don't have many memories from there," he replies, returning his eyes to meet mine. "We were rarely home due to travel league."

"You've always been in the New York area?"

"I did a stint in Montreal my second season, then spent two years in Milwaukee before fighting my way back to the city to Brooklyn."

"What do you mean?"

A horn blares behind us, causing us to scatter on the side of the road. I look back to see a van speeding toward us. Strong arms wrap around me so fast I lose my breath until he sets me down farther away from the pavement. When the brakes are slammed, the tires skid to a stop, and a window is rolled down.

I rush forward. "Why the hell are you driving like that?"

The guy inside laughs, the three hairs his head is holding on to blow back from the wind breezing inside the van. "Plumbing emergency. You know where a . . ." He looks down at an E-pad attached to his dash. "Cottage—"

"Yes, that's where we're heading. I manage the property. It's up ahead on the right. Drive with care this time."

"Will—You got to be shittin' me." Snapping his fingers, he points over my shoulder. "You're Daniel Sutton."

I turn so fast to look at Daniel that my thoughts take longer to catch up. His eyes are secured to mine with some unreadable emotion trapped inside. *Fear?* Nah, what would he be afraid of? *Remorse*? We don't know each other well enough to have regrets yet. Do we? *Disappointment*? It's the only one I can't justify my way out of defending him.

The emotion isn't aimed at me, but more revolving through his expression in himself.

"Daniel Sutton, right?" The guy chirps at him in an annoying tone. "Am I right?"

He doesn't sound like someone who's run into an old friend. This is different. His tone is too excited, bordering on starstruck.

I turn back toward the van, staring at the peeling emblem on the door, and so badly wanting to pick at it. I should know everything about the man standing behind me. He filled out a profile. Did I need details like marriage status or profession? No. Those felt personal and not necessary to accomplish my job. Name, how many adults, how many kids, favorite foods, what to stock, activities they want to do while here, dates of arrival and departure, and can they afford the fees. That is all the information I need.

So why do I feel like this plumber has blindsided me?

I hear the crunch of the dirt and rocks under his shoes and the heat of his hand on my lower back as he comes closer. "Hey man, I'm trying to spend some time with my son and would appreciate the privacy. Do you think you could keep this between us?"

When I tilt my gaze up, the guy looks at me and then Daniel again before he sits back. "Sure, man. Could I trouble you for a photo and autograph, though?"

*Autograph?*

Oh my God. I slap my hand to my forehead as the big

picture comes together. That's why Dolly's been acting like a fangirl. Because she is a fan. How does she know who he is, and I don't?

*Who is Daniel Sutton?*

Apparently, someone famous enough to be recognized in the middle of my nowhere town of Mountain Laurel Cove by someone just looking at him.

Mortification rises like blooming dough inside my chest and forms a lump in my throat.

Daniel replies, "I'll hook you up at the house ahead. We'll meet you there."

"I was dreading driving out here, but it's my lucky day." He pulls away, leaving us to watch as he turns off onto the driveway in the distance.

Neither of us has moved. I feel too dumb to even say anything, much less dare to look into his eyes when he knows I didn't recognize him.

His hand slides up my back and cups my shoulder. "Summer?"

With my head hanging down, I shake it. "I feel so stupid."

"Don't."

"Tell me how to make it go away, and I will."

Coming around to the front of me, he lifts my chin until our eyes meet. "I liked that you didn't know who I was. You treated me . . . like me, like someone normal instead of a celebrity."

"I don't know what you're famous for. I just feel so foolish, like the wool was pulled over my eyes and now the truth has been revealed, leaving me a laughingstock—"

"The truth is revealed, but if it makes any sense, I wish it hadn't been. It felt good to get to know you without my world being a part of it or having an opinion on my love life." He walks onto the road and stops with his hands grasped behind his head. "I hope this doesn't change anything between us."

"It changes everything. I don't know anything about the real you—"

"This is the real me, Summer. I'm still the same Daniel standing in front of you." His eyes search mine with a plea pulling his brows together.

A horn honks in the distance, causing us both to look in the direction of the cottage. I take a breath. "I can't keep him waiting. I need to take care of this."

"Promise me we'll talk when he's gone."

"What is there to talk about? You're some famous . . ." I throw my arms up in the air. "I don't even know why or how you're famous. That's how messed up this is. It feels crappy to be the butt of this joke." I start walking because the anxiety of keeping the plumber waiting is building.

I don't get ten feet from him before he says, "Daniel Sutton. Thirty-five. Dad of Roman." My breath catches, causing me to stop. I don't turn back. I can't, or my emotions will get the best of me. "Professional hockey player for the Brooklyn Breakaways. I play right wing. I live in Manhattan in a penthouse because I thought that would make me feel important. I hate it. I hate being so isolated from the world. I travel too much and go home or to the hotel alone. Most nights. I've never been in a serious relationship because all I care about is my career, which is currently on the verge of being ripped out from under me if I don't fix some shit about my life."

My heart pounds in my ears, competing with his words. I finally turn around, angling my head to the right as I stare at him. "You don't owe me anything, Daniel."

"I want to fill in the blanks, so you know exactly who I

am." He says, "Hockey used to be everything that mattered to me. That changed when Roman was born. But it's a lonely fucking existence to only see your kid occasionally or in the stands and for two minutes after a match in the locker room before the press swarms in for a quote they need for their story on the nightly news."

He just laid his entire life for me to study, analyze, judge if I want to, or soak in and accept him for who he is. "So the whole world knows who you are except for me?"

"Seems so." His half-hearted smirk has my tummy doing flips. Why does he have to be so cute?

The tension I was spinning in starts to unravel, and soon, it's gone altogether. "You make it hard to be mad at you."

Chuckling, he says, "That's not something I've heard before." He rubs the pad of his thumb over his bottom lip as if he's doing some studying of his own as he looks at me. "I'm glad it is with you."

I walk over to him. Hooking my finger around one of the belt loops of his shorts, I look up at him and smile. "Hockey, huh?"

"Yep." His hand rubs my hip like he does it all the time, so natural and familiar on a deeper level, and sends my heart rate spiking. But it's the way he fought for me to stay that has me realizing that if love can be found at first sight, it can be found on an empty country road, with a plumber kept waiting.

It should scare me, but somehow, it doesn't. It's not sleeping with him that worries me anymore. It's too late for me. It's how I keep my heart intact when he inevitably leaves to return to his own life.

But that doesn't mean we can't enjoy ourselves while he's here. Right?

We start walking to the cottage together, because yeah, broken pipes still need to be fixed, especially if I want him to stay here for the summer to keep my bonus. But now I'm wondering if that bonus could also include a summer in his arms.

When we see the small house and the spot where his car was parked, I say, "Your license plate makes a lot more sense. I saw hat trick and just thought you were really into magic."

Under a roar of laughter, he wraps his arm around me and kisses the side of my head. Protective and sweet. *Like I'm his.*

## CHAPTER 11

DANIEL

"Daniel 'The Maverick of Hockey' Sutton. Shit damn, I can't believe I'm meeting you." Shaking my hand like he's trying to test my strength, which happens often, the plumber jerks it up and down.

"It's good to meet you, too . . ." I glance at the embroidery on his stained work shirt. "Bryan."

"With a y. When you sign that autograph, make sure to spell Brian with a y."

I look around, but there's nothing for me to sign. "You got a pad or something to write on?"

"Yeah. Hold on." While Bryan digs through his van, I look at Summer standing at the back of the van, looking around awkwardly. This is exactly what I didn't want. I don't want her to be awkward—well, more awkward than she is—because of my fame. This lifestyle isn't for the faint of heart. I have no choice. She does. And turning her off is the last thing I want to do. "Here you go." He hands me a Buc-ee's receipt and a marker that's seen better days and is missing the cap.

Moving to the hood of the vehicle, he sets it down to

sign, and adds, "Don't forget the y and sign it from Maverick. Then it's like we're buddies. How about writing how I saved you—"

I glare at him. "Do you want to sign it?"

"No, go ahead, Mav."

Bryan, thanks for saving the day.

Maverick Sutton

I hand it back to him and keep walking, more interested in checking on Summer than fulfilling the next demand he comes up with. My good deed for the day is done, so it's time to move on. "Let's go look at the pipes."

"Right behind you, bud." While he tucks his autograph into the van, I find Summer waiting in an Adirondack chair. Her body is at ease as she leans back, her eyes on me since she came into view.

When I walk to her, I see how she looks me over and bites that bottom lip of hers. The attraction between us remains as clear as it was thirty minutes earlier, leaving me to breathe easier. Summer's different from the women I meet, and I don't want to lose this opportunity to learn more about her because I'm famous. Her not knowing who I am was only a perk. A perk that snowballed into a situation.

We need to talk when we have more privacy. I want to check the temperature of how she feels with the information that was dumped on her seemingly out of nowhere. I also want to know what really makes her tick when it comes to this property. It appears to be her sole focus. A goal of sorts.

She manages this place like it's her own business, but

made it clear it's not. Her care and attention are put into every detail, and she gets flustered if things aren't under her complete control. The owner said jump, and she plunged off the cliff to get here. Other than a paycheck, what's in it for her?

Her gaze deviates beside me, and she says, "It's open. The bathroom is in the hall on the right."

When she looks back at me, she holds her phone up with a photo of me taken during a game. Eighty-eight, my jersey number, is on display as I slam into that punk kid who thinks he owns the ice out of Boston. That photo made all the sports channel rounds three years ago. I'd recognize it anywhere. "I looked you up."

I come to stand before her and offer a hand. "And?"

"You're *famous* famous." When she reaches up, she folds her fingers with mine.

"How do you feel about that?" I pull her to her feet.

She stands toe-to-toe with me and raises her chin in the air. She must if she wants to see my face, but I catch a note of tenacity in the gesture. "I think back to all the things you said that made it so obvious, and I still missed all the signs right in front of my face." Our hands are still together when she lowers them to the side, not making any effort to escape or wiggle out of this conversation. "You talked about being on the road. I thought you were in finance or something, and you traveled for your job." She waffles her head. "You do, but because you play hockey. Even Roman mentioned he would only go to games when you were in town. And here I thought he meant because you would take him *to* the game, not for him to watch you play." Turning away from me, she cups her forehead and squeezes her eyes shut. "This is so embarrassing."

"I understand this is a lot of information to take in at once and not something you expected—"

"You fought your way back to Brooklyn after being in Milwaukee." Her blue eyes pierce mine. "Literally, you *fought* on the ice to get traded to the Breakaways. It wasn't just a turn of phrase. And now I know why. Roman." Dropping her head back, she pleads to the heavens. "Save me from myself. It's just so humiliating."

Bending down so we're at eye level, I look at her wrapped up in thoughts that should never be a part of her psyche. She's too good for that. She's too good for me, if I were being honest. That innocence she carries like a backpack doesn't just peek through like sunshine. It shines like a diamond ring. And it's just so damn appealing.

"Look at me, Summer."

"I'm looking right at you, Daniel." Her voice is so sweet that it's tempting to kiss her.

"You don't need saving. You don't need to be embarrassed. You just need to be you. That's what I want. That's what has me standing here right now, hoping the damn pipe gets fixed so we can stay this summer." I stand back up and run the tip of my rough finger along the soft skin of her cheek. "I know you'll offer your house, but you don't need two extra mouths to feed or us crowding your space."

"I'm sure you can buy a few meals, Money Bucks."

Grinning, I chuckle. "I can, but that's not how I want us to get to know each other. I want us to spend time together because we want to, not be forced to because you're too nice. And want to please me." I tack it on at the end, playing into her sweet nature. Low? *Sure*. But I'm so fucking attracted to this woman that it will be hard not to blow through rule three before the sun sets. *If I had my way . . .*

Since I won't because we shouldn't, let's hope we have

the house back soon so she can spend some quality time over here.

"I've looked at the shower and checked the valve on the side of the house," Bryan says, stepping out of the house and disappointingly making me step away from Summer before he runs to the tabloids. There's something about the guy that I don't trust. Maybe it's because he's too buddy-buddy, like he's got something to hold over me.

All I can do is trust that he'll keep his mouth shut like he promised.

Summer starts for the house. "What are you thinking? A new pipe for the shower will need to be installed, but I didn't want to bust up the tile to see how extensive the damage is."

"It's extensive," he says, his eyes going from her and landing on me. "You're going to need a full install of new pipes starting at the entry point from the shower to where it meets the main line."

Summer crosses her arms over her chest. "That doesn't sound like a quick fix."

"It won't be." His eyes deviate from her to me again as he continues, "I'd have to get a small crew out here to demo. After that, one of my guys and I can replace the pipes to the main line."

His disrespect for her pisses me off. I start toward them, and say, "Ms. Season oversees the property. I'm only a guest."

"That's too bad this happened during your visit. You might be able to seek legal restitution if . . ." He points at her. "They don't give you a fair shake for the refund."

"Listen here, pal!" I catch Summer by the wrists just as her arms fly into the air. She shoots me a glare.

Shaking his head like an idiot who walked into the lion's den, he adds, "Sheesh. Women are so temperamental."

*Fucker.*

*Temperamental. Emotional.* My dad never gave my mom a break. He pushed her buttons and yelled at her for reacting. It was always my fault or hers, but never his. And just like the fight that got me kicked out of the house at fifteen, I'm not putting up with shit humans treating women like they're beneath them. "Watch your mouth, Bryan."

Shock wiggles his jowls. "What are you talking about, Mav?"

"I'm talking about treating her with the respect she deserves. She's doing her job, and you're trippin' over your balls trying to impress me for some fucking reason."

"Yeah." Summer crosses her arms over her chest and says, "I've seen more emotion from you fanboying over this guy than I've seen from a tween at a Taylor Swift concert. So watch how you talk to me." There's the spitfire I knew she had in her. Tugging the hem of her shirt down, she raises her chin in defiance. "We won't be needing your services. Good day, Bryan." And there's her sweet side showing out to clean up the mess.

"Hey," he barks. "Slow down there. The lady on the phone told me I had the job if I drove out here. That's an hour and a half each way. I hope you didn't waste my time because you're still going to pay for it."

*How's this jerk not getting the picture?*

This doesn't need to escalate. Before this gets out of hand, I say, "Walk with me." As I turn to walk away, he rushes to my side. "This seems like a complicated job, bigger than tightening a few split rings. You drove a long way, and it's probably not a trip you want to make if the gas is going to eat your profits."

"Hell no, I don't." He looks back at Summer over his shoulder. "And she's already reneging on the deal. I'm not putting up with that shit."

We stop outside the door to his van. "It's nothing but trouble."

"Yeah, it's bullshit. You're right. I don't want this job. Too much trouble." His expression lifts. "But I got to meet you."

"And I got to meet you, Bryan, with a Y." *Asshole.*

Snapping his fingers, he points at me. "Heeeey, you got it. My friends are going to be so jealous."

"But the rest is a secret, right?"

He pulls out his phone to take a photo. "Yeah, no worries."

The photo is snapped. While he studies it, I open the door. "You got a long drive back." When he gets in, I shut the door and punch the lock down. "You take care, buddy."

"You, too, Mav." He starts the engine as I walk back to the house.

As soon as the van pulls away, I see Summer standing there, beautiful as if a weight was lifted.

Her arms are still crossed, but a smile has filtered the anger away. "You didn't have to do that. I can handle a jerk of a plumber."

"I know you can, but isn't it more fun when you don't have to?" I walk straight for her and cup her cheek. Tilting her head back, I lean down because kissing her seems to currently be my only mission in life, and whisper, "Now, where were we?"

Just as her eyes flutter closed, my phone rings in my pocket. Not just any ring, the team's theme song. Her eyes open again as I gently release her. "Sorry. I need to take this."

"That's fine," she says, indicating by her tone that it's not actually fine at all. “I have calls to make too.” She turns, pulling her phone from her back pocket, and walks inside the house.

My phone rings once more, and I answer it. “Hey Coach, how’s it going?”

“Good. Good.” He stalls, letting the quiet linger. “How are you, Sutton?”

“Pretty good. It’s only been a few days since the season ended, so I’m not out of hockey mode yet.”

“That’s what makes you so good.” Coach Spears runs this program like it’s his baby. He’s not just setting the tone and goals, he makes sure his players are in a good headspace. “You’re always ready to go.”

“Yep.” I walk across the deck but stop to glance back to see if I can catch sight of Summer. I can’t, so I head toward the water. “I’m assuming this isn’t a social call?”

“Actually, it is. The owners are having a Fourth of July picnic, a real upscale event hosted in the Hamptons.”

“Sounds fun. I’ll talk to Roman—”

“It’s more of a fancy cocktails, steak and lobster event. Finger weenies—”

“Finger what?”

“You know, fancy shit rich people eat.”

“You *are* rich people, Coach.” The water glides over the rocks on shore as it drifts in and back out again. I stop just before the grass ends and stare out at a few boats in the distance. “I’m also rich people now.”

“Yeah, but we’re not that kind. We had to earn it. Hell, I was planning on throwing burgers and dogs on the grill to celebrate. Now my wife is out shopping for what she calls a summer suit for me to wear.”

The mention of summer has me looking back for the only version that keeps my attention. I chuckle. “The food sounds more my style. Summer suits? I'm not interested."

"They named you personally as one of the players they wanted to see there. It didn't sound like an invite. It sounded like a demand." He exhales. "I know this isn't part of your plans for the summer, but you need to be there. That's a request, not a demand."

"Why?"

"We've talked about this, Daniel. They want to see a new attitude, a softer side to you. Angry isn't doing it anymore."

"Tell that to the other team's goalie. Softer doesn't put a puck in the net. Soft sounds like someone they want to retire." Shoving a hand in my pocket, I say, "So tell me the truth, Rich. What's this party really about?"

There's a pause that I don't rush to fill. I asked a direct question and want a direct response. So I'll wait for it.

I hear him suck air into his nose and hem then haw before he finally relents. "The choice of retiring or playing isn't yours anymore. It's theirs. You can talk shit, but when you talk about your own teammates, me as the coach, or the owners, it doesn't go over well with the organization."

"I don't lie."

"If you want to put skates on the ice again, learn to lie and eat some humble pie and finger weenies. The league wants family-friendly. And you're not for the audience. You have until the Fourth to show the bosses that you're a new man. Bring a date to soften the image because your image is a fucking catastrophe right now." He takes another breath before he asks, "Do you hear what I'm saying, Daniel?"

"I hear you. Put on a good PR show, or I'm going to be retired without having a say."

"That's it, man. The league is changing. You either change with it or get left behind. It's up to you now."

I drop my phone in my pocket, keeping my eyes forward while my head spins. I thought I had time to figure this out, to have a say in my own future, but it doesn't seem like I do. "Soften my image?" I laugh, but find no humor in it.

My shoulder is touched by a warm hand that rubs gently as Summer comes to stand next to me. "Everything alright?" she asks, looking up at me.

She has enough going on. This isn't something that needs to burden her. "Fine. All good." I turn to look back at the house. "So what is the plan?"

"We wait until we get our local guys out here in a few days." Hooking her finger through my belt loop like she did earlier, she tries to tug me close. When my body doesn't pull forward as she intended, she closes the gap. "Looks like you're staying with me."

"I think that's a great fucking plan."

## CHAPTER 12

DANIEL

The beer is cold, and the view is worth every penny. I take another long pull from the bottle of lager, causing the back of my head to tap against the Adirondack chair. Roman was just mastering the art of skipping rocks when the wind picked up, and the water grew rougher. "Good job, buddy."

Summer went to retrieve him so we could grill hot dogs for lunch, giving me time to think about the confusing call with Coach. Why in the fuck would they want me not playing to my full potential?

"What's on your mind?" she asks, sitting beside me.

"Fine."

She laughs. "Daniel?"

Her voice startles me from my thoughts. "What?"

"You answered fine to me asking what's on your mind." Sitting forward, she says, "You've muttered the f-word twice and said Coach under your breath at least three times. I also heard 'soft' in there. So let me try this again. What's on your mind?" She sits back and crosses her legs at the ankles.

Her eyes pivot to Roman regularly, like he's her own, but

when she looks at me, I can tell her attention is fully mine. It settles a piece in my chest I didn't know was out of sync. Roman is my world, but her presence is bigger and more important than either of us could have anticipated. It's like I have an ally for the first time in my life.

Most people don't stick around, or I don't let them. I find myself wanting Summer's company, though. Accepting her like we've known each other for years instead of days.

"I came to the Cove to spend time with Roman out of the spotlight. It's hard to walk around sometimes without getting recognized. I didn't want that to invade our time together. But I also had some searching to do."

"Soul-searching, or are you looking for something?"

Leaning forward to match her, I reach over and rub her knee. "Both. I had a decision to make, but that's been taken out of my hands. It will now be made for me."

She angles closer as if to protect Roman from overhearing. "I don't understand."

"I could play until I'm forty, even forty-five if I can keep my body from losing for me." With rapt attention, she listens as if this is personal for her. "I've been told I'm too aggressive on the ice. My teammates are more kumbaya these days than competitive. I'm not from this generation. I play to win. Whatever it takes. I play my best every game, to get my team one step closer to winning the Stanley Cup again." I grip the bottle harder as Coach's words run on repeat through my head. "I'm supposed to put on a good PR show."

"Why?"

"To show the bad boy of hockey is a reformed man, to soften my image, and make the game more family-friendly to grow the TV audience, according to the owners. That's where the money is made."

"Hockey *is* family . . ." Her gaze drifts away to Roman again. When she looks at me again, she says, "Wait, it is pretty rough. Teeth are flying, blood on the ice. I've only caught bits of games, and I know it can be hard to watch sometimes."

The stab of betrayal digs deep, and I sit back and finish my beer. "You agree with him?"

"No. I just think it's not for little kids. We're teaching them to be nice to each other, to share, not to hit or bite—"

"I've never bitten anyone."

She cracks up laughing. "I'd hope not. My point is we teach little kids about manners and to take care of one another, and then bam, grown adults are beating the crap out of each other on TV."

"Boxing. MMA, Cage—"

"Doesn't matter. Their owners aren't trying to make it family-friendly. Your team's owners are. And if they are, the other owners are as well. It's probably a league-wide push."

"Are you on their side or mine?"

Resting back in the chair, she lifts her heels to the edge, bringing her knees to her chest. Smooth legs and tanned skin. She fits her name better than any other ever could. With her arms wrapped around her legs, she says, "Yours, Sutton. But not because I think they're entirely wrong. I'm on your side because it's your love of this game that brings in the viewers. It's your style of play that keeps you scoring. But mostly, why mess with perfection?" She doesn't just butter me up. She slathers me in the stuff.

"Do you know how sexy it is to hear you say that?"

"I'm hoping very," she replies, taking the last sip of her beer.

"Don't doubt it for a second."

I can feel my blood pulsing through my veins, as if

reaching toward the woman curled up in the chair next to me. We watch Roman as he plays where the lawn falls under rocks that lead to the water. My gaze trails out to the ocean beyond. Without it, the cove would be quiet. Too quiet, if you ask me. But the water rolling in and out is a balm to the chaos in my head, a reminder to slow down. That my problems are less important if I focus on the moment instead.

Not everything needs to be resolved today. It was a request by Coach. A demand by the owners. I don't *have* to listen to either of them, though it is implied I should. They should know by now that I'm going to buck the system. Fans would revolt if I went soft on the ice. Are they really going to sacrifice their star player, who brings in millions in sponsorships, to make a point? Not in a million years.

She sets her feet on the ground again. "What does putting on a good PR show mean exactly?"

It's not like I haven't thought about it, but what that entails is more complicated yet has gotten diluted in the messaging. "It means I have to play nice."

"And nice means? Not saying things you shouldn't, and?"

"Be the golden boy they want me to be. Smile for the cameras. Use my son for photo ops. Be seen publicly with only one woman."

I see her try so hard not to let the shock of my words control her, and she's doing a decent job, but then asks, "Do you sleep with a lot of women?"

"No. But I used to." This isn't a topic I care to discuss, but I understand her interest. "I outgrew sowing my oats in my early thirties."

"That late, huh?" She flashes a grin, and then it's gone again.

"Truth?" I laugh humorlessly. "I had no reason to change."

"Then why did you?"

"Because it wasn't serving me anymore. I didn't feel good, and I wasn't happy. I wanted to be happy for my son. He watches me on TV fighting and pushing plays to the limits. When I was with him, I wanted to feel good, not fighting a hangover or bad mood, and for us to have fun because that's how I want him to remember me."

She sits up and gets to her feet. Coming to stand in front of me, she wedges my feet apart with the toe of her sneaker to slip into the opening. Resting her hands on my thighs, her lips are so close to mine as she eyes my mouth. *The tease.* It would only be a taste, so quick that I would have to savor the swift kiss. But I don't kiss her yet. This isn't how it should be, not with her. It should matter and have meaning, not just playing out my selfish fantasy.

"Caring about your son more than yourself . . . Now *that* is incredibly attractive in a man."

Running my hands down the backs of her arms, I whisper, "Not sexy?"

"*So* sexy." Her breathing jags as she takes in a staggering breath. Moving closer, and closer still, she suddenly stops, standing stick straight with her eyes widening. "Dang it. I need to answer this. Hold my place, I've been waiting for Mrs. Dover to call me back."

Turning away, she grabs her phone. "Hi." She doesn't get another word in before plugging her free ear and then looking down as she toes the decking. "He was such a jerk." I'm not sure if she's aware she's even doing it, but she starts to pace in front of me. "If you had heard him . . . I understand." She glances at me. "He's taken care of." *So she says . . .* I smirk.

She moves toward the house and out of my vantage point. I catch random words drifting back in the wind, such as "ripping you off," and "rude," and my favorite, "I have it all under control."

While she finishes her call, I walk over to Roman, who's plonked himself in the water, and kneel beside him. "Do you like it here?"

He looks up at me. "It's fun. I like fishing. Can we go fishing?" I've fished a few times in life, not enough to consider myself an expert or anything, but enough to get by. "Dolly can show you how to fish. She's good at it."

Though I have no regrets spending time at the cottage with Summer, I could have done without the plumber interaction. "Guess I should have joined you two. I'd like to go fishing with you, buddy."

"We can this summer. I can show you how to attach the gummy worm to the hook."

My head bobs forward as my eyes pop wider. "You use gummy worms?"

"Dolly says it lures 'em right in and makes the fish sweeter to eat."

Rubbing my hand over the scruff that's growing over my jawline, I laugh. Dolly is quite the character. "I bet it does. Hey, so, the pipes aren't fixed."

"Do we get to sleep at Summer's again?"

"Is that okay? It might be a few nights."

"I like the swing." His little shoulders bounce up. "And she's nice. It's okay with me if we stay there." He moves a rock to draw a line in the sand beneath it with a stick. "Dad?"

Picking up a stone, I throw it into the ocean. "Yes?"

When he looks up again, he says, "You told me to never compromise my values."

"I told you that when you were little. Impressed you remember." He nods as a sense of pride rolls through me. "Do you know what it means?"

With his brown eyes staring into mine, he replies, "It means you don't have to play nice—"

"Well, not exact—"

"Or be liked. You just have to play your best, play fair, and know you gave it your all."

That's hard to argue with on the heels of being told to compromise my values. I say, "You've given me a lot to think about, son."

"Why is Summer upset?"

I flip my attention to where she's standing on the deck, hand covering her mouth, and eyes staring into nothingness. "Go on in and pack your things to move over to the pink house for a few nights." I stand. "I'm going to check on her."

He gets up and marches through the lawn to grab a towel from a bench. Wrapping it around him, he heads inside just as I approach Summer.

Her phone is on the picnic table closer to the house, and when she sees me, she lowers her hand. I'm not sure there are words to comfort her when she looks like the rug's been pulled out from under her. I wrap her in my arms and kiss the top of her head. It's not her lips, but I savor the connection just the same. "What's wrong?"

"She's selling."

"Who's selling what?"

Taking a sobering breath, she spreads her arms to free herself and moves a few steps back. Turning once toward the water, she stares for only the briefest of seconds before turning slightly away, lost in her thoughts. She doesn't seem to know what to do before she finally faces me, and says,

"Mrs. Dover owns this cottage and another. She's selling both of them."

"You never did give me the long and short of it. Let's sit down and talk about it."

"I can't, Daniel. I know you're only trying to help, but everything I've worked so hard for . . ." It's the first time she doesn't use her hands to assist her. Her arms hang lifelessly at her sides instead, while her eyes glass over. "Is being sold out from under me."

I hold her hand and pull her to the picnic bench to sit with me. "What do you mean? Why would she do that to you?"

Her shoulders fold over when she says, "That asshole Bryan called her and told her the entire plumbing has to be redone." Such a fucker. "She panicked and called one of the companies who offered her money sight unseen a few months back."

"But you wanted it."

"I have worked my ass off for this property for four years. I did some of the updates myself. I made my sisters help me build this freaking deck in the middle of winter." She turns to me and says, "She promised she'd give me a chance to present my offer and seriously consider what I'm offering since it's more than money." Closing her eyes, she sighs, the wind stolen out from under her sails. She drops her head in her hands.

When her shoulders shake, I move closer and hold her in my arms. Rubbing her back, I say, "I know it's hard to see the light when you're lost in the dark, but I promise you it's going to be okay."

She lifts her head and says, "It's all I wanted. I put my entire future on the line, believing she would give me a chance. One shot, like you said."

"You've taken it, though. Not every shot scores a goal. But there will be others. Those will be your winners."

"You don't understand, Daniel. This cottage is all I have to keep me here. I was willing to sink what little of my inheritance I had left into this property. It was a way to help my family pay the bills one day. But worst of all, when this property sells, they all will. No one will be left in this small town except for us. And then we'll have to go." Rust covers her tone, making it rougher, as tears slip through the words. "High-rise hotels will be built on top of my parents." A sob breaks through as she falls into my arms this time, her cheek to my chest, while fisting my shirt.

Roman walks out with his bag, so I hold up a finger and signal for him to wait inside. He goes but looks back. I don't want to worry him, but this is life. It's okay to show emotion.

I'm trying to understand the full story through the glimpses she's giving me. "Mrs. Dover is not letting you put in a competing offer, or it's a no-bid situation, and she's already sold it?"

"I could put in an offer, but it would have to be higher than what's on the table."

"What's on the table?"

Wiping under her eyes, she sits up and straddles the bench to face me. "Two hundred thousand more than I could ever dream of having."

I rest my hands on her legs and gently rub, wanting to both comfort her and selfishly keep her close. "Can you borrow from the bank?"

Annoyance conveys in her eyes as she turns her gaze somewhere other than on me. Her tongue toys with the corner of her mouth before I'm hit with a hard stare. "I'm not risking our home as collateral, and I'd never be approved for the amount I need to bridge the gap. Without it . . ." A thickened throat has her clearing it unsuccessfully before she adds, "I know it's hard for someone like you to understand money problems—"

"I grew up with nothing but hockey gear. Everything and anything was sold to keep me playing in hopes of hitting the jackpot one day."

"And you hit it." Her patience is worn and threading through her words. I don't blame the urgency she feels to fix the problem. It's her fallback from what I've already learned. "Problem solved."

"I would have rather had a family."

"Me too."

*Shit.* I shouldn't have gone there, not with her. She had the perfect life. I had an angry father who took out his failures on his only son. Yeah, not the same thing. "I'm sorry."

A beat doesn't pass before she's reaching forward to hug me. Slipping onto my lap, she needs this maybe as much as I do. To be close to someone without an expectation of more than comfort feels foreign to me, but I feel it with her. I hold her, knowing this might be the only time, and relish this amazing woman in my arms by kissing her shoulder.

I may not know everything I want about Summer, but I know I can trust her. She's good inside and out. "Summer?"

From against my chest, she whispers, "What?"

I remember my father begging for his cut of my pay. Every two weeks, like clockwork, he showed up. Two years straight. He always called it a loan and would turn around to call me a sucker for falling for it again.

She's not him. She's what's good with the world. What better investment is there than that? I do what everyone always told me not to, and ask, "What if I loaned you the money?"

# CHAPTER 13

## SUMMER

"You can't do that."

I stand, needing room to roam and think through this ludicrous idea with plenty of space to lay out my thoughts to examine them better. Surely, he's drunk, though I know darn well one beer wouldn't have clouded his judgment enough to make such a wild offer.

"Why not?"

"You barely know me, that's why not." I start pacing, seeking a stride that feels right for a situation like this. *There's not one.* So I walk without purpose to get the shock of Daniel's offer out of my system. "These things don't happen to me. It's like winning the lottery and losing your best friend."

"What does that mean?"

"Good always comes with bad, and I'm not prepared for what the opposite of this luck will be."

"Okay. Okay." He's off the bench and blocking my path. Catching me before I dart around him, he holds me still and lowers to eye level. "I wasn't trying to make things worse for you, but I can confidently say that I don't regret the offer. I know enough about you and your intentions to save this town to want to help."

My shoulders ease under the realization that I've been heard. My heart, my dreams, and my goals. A man with a million other reasons not to give the time of day to a small-town girl a world away from his own was listening. The reassurance in his tone lets me know he understands my concerns. "You still can't offer a stranger hundreds of thousands of dollars without strings attached. This is not what most people do, Daniel."

How do I manage my feelings from the reality of being in debt to him? We just met, and he's throwing money at me like he'll somehow get it back. There's no way for me to earn enough to support my family and pay off a loan like that. So as much as I love the feel of him holding me like I'm the only woman in the world that matters to him, I can't take both risks at once. It's either my heart or my head. This is when logic needs to prevail.

Give it a rest, heart.

"I'm not most people." He sure isn't. His gaze softens as he catches mine.

I'm still not sure how he broke through my carefully built walls with unattainable standards to match, but here he is like he conquered the whole damn fortress. "I'm learning that the more we spend time together."

But looking at him sends my heart racing again. There's no restraining a genuine reaction. I cup his face, loving the prickles from the dusting of scruff on my fingertips. "Why are you doing this?"

Reaching over my arms, he cups my face with a grin that can only be construed as he's lost his damn mind, and replies, "Because I want to and because I can."

"But it makes no sense for you. This isn't a good investment, so why waste your money?"

"Are you trying to talk me out of it?" he asks under muted chuckles.

"Yes." I can't manage a smile even from seeing his. The pressure to take the offer and run weighs heavy on my chest. "I can't owe you the rest of my life. I'll never be able to get out from under that debt."

"I'm not investing in the property, Summer. I'm investing in you to keep Mountain Laurel Cove alive." He glances toward the ocean. "Look at this place. I thought everywhere had already been overdeveloped. Not here. This place needs to exist, not just for you but for others to see how beautiful nature really is."

I smile because my heart does. He gets it. He truly understands that if one domino falls, they all do. I can't let that happen. "Careful, or I'm going to start to think you were brought on purpose."

"To save the day? It wouldn't be the first time." His laughter echoes, thinking he really did something there with that compliment to himself.

I can't join him, but it's too real for me. "I'm starting to believe that might be true."

"All clear?" a little voice calls to us. We turn to see Roman standing in the doorway.

Roman's been so good and patient that I feel bad for making him wait around as I spiral over something personal. He's here for a vacation, not to be dragged into my drama. "All clear," I call, checking in briefly with a glance whose smile has stuck to his face like it's glued there and evokes mine in response. "We need to talk more about this."

"We will, but I want you to consider it."

"I am. There's just a lot of details to consid—"

"Can I go?" Roman asks, dropping his bag beside us and startling us apart like two teens busted making out by their parent.

Daniel rubs his hand over his head. "What do you mean you go?"

"You guys are talking, and that's boring." The whine in his tone doesn't seem to go over well with his dad.

"What do we say about being bored, Roman?"

He kicks his foot out and then drops it with a pout of his lips. "Find something to do."

"Yep." He rests his hand on Roman's back. The pats are light with care as if he's rooting for him. "So what are you going to do?"

"Go see Dolly. I can walk down there by myself."

Daniel glances at me with a question in his eyes. "Is it safe?"

"You see how little traffic there is. Ten homes and a dead end don't impress many to drive down here," I reply. "She'd love the company."

"I'm not a baby, Dad."

"I know you're not." He looks at the road once more and takes his bag from him. "I'll bring this down when we return."

I pull out my phone again and text Dolly. "I'll let her know you're heading her way."

He throws his arms around my waist. "Thanks, Summer."

The heart that was shattered slowly pieces itself back together. I hug him. "Go straight there, okay?"

"I will." Glancing at Daniel, he says, "Promise."

Ruffling his hair this time, Daniel says, "On your way, kid. Adventure awaits."

Roman takes off running before Daniel finishes speaking. I come stand next to him, pressing my head to his arm, and say, "Dolly's meeting him halfway."

Daniel's arm comes around me, and he kisses my head. "Thank you."

"I imagine it's hard to let them try new things, to venture farther from us than they have before."

"It's good to do it in a safe way. He can't do this in the city. Mia and I won't let him." There's a scoff that's lacking humor, and he says, "I was running all over the place by myself at his age. Shoplifted my fair share of candy and soda with friends I shouldn't have been hanging around with. By nine, I was busing it to games on my own." Though I desperately want to see his face, his grip is firm, holding me in place. *Purposeful*? Probably.

Other than anger and temper tantrums, I'm certain most hockey players aren't used to showing much emotion. Daniel does with me. He gives me these small peeks into his past and feelings. It makes me feel more connected to him.

Exhaling a deep breath, he shifts his head and then releases me enough to aim his eyes out at the ocean. I'm mesmerized by it every day, fortunate to have it in my backyard. I can't imagine life being lived without the immensity of this beauty in my life.

He crosses his arms over his chest. "I made the mistake of telling my dad I was bored when I was six." No good story begins like that . . . my stomach drops at the thought of what's to come. He peeks over at me. "He beat the shit out of me with my hockey stick and made me practice two extra hours that night without any dinner." Sickness gnaws at my insides, leaving my heart feeling raw and aching. "I was never bored again. My son will never know pain like that. I'll set the world on fire before I let anyone harm him."

Reaching up, I pat his back gently like he did for Roman.

Otherwise, I'd be taking him in my arms. It's what I would want, but what does Daniel need? *Screw it.* I'll take the lead and wrap myself around him from behind, resting my cheek against his back, and hold him.

A breeze picks up, cooling us down, and the closeness soothes me. Listening to his steady breathing becomes a guidepost that he's okay, giving me the reassurance I need. "Daniel?" He hums in reply. He co-parents with Roman's mom, but they aren't on the same page when they're apart. He's on his own, fighting against what he was shown about what a father is and winning that battle. "You're a good dad for breaking the cycle."

He turns, wrapping me up like a present in his arms. Holding me so tight that I can feel his heartbeat against my cheek, he rests his head on the top of mine, and whispers, "Take the offer, Summer." I smile against him because that was said from the heart.

I'd been fighting against the charity he'd offered me because it felt like sacrificing my pride. I don't want his sympathy. I wanted him to give it for other reasons than guilt. Even as a loan, if it comes from somewhere other than feeling sorry for me.

"You won't regret it. I promise. You won't."

"I know."

Pulling back, I want to see his face and those amazing eyes of his. When I do, I say, "Thank you. I'll do whatever it takes to get the money back to you one day."

"I don't want it back. I see the magic in Mountain Laurel Cove like you do." He lifts my chin. "If you can, I want you to keep this town just as it is."

"I'm doing my best." I hug him once more, closing my eyes and finally able to breathe again when my phone buzzes. I let go and look at my phone. Smiling, I tilt my head back up for Daniel. "Roman is safely in Dolly's care."

"Good."

Tapping my fingertips under his, I ask, "Are you as exhausted as I am?"

"Yeah, I should pack up to move my stuff over."

We both turn toward the cottage. He picks up the bag, and we walk together. "I can help."

He shakes his head. "I don't have much. You're tired. Why don't you head back, and I'll meet you over there in a little while."

"You sure?"

"I won't be long."

Sometimes you get a sense someone needs time to themselves. This feels like one of those times. "I can take Roman's bag."

"It's okay. I got it."

I stop on the doormat outside after he enters the house. "Okay." I rock back on my heels and watch as he heads for the bedroom. Thumbing over my shoulder, I say, "I'm going then."

Turning to leave, I take two steps before he calls, "Wait, Summer."

"Yes?" the reply rushes from my mouth so fast as if I needed an excuse to stay a little longer. Right when I turn back, he captures my face in his hands, and my lids flutter closed as his lips press to mine. My head swims in the connection, my body leaning into him, my hands grapple to grab onto his shirt as I hold him like my life depends on it.

Our lips part, and our tongues meet in a tangling twist of rules and breaking them, professionalism, and my personal desires. I toss it all aside and kiss with the desire of a thousand fires burning inside for him.

And when we part, my breath pants from my chest, my eyes opening slowly to find him admiring me with his heart on his sleeve. He whispers, "I just wanted to tell you that."

I hold him as close as I can while this magic lasts. "I'm glad you did." Unfurling my fingers from his shirt, I take a step back and say, "Maybe you can tell me more about it later?"

A sly grin works its way onto his face. "I can't wait."

I start walking backward, smiling like a loon who just scored a fish from the cove. "Me either. I'll see you later." I turn and practically skip off the deck onto the ground.

"See you later, Summer."

I hurry down the road and then just flat-out sprint, filled with the adrenaline from kissing him and the offer to help buy the cottage in play. My thoughts are swirling on the rights and wrongs and the pros and cons when it hits me. I'm halfway back when I come to an abrupt halt.

Out of breath, I look back. I've gone too far to still see the cottage and not far enough to see the house. It doesn't matter. I had a problem, and he stepped in to help. I can do the same for him.

## CHAPTER 14

DANIEL

"Why can't I sleep in here?" Roman's legs dangle off the side of the bed as he watches me drop my duffel bag by the dresser.

"We don't know how long it will take to get the pipes fixed, buddy. I'll camp out on this couch, and you can have a bed all to yourself." I'm thinking I should feel guilty for lying to him, but am I? Is it really a lie? He *will* be more comfortable in the guest room, and I'll be more comfortable in Summer—

"I like sharing with you."

I sit next to him on Summer's bed. "I like sharing with you too, but I took more hits last night from your tossing and turning than I did on the ice the entire last season."

The little smirk on his face makes me think he's not all that upset about taking out his old dad. I tickle his ribs, sending him backward on the mattress into a fit of giggles. "I should," he says, laughing through his words, "have played hockey."

We don't talk about him playing hockey anymore. He never made it to squirt level in the youth league when he was younger. He was a smaller guy on the team at the time, and the hits were brutal to witness. Mia put her foot down, but I didn't disagree. He didn't care about hockey, and it showed when he was out there. Although it's not too late to try again, I'd prefer him to chart his own course instead of trying to mold into mine. "I'm thinking soccer or football might be better for a kid with your skill set. You got a hell of a kick."

"Really?"

I pull him up and then stand, bringing him with me. "You can do whatever you want, Roman. Just finish what you start and don't—"

"Compromise your values. Yeah, yeah." You'd think this kid has been working a hard day and doesn't want the lecture at the end of it with that ho-hum tone. I'll take being the boring dad anytime over what I had growing up.

A knock on the door draws our attention to Summer. She's dressed in the same top and cutoff shorts; her hair is still up, but more strands have escaped the confines of the elastic at the back of her head. There's a shine to her lips that draws my attention to them, making me remember how good it felt to kiss her. With her shoulder against the doorframe, a smile on her face, and looking so damn sexy, she makes it hard to look away. "Am I interrupting?" she asks, her fingers tucked into her front pockets like she's been there a while.

Roman is already shaking his head. "I want to sleep in here with you guys."

Summer saunters in like she's got a few things on her mind that don't include anyone else sleeping in this room with us. Kneeling before him, she takes his hands, and says, "You're going to have a great time in that room. You get the whole place to yourself and all those pillows. Also . . ." she leans in and whispers, "It's been rumored that cookies appear right before bed for good little kids."

"I'm always good. My mom says I make her life easy," he says with pride.

He's old enough not to fall for these shenanigans, but like how Santa doesn't visit if he doesn't believe, sounds like these cookies won't show up either. When he glances up at me, I say, "It's true. You're the best, buddy."

He looks back at Summer, and says, "Do you get cookies in here?"

With a grimace shaping her face, she sighs so sadly that I'm tempted to fall for her tricks. "Unfortunately, no."

"You could if you're good," he says matter-of-factly. This kid is too much, causing me to chuckle under my breath.

"Very true, Roman." She stands still, holding his hand like they're old friends, and taps his nose. "What do you think about you and your dad coming to watch the sunset with me and the others?" To a kid, I'm sure that's not an inviting offer, but I'm not going to push into it. She adds, "Have I shown you the swing out back?"

That seals it. He's already headed to the door. "I want to see."

Summer looks at him over her shoulder. "I need to speak to your dad for a few minutes. Why don't you head down and hang out in the family room with Dolly?"

His eyes dart to mine. I nod, giving him the go-ahead. He runs out the door, and the pounding of each of his steps on the floor echoes into the bedroom.

Summer turns around with a question digging a line between her brows and hanging on her tongue. "I can't stop thinking about that call with Mrs. Dover and your offer."

She's not asking me anything, but I can sense her need

for answers. "I haven't changed my mind, if that's what you're asking."

Moving in, she runs her nails lightly over my stomach. Her touch is intimate, but I wish I wasn't wearing a shirt so I could feel its full impact. "I appreciate it, but I don't know that it feels right. It's too much money."

"I'm not going to force you to take the money." I sit on the bed again, not wanting to tower over her for this conversation. "I hope you do in keeping with your intentions. They're good, Summer. If you can save a place that you love and keep it going for other people to enjoy as well, it makes sense."

"I'll never be able to pay you back. As a rental, it won't generate the kind of income that would let me make a living, care for my family, and pay to fix up this house. Some profits will always have to be reinvested in the cottage for upkeep. In this case, thousands to fix the plumbing is just the start."

I could blow that money in a weekend in Vegas and already donate four times that amount in a year. It's not about the money, but I know what it's like not to have that access, to never dream making that kind of money is even possible. If I say the wrong thing, I come off as showy. If I don't, she won't accept the offer.

And now the lines between us are so blurred that I risk her pulling away as if she'd have to choose only one. *Me or the money.*

Taking her hand, I bring her to stand between my legs. While she doodles on my thigh, I say, "I don't know what to do here, Summer. It's not that I don't care about the money. It's that to me, the cause is worthy."

"I'm the cause?" The affront has her jerking away, losing contact. There's no anger in her words or distorting her pretty face. Something else takes hold, and her eyes glass over. "Instead of daydreaming about boys and going on a first date, I was making funeral arrangements for my parents. Dolly was broken, and the girls were too young." Turning away from me, she walks to the window that faces the oranges, pinks, and blues of the setting sun. She sucks in a staggering breath, as if the tears are ready to fall. "I can't be a charity case again."

"You're not a charity case." I stand, my words getting mixed up in my head as her turmoil reaches me across the room and sinks in. She's wounded by a past that will always haunt her, and I'm making things worse. "I didn't mean to imply—"

"I don't want to be saved, Daniel. I wanted to do this on my own." She turns back, steeling her temperament until it reaches her posture. Amazed by her resolve as she works through scenarios, I remain silent, a sounding board for her. "I paid for my college and part of this house. I don't have enough of my inheritance left to cover the purchase of the cottage. Even if I hadn't had the other expenses, I can't compete with the offer on the table."

Unable to stop the sympathy she hates from storming inside me, I go to her and caress her cheek. "Tell me the truth, Summer. When you talk of your inheritance, is that from your parents' death?"

"It was the life insurance payout. That's what we got in exchange for their deaths." A tear slides from the inner corner of her eye, trailing down her cheek. She had me convinced by her determination, her steady voice when she spoke of the issue. It was all a facade, and I have no doubt she's managed to convince everyone in this town that her brave face is more than surface deep.

It's not. She's just become a good actress. She's surviving

the waves of grief when they roll through. But she's also scarred so badly on the inside from holding it in that it's going to drown her one day. I kiss the trail, then wipe it away with the pad of my thumb, careful not to scratch her with my calloused hands.

The tears dry, and she punches out her chin like she's got something to prove. Not to me. I've seen her strength and what she does for others. Saying anything will make it worse. I won't make her feel ashamed for sharing how her heart feels. "I'm sorry you lost them. Your sisters and Dolly are lucky to have you."

I hear the harsh swallow and see the softening over her eyes. "Thank you for saying that. It means a lot to me." She's not heard it enough. She hasn't been given a thank-you because everyone was trying to survive the best they knew how. She's a caretaker, so that's what she did.

I'm starting to wonder if she can accept care herself. There doesn't need to be a loan involved. I'd give her the money, but I know she'll never agree to it on her own. Playing to her strengths and to what gives her comfort, like control over the situation, is the only way to break through to her. When she moves toward the bed, I walk to the chair in the corner, resting one ankle on the opposite knee, and ask, "What if we put rules in place?"

"The devil is in the details." Hugging one of the four posters of the bed, she drags a small gold butterfly pendant back and forth along a thin chain. "What do you suggest?"

"You set the terms."

"That simple?" Her laughter holds no humor, but she appears to be willing to entertain me by the gentle slope of her smile. "I set the terms, and you agree? That's a lot of money to take that kind of risk."

Dropping my foot to the floor, I lean forward. "What if there's something in it for me?"

"An exchange." Her expression lifts as if she already has an idea. "A thought crossed my mind earlier."

"Okay, throw it out and let's brainstorm from there."

"I need to get comfortable for this." She climbs to the middle of the bed and crosses her legs. Presenting her hand out like a platter, she says, "You're helping me with my problem, which I never pay you back for in its entirety, and I help you out with your problem?"

"What's my problem?"

"Your image."

I sit up when the idea hits like lightning. "Oh damn, you're right." Her smile spreads across her face, her demeanor already shifting for the better. I cross the room in three steps and sit in front of her. "Why didn't I think of that?" Her shrug is so blasé like this is no big deal when it changes everything. "You're the one."

"The one woman you mentioned, right?"

We don't need to get into the weeds of my developing feelings. "Semantics, but yeah."

She scoots closer. "I can be there when you need me, need to be seen, and what? On your arm?"

"On my arm, at events. Are you okay being the target of long lens cameras and being asked ridiculous questions that will sound insultingly personal?"

Pushing up on her hands, she kisses me. It's too fast for my liking, but she instigated it, so I'll take it. "Can I say no comment?"

"It's best if you do."

She grins. "Then I accept the job."

"And the offer?"

Laughing, she playfully shoves my shoulder. "I'm not doing this for fun, you know."

And therein lies the problem. Like she said, with good comes the reverse. I just traded a chance for a real relationship for one that's made for public consumption.

I was never the prize. It was always the cottage. I shouldn't be so surprised, then. I don't think it's a shock, though. I think it's disappointment. Is this what heartache feels like? The connection I have . . . had with her opened my eyes to the possibility of dating.

Just like the sun setting before we could watch it, the potential for love slipped through my fingers before I got to hold on to it. *Now, it's gone.*

## CHAPTER 15

SUMMER

All was not lost even though we missed the sunset. "There will be more sunsets," I say, sitting on the lawn, watching Spring push Roman on the swing.

We had a momentary break for grilled chicken and corn on the cob for dinner that he and Daniel devoured before Roman wanted to swing again—higher and higher by request. But Dolly insisted that we first go on what she calls a "digestion walk." Fall even caught up to the group after a long shift at the hospital.

It's hard for my sisters to coordinate their schedules and be in one place at the same time, so it was nice for Fall to show up in time to meet Daniel and Roman. And so tempting to pull her aside to share the details of the agreement. If I'm going to be photographed, I'll need to warn them anyway. The words didn't come when I needed them to, and where no one else would hear. If I voice it, it makes the situation real. And I think another night to sleep on it will do me some good.

We reached the marina at the edge of town, walking the docks, and having a quick chat with a friend coming off his boat before turning back. Now, settled under the moonlight in the backyard watching the lightning bugs and the stars come out, I lean forward to peek over at Daniel sitting on the other side of Dolly. She plonked her chair in the middle of us for some unknown reason. That's what we get for trying to pretend nothing is going on between us. I would rather be in his lap than in the grass, but so much has happened that it's probably best that we keep it low-key for now. "I said there will be more sunsets," I say louder as if he didn't hear me the first time.

"Gracious. What in blazes are you shouting about sunsets for, honey?" Dolly grips the arms of her chair like she needs them to ground her after jumping out of her skin.

Daniel's chuckling before his eyes meet mine. "There will be. Every night, technically."

"I didn't know if Daniel heard me."

"Who didn't hear you? I'm sure Mr. Taylor and Mrs. Browley up the road heard you." Patting her chest, she sits back, muttering, "About gave me a heart attack."

I think that's my cue to get ready for bed. With Daniel being in the room, I need to get a head start anyway. Standing up, I dust the back of my shorts off. "I'm going in. It's almost ten, and I want to do a face mask."

Daniel appears to be working through my words like they're code for something else. I add, "It's a jelly mask." I'm not sure that helped pull him from the path his mind was already traveling like a bloodhound on the scent. "Peach. Vitamin C." I shake my head. "Forget it. Night, everyone."

A chorus of "night" and a giggle from Roman is heard before I trek upstairs. I kind of want to take a bath. It would feel so good after running around all day. I glance toward the window that overlooks the others and decide. "A quickie."

After turning on the water in the bath, I strip down and twist my hair up again, this time higher so it doesn't get wet. I pull a mask from my mask organizer and smooth it on before dipping one foot, then the other, and slowly sliding under the water. The water hits the peak before it spills over, so I turn it off, then rest back on the bath pillow and close my eyes so the mask can do its job, and I can relax.

My muscles give in under the warmth of the water, but my mind is still swimming around the agreement Daniel and I made. Have logic and good sense gone out the window? Am I desperate enough to be one-half of a public spectacle of a couple to buy the cottage?

*Yes.*

*And yes.*

I'm not seeing any other way to get enough money in time to fight the other offer. I can't ask my sisters. They have their own lives and dreams to pay for. This is it. Daniel is the only option I have.

Beads of sweat form at my hairline as the heated water sinks into my skin. I'm surprised to see some bubbles remain. Clearly, I've not been in long enough if those haven't disappeared. Closing my eyes again, the worries of money and broken pipes, and faking it for the cameras fade away. But the idea of being on Daniel's arm stays. Like the first time I saw him, the memory has me biting my lip. Counting those abs has my hand shifting under the water and between my legs. My heart thumps as my body embraces the desire I have for him.

I stop and look back over my shoulder. I'm not worried about him walking in while I'm bathing. The suds hide enough. But catching me masturbating is a whole other story. Holding my breath, I listen.

Normally, my sisters sound like a stampede on these

wooden floors. I'm greeted with silence, which means they're still out back. *Good.*

Closing my eyes again, my thoughts go back to the first time our eyes met, an intensity like I've never felt before washing through me to take notice. Rubbing slowly over my clit, I can still feel the spark from when we first touched. When I was leaving and peeked back over my shoulder, I was met with a promise and a dare, as if he were my savior and the forbidden.

I tease and circle, rub and touch—

"Would you like company?"

My body flails as my legs slip out from under me when I hear his voice, the water splashing while I struggle to secure a hold of the sides of the tub. I catch myself, but not before the bubbles end up in my eyes and dissipate in the water. "Don't look."

"If it makes you feel better, I've seen a naked woman before."

I swipe the suds from my eyes before they start burning. "It doesn't, Daniel. Go."

"Okay. Okay." He walks away with heavy steps, and the door protests as it closes.

Turning on the faucet, I pour more bubble bath under the running water, letting it spread so the cooler water tempers the hot water I've been lying in. I pull off the mask, wad it up, and stick it to the edge.

I don't know what he saw, but he's the only thing that's inspired me to feel anything sexual in an unhealthily long and dry stage of my life. I should be embarrassed for what I was doing to his memory, but I can't seem to muster the energy. It felt too good to be ashamed. "Daniel?" I look back when the door cracks open, but it's not enough to see him. "Don't leave."

"I'm here. What do you need?"

Gnawing on the inside of my cheek, I fear being rejected. I don't need the blow to my ego right now. Or ever. But the question is loaded. He just doesn't realize it yet.

*Do I ask?*

*Should I?*

What am I doing? *Oh God.*

I've lost all better judgment around him, and why? Because he has a great face, hands that I am desperate to feel cradle my body, and a soft side for me that apparently doesn't exist for anyone else. He knows my situation on the drought scale. He understands how my type A personality fits into my neat-and-organized small-town life and accepts me for it. He even feeds it by whispering sweet nothings, like suggesting we make rules and follow them. I have the perfect guy asking how he can help me.

Please Lord, don't let him reject me. "Can you help me with something?"

"What is it?" he asks through the one-inch opening of the door. "Do you need a towel?"

"No. I need . . ." I turn off the water again and sit back, covered in bubbles. Taking a breath, I ready myself for the worst, bracing the iron side of the claw-foot tub, and—

"Are you okay, Summer?"

"I'm fine," I reply, losing my nerve. *Just do it.* "Can you come in here?"

The door slowly creaks open with his finger still in the air from pushing it open. "How may I be of assistance?"

Lying back in the tub, I keep my eyes forward while he remains behind me. "Did you see anything?"

"Other than you bathing?"

I glance back, seeing him leaning against the door with

his arms crossed and admiring me like I'm prettier than any sunset, and ask, "Is that all?"

He smirks. "I saw you master-bathing."

"Daniel!" The water splashes up the sides when I howl in laughter. "That's such a bad joke."

"Made you laugh, though." His tone is as lighthearted as he makes me feel.

*Happy.* "I'll give you that." The earlier nerves rippling through me have disappeared, and I'm left with a smile and a desire to spend more time with him. Sexually and not sexually, but in that order. Do I cross the line from what this is—*playful?* —to more? We've kissed, so I know the attraction is mutual. I take a breath and try again. "I was . . ."

"You were what?"

"No, I was saying I *was* master-bathing." I feel ridiculous repeating it, but his chuckle echoing in the small room makes me glad I did. But I'm not brave enough to ask this to his face and that great jaw of his, the eyes that stare at me expectantly, *and just say it, Summer!* "Maybe you could—"

"Lend a hand?" His tone is optimistic while I'm still second-guessing myself.

*What am I doing? What am I doing? What am I doing?* "Yes." I drop my head into my hands, cringing as I wait for him to either laugh, run out the door, or accept the mission.

The sound of his footsteps draws me to peer through barely spread fingers. Daniel kneels beside the tub and pulls my hand away from my face. "Are you asking me to touch you, Summer?"

I nod, my breathing too erratic to speak.

"Do you want me to make you come, Summer?"

Unable to breathe at this point, much less think coherently, my head bobs up and down like a dashboard ornament.

He gets on his knee. "Lie back and close your eyes."

I lick my lips and get comfortable. Looking at him once more, I commit everything about how he's looking at me to memory and close my eyes. I hear the dip of his hand and feel the water as it laps over my chest like it does in the cove. The back of his hand slides across the top of my thigh before I bend the other, and it jumps to slip down the inside of that one. His knuckles brush gently over my lower belly before he goes lower. "You have an incredible body," he whispers as he slips between my legs.

His breathing deepens along with mine as I angle lower and then butterfly open my legs for him. He sucks in a sharp breath, his tone dropping to a sinful, almost growl. "Good girl." My heart flutters, and I swallow hard as my eyes pop open. He's watching as his hands explore with a worshipful awe softening his features as his Adam's apple bobs. I never thought I'd be into dirty talk, but I'll never be able to unhear those words from his lips, to unsee the pleasure mapped along his features as if he's the one experiencing this.

Two fingers dip between my lower lips, exploring tenderly as I close my eyes again. His fingers bend, teasing, and I'm torn between accepting this or stepping out of the water to beg him to take me instead. I bite the tip of my tongue to keep from moaning and grip the sides of the tub to keep from grinding myself against his purposeful journey. "You are so soft," he murmurs. "So responsive."

"Mmm," I respond breathlessly as the tip of his finger circles my entrance and dips just enough to make me gasp and hold my breath.

"Breathe, Sunshine."

I take a breath, and just as I exhale, a finger dives into me. My eyes fly open as I slam my hands on either side of my hips, my body clenching, and my knees knocking together.

He's smiling at me with a brow raised. "Are you okay?"

My swallow is so loud, I'm sure he can hear it, and the nerves that have returned. "I'm okay." I lie. I'm caught between panic and the need for him to move a little.

"I might," he starts, shifting his weight, "be losing blood to my hand." His other hand reaches for my chin, and he runs his fingers along my jaw. "Take another breath for me and try to relax your legs. Can you do that for me, Summer?"

"I can do that." *I don't know if I can.* "I think."

Leaning closer to my head, he nuzzles my cheek, his tone lower, gentler. "No, you can. You're ready. Look at you opening for me, and so aroused. I want to taste you, Sunshine."

"It's been a long time," I whisper, wishing I still had the confidence from a few minutes ago when I asked for his help.

"D4. I remember." He nibbles at the lobe of my ear, and the shock of it sends ripples of pleasure through my body, pebbling the skin exposed above water, and loosening the tight muscles gripping his hand. "That's it."

I can feel his smile against my cheek, but he doesn't immediately move his hand. Instead, his thumb finds the bundle of nerves, and he gently glides it over my clit. His other hand reaches for my chin, turning my attention back to him.

"Who needs hands for hockey?" he says, unable to stop his smile or evoking mine, causing me to melt into him.

His smirk is cocky, like he knows exactly how to give me what I need. I can choose to trust him, to take the leap, but I also know he would stop if I asked.

The tip of his finger runs gently around my entrance, teasing my clit before dipping lower again. This time, his eyes stay locked on mine as he slides into me.

I need to see him too much to close my eyes again. Pulling out and moving in again. When I reopen my eyes, I'm not met with his browns like I expect. I catch him in a moment with his eyes closed and mouth open as his breathing jags and his chest rises. In a quick fall, he exhales, opening his eyes and latching onto mine. "You're so fucking tight."

He pushes into me faster, and I find my hips moving to meet each thrust. The water splashes, but he feels too good to care. The flick of his thumb against my clit makes me jump, but the soothing pressure right after has me sinking back into pleasure. Until it becomes too much. His pace, the care, the tease, and the gentle pinch send me into my head, pulling me away from here and the feel of Daniel consuming me.

"You're stunning," he groans. "Taking my fingers so perfectly."

"So good," I utter as I chase the euphoria and succumb to the rapture. My thoughts dull as a current of electricity sparks every nerve ending to life again, leaving me sinking into the tub until I breathe a sigh of relief. I lick my lips as my head rolls to the left to look at him. "That was amazing."

His hand travels over my hip and holds my side. Leaning over, he kisses me with reverence in the pressure. When he's staring into my eyes, he whispers, "It was incredible to feel you wrapped around me, and to watch you come." Kissing my forehead, he sits back. "It was amazing." He stands and reaches for the towel hanging nearby.

It's hard to miss his erection, and he doesn't try to hide it one bit. He also doesn't ask me to return the favor even though I'd be more than happy to. He places the towel over the faucet and says, "You need anything?"

"No. I'm all good." And smiling like a fool.

"I'm going to head down and get a glass of water." He's already in the doorway when he looks back. "I also want to see if the rumors of the magical cookies are true. I'm stealing one if it is."

I'm too happy to contain the laugh that's itching to come out. "Grab me one if you do."

As soon as I hear the bedroom door close, I lie back with my arms wide. "So this is what heaven is like."

There's still much to work out on a professional level with this deal we've struck, including a call to Mrs. Dover first thing in the morning. On a personal level, though, I've never been happier.

# CHAPTER 16

## DANIEL

"Your middle name is Sky?" I rub her back, holding her in my arms in bed. "Summer Sky Season?" It probably shouldn't surprise me anymore. "Your parents went all in."

She giggles against my chest, her finger never slowing from drawing figure eights across my skin. "Yep. They did." I didn't think I'd be in her bed tonight, but it made no sense for me to be on the couch after what happened in the bathtub. Her words. *Not mine.* I would have been sleeping on the sofa if she hadn't flipped the covers open and told me to get in. "Want to know what my sisters' names are?" She tilts her head up to look at me. "Ready?"

I've met two because they all seem to be running on different schedules. Understandable at the point they each are in their lives. Summer, as the oldest, is eager to carve out her place, to have something all her own, and to put her energy into. I'm thinking it's because she's losing the role she's played in each of their lives. I have years with Roman before he takes off for college or pursues whatever he decides, but that doesn't mean I don't know the absence is coming. Faster than I'd like. Transition is hard, but it's life. "I'm ready."

"Summer Sky. Autumn Leaf, Winter Snow, and Spring Lily. We tease that Autumn won the lottery with her name, so playful nicknaming led to us calling her Fall when we were little. It just stuck. Now, if we dare to call her Autumn, she'll correct us."

"It's impressive and original."

Pushing up, she rests her weight on her hand. "You called me Sunshine?"

I'm not sure of the question posed. I act on instinct in hockey, and I'm smarter than I've been given credit for, usually underestimated as a dumb jock. With Summer, though, I do what I never do and follow my heart. "You are. Every time I see you, it's like the sun has come out."

Her gaze dips down as if the compliment is too much to hear, though her smile gives her away. I reach up and touch her cheeks that are warm for me. "What about your parents? What were their names?"

Her eyes flick back to mine, brightening her entire expression. "You want to know my parents' names?"

"Of course, I do."

Angling toward me a little more, she says, "Faith Loving." The inspired tone prompts her smile to grow, as if hearing the name itself created it.

"That's beautiful."

"She was. She was so beautiful. I can sometimes still hear her laughter. It used to ring through this house, reaching every corner." Her gaze drifts to the room around us, and she sighs. When she turns back, she says, "My dad was Charlie. Charles officially. Charles Duke Season. Charlie Season and Faith Loving." She lies back in my arms, her breathing even, which I prefer. With her hand flattened to my stomach, she keeps her head down. "Do you want to talk about your parents?"

"No. I like your world better." The response feels like a betrayal. My mom deserves better than to be lumped in with my father. Draping an arm over my head, I say, "My mom is Janie. That's what everybody calls her." I glance at Summer. "Janie Sutton. She wasn't perfect when I was growing up and had her own struggles with my father, but she did the best she could. She's better without him, even as a mom."

"When did they divorce?"

Running a hand through my hair, I've carried the burden of their relationship most of my life. "She stayed until I helped her get out. I bought her a place of her own."

Summer slides up next to me, her head resting on the seam of the two pillows to stay close. I glance at her and can't find an ounce of judgment in her fine features. I do find an assuring smile, forgiving at the ends like the corners of her eyes, leaving room for me to say what I need to get off my chest. "I've never really talked about this stuff." There's a pause. When I look at her again, I can see the hesitation and concern deepening her blue eyes. "I feel okay with you."

She presses her palm to my cheek. I lean into it, and she asks, "Why don't you talk about it?"

"There was no one to talk to."

The release of a heavy breath has her lowering her hand and slipping it against mine between us. She whispers, "You can talk to me, Daniel. I'll always listen."

I reach up and take her chin between my thumb and forefinger, studying her the way her eyes hold truth to the offer. "Where'd you come from?"

"I was right next door." Her smile shines light into the darker corners of my heart like I'm seeing the sun rise for the first time. *Sunshine.*

"I'm starting to think you're heaven-sent." I lift to kiss her once. It's gentle like she is and as sweet as the taste of her.

And then she kisses me, letting her lips linger against mine. When she leans back, she says, "I've been right here all along."

The urge to kiss her again, to deepen it, and run my hand over her body to make her come again is potent. The need to be inside her and claim her in ways that make her mine is even stronger.

As much as I want to make love to her, I can still hear one of her sisters' electric toothbrushes buzzing from the bathroom down the hall. Another just arrived home, and tiptoeing apparently isn't a thing around here. Every noise is an echo for someone else's ears. I don't want to be quiet with Summer. I want to feel every inch of her and hear each moan and my name falling from her lips from ecstasy.

When she can't conceal a yawn, I slide down the mattress, bringing her with me until we're lying down again. I can't make love to her, but I have the privilege of spending the night holding her.

Cuddled into the crook of my arm, she says, "It won't be hard to act like your girlfriend for the cameras."

I peek at her out of the corner of my eye. "You don't think so?"

"No. It'll be like we are right now. No acting required."

I don't remember the last time I had a girlfriend. Mia and I never got there. There might have been one or two in college, but after that, they were more of a distraction than a benefit to my life, especially as my career was taking off.

With Summer in my arms, this feels right. *Right timing. Right place. Right girl.* She's right. "I like that."

"What's that?"

"The no acting required." God, I love her smile. I kiss her forehead and say, "Sweet dreams, Summer Sky."

"Sweet dreams. Wait . . ." Popping back up on her elbow, she says, "I don't know your middle name."

I've been dreading this. "Don't laugh."

"I'll give you the same courtesy you gave me."

Chuckling, I scrub my hand over my face. "I knew that would come back to bite me in the ass one day." It's not like she can't find it online. I glance at her and just say it. "Stanley."

She mulls the name, as if it doesn't quite make sense. "I don't get it." Her eyes widen. "Oh, is that your trophy? The chalice?"

My laughter is louder than I intend, but God, I hope she never fucking changes. "Yeah. The Stanley Chalice." Still chuckling, I hold her closer. Kissing her head once more. "Good night."

"Good night, Daniel Stanley."

I'm still smiling after I reach over and turn out the lamp on the nightstand. Settling in with her, I ask, "Are you tired?"

She bursts out laughing. "I am. Go to sleep."

"Yes, ma'am." I close my eyes, but I open them again, waiting for them to adjust to the dark so I can take another look at this woman. I can't think of anything I did to deserve her, the grace she's given me, or the way she sees me as everything I've not been. I'd been thinking I was sent here as a punishment. It's a reward. *She is.* And holding her now is an honor I didn't earn. But I will. "Are you asleep?" I tease.

"Daniel." She giggles right after, and her arm tightens over me. "Good night."

~

"SUMMER? SUMMER."

I open my eyes to the sound of my son and swirls of paint on the ceiling I didn't see last night. They're pale yellow and vibrant in the daylight. He calls her again, his voice too distant to be in the house. I sit up and look around.

The bed next to me is empty, made up like no one slept there. The room is clean, not too much clutter, but things are here and there—a desk with necklaces hanging off a mirror's edge, and makeup in a bin propped on top. A leather journal and black mother-of-pearl-looking pen. I bought my mom a pair of earrings with that same design one time.

"Your turn." Roman's giggles stream through the window with sheer curtains and a chain of stained glass green leaves hanging from the top of it. Flipping the covers off, I go to look out in time to catch Summer flying off the swing under the tree near the water. She makes a perfect landing as my kid cheers. He makes everyone feel like a hero.

Resting my palms on the sill, I feel different, like a switch inside me was flipped.

It could have been making her come in the tub. I take pride that I ended that drought, though I'm not sure if that's the only dry spell she meant.

My guess is that waking up in the middle of the night holding her did the damage. How am I supposed to sleep alone now that I know what it's like to hold Summer Sky all night?

And to see her with my son, to see how carefree he is with her, and being here in the Cove makes me feel like I'm finally doing something right by him. *And me.* I needed this without realizing it—until I was in the middle of a place only found in storybooks.

Summer leans down, cupping her hand to Roman's ear before they both look up and wave. Guess I'm busted. "Come on, Dad," he says. He doesn't have to ask me twice.

I need to take a shower and eat something because I'm starving. But I pull on my shorts and shirt from yesterday since they're handy and brush my teeth. No way am I missing this opportunity with them. Or kissing Summer with morning breath.

Rushing down, I hear the kitchen door swing open like I've lived here my whole life, and Dolly saying, "Don't run in the house, Daniel," from the other side of it.

I slow. "Sorry, Dolly." But as soon as my feet land on the back patio, I'm running again. Scooping Roman in the air, I spin him and then give him a big hug. "How're you doing, kid?"

"Good." Settling with his legs around me, he leans back, knowing I'll never let him fall. "I got cookies last night."

"Oh yeah? So the folklore is real?"

He pulls up with his arms wrapped around me. "I got two with M & M's in them. There were four cookies, but Summer said the elves must have taken the rest."

My eyes meet hers over his shoulder to catch her holding back her laughter. I look into my son's eyes, never seeing them so clearly until now. "Sneaky little devils."

When I set him down, he's off to the swing again.

I steal the time to look at Summer in her sundress. The skirt is blowing along with her hair as she uses her hand to shield her eyes when looking at me. "How are you this morning?"

Her smile flows onto her face so naturally when she looks at me. Mine does the same when I see her. "So good. How are you?"

I've wondered if I should hold back and keep my feelings under wraps, not only for others but for Roman. But I know my son. I know he wants to see me happy, and damn, this woman makes me happy. I pick her up just to see that blue sky and her matching eyes at the same time. "I liked last night with you. A lot."

And when I lower her down the front of me, I get a quick kiss before she looks around to see if we got away with it. "Me too, and not just because I benefited." Tapping my chest, she adds, "Although I really, really did." Her eyebrows pop at the end as if she has all sorts of things not appropriate for others on her mind. "How'd you sleep?"

I step back, though all I want to do is invade her space to keep her close. "Couldn't have slept better."

"Watch this, Dad." That singular phrase probably ends in an ER trip more times than not. I watch but brace myself.

I turn in time to catch Roman jump off the swing midair and land on the lawn. "Great job, buddy."

"Maybe I should do gymnastics?"

From hockey to gymnastics? Not the most direct route, but if it makes him happy, I'm all for it. "Talk to your mom when you see her next."

Dolly calls to us, "If you're hungry, come get some breakfast."

Summer asks, "Are you hungry?"

"Starving."

Roman runs to my side and holds my hand. "Starving." *The little mimic.*

Ten minutes later, we have full plates and a full table, though Fall is missing again. She left before the sun rose, I hear, to make another shift at the hospital. And Winter is out with the bees collecting honey. "You're running a bee farm?" I ask after drinking some orange juice.

Summer nudges me. "Winter will correct you and call it

an apiary or bee yard. I don't know what her issue is with the bee farm, but I think it's funny she cares so much."

"It's her business," Spring says. "What's the update on the water situation at the cottage?"

"None," Summer replies. "The guy was a con artist who planned to bilk Mrs. Dover out of her last dollars. The update I do have is still being worked through." She glances at me with the smallest shake of her head to keep the messaging aligned.

I'm the last one she needs to worry about. I'm the king of keeping things private. Comes with the territory.

Summer takes a sip of her coffee as the group goes quiet, too busy eating for conversation. She sets her mug down, and says, "I think we should go into town later."

## CHAPTER 17

SUMMER

"You ready?" I park a block down from the store and look at Daniel before we get out. Sunglasses on, ball cap in place, identity not hidden in any way, but I understand him wanting to try.

"As I'll ever be." He didn't want to come, not because he doesn't want to visit downtown Mountain Laurel Cove or hang out with Roman and me. He doesn't want Roman subjected to fans, or, worse, have photos of his son plastered all over the internet.

I can't relate to what he's experiencing. It's unique for someone in his position. But also, at six-four and displaying those shoulders, he's not exactly able to blend into a crowd. So I get his hesitation. But for us, he came charging out of the house ready to tackle fame head-on.

Popping out of the car, I open the back door for Roman to climb out. We don't make it onto the sidewalk before I'm waving at Joan from the coffee shop located up the road when she passes us. She does a double take at Daniel but doesn't stop to chat, thank goodness. "See that store ahead?

The Honey Hive?" I lean down to whisper to Roman, "That's my sister's shop."

"Is there honey?"

Standing back up, I reply, "Oh boy, is there honey. Honey in everything."

Daniel keeps his head down and asks, "Which sister is this?"

Over my shoulder, I whisper, "Winter. She's a mogul in the making. I swear she'll have a honey empire one day."

He laughs as he strips his sunglasses off and opens the door for us. "I have no doubt, if she's related to you."

Heading straight for the counter, Winter hands a bag to a customer and wishes her a good day when she lays eyes on me. "In the market for some honey?"

"Sure am," I reply, tapping the counter and glancing around the store. "What's new?"

"We got this nougat honey bar that I can't stop eating." Reaching around, she takes one from a wooden display rack. "It's wicked good."

"Wicked, huh?" I laugh. She graduated from Boston University last month and brought home some of the local vernacular.

"Want to take one?"

"Bring a few home tonight."

Despite a few other customers browsing, her eyes land on Daniel and Roman with their hands pressed to the ice cream counter as they study the selection. I smirk, my gaze following her as my shoulders relax. Leaning closer, she whispers, "These are the tenants for the summer?"

It's only been a few days, but calling Daniel a tenant feels like such a disservice for how involved we already are. "They stayed with us for the past two nights. The pipes are broken over there."

"Spring filled me in. So he plays hockey, huh?"

"He does." I look over at him just in time to catch him wink at me.

Resting her arms on the counter, she says, "In Boston, they call the groupie girls who chase hockey players puck bunnies."

"No." *But I'm not sure either . . .* My mood infects my hunger, so I grab a candy bar from the display and rip the top of the wrapper off. "I need this, after all." Taking a bite, she's not wrong. From the first taste, it's delicious, but it doesn't make me feel better like I hoped. Does accepting Daniel's offer make me a groupie?

Stealing another glimpse of Daniel, I'm frustrated we haven't found time alone to work out the details. It would be easy money for me. I don't have to pretend to care about him. I already do, he and Roman both. But I hadn't been thinking about other women in his orbit, not really. Wonder if I should. "It's good," I say, once I swallow. I take another from the rack, feeling the need to stock up on comfort foods. and shove it into my pocket.

"Are you going to give me the details or what?"

No way would she know. I haven't spent any real time with her in the past few days, and I haven't told anyone about the arrangement. I don't plan to either. I can only imagine the lecturing I'd get if my family knew I was selling myself in exchange for money. Wait . . . that sounds so much worse than the idea I came up with or the offer I've accepted. "What details are you talking about?" I play coy.

"You and the hockey player, silly."

"Oh." I laugh like we're sharing an inside joke to throw her off. "I'd need more time than I have to share those details."

She clucks her tongue at me. "Give me the short version."

I step aside when another customer comes to the checkout. "Trust me, you'll get an earful soon enough."

She rolls her eyes, then smiles at the customer. "You are going to love this honey. And you can order online when you run out. That will be $7.45." Then she turns to me and mouths, "Tease."

*"Good girl"* plays on repeat in my head, my body reacting as if he was still touching me. I take a deep breath. Yeah, my sister has no idea of the teasing capabilities of that man. He has it down. I was so close to asking if he wanted to mess around some more last night. Overthinking it got in the way.

I slide down to the far end of the counter, bumping my hip against Daniel. "What's on the menu?"

He shoots me a look that tells me he sees a lot that is tempting. It takes so little for him to fuel the fire inside me and the flames to reach my cheeks. "I was thinking later we could—"

"Hi," my sister says, bursting the bubble we had floating around us. Holding her hand over the counter, she smiles with her eyes wide on him. "I'm Winter. Summer's sister."

"Daniel," he says, taking her hand, then patting Roman's back. "This is my son, Roman."

Winter hovers over the glass display. "What looks yummy?"

Roman doesn't hesitate and taps the glass. "Honeycomb chocolate."

"That's my favorite. Cup or cone?"

"Cone." She's already reaching for a cone as if she knew the answer.

When she starts scooping, she peeks up at Daniel. "And what looks yummy to you this summer?"

"Excuse me?" His brows squeeze tight.

Winter's laugh grips her as she bends to catch a breath. "Sorry," she says, a hand reaching over the top of the counter to signal she's going to live. I'm just here, mortified, while she finally gets a hold of herself and stands up. "I didn't mean my sister . . ." She starts laughing again. "I meant what's going to be your treat this summer, like the season. Oh God, I'm making this worse."

"You are," I deadpan, knowing she absolutely meant me with that loaded question. "I'm regretting visiting you today."

She breezes her hand in the air like this joke is gonna go on forever. "No. No. I'm sorry." Laughter still interrupts every word.

I glare at her, though I must admit it was a good play on words. She gave it her full effort despite telling us it wasn't planned. I know Winter better than that. "I'm not sure how sorry you are," I say, then plaster a fake smile on. "But you're going to be, little sis. Now get the man his ice cream." I laugh.

"I'm going to try the orange honey vanilla." His eyes dart between us as he studies us. "Visually, you and Winter are opposites."

"Like the seasons." I walk to a new lotion I've not seen in here before and use the pump.

"Remarkable."

"As if my mom knew before she met us."

Winter hands him his cone. "Sorry to hear about your vacation being ruined."

"It's not ruined." His little finger grazes the side of my hand just hidden from view from my sister. "We're coming out ahead, if you ask me."

Her eyes flick to mine, and we share all-knowing smiles. "I know Summer will take good care of you. She's the best."

The bell chimes above the door as a group of women from the local ladies' club walks in. "Hello, girls," Mara greets with her arm thrown in the air with flair. For twenty-five years, she's voluntarily run the playhouse because of her love of the dramatics.

We've known her since the day we were born. She's always been a friend to the family and came to help Dolly with us when our parents died. I give her a tight hug because it's been too long. "How are you?" Her signature scent of Shalimar still provides comfort in the memories of her spending time with me when I was little.

"Wonderful, darling. We're here for the best ice cream in town." She spots Winter at the back of the store helping another customer. Tourist season is in full swing. Our town needs the monetary injection. "You know what I like, dear."

"One scoop Ube Honey and one scoop of orange honey vanilla coming right up."

Mara strolls over while the rest of the group heads toward the ice cream display. "How's your Dolly?"

Folding my hands in front of me, I reply, "She's doing good. Keeps busy."

"I've tried to get her to join the ladies' club, but she always has something else going on. We need her moxie to liven things up. I bring them here to get a sugar rush, but it wears off before we can get into any trouble." *So much like Dolly.*

I laugh and lean in conspiratorially. "I'll talk to her."

"Thanks, Summer." Moving on past me, she looks Daniel up and down and then glances at me and whistles. With a completely non-covert nod toward him, she says, "If you're looking for love, Summer, check him out."

As if I don't get this enough at home, now I'm subjected to it downtown. *Sheesh.*

Roman asks, "What does looking for love mean? I thought it just happened. *Poof.* Like you and Summer."

My eyes fly to Daniel, a message of "oh shit" silently exchanged between the two of us. While I stand there with my mouth wide open, he plants a knee to the floor, facing his son. "Love can happen in an instant. Even without looking for it." His eyes slide to mine before he looks at Roman again. "Summer and I aren't in love."

"But you kissed."

Daniel stands and digs his wallet from his back pocket. Eyeing me, he says, "I can pay you back for the ice cream, but I think it's best if I talk to him in private."

"It's on us," I say, seeing the concern in his gaze.

Tucking it back in, he says, "Thanks." He takes Roman's hand and leads them outside with ice cream in their other hands.

I look to see if Winter was a witness, but she's busy scooping ice cream for the ladies' group. Slinking up to the counter, I say, "Put the ice cream on my tab, Winter."

"You don't have a tab," she replies, cocking her eyebrow.

"In that case, thanks for the ice cream, sis."

She's already moved on to feed the crowd to bother with my antics. I walk outside and look in both directions. I find the two of them sitting on a bench in front of the marina two stores down from the Honey Hive.

I start to walk over to them, but stop. Should I? Is this time they need alone? Roman is eight, so it makes sense that things are black and white. But Daniel and I are stuck in the gray as we work through things. How do you explain that to a kid?

There's probably not a way that will make sense to him.

Daniel sees me and waves me over. I go, but I'm much more cautious. The last thing I wanted was to confuse his son. We are moving fast, and love shouldn't be a part of the equation, not at this stage. Doesn't mean I'm not susceptible to the notion. I am, so easily. Maybe I'm the problem. I asked him to touch me last night *like . . . like. . . like* a puck bunny. Good Lord, I didn't even know he was a hockey player.

My heart beats faster, telling me I'm lying to myself. I am. My heart knows good and well that the feelings developing are real.

I stop near the bench, taking tentative steps until Daniel says, "Come join us."

Roman's ice cream is almost gone, but Daniel's is missing altogether. Guiding my way to the opening seat puts Roman in the middle of us. Daniel's arm comes around the back of the bench, and he rubs my back before pulling back. "Roman and I were just talking about what love means."

"I see."

I'm not sure I have a right to feel awkward. It was an innocent assumption on his part. Daniel saying we're not in love doesn't hurt me. It's the truth, even if feelings are simmering under the surface. But I still do. I hate to put the burden on Daniel to explain our relationship, which happened faster than a runner setting a new world record.

Roman looks up at me. "Like turns into love. Friends can do the same, but some friends are just friends and will stay that way." He licks his ice cream before it drips.

My lips part in awe. "Umm . . ."

"Can I go see the ducks now, Dad?"

Patting him on the back, Daniel says, "You're free to go, but don't go too far down the dock. Stay close, buddy, okay?"

"Okay." He pops up, finishing his ice cream and

munching on the cone while stepping down to the lower dock near where the ducks wait for visitors to feed them.

Daniel's hand caresses my shoulder. When I look at him, I say, "I'm impressed how you got out of that one."

"It wasn't about getting out of it, Sunshine." Scooching over, he sits with our legs bumping together. "It was about teaching him that it's okay to take the scenic route in relationships." He gives me that smile that's graced the covers of magazines and headline stories. It's winning for a reason.

"Are we taking the scenic route, Sutton?"

Wrapping his arm over the back of the bench again, I can feel how much he wants to put it around me. I want the same, but we're in the middle of everything, sitting here where everybody can see us. "I don't know. I'm starting to believe I was led here for a reason."

Angling toward him, I peek at him out of the corner of my eye. "What would that be?"

"To find a hidden investment."

"Ah." I tilt my shoulders away again and watch Roman toss pieces of his cone in the water for the ducks. "The cottage."

"No, Summer. You. The cottage is just a good cover."

My gaze runs back to his, and if I could, I would kiss him right now. But displays at home are one thing. Kissing in public is a whole other. "Do you mean that?"

"I always say what I mean." *I believe him.*

My heart beats strong. I want to touch him, to kiss him, and to be held in his arms again. Reaching over, I slip my hand between our legs and scrape my nails over the cotton of his pants. With his eyes ahead on his son, he whispers for my ears only, "Did I tell you how much I liked kissing you?"

"I think I missed it if you did." I quirk a silly grin at him. "Tell me again."

"Hey, Summer," a familiar voice cuts through the conversation from behind us.

I turn to the side to see the face that matches that voice. "Hey, Brandon. How's your mom?"

He stops and looks back. "She's doing well. I'll let her know you said hi."

"You do that. Take care."

When I settle back onto the bench with Daniel next to me, I glance over at him. His eyes are still stuck on Brandon, though. "Friend of yours?"

Dropping my head in hopes of pulling his attention back to me, I ask, "Do I detect a note of jealousy?" It's not so blatant but fun to call out.

"Just curious," he says, his eyes still tracking Brandon as he walks away. "I was under the impression this town was retirees and—"

"And not hot firemen?" He leaves me no choice but to tease when he wants to ignore the question.

"He's a fireman?" *He's definitely jealous.*

Generally, I've noticed that Daniel is pretty laid back, so it's cute to see him get a little wound up. Makes me want to see how he is on the ice if he's being told to soften his image. "And a paramedic. Our town is lucky to have him."

Standing up, he tugs the bill of his hat down his forehead and pulls his sunglasses from where they're hooked on the neck of his shirt. "Did I mention I'm a professional hockey player?"

"Not at first." I stand, turning around to lean on the railing to face him.

"MVP seven times in my career," he states like he's on a mission to prove himself. Men. I grin and let him. "I know you're not into hockey, but that's the second all-time record."

*Should I?* Probably not. But I can't resist, so I ask, "Who holds the top spot?"

Annoyance gets the better of him, and he huffs. "Wayne Gretzky."

I toss out a casual shrug. "Did either of you ever rescue a kitten from a tree?" I bat my eyelashes before Roman runs up the steps to join us again.

Daniel sweeps in front of me, picking Roman up. "How were the ducks?"

"Hungry. Can we bring food next time?"

"Sure. You ready to go?"

"Yep."

Holding Roman's hand, they're about to pass me when Daniel stops, and says, "I don't know about Wayne, but I have the key to the city of Philadelphia after saving a woman from a car that caught fire outside the arena."

"Brandon doesn't stand a chance against you, Sutton." Pressing my hand to his chest, I smile to myself, happy as a clam. "And just for the record, you never had anything to worry about. Brandon Culver has been in love with my sister Fall since they were in middle school." I pat him and then drop my hand to tuck into my pocket. "And he's not my type."

Roman slips from his hand and runs to the car while we keep a steady pace together. "And what is your type exactly?"

"Tall and ridiculously handsome hockey players that are too generous for their own good and have a wild jealous streak when it comes to local firemen slash paramedics talking to their summer landlord." Feeling quite smug for coming up with that one, I grin up at him in challenge.

"Wow, what a coincidence." His knuckles brush against the top of my hand, the electricity still present in the lightest of shared touches. "I happen to know a guy who fits that criteria."

"Oh really?"

"Really." When I stop on the driver's side, he keeps walking around the car and opens the door. Looking back at me, he chuckles. "Guess it's your lucky day."

He gets in the car, leaning over the seat to check on his son, and leaves me on the sidewalk trying to catch the breath he stole right from my chest.

How is this my life? Surely, I'm dreaming, and if I am, I never want to wake up. "Lucky me, indeed."

# CHAPTER 18

SUMMER

"Mrs. Dover . . ." I take a quick breath to temper the panic in my voice and keep the words from rushing out of my mouth. Each cold drop of condensation rolling off the bottom of the glass of lemonade is a shock to the system when it lands on my bare leg. I shift to have it drip over the grass. "I understand the hassle. It's a hurdle I'm ready to overcome. As I've said, you won't have to do anything other than reconsider selling it out from under me."

Taking a slow sip of her lemonade, she rests an arm on the fence. Her eyes haven't left the field or Bessie grazing on the hill in the distance, giving me the distinct impression she's not looking at me on purpose. It's disconcerting to plead a case to someone who shows no interest. This is going south so fast that it causes my heart to sink. I came here feeling ready to take on the world, strong in my intentions and purpose after rehearsing what I needed to say. Now, my confidence is slipping away just like this opportunity is. *Again.*

Standing next to a bucket of carrots, she says, "It isn't out from under you, Summer." Shielded under a large sun hat, she finally journeys her gaze my way. "I never promised you the property."

"You promised me a chance."

"This *is* your chance." Her tone has never been firm with me until now, but it's the chill that I find unsettling. She's known me my whole life, but she's choosing to side with strangers. The sting burns as the realization sets in. I may not win this battle. She says, "I'm giving you a chance right now. I haven't signed any paperwork yet. Give it your best shot."

"I can't just throw out numbers. I wanted to put together a presentation. I've worked on it, but with the summer tenant and dealing with the water situation, I've been distracted."

Angling toward me, she props her boot up on the bottom rail, paying no mind that it's stretching the hem of her dress to the limits. "I heard you were walking around downtown yesterday with someone on your arm. Would that be my guest?"

My immediate response is that I should be insulted she's insinuating I would mess around with her guests. She's not wrong, but I don't need it to thrown in my face. It's the image of me hanging on Daniel's arm like I'm a . . . a puck bunny that gets me. "I wasn't on anyone's arm."

"I'll take that as a yes to my question." There's no smile or friendliness when she looks me in the eyes. "Your hospitality ends when you hand the guests their key. I thought that was self-explanatory." She digs the heel of her boot back into the dirt again. "I also expected a refund request from the guest since they have no water. Tell me . . ." She leans closer. "How are they making do over there?"

I could lie, but if she's already heard about us being in town yesterday, the rumor might have gotten around about the arrangements Daniel and I made for him and Roman. Though I'm not sure how. My sisters would never spread gossip about each other and Dolly . . . *Oh Dolly*, I rub my temple, remembering how she ran errands yesterday. She'd never tell one of our secrets, but we didn't tell her not to say anything about them staying with us either. No point in fibbing if the truth might already be out there. "They're using our bathrooms."

"That's awfully courteous of you. And the sleeping arrangements?"

There is no way in Hades I'm sharing intimate details about Daniel and me. The act itself isn't as illicit as it would sound when saying it out loud. Even last night, we could have amped things up another level, but we didn't. It was nice and romantic to be held in his arms without feeling the pressure to go further.

I don't know how he's so patient with me. It's so different from any other relationship I've been in, which seemed to be more about them getting sex than learning who I am. Daniel is the opposite. Our souls are growing closer as our bodies do. It's a slower pace and just my speed. "We're getting off track, Mrs. Dover—"

Her laughter interrupts my train of thought. "Summer Season, I didn't take you for a wild child like your grandma." Dolly would flip if she heard Mrs. Dover call her that. I might have to tell her if this deal goes sour. "Listen, you lure that man in and hook 'em on a line. Not many come through this town, so when the gettin's good, you better get you some." She starts for the farmhouse, continuing like I'm right beside her. "Wouldn't you rather settle down than mess with a house that most likely needs to be torn down?"

I hurry to catch up, not wanting to miss a word. "No. I wouldn't rather that. I would rather we continue the traditions of this town and secure my family's place in it."

She stops on the second step leading to the front porch and turns, steadying herself with a hand on the railing. "A word of warning. Nothing lasts forever. I didn't expect to be spending my golden years alone with a cow for company." Her gaze drifts back to the pasture, and she laughs. "Bessie's a good listener." When her eyes return to mine, she says, "Change happens whether we like it or not. You might not be able to save your family and the town. It might be one or the other."

"I'm going to try."

"I like your moxie, dear." She starts up the steps and lands on the porch. "It comes down to money and contingencies."

"Contingencies?" It hadn't occurred to me to look beyond the purchase price. Of course other things are in play. Those will make it more appealing for her to accept or whittle down an offer from the bid. Most likely mine, so what can I add that would give me an edge?

"The current offer comes with no contingencies or inspection needed. I wouldn't have to fix the pipes. It would sell for above anything I could dream of asking around here and as-is."

I can't wrap my head around the fact that I would have to pay more than the offer and still invest money into getting it fixed. I feel ill, knowing that's not possible.

Mrs. Dover returns to the bottom of the steps and takes hold of my upper arm. "They're not coming out until after the Fourth of July. Give it some thought and let me know what you come up with. I realize it might be out of your ability to afford, but for me, that's money I can't turn down, especially when I'm looking at a mountain of issues to fix to keep it going."

"I'll think about it." I'd been putting off mentally digging into the details of what I'll be committing to both financially and personally with Daniel. I don't want to owe him or anyone money. But how will that shape what feels like a relationship in the making? I like him. Will that be what it ultimately comes down to? *Daniel's money or Daniel?*

I don't like the way this is turning, but it seems unavoidable. A hard decision must be made. I just hope I have time to dig through the details of his offer and my heart before having to decide. "Thank you, Mrs. Dover."

She starts back up the steps and stands on the porch, an obvious hint that it's time for me to go. "You take care, Summer."

I get in my car and start the engine just as a wave of harsh reality washes through me. Owning the Cove Cottage might not be possible. That sparks a streak of stubbornness, a desire to prove her wrong. I'm not ready to give up this dream.

Startled by a knock on the door, I jump back to see Mrs. Dover standing there. I roll down the window. "Mrs. Dover, what is it?"

"July thirty-first. That's the date they're coming with the contract." She taps the hood. "I'm rooting for you."

Although I can't say I feel she truly is, I reply, "Thanks."

When she walks away, I start driving home.

A deal is already in the works, but something made her want to share more details. Maybe she is rooting for me.

With more than a month to decide whether to jump into this bidding war and make an offer, I can breathe easier knowing I have some time.

Is this a good investment for my inheritance and

Daniel's money? It's not. I've said as much. There's no paying back a loan. Does my pretending to be his girlfriend really justify the money?

My gut knows this is wrong. My head can't rationalize spending that kind of money when it comes to owing Daniel. But my stinkin' heart keeps me fighting.

When I pull onto the driveway, I don't see Daniel's car. My heart picks up, sending it straight into panic mode. What if he's gone? *For good?*

Him.

Roman.

The offer he made.

*Would he leave without a word?*

I don't think so, but I hold my breath until I see his black sports car parked in the no-parking zone and can breathe again.

They don't notice when I pull in or park the car. They're busy having fun in the water—splashing and chasing each other. I'm sitting here wondering when my life started depending on Daniel Sutton.

I don't know what spell he's put me under, but there's an instinct to fight it either way, which is so unlike me. *He's* so unlike me.

I'm all about rules. He's all about breaking them.

He has more money than I could dream of having. I'm relying on the last of my inheritance and a bonus his stay would give me to pay my bills.

I like order. I'm certain he's into a bit of chaos. That might just be to rattle me in teasing, though.

He oozes sex appeal and has those abs. I have no comparison.

. . .

Those differences shrink at this moment. Seeing him play with Roman, remembering how he speaks to him at his level and never down to him, and watching him be the dad he never had tells me the real man he is.

I haven't seen the side that needs to soften.

I've not experienced the part of him that only lives for his sport.

He's treated me with nothing less than respect, even taking it slow like our relationship matters to him more than a casual hook-up.

And he's taken to my family like they're his own, and they've brought him and Roman into the fold without an ounce of hesitation.

Adding all of this up is getting me closer to the cliff of falling for him. My toes are already hanging over. My heart isn't far behind.

Daniel sees me, standing in water that reaches his knees, wet from swimming, and looking like an Adonis coming from the ocean. He waves.

I wave back, feeling seen, not just literally but emotionally. I'm not one of the Season Sisters, the orphan of a tragedy, the one holding the family together. I'm Summer, and he accepts me as I am. Rules and all.

Prince Charming showed up. I deserve this. *I deserve him.*

Meandering my way over, he keeps his eyes on me the entire time. Sometimes they dip lower and linger, but he smiles when I get close. "Hey, you," he says, coming out of the water to greet me with a kiss.

Nothing's cooled between us after the Roman love talk at the docks. He got it. We're friends who have feelings that could turn into more. An eight-year-old doesn't need more information before Daniel and I figure it out.

He asks, "How'd it go?"

"I think I need all the options laid out and crystal clear. Can we go over the details?"

# CHAPTER 19

## DANIEL

"Instead of a set amount of 'dates,' what if we go with a period of time that's required to be seen together?" Summer rolls her head against the back of the chair to face me.

Rubbing a hand over my face, I mumble, "I'm in the weirdest timeline." I tip the beer bottle back and take a long swig.

"You're telling me." Turning away to watch Roman floating on a raft tied by a rope to the closest tree, she adds, "Do you know what a puck bunny is?"

Beer spews from my mouth. "What the fuck?" Why do I suddenly feel like I don't know this woman?

Without looking back, Roman says, "You owe the swear jar five bucks."

"At this rate, that jar is going to have your college paid off before you turn ten."

"Then you can buy me a Lamborghini." What the hell with this kid? I don't recognize either of them right now.

Summer's busy laughing. It's good to hear it again.

"We're a Ferrari family, Roman. We can dabble with Maseratis, but never a Lamborghini."

He turns so fast on the float that it rocks beneath him. Car talk is what gets his attention? I'm learning all kinds of stuff about him on this trip. "That's not fair!"

"It is when Ferrari is one of my sponsors. I got the car and a big paycheck last year. I'm loyal as fuck to that brand."

He lies back down. "That's another five bucks."

"Fuck me," I mutter.

"Fifteen," he shouts, tucking his hands behind his head like he's got it made in the shade, which he does.

I turn to Summer, thumbing over at my son. "Do you believe this kid?" I grin, not able to pretend I'm not enjoying every second of this with him.

"You only have yourself to blame. He takes after you."

"That's for sure." I take another drink. "You didn't know anything about hockey before, and now you're asking about puck bunnies?"

"Yeah. I heard about them and . . ." Dragging the butterfly on her necklace back and forth, she returns her eyes to mine when she says, "Will I be accused of being your bunny?"

"No." Simple answer that I hope ends this line of questioning. It pisses me off that it would even cross her mind. "Whatever idea you got for comparison, there is none. You're nothing like them. End of story."

"Is it the end or is this the beginning?" She reaches over to run her fingers over my forearm. "What makes me different from them? Please tell me so I can be prepared."

"You don't need to prepare. You arrive with me and smile if you want to. We don't have to listen to the photographers' demands. I rarely do. Showing up is enough." Her gaze drifts out to sea as she appears to mull it over. "Just be you, Summer. That's all you need to be."

But then she turns to me and asks, "So $250,000 for a few dates in public? Is that all we're saying? No other strings, no timelines, no payback. Just my time for the money?"

"Maybe we can rephrase it. You're not a call girl."

"Okay, you're gifting me a quarter of a million dollars to expand my family's property and to protect it from greedy venture capitalists. In return, I show you the way to play nice when in public. Is that better?"

"Definitely. I sound like a fucking hero who's saving a small town from demolition."

"Twenty," Roman shouts.

"I'm going to go broke with him around."

"It's okay," she says. I hate that her touch disappears. "I think we summarized it pretty well. We don't need to overcomplicate it." She sits back, and I already miss her touch. "I'm getting what I want. You're getting what you want. It's settled. It's a win-win." Although she doesn't sound like there's an issue from listening to her tone, she doesn't sound happy either.

"Yeah, it's a win-win," I repeat, closing my eyes. Bothered that she sounds more resolved than relieved, I can't keep them closed. I gave up on trying to read women's minds years ago. I sit up and angle toward her. "Why does this not sound settled?"

"Because it's not. I'm trading a relationship for my dream. It sucks."

"I don't understand. What relationship are you trading?" I reach over and cover her hand with mine and give a gentle squeeze. "That's not what we're doing here."

"Explain to me how it's not?"

"It's just not." I glance up at a cloud that's moved in overhead while my words stumble over my feelings.

She sits forward, bringing her closer to me. "If I'm dating you in exchange for you giving me money to buy the property, that's not real. That's a negotiation and a deal."

I look back at her, knowing she deserves more than a thoughtless answer to appease her. She deserves to know how I feel when I'm with her. "I'm not a wordy guy. I play hockey because I sucked at writing papers. And because I was damn good at it. But if I give this a try, I'd tell you that I like what's happening between us. It's not something I've experienced or thought I'd have. With you, I do." I take a breath and just go with the words that want to flow. "You're not dating me for money, Summer. I hope you're dating me because you're on the same page as I am."

"I am." Leaning forward, she rests her arms over mine, holding me as close as these large Adirondack chairs will allow. "I was overthinking it."

"I can see how you got there, but I'm giving you the money. You're not dating for it. But I appreciate you helping me out." I kiss her tenderly on the lips, wanting to deepen it so badly. Not the time. Not the place. Not the right circumstances. "And please never bring up puck bunnies again. You're in a whole different league, baby."

She laughs. "I think I'm honored." Getting up, she comes to sit on my lap. With her arms wrapped around me, she says, "Thank you for the gift. It's life-changing."

I cup her cheek and slip my fingers into her hair to guide her back to my lips. This time, her mouth parts for me, and our tongues meet, slipping into a breathless caress. I end it before it goes deeper. Although his attention is somewhere else, Roman is near. She licks the corner of her mouth, and whispers, "Thank you."

"For what?"

"The money, the kiss, the way we communicate, for booking this cottage so we could meet." Her smile is soft, but it's no less potent.

She's going to devastate me one day. Whether it's me leaving or her going, I can already feel it. Though she'd probably argue I'm doing the same to her. Getting so close, so fast comes with a large dose of consequences and a detriment to my weakening heart.

"I don't have to think about anything from my bills to my meals. Even Mia takes care of Roman most of the time. I just get to be the fun dad. Doesn't mean I don't want to be more. More in life other than a hockey player."

"MVP seven times over," she says, smirking at me.

"More than that to someone, to matter more than my stats." I move in closer again, realizing I just can't stay away from her or those lips. "When it comes to you, Sunshine, I want to be involved, not a bystander."

I see the breath she takes, the gentle close of her eyes as she soaks in my words. When she looks at me, she says, "I want that, too, but how do you see yourself doing that?"

The conversation with Roman about what love is has come back to me tenfold. This is love. I fell for this woman the moment I met her. "By starting now. I want a relationship with you."

Her arms tighten around me. "We have one."

"Officially. Will you be my girlfriend?" Why do I feel like I'm fifteen, asking a popular cheerleader out on a date again? She said yes. Will Summer?

"You want me to be your girlfriend, Daniel?" It's not teasing, but her tone tells me she's definitely having fun with this. Good. This should be fun, or why do it?

I chuckle. "I want you to be my girlfriend, Summer."

"Sure."

Feigning the deep wound she caused, I sit back, cocking an eyebrow at her. "I lay my heart out in front of you only to have it driven over like roadkill?"

Laughing, she glances at my son—always keeping a watchful eye with me. When she collects herself, which takes long enough for me to check the time, and then on Roman to see he's still content, I start wondering what time is too early to take this beauty to bed without it looking like we're sneaking off to have sex. I'm thinking that once Roman is in bed and the cookies have been delivered, it should be late enough.

"The job comes with perks," I add to entice her a bit more to say yes.

She kisses my forehead and then catches my eye. "I'd love to be your girlfriend. No perks required."

I shrug. "Perks come with it anyway."

"So . . ." She kisses my lips this time like it's the first time we've kissed—burning heat that will turn into so much more when we unleash it. Plucking her mouth from mine, she wipes just underneath her bottom lip. "What happens now?"

"I don't know." I grin, looking ahead, wondering that same thing. "I'm new to this relationship stuff."

"I thought you'd dated a lot."

"Define dated."

My shoulder is whacked under a roll of her laughter. "You're the worst. I don't even want to know how you'd define that term."

"It would be best if you didn't." I chuckle and get to my feet while setting her down on her sneakers. Holding her hand, I bring it to my mouth and kiss it twice. "So I've been thinking . . ."

The hope in her wide eyes as she leans against me has me hoping she will always see me in this light. "What have you been thinking?"

"I was thinking we should have steaks tonight."

She escapes and starts marching toward the cottage. "You really are the worst, Daniel Sutton."

"I may be the worst, but I still got the girl."

"Fair," she calls over her shoulder.

Feeling mighty fucking good right now, I walk the rope and start pulling it in. "Come, Roman, we need to get back and clean up before dinner."

"Do we have to?"

The raft is grounded on land when I walk over and give him a hand up. "You sure did take to the cove life quickly."

He lands on his feet in front of me. Pointing at the water, he says, "Look out there."

I bend beside him so I'm eye level, and we take in the ocean. "What do you see?"

"Nothing." His eyes pivot to mine, and he asks, "Do you hear that?"

Glancing up at the treetops, I ask, "The birds?"

"Yeah, and when they're quiet, you can hear the wind through the trees."

I think he had an existential moment out on that raft. "What do you think about that?"

"One day, I'm going to live somewhere I can look out and see for miles and listen to the birds sing." That's not New York City . . .

"It's pretty great, huh?" He nods and throws his arms around me. "I love you, Daddy."

Wrapping him in a big hug, I kiss the side of his head. "I love you, buddy."

When he releases me, we start toward the cottage to

gather our things. He looks up at me again. "Mom has a boyfriend."

"I know. David's nice, huh?"

"Yeah." He smiles. "But you have Summer."

I laugh, feeling every bit of the pride and joy that comes with getting the girl of your dreams. "I sure do."

A message pings on my phone. I stop, pulling it from the pocket of my trunks. I only see the preview of a headline to know I need to check this. *Is it Time for Daniel Sutton to Retire?* "Go get your stuff together. I'll be there in a minute."

I watch my son run inside, then look back at my phone again. Expanding my agent's message, I scan the article, picking up on words like *retirement, best is behind him, what age is too old,* and other shit.

This is a hit piece. I can smell it. The ultimatum is back in play, and they're making sure I follow the rules this time. *Fuck that.* The only rules I'll be following are—

"Everything okay?" Summer asks, standing in the doorway.

They can float these retirement ideas out there all they want, feed them to the press by anonymous tips, but no way in hell am I going down without a fight. *Fuck them!*

If they want to play, let's do this.

I wave to her. "All good." It is with her by my side.

# CHAPTER 20

## SUMMER

"Roman only left one cookie for the elves tonight." The bedroom is darker than I expected, but enough light trails from the bathroom door being cracked open that I have a clear view of Daniel in bed. It's a great way to be greeted. "I got it for you."

His chuckle reaches my ears before my eyes fully adjust. "His teeth are going to rot from eating cookies before bed."

"We only thought it would be a few nights." I set the cookie on the nightstand and slip my robe off, hanging it on the hook by the bathroom. Dressed in a thin cotton pajama set, I hip bump his legs to get him to scooch over on the bed. "Not all summer." I really like having him here. I love the excitement that bubbles up inside me as I get closer to the bedroom, knowing he's waiting for me. "We could make something else up, if you want. Something that won't give him cavities and the sweetest of dreams."

Leaning against the headboard, he reaches over and rubs my hip. "Have we overstayed our welcome?" His voice is quieter than usual, even when we talk at night. I brush hair away from his forehead and reveal a tempered smile. It's there, but boy, does it need inflation.

"No. In fact, I've heard the opposite from everyone. They want you to stay, but don't know what you'll do since the cottage isn't getting fixed."

"What happened to the local guys and your second cousin once removed?"

That he even remembers that is hilarious. He's becoming a regular old townie at this point. "Twice removed, and Mrs. Dover called them off since she's selling."

"But if you're buying, it still needs to get fixed. So let's get it fixed."

"It's not a done deal just because we offer more money. She mentioned contingencies—"

"Then don't put any contingencies," he snaps, sitting higher on the bed. *Away from me?* "And close the deal."

Standing up, I give him the space he so clearly desires, but I can't stop staring at him. I look back at the door and then walk out of the bedroom, shutting the door behind me. I wait.

"Summer? Come back in," he says from the other side.

We all have off days. The day with him was great. He's just having a moment. I knock this time even though it's my own bedroom, giving us a redo. He says, "Come in." The response is much lighter this time around.

When I open the door, the lamp is on, and his mouth is full. Only crumbs remain on the nightstand while he chews. Pressing my back to the closed door, I lock it and bite the inside of my lip to keep from smiling. "Hi, I saw your light on, so I thought I'd stop in."

"Glad you did," he says when he finally speaks.

So handsome—the light shining in his eyes is a beacon

calling me to him—waiting for me like his night just got better with a smirk that wasn't there earlier. When I approach the bed, he shifts to the side this time, giving me ample room to make myself comfortable next to him.

I climb on the bed, but I don't sit next to him. I crawl on my knees and straddle his lap. I'd love to adjust, but I just want to kiss his upset away so badly that I cup his face. Tilting his head back, I lean in and kiss him. Our lips mold together like a confession whispered from my soul to his is exchanged in the connection.

The feel of him hardening under me inspires me to rock into a better position. Large hands take hold of my ass and give a good squeeze. We're already breaking new ground, crossing lines we haven't before. The feel of him is both familiar and new, spun into the burning desire I have for him.

I roll my hips on top of him. The hardness feels so good against my clit that I do it again. And again, until I slide my hands to his neck, resting my head against his, closing my eyes as I try to calm my racing heart.

Running a hand over my shoulder, then caressing my jaw, he whispers against my cheek, "We can't do this here."

I lean back, still holding on to him. Sliding my hands to his shoulders, I search his eyes for the answer that doesn't seem to be obvious to me. "Why?"

"Listen." My breath is heavier than I'd like, so I hold it and turn an ear toward the door. The sound of *Jeopardy*, the tick of the clock at the base of the stairs, the creak of the floors, and a good night exchanged between two of my sisters. Every sound is so prevalent and louder than it should be.

I haven't paid attention to the noise in years. With this

many people living together, it's just always how it's been. "I don't even hear it anymore."

"I can't stop listening to every sound that slips under the door. I kiss you. Someone laughs. I slide my hand over your body, and the theme song to *Golden Girls* kicks in. I made you come, and someone dropped something heavy in the kitchen. There's no privacy."

He's not wrong, and that throws cold water on the embers we were breathing fire into. Sitting back, I lose the energy to sit straight, so I slump and ask, "You don't want to do anything?"

After pushing forward, he slides a finger over the outline of my lips, then follows with the softest kiss. "I want to do everything to you, but not here. I only want to hear you when we're together, especially the first time."

The sexual attraction has been there all along. Daniel made me feel so good in the tub. It was incredible, but it doesn't change the growing need I have for him or to give him the same pleasure he gave me. Regulating my reactions isn't something I want to do.

But giving is better than receiving, so I slip the little top off over my head and let it fall to the floor beside the bed. Those brown eyes that hold the light inside even when it's darker in here drift down my body. His hands follow until he's cupping my breasts like he held my face—with favor and adoration.

Reaching around me, he grabs my ass again and pulls me toward him in one swift tug. We kiss, and when his hands slip up my front to my breasts, he kneads them like I'm precious. The pressure firms, and when the tip of his thumb rolls over my nipple, shock waves shoot straight to my center. My body clenches in response as a craving is awakened. It would be so easy to lose myself and melt into his kisses. I don't. I prop up on my knees, still kissing him with a building fervor when our tongues tangle together. And then I slip off to the side of his legs to station myself beside him, our mouths never losing contact.

I scrape my nails down his chest, momentarily distracted while running them through the hair on his chest twice before moving my hand lower and dipping under the waistband of his boxer briefs. A heavy but restrained hum greets me when I slide my hand over his length.

His eyes are locked onto mine like he'll miss something if he blinks. With my fingers wrapped around his erection, my own desires magnify, making me wish his hand was touching me. As much as I want that, I want this to be about him more.

Angling toward him, I push the covers down his legs and start pulling the waistband down. He lifts enough for me to free his cock. He doesn't hide or shy away. He runs his hand up my spine, hovering at the back of my neck. "I want to be in your mouth, Sunshine. Will you do that for me?"

That husky voice of his about does me in. I squeeze my thighs together as I station my hand at the base of his length, holding it up ready for me. He's smooth and so large that I analyze angles before bending forward. I lick my lips and take the head of his cock into my mouth.

It only takes that contact for his head to snap back, digging into the padded headboard. Mouth open. Eyes closed. That earlier hum now caught in his throat.

I swirl my tongue under the cap and then cover more of him by sliding down inch by inch until my lips meet the top of my hand. I breathe through my nose and relax my throat, going deeper as my mouth follows my fingers. Tightening my lips and hollowing my mouth, I suck as I slide to the end again. His hand at the back of my head only encourages me to go deeper.

Catching a breath, I slide him back into my mouth. This time, I don't go slow because I want this man to fall apart for me like I did for him. Bobbing, I push my limits, eliciting a moan from deep in his chest. "Feels so fucking good, babe. Don't stop, okay?"

He's steel and smooth as I use my tongue along the top of his cock. His low praises send goose bumps down my back. *Powerful.* My confidence explodes as I bring him to his knees. *Invincible.*

Adjusting my position, I ease my throat. He thrusts experimentally, and we find our rhythm together. "You're taking me so deep, Sunshine. Just like that."

Pulling my hair together in his fist, he moves to the side, and I peek up at him. His eyes are hooded, his mouth slightly open as he sucks in a breath and bucks his hips. He's never been more attractive. More . . . mine. My core clenches, aching for him in the ways I hoped we would connect tonight. But this is so good. "That's it. You're doing so well for me. You're taking my cock like you can't live without it." His breathing is erratic, chest pumping for air as much as his hips thrust for me. "Good fucking girl. Relax for me."

His ab muscles tighten under my touch as an orgasm starts ripping through him, the current too strong for him to pull back. Grinding his mouth shut, he chases his release before it escapes.

I suck harder each time I slide up his length until he starts losing the control he's holding tight to. "I can't stop . . . Come so hard . . ." The words are as ragged as his body as he fucks my mouth like he'd fuck me.

I'm so wet, and the tingling is becoming too much. I push it aside, but the raw desire I have for him consumes my thoughts, and my body reacts instead. Fingers dig through my hair, pulling as he pushes, meeting me for every thrust.

His hand dives into my shorts, taking no prisoners. When his fingers slip through the yearning I have for him, I lose my control and bob harder just as he pinches my clit. My body releases as if he'd demanded it. My name rolls off his tongue in a chant or a prayer, I'm not sure. My senses are so overwhelmed that up becomes down and left turns right, leaving me to spin in the ecstasy.

But with him deep inside my mouth, I swallow, my throat embracing him until his gifts run dry and he pulls out. Dragging me into his arms like I'm a rag doll. I am devoid of energy to think, much less function with any physical competency.

Curled on top of him, I close my eyes, my jaw hurting, and lying in the aftermath of our pleasure. My breathing is as uneven as his and not stabilizing anytime soon.

His fingers pull my chin up. My eyes follow, meeting his again. His lids are lower, dragged down from what we just did. He says, "Do you know how incredible you are?"

"No. Tell me," I joke.

"You're fucking amazing."

I'm grinning, but laughing takes more effort than I'm capable, so I hum like he did earlier. Putting my head on his shoulder, I whisper, "You're so amazing."

Stroking my hair over my shoulder, he says, "You know what surprises me?"

"Hmm?"

"I'm surprised that I lasted as long as I did. That was so good, Sunshine."

I feel the pride he's instilled in me by finally lifting my

hand anchored to the mattress and seeing the smile that looks like it's going to be there a while. I say, "You know what surprises me?"

"What?"

I laugh. "That you know the theme song to *Golden Girls*."

"Lots of time stuck in hotel rooms with no streaming." He chuckles, then rolls me onto my back, hovering over me. "But do you want to know what really surprises me?"

Running a finger from his temple to his jawline, I say, "Tell me."

He's above me, looking as smug as a thief who got away with the crown jewels with that smirk on his face. "That you could keep from screaming my name."

"That was a miracle." I laugh too hard to keep quiet any longer. "Trust me, though. When we're together for the first time, you'd better take me somewhere else because I won't hold back."

"I'll take you to the moon and back, babe."

I grin because I believe he will if he can. "The cottage also works." Staring into those mesmerizing eyes of his, I add, "Or your fancy place in the city."

Pushing my hair back from my cheeks, he kisses my neck and trails higher to my ear to whisper, "How about both?"

His sweet attentions have me closing my eyes and floating in the dream of us together like this more than tonight. "You got yourself a deal, hockey player." Opening my eyes, I'm met with a sea of serenity seen in his. My heart squeezes, so I tighten my hold around him. I kiss him, wanting to hold on to this—the quiet and calm, the peace and tranquility—found in my arms.

This time, when our lips part and our breathing evens, I

kiss his cheek, and whisper, "You can tell me anything, Daniel."

The rough of his scruff grazes across my cheek when he turns to look at me again. He doesn't say anything, but I see the tug-of-war in his eyes. Caressing his face, I say, "I want you to talk to me." Our eyes are as connected as our bodies. "Will you tell me why you were upset earlier?"

## CHAPTER 21

DANIEL

She's an angel sent to save me. There's no other way to explain why this perfect woman would have anything to do with a guy like me. *I'm trouble.* It's always been that way since I was young. I heard that more times than I ever heard I love you.

I fought to be a good dad to Roman, rejecting everything I learned from my father because I knew there had to be a better way. I studied movies and read books when I found out Mia was pregnant. I've worked my ass off to be the dad he needs. The role model part is still a work in progress.

I can do the same now. I can be a good partner for her. Someone she can rely on and trust, most importantly. I want to be that man for Summer. But that means pushing past the parts of me that don't make me a better man or boyfriend. Silence helps no one. I learned that from my mom.

So looking into her pools of blues where I can swim freely and be myself, I swallow down the fear of rejection, and reply, "The PR machine has started in on me."

The knit of her brows is overshadowed by the concern floating in her eyes. "I don't know what that means."

"It means the higher-ups, but more likely, the owners are trying to control the narrative to make sure I play by their rules."

She smiles. Not the reaction I expected. "Have they met you?" Her laughter tinkers through her words as she strokes my cheek. When it settles, she says, "They can do whatever they want. We're about to show them who's really in control."

I've gotten glimpses of this feistier side of her, mainly regarding the cottage. It's sexy, but more than that, it's incredible to hear the conviction in her voice. At the mere mention of a battle ahead, she's willing to fight for me. No questions asked. Not needing more details to think about it. A simple threat in my direction has her readying to protect.

The words haven't been said aloud, but if that's not love, I don't know what is.

I roll off to the side and switch off the lamp before readjusting in bed. "Maybe we show them in the morning, though."

She curls against my side, her giggle wiggling between us. "Sounds like a good idea."

We lie there in the dark. I can tell she's awake like I am by the gentle tapping of her finger and the brush of her eyelashes against my skin. I shouldn't say anything. It would be wise to just go to sleep, but my thoughts are running rampant with different ways I should be handling this situation. My agent sent that message with not so much as a word of advice. So I turn to the person I trust to have my best interest at heart. "Summer?"

"Yes," she whispers, her finger stills as she spreads her hand to rest on my chest.

"Don't change for them, okay?"

"Who?"

I kiss the top of her head. "Anyone." She's so perfect, I don't want her tainted by my reputation. "Good night."

"Good night."

~

*Five Days Later . . .*

I dry my hands, then hand the dish towel to Roman. He tosses it to the kitchen counter and crosses his arms over his chest. "Why do we have to do the dishes?"

"Because that's how we contribute. Dolly, Summer, and her sisters have treated us like kings since we got here—"

"I like being king."

His feelings are much different from mine. I wasn't taught to clean or to help. I was taught it was a woman's work and stayed out of the fray. Being here changes things. I want to help. I like being in the fray. And Roman will get over it. He doesn't need to be spoiled, which I know Mia doesn't. This is a good reminder for him. "They've opened their home to us. We can do a few dishes." I grab his tossed cloth and drape it over the sink like I've seen Dolly do. "Anyway, we're done. Go play."

He runs out of the kitchen, as if his right to play will be revoked if he lingers too long. "Bye," I say to a door already swinging closed.

I take a chair and sit. The quiet is a good time to think. The door swings open, and Roman peeks back in. He's already smiling. "Bye, Dad."

Now, I'm smiling. "Come here."

He comes back in and right into my arms. I embrace him with my life and career rolling through my head. My childhood and the sacrifices I made to play hockey, the events I had to say no to because I was busy becoming great, and the life I didn't have time to live through the first year in the league. I never think about it, so it's odd that those memories are coming back now. But with my son in my arms, I realize the parent he needs is important. It feeds my soul as well as his.

I can only be so lucky that he takes my presence in his life for granted.

When he starts squirming, I release him. Summer walks in and stops with the door in her hand. Her soft smile gives me the peace I need to know everything will work out. She's also said it like five times today.

Roman runs past her. "Hi, Summer."

"Hi, Roman," she replies, watching him run toward the front door. "Tire swing?"

"Yes, ma'am."

She turns back to me and lets the door maneuver closed by itself. I say, "I've never heard him say that before."

"He's a fine little gentleman." When she laughs, she adds, "And you can blame Dolly." She pulls out a chair across from me and sits, holding her hands in her lap. "What will his mom think about that?"

"She'll probably laugh and tell him not to call her that." I don't know if it's right or wrong to talk about Mia with her. Summer is going to be in my life, so they should know about each other. "Mia has a boyfriend."

"Oh."

"They've been together for a few years." I rest my arms forward on the table. "He's a good guy, and he treats Roman well. He'll even bring him to some home games so he can watch his dad play."

"It's nice she's found someone who treats both of them well, and you." Her eyes search mine as if she senses there's more to this than I'm sharing. How does she know me so well? "What's going on?"

I've been protecting her, smiling as she showed me the apiary, quiet as she worked on a presentation she might get to give, and walking in a daze, somehow believing that everything is going to work out. It always has for me, so that seemed logical.

Not anymore. Five days after reading that article, my anger hasn't subsided. It's grown. My agent's avoidance of my calls adds to the frustration. My time here is spoiled by checking my phone and scanning websites to see when the next sabotage will drop.

"I haven't gotten a call or text that indicates my agent gives one shit about my career, much less two."

"Is that why you've been distracted lately?"

I shouldn't feel guilty for caring about my career. "Taking action from the Cove makes me feel like I'm betraying the trip with my son and doing something wrong behind your back."

She shifts in her chair, but her expression doesn't tense. "You're not doing anything wrong. I couldn't take off months without working. If I could, I totally would." She glances at the wallpaper and chuckles. "I guess the Cove has an offseason, though. Winter is rough without the tourists."

I try to laugh along with her, but my heart isn't in it. I know she's working hard on her own goals, though she's never hesitated to help me with mine.

Summer isn't just a friend I've grown close to, or someone I'm insanely attracted to, though she is both. She's become someone I can talk to, so my stomach shouldn't drop like it just did. I reach across the table and hold my hand out for her. "I need to make a quick trip back to the city. A couple of days max for meetings and to get things back on track."

"What brought this on? The PR stuff? Isn't the best way to fight that by controlling the access they have to you?" She glances out the window above the sink, and when she turns back, her eyes hit mine hard. "No one knows you're here."

My hand remains empty of hers, and although it's hard to feel the sting of rejection, I fight it and leave it in place. "They're putting out that I'm on the verge of retiring. That does damage. It gives the impression that I'm not playing at the level I used to and that I'm hiding from the press on purpose."

"I don't know your levels. I wish I did, but what more do you have to prove?" She slips her hand in mine, and when her fingers curl around my hand, I breathe easier. "You have the accolades to back you up."

"It devalues me as a brand. I could lose millions in sponsorships."

"You're not a brand, Daniel." Her grasp tightens around my hand. "You're a man, a human with real emotions."

"I'm a brand that employs fifteen people full-time to run this career."

"I don't understand. You're rarely on a call." Her gaze drops to our hands. "How are you running a business . . ." She looks up again. "If you've spent the time here relaxing with your son? And with me?"

"I don't handle the day-to-day decisions. I show up where I'm supposed to be and when I'm told."

Detecting a touch of gray around the edges of her blues,

she appears to be lost in thought. Her gaze intensifies when she asks, "What if you didn't?"

"Didn't what?"

"What if you didn't show up where they told you to. What if you showed up unexpectedly? What would happen?"

"The paparazzi would have a feeding frenzy, and I'd hear from my agent."

"And then what?" I can't seem to think of a damn consequence that I don't suffer, even when I do as I'm told. "Your agent has chosen The Breakaways franchise. I read that his agency consults not only with that franchise but also with the hockey league. My guess is they are his priority."

I lean in closer, as much as the table between us will let me. "It's always about money. I've made him enough to pay off his homes in Aspen and Cabo San Lucas five times over. They have a setup so enriching, his great-grandkids will never have to work a day in their life, and they haven't been born yet." She's brilliant. "So if I show up in the city without giving notice—"

"Effectively catching everyone off guard."

"I take back control and get my own team in order." When she leans in conspiratorially, I know it's about to get good. "Or we can put our plan into place and force them into defense off the offensive line."

I grin. "See? I knew you were a hockey fan."

"Well," she says, her shoulders pumping twice. "I know a little something about football." She rolls her eyes. "Not by choice." I'm blaming Dolly. She's a sports fanatic disguised in grandma clothing.

But hearing sports terminology, even if it is football, only amplifies my attraction to Summer, leading me to realize this trip could do double duty. We will finally have the privacy we want and need. Selfish? *Maybe.* My favorite pastime has become getting her off. But we should get medals for the restraint we have to hold back.

"How do you feel about a trip to New York?"

Sitting back, she's relaxed with the ease of a smile on a lazy Sunday, situated front and center. "When are we talking?"

I turn our hands over and back again. "An hour?"

She laughs. "I'll have to check my schedule." She pretends to flip through the air. "Oh look. I'm free. Since Rodgers bailed on the pipes as above his knowledge, the other guy can't start anything until this coming Wednesday. We'll be back by then, right?"

"I'll get you back by then." I stand, evoking her to do the same. Her hand is still in mine as I come around to her to hold her in my arms. "Is it wrong to be this excited to wreak havoc on people I thought I could trust?"

"Probably, but they've already chosen a side. So they already broke the trust."

I lean down to kiss her, sliding my hand from the side of her neck to the back of her head. Her lips have become more home to me than my penthouse. And when we part, I whisper, "I can't wait to make love to you."

Staring into my eyes, she holds my shoulder. "I want nothing more." I believe her.

We step apart. The kitchen of a busy household isn't really the place to get us wound up. I clear my throat and say, "I need to call Mia to see if Roman can stay with her while we're there. I know she misses him, and he misses her, but I don't know her plans."

The kitchen door swings open, and Dolly, on a mission, goes straight for the fridge. "He can stay with us if he wants. It's only a few nights."

Two immediate thoughts: *Oh shit.* How much of our conversation did she hear? I glance at Summer, whose eyes are currently squeezed closed, certain she's in a state of mortification. I guess it's good I didn't say how I really felt—that I want to fuck her until she forgets her name and only remembers mine.

Second, the idea of Roman staying isn't something that crossed my mind. "I would need to talk to Roman."

As if on cue, Roman runs in—red-faced from the heat—and straight to the cabinet where the cups live to retrieve one. "Can I?" I'm thinking these two are working together. I really fucking hope he didn't hear what I said to Summer. Dolly is one thing and rough enough. My son is a whole other thing that will lead me to have to talk about the birds and the bees, and that's not something I want to get into this summer.

"That's a kind offer, Dolly, but that's a big change to your day."

"Roman is a highlight of my day. It's fun to have a kid in the house again."

I look at Summer, who seems good with this plan if I am. "I need to check with Mia, but I'm sure his mother will be fine with it."

Filling the cup with water from the faucet, Roman says, "I already asked, and she said it's okay if I'm good with it. I'm good with it, Dad." He starts chugging water like he's about to be charged for any left over.

Scratching the back of my neck, I'm starting to wonder if the joke is on me. "I just decided to go to the city five minutes ago. When did you ask?"

"Yesterday."

Should I be concerned that my kid is functioning a full day ahead of me or that he might be psychic?

He starts giggling like he's in on a joke I'm clearly not in on. "You always take a meeting, so I was just talking to Mom about it and asked."

That doesn't make me feel good. I go to him and kneel. "I don't have to go."

"No. This time, it's okay. I want to stay. Dolly said we can stay up late and watch movies, eat candy for dinner, and—"

"Did she now?" Summer asks, shooting her grandmother quite the look.

"You survived somehow," Dolly replies with a roll of her eyes that's way too familiar.

When I turn back to Roman, I ask, "Are you sure?"

Setting his cup in the sink, he says, "Yep."

Summer walks to the door, and says, "I'll let you guys work this out. I need to figure out what I'm wearing for the big city, and pack." She's gone before any of us can say another word. But through the swinging door, she asks, "Who fixed the loose baluster?"

Roman hurries after her. "Dad and I did yesterday." He took pride in the job we did, but to hear it in his tone is double the reward.

I look at Dolly when it's just the two of us. "Are you really okay with this?"

"I'm really okay with this. Roman is a joy, polite, and brings life back into the house again. And you've done that for Summer. I'd like nothing more for you two to have the time alone you need."

Pushing out a breath and a chuckle, I grasp the back of my neck. "Thank you, Dolly."

Before I reach the door, she says, "Summer is strong, I'll give her that."

I turn back. "She is."

"It would be nice if she didn't have to be so strong all the time. When she lets her guard down, take it as the honor it is and protect that heart of hers."

"I won't hurt her."

Our eyes stay unblinking until she breaks our gaze. Giving me a cheeky grin, she says, "Best not. I'm the last person you want to deal with." She pulls a bowl of veggies out of the fridge to set on the counter. When she looks back at me, she adds, "Go show her a good time. She deserves it."

"I will."

I leave the kitchen and text Mia:

Did Roman ask you about staying in Mountain Laurel Cove when I come to the city?

She doesn't reply right away, so I start up the stairs to pack my bags. Before I reach Summer's bedroom, my phone buzzes with a message:

He said he's having the time of his life, so if you trust the family, I'm okay with it. How long?

I type:

Two nights.

Mia:

I'm good with that. He's loving it and said some days he doesn't play video games at all.

I reply:

He's having an analog summer, and it's been great to see him so happy playing outside. He never wants to come in.

Mia:

I'm happy to hear that. I'm heading out, but I wanted to tell you that I'm glad you two are having this time together, Daniel.

Me:

I am too.

Mia:

Have a good trip.

Me:

Thanks.

There's a lot to accomplish in a short time, but having Summer with me and the private time alone have me ready to take on the world. *New York, here we come.*

## CHAPTER 22

DANIEL

The reserved parking spot underground didn't faze Summer. She said nothing about the private elevator that's reserved only for the penthouse. But . . . I feel exposed when the elevator door opens, and we're greeted by the expansive view of the city and the Statue of Liberty in the distance. Not because I don't get a high every time I see it, because I still do. It's a daily reminder of what I've accomplished.

I don't want anything to change between us when she experiences my lifestyle, though. I get that it will be a shock. But I've never lied to her. So I'm nervous about how she'll react.

"We're here," I say.

"Why so ominous?" She laughs, but I spot her nerves in the breaks of it.

If I weren't carrying our luggage, I'd hold her hand. "Not ominous." I take a breath just as the door slides open. "I'm glad you're here."

Her eyes pivot forward through the golden light flooding into the elevator. She doesn't move. Not one step is taken, though her mouth hangs wide open. I set a bag down and lift her chin. "We're here," I say, hinting at next steps.

The elevator door starts to close, spurring her into action. "Oh." She hops off, throwing her hand in front of the door to hold it open for me. Giving me the sweetest smile that I hoped would travel with us from Mountain Laurel Cove, she says, "That was close."

My smirk is automatic, shoulders relaxing as she spins in a circle in the entry. Saving me isn't something she realizes she's done, but I'm beginning to believe she has and not just from the elevator closing on me. "Make yourself at home."

When she turns around, the light doesn't just shine on her face. Her entire body seems to lift in a breath of air. "This isn't a home." She peeks at me. "It's like a hotel." Rushing forward, she heads straight to the windows. She's about to press her hands to the glass but stops herself. "I'm afraid to touch anything."

"Don't be," I say, setting the bags down at the opening to the hall. I walk to her. "Everything is replaceable except you." Wrapping myself around the back of her, I rest my chin on top of her head and appreciate the view. When I dip my head to the side and kiss her temple, she eases into me, wrapping her arms over mine.

"You're doing a good job of getting me into bed, ya big charmer."

"I wasn't even trying. That's just my skills, Sunshine. Wait until you see me on the ice. It gets really good then."

Turning in my arms, she slips her arms around my neck and leans back to catch my eyes. "When will I get to see you in action?"

I grab her by the waist, tossing her over my shoulder

under squeals of laughter, and start back toward the bedroom. "Now's a good time."

"Daniel!" She flails in laughter, arching her back with her impressive ab control. Collapsing over me, she smacks my ass as hard as she can by the energy she puts into it. "Romance." She cracks up, unable to hold a straight face, and sends her laughter bouncing off the walls.

Spinning her down to her feet, I slide my hand around the side of her neck, holding her hip with the other. "You want romance?"

"What girl doesn't want romance?" Her lids are heavier, her blinks slower as she melts in my arms.

"I can give you romance." I kiss her because she deserves a good start to this night, and she deserves to be appreciated after the silliness of before.

Her hands slide over my shoulders, bringing me closer to her. When I pull back even a millimeter, she says, "I'm suddenly wishing we didn't have plans."

"I can cancel."

A soft laugh and matching smile have her holding on as she leans back farther in my arms to look at me. "We only get one shot at this, remember?"

I'm not sure if I find it sexy that she's quoting me or impressed that she used it against me. Both. I nod. "I remember. We'll pick up where we're leaving off later?"

"Something to look forward to."

Leading her into the bedroom, I catch the time. Traffic was worse than expected, pushing us to arrive at the event sooner rather than kicking back and chilling together. "Do you have a dress?" I ask. "Like a dressy one?"

I'm not sure if that's horror I see in her eyes, but she rapidly blinks before her gaze shoots out the window and ricochets back to me. "I have a dress. I packed two. How dressy?"

I pull my phone from my pocket and find the invitation. Showing it to her, I say, "Medium?"

Her eyes flick from the phone, then she grabs it from me to read for herself. Flashing the screen in my direction, she says, "I don't have anything that would work for this attire." Her arm flails out. "Do you have a tuxedo lying around?"

"Not lying but hanging in my closet."

Shaking her head, she says, "Of course, you do." A heavy sigh leaves her chest weighted down. "Why would you not tell me? My sisters had options. I have nothing in my suitcase that works for formal attire."

"You don't need to worry. Let me make a call."

"It's that easy, huh?" She sits on the bed and flops backward, a moan of ecstasy escaping her. Rubbing her arms over the blanket, she says, "How is it possible to have this perfect mix of soft and firm in one mattress?"

"It heats too, which is great for my muscles and recovery after a game or getting home from traveling." I scroll to favorites in my phone and call the building's concierge. "Ray, it's Daniel Sutton."

"Good evening, sir. How are you?" He's always chipper, which I appreciate.

"Good. Good. How are you?" I return to the living room to finish the call. Money isn't something I want piling up between us. Beside us is a different story . . .

"I'm doing fine this evening. How may I help you?"

I walk to the kitchen and back, keeping a steady pace. "My date and I have a last-minute event tonight. She needs a dress that fits for formal attire. Any suggestions?"

"Let me make some calls," he replies without hesitation. "I'll ring you right back."

"Thank you." I hang up and return to the bedroom, where I find Summer sitting cross-legged in the middle of the mattress, staring out the picture window. "Hey there."

She looks over with a smile blooming as soon as she sees me. "I'd never turn on the TV if I lived here. There's so much to see." She climbs off the bed. "Do you sleep with the shades open?"

"No. I don't want to get up with the sun," I reply but realize she never closes the blinds on the small window in her room. And it hasn't bothered me at all. I've pulled her back into my arms at daybreak when I found her awake. "We can leave them open if you want."

"I'd like that." She slips off the bed and comes to me. Fisting my shirt, she lifts on her toes and asks, "So what are we doing about the attire?"

My phone rings. Holding it up, I reply, "We're about to find out. Hello?"

"It's Ray, Mr. Sutton. I have great news. I've organized a car to take your date to A La Maison in Soho. They'll have makeup and hair ready to receive her as well. How much time will she need before she leaves?" I look at her, wondering if this is more than she'd want. Covering the phone, I ask, "There's a shop that has dresses. They'll do makeup and hair unless you prefer to do it yourself."

She hops up. "Sign me up. Do I have time to shower first?"

I nod, still covering the phone. "Yes. Twenty minutes?"

She hustles toward the bathroom. "I'll be ready."

"Twenty minutes. Thank you, Ray." When she closes the door, I lower my voice and add, "Make sure everything is charged to my card. She'll try to pay. Don't let her."

"Yes, sir."

"Thank you again."

"My pleasure, Mr. Sutton. Have a good evening."

"You, too." He more than earns a holiday bonus every year because he never lets me down. With everything set up, I pour a glass of bourbon. I don't like events that require a tux, but since I'm not driving and have no clue what the plan is tonight, I need a drink.

Summer pads down the hall with bare legs and feet, a "fresh from the sea" tee that I have no fucking idea what that means, and looking fucking gorgeous. I don't see the woman I've been falling for from a small town where I found myself spending the summer. I see my tonight, my tomorrow when I wake up, and my future.

My chest tightens as she comes to me and climbs onto my lap. "Thank you for setting this up for me." The image of my future wrapped up in this woman still has me in a chokehold, and I struggle to speak. She bends and kisses my cheek. A burst of excitement bubbles up, sending her to her feet. "I've got to run, but I'm so excited about tonight."

"So am I." I follow her back to the bedroom as she pulls on a pair of shorts. "I'll pick you up from the store."

She slips on her sneakers. Looking up at me, she nods. "I don't know what time I'll be ready."

"Don't worry. It's handled." I walk with her to the door. "You just enjoy yourself."

Turning suddenly, she takes my hand. "I will." Lifting to kiss me again, she says, "Miss me, okay?"

"I already do."

Holding hands, we walk to the elevator. I push the button. "Select the lobby button. Ray will help from there." The door opens since it waits where it was left. I grab her and kiss her like it's the last time, but when our tongues mingle, it still feels exciting and new.

She pulls away, leaving me breathless as I watch her

back into the elevator. She pushes the button and looks back at me. I shove my hands in my pockets, the emptiness of my arms reminding me how I was lucky enough to hold her. "See you later, Sunshine."

Lifting her hand, she waves. "I'll see you later, Sutton."

The door closes, cutting between us, and leaving me staring at a silver door instead of her beautiful face.

I turn around, the air shifting in her absence in an apartment she has only inhabited for less than an hour. Or is that me who's shifted? I retrieve my drink and finish the small pour when my phone buzzes with a message from Ray, letting me know Summer is on her way and confirming the pickup time.

It doesn't take me long to get ready: a shower and shave, getting dressed, and then time to hang out, waiting until I can see her again.

When the car finally pulls up to the curb outside the shop, I get out, straighten my jacket, button the front, and wait outside the door. Those earlier nerves are back. I stare at my shoes, seeing a spot that was missed when shining. The door opens, and I look up.

"Oh shit," I whisper.

The black dress fits like a custom-tailored glove around her torso and chest. The skirt flares out from her hips, with the fabric longer in the back than in the front. Her shoes give her a good four inches from her usual height. The red lips are showstoppers, but it's her eyes I can't stop staring at. Brighter than I've ever seen. She slightly leans on her ankle, her face scrunching. "Do I look okay?"

"Breathtaking." I close the gap, wanting to kiss her so badly but not wanting to ruin her makeup. Her neck is bare, so I kiss her there and then her exposed shoulder. "You're the most beautiful woman I've ever seen, Sunshine."

"Really?"

I don't know how a woman as gorgeous as she is could question any man's attraction to her. "You're stunning, baby." With her hair pulled up and fastened at the back, I'm given the full view to admire the way her cheeks blush for me. Holding my arm out, I ask, "You ready to be seen on the arm of the baddest boy in hockey?"

Hooking her arm around mine, we return to the car. "You're no boy, baby. You're *allll* man."

"God, I love you for that." The words come out before I can think twice. Her feet stop just short of climbing into the car. I see her chest rise and her lips part to release a breath. Will ignoring it make it better or worse? The woman makes me laugh more than anyone. It was said in jest. She understands that. *Fuck.*

Ducking her head, she slides into the back of the vehicle. After shutting the door behind me, I take her hand and hold it between both of mine. "You really do look beautiful, Summer."

"You look handsome." The little tension that tried to seep between us doesn't develop into more, and she says, "I had the best time. We drank champagne and had cheese and berries. One guy was doing my hair while another woman was putting on my makeup. I've seen it in the movies but was never treated so special. Thank you, again. Oh . . ." She pushes her ears forward. "I got your present. You didn't have to give me anything."

The diamonds are impressive—one in each ear. I'm thinking Ray is working overtime for that bonus this year. "I'm glad you like them."

She looks out the window, then back at me. "What are we going to say?"

"Doesn't matter because anything I say will be twisted

online before we get back to the penthouse tonight. So I don't want to script ourselves. Let's have fun without the pressure. How does that sound?"

Latching onto my arm again, she pulls herself closer, sliding across the leather seat. "Sounds like a perfect night."

We're hurried out of the car on arrival and shuffled down a short red carpet to take photos. In a flurry of chaos, managers and agents, celebrities and their entourages surround us. Summer presses against me and whispers, "Don't leave me."

"I won't." I keep Summer close, holding her hand and anchoring her at my side when we're guided to the press.

The flashes are blinding, and I hear my name shouted in ten different directions. The reporter upfront asks, "Everyone wants to know. Are you retiring, Daniel?"

"No. Why would I retire when I'm at the top of my game? Gretzky was three years older than I was when he retired. Gordie Howe was fifty-two."

The microphone is pulled back, and the reporter says, "You're not a Gretzky."

When the microphone is shoved back in my face, I'm about to take it to shove it up his—

"You're right," Summer says, stepping out to give herself some room, though holding tight to my hand. "He's Daniel "The Maverick of Hockey" Sutton. Seven-time MVP, which is two shy of Gretzky. He had the highest contract for the longest term in history. Between his power play goals, hat tricks, and assists to saves, you're looking at a future hall of famer, and you should learn to speak to him with the respect he's earned."

*Oh shit...*

The press line falls silent, prompting others on the red

carpet to look around to see what happened. She slinks against me again, and whispers, "Did I break them?"

The hurricane of questions hits hard and fast.

*"What's your name?"*

I take this one. "This is Summer, my girlfriend."

*"How long have you been dating?"*

Laughing, she glances at me quickly and then leans in to answer, "Since we met."

*"Hey Summer, are you a fan of hockey?"*

Summer replies, "I'm a fan of Daniel's."

A lady wrangles us, sending us in the direction of the party, and tells them, "That's all, folks."

While we're walking, I say, "I'm a fan of yours, too. The biggest." I bring her hand to my mouth and kiss it. "If we wanted people talking, that should do it."

She clasps her other hand around our already secured hands. "Are you mad?"

"No, I'm impressed. You handled them like a pro."

"It was so rude. How dare he talk to you like that?"

"You don't take any shit." Chuckling, I add, "I need to put you on my payroll."

I twirl her in front of me and back into my arms just after we enter the party. Bringing her in for a kiss, I whisper, "I've never been happier than when I'm with you, Summer Sky."

Her expression softens into one I see often in Mountain Laurel Cove, and a smile embraces her lips. She touches my cheek before she kisses me again. "I'm so happy I feel like I'm floating on cloud nine. But you know what would make me even happier?"

"What is that?"

"Seeing you in all your glory on the ice." Warm weather isn't conducive to a cold-weather sport, but I usually practice every day. This summer was just different because I chose to spend time with Roman instead.

She has a way of making me feel worthy of her time and attention. *Love one day?* I cringe at what I said earlier. Not because it was untrue, but I would never want to tell it as the punchline to a joke. Fuck, what a loser. Maybe this can be my second chance. "I can do that for you sometime."

The buzz in my pocket makes me smile, but I'm not answering it. I know who it is, but they didn't care before, so they can go fuck themselves now. "I want a drink and then to show you off to everyone here. How does that sound?"

"Sounds like a good time to me." *God, I love her.*

"I CAN'T BELIEVE I met Brad Pitt." She practically swoons when she says his name for the tenth time tonight. "Did you see him in that F1 movie? He was so good."

"He'd be great in a hockey movie." I eye her in the darkened cab of the vehicle. She's busy watching the city go by outside, so I continue, "Wonder why he was never in one?" I loosen my tie and unbutton the button pinning my collar together. "Maybe he can't skate." She looks at me like she's figured me out—her smile remaining small with the slightest upward tip at the corners and brows raised just enough to signify her amusement but not enough to reveal more. "It really takes some talent to balance on two blades on ice, of all things."

"Of all things," she adds like she's fully invested in this story. Or she's pulling my leg.

"But to also add in a large stick and perform at top level in a sport—"

"Brad Pitt could never." I'm not sure what's so funny, but

Summer's arms are wrapped around her stomach like she's going to tip over in laughter if she doesn't hold onto herself.

"That's what I'm saying."

She pats my arm. "You're half his age, so I think it's safe to say your role in future movies is secure."

*Huh?* "That's not what I was getting at."

Wrapping an arm over my shoulders, she scoots onto my lap. "What are you getting at?"

"That I'm a jealous son of a bitch."

She whispers, "There's no need to be jealous of Brad Pitt. I only got a photo with him." She kisses my neck. "But you're the one I'm going home with."

"Damn right." The heat of her lips against my skin has me craving to taste her again. I'm already getting hard when her hand rubs over my dick. "I can't wait to feel you inside me, Daniel."

*Fuck.* I look out the window to get an idea of how much longer it's going to take to get to the apartment. Two blocks too many. I turn back, capturing her lips with mine and sliding my hand under the fabric of the dress. It's not lace or cotton I discover with my fingers. It's her sweet little pussy wet for me. "Have you been like this all night?"

Rolling her head to the side, she grins, the little minx. "I have, just waiting for you to touch me."

"Naughty girl, what am I going to do with you?"

"I have a couple of ideas."

We don't waste time when we arrive in the building. I pin her against the elevator, nipping at her jaw and wanting so badly to fuck her right here and now. The door slides open, and we look at each other. "This is it, Sutton."

"It sure the fuck is, Sunshine."

I take her hand and spin her to the wall of my apartment, her back pressed against it as I kiss her down her neck and chest before I'm blocked by the dress. Her tits are trapped in black fabric that fits so tight to her body, I'm thinking they sewed her into it. "Turn around." I grab the zipper, but it doesn't budge.

Her breathing grows jagged, and she asks, "Is it stuck?"

I'd fuck her right here with the dress on. I'm pretty sure she wouldn't appreciate that, though. At least not for the first time. The second time is still in play.

I tug at the zipper again. "It is."

My dick is so hard that it hurts being stuffed in these pants. "You have two choices. Take the dress off, or I'll rip it from your body."

I want to fuck that open mouth of hers, to come on this fucking dress like that would teach it a lesson. "Please try once more."

This time, I pull the fabric taut north to south and tug the zipper down. The teeth open wide, and I hear a huge sigh of relief from Summer. We haven't even made it out of the entryway before I'm pulling it off over her head. She's left standing in a lace corset and nothing else but her heels.

*We're not making it to the bedroom.*

# CHAPTER 23

## SUMMER

"Spin for me." The gruffness of Daniel's voice is almost as desperate as I feel. Turning slowly, I peek over my shoulder to catch his expression softening, his lids lowering as he pinches his lip between thumb and forefinger. Pure need. His desire drives mine, pulsing between my legs. I've never felt more beautiful. *More powerful.*

His hands fist at his side, but his expression is anything but angry. The press of his gaze lingers on my skin like a caress, and owning that I can do this to him is an aphrodisiac. I want to show off, to feel his hands on me. I stop when my eyes are on the wall in front of me. My nipples peak, my body on alert. I close my eyes to stave off the need to touch myself. *Resist, Summer.* The pull is strong, my clit aching for him. I wanted to drop him to his knees, but I'm about to be the one begging.

I clench my core just as his hands warm my hips and slide around to my front. His body presses against my backside, his steel pushing against my ass. The tip of his finger slips through my folds. One circular glide over the bundle of nerves has me dropping my head and trying to catch my breath.

He peppers kisses along the back of my neck before licking the base of my ear. "You're so wet for me, Sunshine. Do you feel what you're doing to me?"

I slam a palm to the wall to keep myself upright. I would let him take me here. Lifting my head and raising my chin higher, I open my eyes and tilt to the side to give him more access to my neck. "I'm so ready for you."

I'm spun so fast around that if he didn't catch me, I'd fall. He cups my face, pushing my back to the wall so he can pour his determination into his kiss and steal my breath. He pulls back as if he was yanked by something greater and takes my hand. "I'm not fucking you here. Not the first time."

Tiptoeing over the dress puddled at my feet, my gaze travels to Daniel's lips as he grins. It's a mix of desperation and unseriousness, and he pulls my hand, racing us toward the bedroom. I can't stop the giggle that bubbles up, but he rewards the sound with a glittering of his eyes. Pride, maybe? We round the corner, and he swings me into his arms, like he can't miss a moment of touching me.

Enough light streams through the windows that we don't need the lights on. Just me, Daniel, and NYC.

"Summer?"

I turn back to see him unbuttoning his shirt. The jacket and tie, and the shoes and socks have already been discarded as I play out my *Pretty* Woman fantasy, other than me being a hooker. "Yes?"

"Walk to the bed."

We hold our gazes steady before I break protocol to swish my hips. I start to climb on, but he says, "Two feet on the floor." I glance back, feeling so small town when I don't understand. "Face the headboard and bend forward." The emphasis on bend has my heart beating faster.

HE WANTS me on display for him. My mind can't seem to process this level of confidence in his sexuality. Can I muster the same?

I'd never done anything with a lamp on, much less in a glass box for anyone with binoculars to watch. But also, I have never had anyone look at me like someone special. If this is what Daniel wants, I can do this for him. I lean forward, propping myself up on my forearms, running my hands over the blankets, then gliding them back to me to position my legs, leaving my ass in the air.

Without seeing what he's doing, my hearing heightens. The sound of his zipper and then pants falling is the pinch of reality that has me squeezing my thighs together. Anticipation zips through me, needing to release it somehow. I lift one foot, then the other, before standing firmly on the floor again. My throat is dry, and my mouth is open as my breathing gets heavier.

He places a hand on my lower back and presses kisses along my spine. "Do you know what a bad girl you are for making me wait to taste paradise again?"

Goose bumps ripple down my arms as my body readies for him. "I do." I don't even know what I'm saying, but the words were evoked from the tip of my tongue. His hands slide over my ass and down as he kneels behind me. "I'm going to make you come so hard, baby."

His hands slide between my legs before I can clench, opening me up for him. Leaning my head back, I close my eyes as I suck in a harsh breath. "Oh my God."

I'm met with his rough stubble that's grown in the past

few hours, two fingers exploring and teasing my clit, and his mouth exhaling hot breath against my wet center. His tongue licks me from entrance to clit, flicking it, and then kissing the sensitive spot like he'd kiss my mouth. A suck and tug has my knees weakening, but his head being between my legs is too much. I fall face down on the mattress. Angling my head sideways, I say, "I needed to lie down."

He chuckles, the vibration inching me even closer to release. "It's too much, Daniel."

Although he sits back, his hands stay secured to my inner thigh while the other explores like he's discovering new territory and ready to mark me as his. "Do you want me to stop?"

"I've not killed before, but if you stop, I'll spend the rest of my days on death row."

Standing, he says, "We can't have that. The world's not ready to mourn a sports legend before his time has come." He slides his hands under my arms and lifts me to my heels like I weigh nothing. Kissing my shoulder, he starts unclasping the eyes from the hooks that hold this corset. Breathing becomes easier with the release of each as his hands trail down my back. "I want you to wear this for me again. Will you do that for me?"

The need to please him is so strong in my bones, the thrill of turning him on is consuming and utterly intoxicating. "Yes, sir." My throat closes from the horror of my small-town manners kicking in with such ill-timing. "I didn't—"

"I like it." A growl rumbles through his chest as the corset comes free, and he smacks my ass. "On the bed. I'm going to make you feel so good."

He already has . . . I thought I wanted romance, but I'm finding the sting smarting my ass awakens desires I didn't know I had. I climb so quickly onto the bed and fall flat on my back. He slips off each of my shoes slowly, dropping them to the floor without care as he climbs onto the bed after me. Taking my ankles, he pushes my legs up and anchors them over his shoulders.

I don't know who I've become with him, but I can't summon shame in the act of being spread apart for him to trace the lines of my body and up the center until our eyes meet again. His fingers run through the desire he's elicited between my legs, then he brings the tips to his mouth to suck them clean. "Paradise."

My chest inflates as I watch him savor me like a specialty dish created just for him. His eyes lock on mine when those same fingers circle my entrance and then enter, forcing the breath I was holding to expel. "Ah!" My back arches on the high note.

The shock of the fullness has me breathing through it, willing my body to adjust so I can think clearly again. Pulling out slowly, he says, "You're doing so good, Sunshine. I can't wait to feel this tight pussy wrapped around my dick." Two quick thrusts and a spin of his thumb over my clit have me digging my heels in and unwillingly sliding higher.

The vacancy he leaves when he pulls back causes me to lift my head. Tucked under my legs, his brown eyes have never been darker with need while staring at me. Dipping down, he replaces his mouth with his hand, fucking me with his tongue without warning. I fist the blanket, needing to hold on to something to ground me to this world and this man. I will never survive feeling less than the ecstasy I'm experiencing under his care.

It takes no more than two taps on the place I yearn for him the most to send me over the edge. "Daniel . . ." The vibration of a groan against me sends me skyrocketing into the stars as my body fights to stay in this state forever. Floating in the satisfaction, I start a quick descent too soon back to the here and now.

The weight of him carries as he places kisses up my stomach to my chest like crumbs that will lead him home again. His mouth covers mine, the sensuality of tasting him and me, and that he's all mine twists my thoughts as I wrap my arms around his neck to deepen it.

But holding him so close, the need to feel him grows greedier and more demanding. "Daniel?" His head only lifts enough for our eyes to latch. "I want you inside me."

Reaching between us, he's positioned right where I want him. A taunting push to only bury the tip, his breathing comes as jagged as his words. "Tell me you're on BC."

"I am."

Swift without relent, I'm pierced, my body so his, and my mind living the paradise he speaks of. He stills, his mouth open on my shoulder, the hot air from his heavy breaths splaying over my skin. With my arms tight around him, I open my eyes in time to catch the struggle as his expression filters through pleasure. I understand the pain of it feeling so good. Too good.

I'm so full I don't think I can take more, though I want to. I need him to thrust into me, to claim me in a way I've never wanted before. I rub his back and whisper, "I need you to move, Daniel."

A smile glides into place as he pushes up and pulls out of me. His eyes stay on me, traveling down to watch my breasts bounce with each thrust before taking the tip in his mouth and toying with my nipple between his teeth. A sharpness shoots through me, making me push for more of the pleasure as he fills me.

"Ah, yes." I moan as the yearning for more becomes too much. "Fuck me, Daniel."

His head lifts again, a chill breezing over the wetness on my breast. "You want me to fuck you?" I smile from the eagerness in his tone.

"I want you to consume me, and I want to come with you."

As if that's the permission he's been waiting for, he smirks, then kisses me. When our tongues are deep into tango, he rests his hands on the bed above my shoulders and shoves in. The second time, I'm meeting his thrusts, impatient to feel the bliss of release again. It only takes a few for us to fall into a rhythm. The race toward an imaginary finish line picks up with our breathing. When our lips part, we both take a breath without missing a beat with our hips.

His hands grab my breasts, each squeeze and knead leading to an urgency of satisfaction. Thrust for thrust, lines blur. The conflict of wanting to feel this always and hitting a peak rages in my mind as my body works with his.

He licks and kisses my neck, dragging my attention there, but when his hand dips between us, my devotion to that maneuver is set.

It won't take much. Filled to the hilt with more than I've ever felt, the tips of his fingers leave fires trailing behind every touch as he slides over my body. The slick sounds of our bodies connecting become a steady melody amid the chorus of moans and the soft chants of his name, intermingling on my lips.

"You are perfect," he says, each word punctuated with a thrust. "Your pussy fits me like a glove. So. Fucking. Beautiful."

"Please," I beg, the response coming so fast that I do a

quick mental check, but the slower pace seems to be the only thing keeping me from diving into the abyss.

"Hold on to me." When his lips drop to my ear, he whispers, "Remember how much I care about you."

The words make no sense until he juts into me without regard for time and space, the bed, my body, the chase, and release. Nothing. Everything. Up and down. Sideways. The repetition coaxing the tightening deep inside to unwind in a wild tornado of emotions. "Yes. Yes, Daniel. God, yes."

Digging my nails into his back, he jerks. With his head next to mine, his breathing has become as erratic as his thrusts. "I'm close."

The room spins as my mind muddles, the string releasing the spinning top inside, sending me free-falling. A bite to my shoulder breaks through. "Don't stop. Don't stop."

The tremors strike, a tornado ripping through in full destruction of everything in its path. My body squeezes around him until his heat penetrates. "Fuck, Summer. Fuck." My name rolls off his tongue in praise and adoration as his body follows the wild inclinations of instinct. "Summer. Summer. Summmm . . . *Ah!* Oh fuck."

My body's trembling subsides as I sink against the mattress. His weight pushes me deeper into the memory foam, and I love it. The full weight of the energy we've lost together is exhilarating. But holding him soothes my racing heart, and I kiss the top of his head.

When breathing becomes too hard to sustain, I rub his back, and whisper, "Daniel?"

He rolls to the side without me asking, our bodies falling apart, making me miss him already. But there's no space between us when he brings me to him. Kissing my forehead, he whispers, "I love you."

No laughter follows. This time, it's not a joke.

Shifting my head to see him, I wait until he finally takes a breath and looks over. There are no visible nerves to pinpoint, only a strong fear of rejection tainting the warmth of his usually welcoming browns. "You love me?" I wince. Why'd I ask that?

He smiles. "I do. I love you, Summer."

I was always warned not to proclaim declarations too loudly because you might jinx them. But I wish the entire city of New York could hear him and my response. "I love you, Daniel. So much."

We meet in the middle and kiss, sealing our shared feelings. But when I lie back, still not recovered from the activity, he asks, "What are you thinking?"

"I'm thinking how this feels like a fairy tale. What are you thinking?"

"How long will it be before I'm inside you again." I want to nudge him for that, but honestly, same.

## CHAPTER 24
SUMMER

"Why don't you have anything on your nightstands?" The surfaces are too clean, sterile even. I'm lying on my side facing the window, and my eyes are drawn away from the incredible view to the nightstand beside me. Knowing there is a matching one on his side has me wondering where Daniel Sutton's personality is found in this apartment. "You don't even have lamps on them. You have wall sconces."

"The horrors," he deadpans. I almost thought he was asleep, but apparently, his humor is up and active. "I do." His tone is defensive as his arm tightens over me, dragging me into his fold. Though I love lying in bed wrapped in his arms, he's a hot box, so I've been slowly gravitating away to put some air between us. "There's a phone charger and my phone."

Sadly, I think he finds that funny.

I roll to my other side. I'll never understand what I did right in this life to be the one lying next to him. "There are no cookie crumbs, no journal, no random books that you've started but haven't finished, no framed photos, no jewelry you forgot to take off before getting into bed. There's not even a glass of water, let alone a fancy French bottle of water, in your case. No lotion, and—"

"I get it. You don't approve of my clutter-free apartment."

"It's beautiful, but your heart and soul live somewhere else."

He kisses my shoulder twice before closing his eyes. "They're right here. In my arms." Snuggling against me, I watch the exhale that tells me sleep is upon him.

He needs rest. So do I, but I worry about the life he's living in the city. I shouldn't. He's a grown man and has lived like this his whole life. But in Mountain Laurel Cove, he fits right in with the stuff that's around, nosing through yearbooks on my shelf, and studying the detailed woodworking of the kitchen cabinets. He's never said a thing about clutter or looked bothered.

Caressing his cheek, I ask, "Do you feel at home here?"

He opens his eyes with a lazy smile forming. Tapping my heart, he says, "I feel at home here." It's a good answer. Charming, but I'm not convinced it's the truth.

His phone buzzes like it has, off and on, for the past few hours. It woke me up earlier, and I've been awake ever since. Maybe it's a sign to let this go. I'm still curious, though. "You're not even tempted to check it?"

"Not really. I don't care what they say about me in the media. But if you want to look, you can."

"What if it's your agent again?"

"More reason not to check. I'm firing him in the morning." He sighs, but then leans forward and kisses my forehead. "Tonight, I want to sleep."

Raising my free hand in surrender, I say, "Hint taken."

I close my eyes, willing my turbocharged brain to relax and let me sleep. After a torturously long time of forcing my eyelids to stay closed, I pop open my eyes. "How are you going—"

"You didn't even last ten seconds."

"Really? Felt like ten minutes."

Propping up on his elbow, Daniel brushes hair that's escaped my scrunchie back from my face, and says, "You're not going to sleep, are you?"

"Probably not. There are all these sounds outside, and I thought I heard someone slam a door shut in another apartment."

"You didn't. The floors have soundproofing, and the windows are the highest-grade thickness allowed in buildings that are also completely soundproof."

My imagination got away from me. There's nothing for my mind to focus on, so it made stuff up. Everything around me is so unfamiliar except for Daniel. But this is him in his world, not mine. "Maybe that's the problem. It's too quiet. There's no breeze through the leaves or water at the shore. There's not even a buzz from an adventurous bee who left the apiary to explore—"

"Summer." Falling backward, he hits the mattress and his head lands on the pillow. "Ugh." Shifting to look at me, he asks, "What do you need to sleep?"

"I don't know." I half shrug, blocked by the bedding. "Fresh air and—"

"Come on." The covers are flipped off both of us in one swift motion, and his feet land on the floor like a man on a mission. I don't move, a little worried that I've driven him to madness. Holding out his hand, he says, "Trust me."

"Since you put it like that . . ." I take his hand and slip out of bed. He leads me into his closet and gives me a T-shirt he pulls from a hanger. I'm not sure what in the Christian

Bale *American Psycho* he's got going on in here, but tees should always be folded.

I slip it on over my head, and then the boxers that he handed me right after, while he pulls on a pair of sweatpants and nothing else. Okay, I'm softening to this idea he has if I get to ogle him in sweatpants that highlight all the good stuff that's under them.

"Where are we going?"

"You either trust me or don't."

"You're so bossy when you're tired." Realizing that shouldn't stir a tightening in my belly, but here we are. I'm blaming the sweatpants.

Taking hold of my hand again, he has quite the clip of a pace for someone who claims they're so tired. Sure, it's 3 a.m., but who walks this fast? New Yorkers. I rest my own case.

"I never gave you the tour." *Oh.* Okay. It's as good a time as any, *I suppose* . . . I will never figure this man out. He taps the door across the hall. "This is Roman's room."

As we hurry past it, I say, "Guess I can actually see it in the morning. Don't let me stop you."

Pulling me behind him, he points at the next door. "Guest room. There's a bathroom in each bedroom."

"My sisters would kill for my room. Simply for the en suite bathroom. I used to lie awake at night, wondering which one was going to do me in so they could steal my bedroom after the funeral."

I run into the back of him when he stops abruptly. Peeling myself off, I ask, "What happened?"

He turns around and stares at me like he can't make sense of my face. I'm checking if the shape of my nose is still the same when he asks, "Are you serious?"

"About what?"

"Your sisters possibly killing you for your room because it has a bathroom?"

My laughter spills through the hallway, leaving my shoulders rattling under the pressure. "Don't be ridiculous. Of course not." Then Spring comes to mind . . . I laugh again. "Though the youngest is awfully talented with a chainsaw. Spring won the ice sculpting contest at the holiday fair two years ago. She was the youngest contestant to ever enter and to win."

"What did she carve?"

"Our old neighbor Bill—"

"I can't with you, can I?" He's off again, dragging me along with him like a bee has gotten in his bonnet.

"Well," I say, bobbing my head side to side. "In Spring's defense, and to be fair, that neighbor was quite the jerk. He used to drag me around by the hand a lot like you are now."

Coming to another stop, he ruins any kind of gravity he was striving for with his chuckles, and he scrubs his free hand over his face. Standing in front of me, he huffs with a big old smile on his face before cupping mine and kissing me. "I've never known anyone like you."

"Is that a compliment?"

"Yes."

Lifting onto my toes, I kiss him quick like I'm getting away with a stolen piece of candy from a shop. "Thank you."

"You're welcome." His token phrase is back in action, I hear.

Batting my lashes, I add, "And because curious minds want to know, the winning ice sculpture was a hagfish."

"I'm not sure I was *that* curious."

"It really just looked like a penis. The judges were all women, though, that year, and agreed it was a fantastic likeness."

His expression scrunches his nose almost to his forehead. "To a hagfish or a penis?"

"Both."

Pulling us forward, he grumbles under his breath, "Just leave it next time, Mav."

I skip ahead to catch up, wondering where the tour is stopping next. "You call yourself Mav?"

"Huh?" He stops with his hand on the knob of a closed door off the entry.

Standing with the tip of my big toes pressed to his, I say, "You said, and I quote, 'Just leave it next time, *Mav*.' You called yourself Mav."

"You don't talk to yourself?" He scratches the back of his head. Maybe this conversation is a little much for the time of day.

"All the time, but I use Summer or Sum."

"Well, mine is Daniel or Mav. Same thing." Not really, but I'm thinking this isn't worth the tit for tat. Reaching up, he slides his fingers along the doorframe and pulls a key down. "Safety measures with Roman around." He unlocks the door and guides me in before him.

I scramble to turn around, grabbing onto the drawstring of his pants. I'm a terrible person for thinking there's a chance he's locking me in here for the night, right? *Yes, Summer.* I shouldn't have let *American Psycho* enter my psyche. Now I'm all twisted with mistrust, which is misplaced in Daniel's case. He's been inside me. Trust has been established.

As if everything else was left in the entry, he smiles like he did earlier when he first woke—*correction* . . . when *I* woke him up. Sweet and sleepy at the same time. "Turn around," he whispers.

His arms come around me when I do, holding me to his

chest as if I'm precious to him. Moonlight shines inside, lighting up the room. "This is my office. Sometimes I need fresh air, too."

I grin. It feels like we took the scenic route, but we got here in the end. He was listening. The room is larger than I would have expected for a home office and bigger than our family room at home. Creamy fabric-covered couch that looks like the perfect spot to take an afternoon nap. If it's raining outside, even better. The desk is modern wood and so large that visions of getting naughty come to mind. Paintings hang above the couch and are opposite a fireplace. *So cozy.*

But it's the large patio that has me standing in awe. Words won't do the beating of my heart justice.

He whispers in my ear, "Want to go out there?"

The excitement heard in his tone transfers, and I nod. "Yes, I do." Calling him charming didn't do him justice. He knew I wanted fresh air, and like magic, he gave it to me.

Shifting around me, he goes to the door and pulls a rod from the top of the frame and unbolts it. Pushing forward, wind slips in through the opening. He holds it open for me. I wouldn't say it's the size of a basketball court, but I don't know those measurements, and it's massive out here. My eyes return to him on a swivel. "How do you have a pool up here?"

He grins. "Just do. I wouldn't suggest skinny-dipping unless the underwater lights are off. Unless you're an exhibitionist."

"You've met me, right?" The pool is tiny, but it's enough to enjoy an afternoon if you need to cool off.

Chuckling, he says, "I have. Just letting you know it's an option." He lets the door close and starts toward the turf-covered area. I follow him to a row of four lounge chaises.

He grabs towels from a cabinet and a blanket from a large trunk. "I thought we could lie out here. Horns aren't the same as the ocean, but maybe it can help you sleep."

I just fell for this man all over again.

Dragging two together, he spreads the towels down and then sits, patting the spot next to him. So stinkin' cute. I lie next to him as he reaches over me to tuck the blanket in on the other side of me before he snuggles close under the covers. "What do you think, Sunshine?"

His eyes have a renewed energy, lifting his expression and bringing it to life. He did this for me, brought me out to get fresh air, but it sure looks good on him.

He leans over and kisses me. Even when deepened, there's no intent behind it other than connecting. It's not a base to lead to a home run or a puck to a goal . . . wait, not sure that makes sense. I need to learn about hockey quickly.

I cuddle in the nook of his arm, resting my head on his shoulder. "Thank you." I flip my index finger up. "And don't say you're welcome."

"You are, though." I don't have to see the smirk with the smugness all over his response.

"Good night." I'm pulled to say more. Even though it was said in the aftermath of making love earlier, this is love. This is the kind found in the day-to-day that reminds someone they're not alone. *We're* not alone anymore. "I love you." I don't whisper. I let the wind overhear my heart speaking to his and whisk it away, so the world knows.

"I love you, too, Sunshine." His lips meet the crown of my head, and warmth blossoms in my chest.

The sound of the city lulls my body into relaxation, but it's the safety of his arms that has me falling deeper—into sleep and into love with him.

"Is the blindfold really necessary, Daniel?"

Leading me by both hands toward him, he replies, "Yes."

"I'm not saying I'm against being blindfolded and getting another smack on the ass from you—"

"What?"

"What?" We're not moving, so I'm thinking he caught what I was throwing down.

We start moving again. "We're revisiting this conversation another time."

"I'd rather revisit you pene—"

"The Maverick of Hockey." *That's not Daniel.* I try to free my hands, but he's holding them like he knows I'm freaking out.

"How are you doing, Billy?" Daniel asks.

"Good. Good," this Billy guy replies. "Is this the little lady?"

"It is." Aw, Daniel says that with such pride.

Clearing my throat, I say, "I'm right here. And thank you for the compliment, Billy."

Daniel comes closer but still holds my hands so tight I can't shake them free. "Promise to leave on the blindfold, Summer?"

"Yep," I lie like a dog getting away with the Thanksgiving turkey.

As soon as he releases one, I reach for the blindfold. His quick reflexes have my wrists trapped in just one of his hands. "Disappointing," he says with a chuckle.

"What can I say? Being at someone else's mercy isn't my favorite."

"Trust me, you're going to like this surprise."

I hear a metal door protest when it's opened. My mind

reels through fifty different scenarios of where we might be, from jail to the top of the Empire State Building. I have no clue, so I might as well go with the flow. "Well, let's get on with it, then."

We move forward. I hear the door close, but this time, the lock doesn't get bolted back in place. There's that silver lining. When we find our way into another area, it's more echoey. "Hello?" I call out to test if my voice comes back to me.

"What are you doing?" He can't hide the amusement in his tone, though it kind of sounds like he's trying to.

"I don't know. Trying to figure out where you brought me."

"You're going to know very soon. Come a little farther." I walk forward with confidence. He's not going to let anything happen to me despite the hard time I'm giving him. "Stay right here."

I hear him shuffling and what sounds like a box he's digging through. Daniel slips a wide knit headband over my head, covering my ears. "You know it's almost the end of June, right?" I was starting to sweat in the layers he forced me to wear out tonight. I'm comfortable in this room, though, and even feel a little chill on my nose and exposed hands.

"I do know that."

A scarf is wrapped around my neck. "If you're going to strangle me, can I at least remove the blindfold?"

"No. Keep it on. Only a minute longer, and then all will be revealed. Hold out your hand."

I hold out a hand. "Oh my God. Are you about to propose?" I'm kidding. Now if I could only see his reaction. I bet it's epic.

Slipping a glove on me, he laughs. "You don't need that kind of jump scare."

"I'm impressed that even hearing the word proposal didn't send you running."

My face is cupped and tilted up. His lips press firm to mine in a heated kiss. Just as my lips mold to his, he disappears. "Other hand."

I huff, holding out my other hand for him to slip a glove on it. The movement I was hearing stops, his breathing even. I stand there and wait, wanting him to have his moment. Whatever is about to happen, I know he's put time and effort and a whole lot of consideration into surprising me.

The swift cool air drifts across my face when he shifts in front of me, and asks, "Are you ready?"

I can't wait to see the smile that I hear in his voice. "I'm ready."

The blindfold is lifted to rest on my forehead. Daniel is always a nice surprise, but he's blocking my view. When he steps aside, my hands fly to cover my mouth when it drops open. I pivot my gaze back to him, who knows by the smirk on his face that he's done good. Darn good.

I glance at the box stuffed in an arena seat and see white ice skates still inside. Tears flood my eyes, and even when I tip my head back, I can't keep them from falling. "You brought me ice-skating?"

"Figured we could skate together since we're a long way off from preseason."

He flips a seat down for me to sit. I take in the rink and the arena, the scoreboard, and the large speakers, their penguin mascot painted under layers of ice, and the team's logos on the sides. "This is where you play?"

He sits next to me to start putting on his skates. "This is where I play."

The tears should have subsided. I don't know why, but I feel closer to him than ever, being here. Leaning over, I hug him. "Thank you. Thank you for bringing me here."

"It's fun you're here, Sunshine. So I guess I should have asked. Do you know how to ice-skate?"

*Oh boy.* "It's been a while, but I sure do. I was Frosty the Snowman in our school's production in third grade. It was a live show on ice."

"I can't wait to see those moves."

"Yeah, watch out. Literally." I laugh just as the crackle of speakers is sharp to the ears. A pop song soon comes through. Removing the blade covers from his skates, he backs onto the ice. I take one off and then the other just as the song changes from upbeat to . . . My heart catches in my throat. "Are you romancing me, Mr. Sutton?"

"May I have this dance?"

I take his hand and step onto the ice. I want to say it's like riding a bike, but I'm grateful the sides of the skates are reinforced to keep my ankles from breaking.

He asks, "Can you skate backward?"

"No." I flash a humorless grin. "Absolutely not."

Moving his hands to my waist, he says, "Hold my shoulders. I got you."

He's got me alright. It's been so long since I skated. With him, I feel like I skate all the time. We spin around the rink, taking it wide. He rarely looks back as if the size is burned into his memory. Our hair is blowing from the speed, our eyes locked together. My mind is concentrating on staying upright, but I have a feeling he skates by instinct. "What do you think?" he asks, not slowing as we take another lap around the rink.

"I think you know how to win a girl's heart."

Pulling me closer again, he lifts me into the air, spinning faster with me in his arms. When he lets me slide down so our eyes are equal, he whispers, "I don't want to be apart from you."

When the song changes to another melody, I slip lower, my skates landing on the ice again. "I don't want to be apart from you either." I look toward the seats, the reminder all around us. Our worlds aren't the same. "We have time to figure things out."

He slides his arm around my lower back, holding my hand in the air with the other. "I know but—"

"No buts. Not yet. Please. I just want to be with you, Daniel, at this moment right now."

We start skating slowly, our gazes only on each other as we dance across the smooth surface. With his secure hold of me and the wind in our hair, he makes me feel as if I could do this, like I am doing it, soaring across the ice like I could almost fly. Slowing in the center of the rink again, he loosens his arm from around my waist, and I spin slowly like a ballerina. And caught before there's any possibility of falling.

And when I'm brought into his arms again, he holds me there—my body in his arms, my gaze, and my heart in his hands. "Promise me tomorrow, Summer. Promise me when we leave here, we'll still have this together."

I'd like to kiss him, but when the blade slips, he catches me. So I hold onto him, knowing he's got me just like he said, and whisper, "We'll still have this. I promise you. Tomorrow is just one of many days ahead. We have forever."

Caressing my cheek, he kisses me and then his embrace keeps in his arms. "I'll take forever, Sunshine. That's how in love with you I am. I'm lovesick for you."

It's like those earlier tears were just waiting in the wings and come back uninvited. It's not the tears I'm worried about, though. It's my heart. I've been spoiled to only know this side of him, the one that opens up and shares what's on his mind and heart. I don't see the bad boy of hockey or someone that needs to change anything about himself.

So it's easy to pretend today is all that matters with him, to make promises of forever with any hesitation. But there will come a time . . . I don't want to think about it. I shake it off by wiggling my hips for him to earn a laugh and to keep my tears and broken heart at bay. "You're in luck. I just so happen to know the cure for that."

His smile returns. "Oh yeah?"

Patting his chest, I say, "I'll fix you right up and take good care of you."

"Promise?"

The promises reveal a deeper need. I feel it too. A hint of desperation to keep things the same when we both know they're going to change before we're ready. It doesn't make it any harder to give him the world and my soul. "I promise." I'm going to do everything in my power to keep it.

## CHAPTER 25

DANIEL

The sisters I was warned to avoid are waiting for us when we pull onto the property.

Spring has her arms crossed over her chest while standing on the steps of the back porch as if she has a bone to pick. Winter has a beekeeper's helmet tucked under her arm, looking like we're holding her day up.

I scan the area for Autumn and Dolly. I spot Autumn, but Dolly is missing, which is out of the ordinary.

*An ambush?*

I'm not scared of anyone my size, or even bigger. But women, especially when they're amassing, make me a little nervous.

I finally spot Autumn at the far side of the yard, where my son is currently flying off a swing ten feet in the air.

I can handle having a tooth knocked out, getting a bloody nose, or a broken bone. When it comes to my son, I prefer him in one piece and the way he was when I left him. Not that I can blame the Season Sisters. He's clearly been working on his dismount for the past two days while we were gone.

*I exhale when he lands it.*

Roman comes running to the car as soon as I park and cut the engine. I open the door just in time to catch him jumping into my arms. In the city, he usually smells of the soap used to wash his school uniform. Out here, I pick up the subtle scent of sweat and adventures he's had playing outdoors. He's getting the childhood I want for him. "Hey buddy, missed you."

"Missed you, too, Daddy."

Summer comes around with the garment bag protecting her dress in one hand and rubs Roman's back with the other. "Good to see you, big guy."

With his legs still wrapped around me, Roman leans over to hug her and rest his head on her shoulder. "I'm glad you're back." Popping back up, he giggles. "I got good at jumping off the swing."

"I saw. You were really high."

I set him down, and he dashes to the house. "Time for sweet tea," he announces from the porch like his last name is Season and not Sutton. Seeing him happy always overrules my sensitive ego.

Opening the trunk, I pull our bags from it. Summer says, "They know."

I look up, not sure what the hell she's referring to. "Who knows what?"

"My sisters. They know about New York."

Her eyes stay on her sisters, who haven't so much as said hi, much less greeted us in any form. I can't even say I've seen a smile out of even one of them. After shutting the trunk, I grab the handles of the luggage. "It's not a surprise. We told them we were going."

"Nuh-uh. They know." She whispers, "Everything. We all

have a sixth sense when it comes to each other. You can't keep secrets in this family."

I'm learning that, as level-headed as Summer is, her imagination gets away with her sometimes. I'm not sure if I should encourage it, but when in Rome . . . "What secret were we trying to keep?"

We start walking toward the house. Out of the side of her mouth, she whispers, "They know about—"

"That must have been *some* getaway," Spring says. All three hold up their phones with a different gossip page on each screen. Oh that... Not so much a secret since I knew we'd make headlines, but I can see how it might have come as a surprise to someone not in the loop. Or three specific someones used to being all in their oldest sister's business all the time.

Winter's looking at me when she asks, "Want to fill us in?"

Our bags in my hands, I give the firing squad my best paparazzi grin, hoping I live to kiss Summer again. "Did I mention I play hockey?"

"Nope," Spring replies, sitting down as she shoots Summer a fire-fueled look. "Neither did our sister."

Summer takes the first step. "I thought you already knew." Defensively, jabbing her chest, she says, "I was the only one in complete darkness when it came to Daniel."

Winter shifts, sets her hat on the steps, and moves to stand near Autumn. "We knew because we use this thing called the internet." Her sarcasm is on point.

I shrug, glancing at Summer. "She has a point. It is odd you didn't know who I was."

"Wow." She's shaking her head as she ascends the steps. "They turn on you so quickly." When she reaches the top, she turns back with a big grin on her face. "As fun as this is to tease me, the event was at the last minute. I have to tell you about the princess treatment."

Autumn sweeps in and takes the garment bag off Summer's hands. "Can I borrow this dress? It will be perfect for a charity event that the hospital has coming up." I'm assuming the question is rhetorical since she's already walking away.

Standing up, Spring dusts her backside off. "I'll admit," she starts, looking at her phone again, "you look beautiful, sis." When she glances between us, her expression morphs into her usually sunnier disposition. "You guys really do make a stunning couple." Coming down the steps, she shoots me a doe-eyed look as she passes. "And if you have any teammates that like small-town girls, you know where to find me."

"I'll keep that in mind next time I see the team."

She says, "Oh, especially that number twenty-four. He's hot."

Twenty-four? "Dave Mackley?" Summer and I look over our shoulders at her. I say, "He's engaged."

Spinning, she laughs. "He's not married yet."

"Spring Lily!" Summer snaps. "That's terrible." Annoyance tugs her brows together, and she rolls her eyes.

"Double-naming me? I really struck a nerve. Anyway, I'm just kidding," Spring starts laughing again. "I'd be okay with thirty-seven." Apparently, she's memorized the entire Breakaways roster. "And I already confirmed he's single."

"LeBeaux is an asshole. No way would I do that to you."

Her arms fly from her sides with car keys in one hand. "Maybe I'll just stick to guys in the tri-county area. Gotta run." Walking backward, she smiles. "And welcome back, lovebirds."

Summer says, "I'm starving, unless you two want to have

fun at our expense?" Her tone is light, and I love seeing her so happy.

Autumn says, "I'm good."

With her hands up in surrender, Winter adds, "I'm good as well. Jealous, but good." Hooking her arm with Summer, she starts dragging her inside. "Now tell me everything. Do they shout your name on the red carpet? Did you meet any celebrities?"

"Oh my God, I met Brad Pitt . . ." she replies before the screen door closes. The man could be my father, and she's drooling over him like he's, well, like he's me.

The screech of the door opening again has me looking up. "I forgot to tell you something, Daniel."

"How you picture Brad Pitt in your head when we're making love?" I deadpan. "That's why you come so fast?"

She laughs as she crosses the porch to me. "You know none of that is true. Why would I have to imagine him when I have my very own heartthrob?" Wrapping her arms around my neck, she hugs me. "But I did forget to tell you what an amazing time I had in New York with you."

Having an apartment to ourselves, having her to myself spoiled me in ways I didn't expect. "I did too." She fits so perfectly into my world like a puzzle piece that's been missing. She's exposed the cracks in a world I thought I had built of steel, that was supposed to be impenetrable. The dad, the player, the man—she's exposed that I'm also human and need more than air, water, and hockey to survive. *I need her.* "It was nice being just the two of us."

She's brought parts of me back to life that have been dormant for years.

This place and her family bring her to life.

Bridging our lives won't be simple, but it will be a masterpiece when it's done.

Rising onto her toes, she kisses me, but holds my face in her hands afterward while her eyes search mine. "And I love you. Three words Brad Pitt will never hear from me."

"I like that. Both parts." *Jealousy misplaced.* Look at my girl choosing me over that other guy who we shall not name anymore. "I love you, too, Sunshine."

Reaching for a bag, she says, "I can help, you know?"

"Got it covered, and I'm right behind you."

My phone rings. It's the ringtone that didn't disturb us in the city. My agent sent plenty of texts, but he was smart enough not to call. "I'm going to take this first." She nods before returning to the house. I set the baggage down on the porch and walk toward the water for this conversation. "Hey, Jimmy."

"What's going on, Daniel?" What I used to consider happy to be working with me now sounds like an effort to sell me a lemon of a used car. "How's summer treating you?"

I cover the last few steps before stopping and staring ahead. "Listen, I know you saw the event coverage."

"I did. That's quite the spitfire on your arm. Red-hot candy."

My blood shoots straight to boiling. "Watch your mouth, Jimmy. She's not arm candy. She's my girlfriend."

"Oh whoa, whoa. Didn't know you were dating anyone. Apologies." He's so fucking slimy, every word spoken is faker than the previous. I don't know how I didn't see it before. Or maybe I ignored it since he's good at his job. "I can meet her on the Fourth. I think the owners will be happy—"

"I don't give a shit about the owners when it comes to my personal life."

"I hear you. I hear you loud and clear, buddy. I want to touch base with you. We're going into negotiations at the end of July and—"

"We aren't."

There's a pause, and a buzz as he says, "Hm." Voices pull my attention back to the house where the three sisters are talking with Roman in the mix. Winter grabs her beekeeper's hat, and Summer waves before they head toward the woods. The woods past the shed, where I was forbidden in rule number two? "Yeah, it's right here on the calendar. July thirty-first. Ten a.m."

Dropping my head, I grind my teeth just listening to this asshole. "Let me be crystal clear. *We* aren't. You let them put that story out to damage my career in hopes of what?" I look up again, my future brighter now than it's been in years. "Twisting my arm to make me bend to their demands? Fuck that and fuck you. You're fired for fucking me over with the team and league." I hang up and tuck my phone back in my pocket.

I feel a lot lighter already, a hundred and eighty pounds lighter, actually. Puts a new meaning in free agent. He's free to piss some other athlete off because it won't be me anymore.

I head for the woods to find where they snuck off to. The trees grow denser the farther you walk into them. I find a path they've worn into the earth and cut over to it to follow. Is it wrong to want to see what they're up to before announcing my arrival? It's not spying per se. They took my son with them. But my curiosity is getting the better of me the deeper I travel into the woods.

The infamous shed I was warned about doesn't slow me down. I can't imagine it has more than a few rusted tools stored in it, given how it's barely standing. Walking a bit more, I stop when I hear their voices. They're too far to understand the conversation, but the laughter is distinct. I only walk a little farther before the trees widen apart, giving me a peeping Tom's view of the wide-open field ahead and making me smile.

Seems odd to warn me when it's only a bee farm. The apiary is bigger than I imagined. Now I'm wondering if the Honey Hive shop is only using their own actual honey. Summer mentioned Winter being a mogul in the making. I'm beginning to believe her.

I start walking again, this time making myself known. "Summer?"

"Over here." I see her waving from a corner near a tiny house. What? Who lives here? Why does it feel like these women have more secrets than truths? The mysteries abound with the Season Sisters.

Dressed in full beekeeper gear, Winter walks around a bee box with a canister to smoke it out.

Roman is by her side when Summer signals me with her arm to move to the far side of the field, and yells, "Walk around."

I don't see Autumn at all, and Dolly never left the house. When I reach them, I have more questions than we probably have time for. So instead of asking, I say, "So you have a bee farm . . ." I leave it open for her to fill in the gaps.

"You knew that."

"I thought you had a box or two." I wave my hand toward their impressive setup.

She laughs. "It's not quite the size of a typical commercial-sized farm, but it's grown a lot. Winter is up to fifty boxes."

"That's a lot to manage on her own."

"We help out." She pats Roman's shoulder. "Come on. We must keep you safe." She heads for the tiny house but looks back at me over her shoulder. "He's not allergic to bees, is he?"

"He's going into the beehives?" Staring at Winter, I watch her swat, not making me more comfortable with this idea.

She grins up at me. "He's not going *in* the beehives. He's walking around with my sister to learn about the boxes." She tells him to go on inside the house. When he does, she rests her palm on my chest, and whispers, "He'll wear a beekeeper's suit. It's safe. I've never been stung wearing one."

I glance at the house and then back at Winter. Thinking about Roman surrounded by concrete and high-rise buildings more than nature, I come around to the idea. I'm not so stuck in my ways that I can't change. *If I want to.*

"He's not allergic, but I want him safe."

"He'll be safe." The house is full of supplies, holds Winter's office, and is where the honey gets jarred. It's a nice space they've built out here. Summer has tucked Roman in Springs' old bee suit that she outgrew a few years back. It fits well, but I have her give me the tour to see how secure it is at keeping things out.

As soon as he's off to catch up to Winter, Summer asks, "Are you doing okay? It sounded like an upsetting call earlier."

"I fired my agent. I'm not upset, though. As you know, it was coming." Winter is taking Roman under her wing, showing him how to use the canister, when I add, "Did you hear much of the conversation?" I'll bury him if she overheard any of the arm candy crap.

"I heard the f-word a few times but nothing else." Coming a little closer, her pinky wraps with mine. "But I asked how you're doing? It may have been time, but it doesn't make severing a relationship any easier."

I hadn't even picked up on the question before I was off and running, talking about the bad stuff. She listens to my stories, but she cares more about me. I wrap my arm around her, wondering how I'm worthy enough of this incredible woman loving me.

Autumn comes out of another part of the woods. She wipes under her eyes and then walks a wide berth around the area where we're standing.

Summer troubles her bottom lip while fidgeting with her shirt. Concern has tightened her expression, but when she finally looks at me, she says, "I want to share something with you, something personal, if that's okay?"

Seeing how affected she is, I don't make jokes. Not the time. "I'd like that."

She takes my hands when we're a fair distance from the bee yard, her steps growing more tentative, and she only glances back at me once before we reach another clearing. I look up at the sky and then down around the perimeter to see if trees existed here or if it's a natural oddity in the middle of the woods. Doesn't appear to be created by anyone. It's just this way.

Flowers fill the small area as if they're not allowed to grow anywhere else. White and yellow daisy petals catch in the slightest breeze. Summer stops at the edge and stares ahead. It's only then that I see the headstone hidden among the flowers.

The fun I thought we were having drains from the realization of what this place is. Keeping my eyes back on Summer, I ask, "It's okay if you don't want me here."

The warmth of her hand bonds mine to her. And her soft smile works overtime to make me feel welcome. "I want you here. Will you come with me?"

I nod, and we start walking again, stopping at the spot where the tall grasses are trampled from time spent here.

## FAITH AND CHARLIE SEASON: FOREVER TOGETHER.

**Forever in our hearts.**
**Forever living through their daughters.**

"They were in a car accident. Is it wrong to hope they were killed instantly?"

A bit dark for her to think about, but I'd want the same. I wrap my arm around her shoulders. "No. No one wants their loved ones to suffer."

Her parents were young when they passed, one year younger than I am now. I can't imagine how that impacted Summer and her family, but I get glimpses of it. She's never grieved. And from what I've learned, there was no time. That's why it knocks her sideways sometimes.

Tightening my arm around her, she slides her arms around me, and I kiss her head. My heart breaks for her, not only for the loss but the pain she holds onto like it will bring them back if she doesn't release it. "It's okay to grieve, Summer."

"It's not." I can hear the hurt in her tone, the sniffle she tries to hide, and feel the wetness from her tears seeping through my shirt.

"You don't have to be strong all the time."

Her swallow is hard, her arms tightening around me. "I do."

"What happens if you're not?" She doesn't respond. Rubbing her back, I whisper, "Nothing. Life will go on." I kiss her head once more. "You don't have to travel life's path alone."

Her head jerks as she pushes back from me. "What did you say?"

Confusion rankles my brain as I stare at her trying to figure out why she's upset. "I was just saying that I'm here for you."

"No." Her head is shaking so much that I'm worried she's going to hurt herself. "That's not what you said, Daniel."

I reach for her hand. "What's wrong?" She doesn't pull away when I catch hold. Good sign, right? Unable to do anything more than stare at me like a ghost who's come to haunt her, I say, "You don't have to travel life's path alone. I'll always be here for you. That was what my mom wrote in a card she gave to me the night before the hockey draft."

She slams into my arms, tears flooding her lids and falling. Through sobs and laughter mixing, she says, "That's what my mom told me." Looking up at me, she rests her chin on my chest. "She told me that two years before she died."

The tears have slowed, and her smile has bloomed like the wildflowers. She reaches up and palms my cheek. "My parents would have loved you."

# CHAPTER 26

SUMMER

*ONE WEEK LATER . . .*

I can't stop staring at Daniel. *Not that it's a chore.* But it is bordering on creepy tendencies . . . if I'm caught.

I'm starting to wonder if it wasn't a coincidence that he came to Mountain Laurel Cove, that the pipes broke, and that we ended up shacking up, which led to love.

*Dots connected.* I think my mom had a hand in this. It's all just a little suspicious how well it's worked out. Almost like it was planned. I look up at the ceiling of the cottage with my hands in prayer. "Thank you," I whisper, hoping my mom hears me.

"Everything?" Daniel asks, hovering over the plumber in the bathroom. "The entire bathroom, Willie?"

Willie replies, "The plumbing for the entire house. Whoever did the work the first time didn't seal the pipes properly, and if I'm being honest, used the cheapest supplies they could. I'm sure you were charged a pretty penny for it, though."

I dipped into the hallway when the guy's pants hung

lower in the back than I was prepared for when you hear "plumber's crack." But leaning against the hall, the view from here has been incredible.

Six-four.

The thick hair he combs his fingers through when something's on his mind.

Those shoulders that held me like I weighed nothing.

*That smile* . . . If I have a say in when and how I leave this earth, that's what I'd take to my deathbed.

Willie hands him a card. "Get other estimates. I bet I can match it if they're using the same grade materials I would. My work will last you the rest of your days in this place. I guarantee it." That shouldn't make me laugh. Easy guarantee to toss out if we're no longer here to make the claim.

Daniel rights himself and looks at me, giving me that smile I know has broken a million hearts. Not mine.

When he turns back, he says, "Thanks for taking a look. We'll talk and get back to you."

Daniel walks him out, leaving me to feel a lot like we're playing house. I like it. I like having someone around to help me out, especially when it comes to contractors. I sit on the couch, tucking my legs under me and listening to the send-off, and watch as he shadows the windows when he passes by. He shuts the door behind him. "What do you think?"

"I like him. My gut trusts him. And," I say on the verge of a sigh, so tired of dealing with this plumbing stuff. "I don't think there are many others qualified who can do a job out here in the Cove."

Sitting too far from me on the other end of the couch, he says, "I agree. And you said he came recommended? Seems like a safe bet. We can get a few other estimates, but I think it's going to lead you back to him to do the job."

I stretch my legs out, my heels pressing against his leg.

He picks up my feet, setting them on his lap, and rubs. The man knows the way to my heart. "I'm not doing anything until I own it, but he said his schedule has an opening on August first. Starting the day after I buy it isn't too soon." I laugh, scooching lower on the couch, resting my head on a throw pillow. "Should we go back before Roman gets up from a nap?"

"I'm still surprised he took one."

"The swimming did him in." Tossing my arm above my head, I'm here wishing we had time for a nap without the sleeping and definitely naked together.

His hand moves to my leg, rubbing over my shin and higher to the knee. "We have a little time." I love when we're on the same page. That's more often than not these days. Daniel loves waking up and sliding into me when the house is still asleep. An unhurried meeting of our bodies while the birds sing outside and the sun rises makes a beautiful start to the day.

Nighttime holds so much romance for me. The reconnection of slipping under the covers to come back together after a long day. The moonlight helps me relax, and the calm quiets my mind, allowing me to experience our bond on a deeper level. A little forbidden and a lot sexy, and love that's flourishing so fast I can't always hold off as long as I want, and the release hits hard.

His hand slows over my thigh as his eyelids wane, a tell that he's not in such a hurry either. When his fingers dip under the hem of my short dress, I let one of my knees fall to the side, allowing more access to where I want him most.

My heart beats heavier in my chest, my lower belly winding tighter. It's the tingling between my legs that has me closing my eyes and only wanting to feel him. We're rarely alone, and when we are, it's in my room with my entire family home.

"The door is locked," he says, the tone matching the mood—naughty and like we're getting away with something. "Why don't you take off what you got under there?"

Not a question, which is good because I took it as a request and already have my fingers hooked around the sides of my underwear. He's undoing the button and zipper of his jeans and sliding them down his thighs. Daniel still looks at me like it's the first time, never wavering from complete adoration.

I come to him and straddle his lap. Lifting, I feel him positioned and slowly slide down his length. How I feel complete every time we do this reminds me of how empty I feel when we're not entangled together. Resting my arms on his shoulders, I put my head to his cheek, breathing through the stretch and acclimation. I love this. I love this with him so much, any pain washed away by the pleasure.

He kisses my cheek, whispering against my skin, "I will never take you for granted, my love."

*My love.* I drink in his words, rolling them around my tongue to see if they taste as good as they sound. The softer edges and sweet centers of those two words slip past my stomach and head straight for my heart. The urge to please him, to give him everything courses through my veins, revealing the need to tell him, "I love you."

Rocking slowly on top of him, I lean back to keep my eyes locked on his as the sensation of owning him as much as he owns me takes hold. He sits up, taking control of my hips and moving me faster as he whispers, "You're so good to me, baby. Fuck me just like that. Yeah, keep going."

His words encourage, filling me with a boldness I didn't have before. "You're so big, so full inside me." I lift and devour, rock and embrace, squeezing so hard to push him closer to his release just to watch him fall for me all over again.

Watching his mouth fall open and his eyes close because of me weaves into my veins, tying us together.

I betray myself. The feel of him claiming my insides as his gaze hooks me into the daze of deep breaths and darkness, the chase and reaching the peak, before the simplest touch of his fingers to my clit induces my orgasm.

A wave of tremors swims through me just as he grabs my hips, lifting me before dropping me back down to an eruption of moans and swears, Sunshine and him coming. And when my body has no bones left to keep me upright, I collapse onto him with my head on his shoulder and him tucking me into the fold of his arms.

He kisses my head and temple, my nose, and the sweetest of kisses is brushed against my lips while he tries to regulate his own breathing.

Our connection is otherworldly, kismet, nothing I've ever felt before or knew existed before Daniel. Our love, that's eternal, greater than either of us has ever experienced.

*Time is a bitch, though . . .*

"We should go before someone comes looking for us," I say, not moving a muscle and wishing we could stay like this. At least a little while longer.

Using a bottle of water to clean up on the side of the house is not one of my best moments. That the water is French makes me feel a little fancier as I get the dirt off my legs after it splashed me.

"Shortcut through the woods?" I ask, ten steps ahead. I'm now convinced that whoever said shame should be a part of the aftermath of intercourse when walking home wasn't having great sex.

Just on this side of the special place where my parents are buried, Daniel asks, "What's that?"

I stop and look back at him. "What's what?"

"That sign on the tree?"

I look in the direction of his gaze, but there are a billion trees to sort through. "What kind of sign am I looking for? An animal, a bird, a wanted sign for someone on the run from the law? X marks the spot? I'm going to need more information here."

Chuckling, he says, "No, it's not treasure. At least, I don't think it is. I'm talking about that carving." He steps over brush and brittle branches that are crushed under his shoes when he deviates from the path. I follow, figuring there's not a foot of this property I haven't stomped through at one time or another. He taps a tree. "This."

Looking up at it, I'm stumped. "I haven't seen it before. Doesn't look new since the bark is healed. Lift me up, so I can see it." He picks me up from under the arms, holding me so close to the tree that I push back just so my eyes can focus. "CS #7. *Huh.* Down please. It's extra odd because it's so high. Who would carve a message that most people will never see?"

"No clue."

"No idea," I hum under my breath. Reaching up, I run the tip of my finger along the scraped letters. "C-S. Charlie Season." This makes no sense. "Is it a marker?" I look up at the treetops only to find leaves and branches, and nothing out of the ordinary.

"Number seven? It's got to mean something. It's too specific not to."

"Seven trees? The seventh from the ocean? Or the road?" Even from where I'm standing, I can tell there are more trees than that in every direction. No signs of tampering or other carvings, no markers or anything that would give us any indication to what this means. Glancing back at Daniel, I say, "It's here to mark something, to signal to someone. Or do you think it's random?" I turn my gaze back to the carving.

Reaching over my head, he touches it as if it will help him come up with ideas. He moves his arm around my lower back. "C-S. Charlie Season."

Hearing him say my father's name shouldn't overwhelm me as much as it does. A lump clumps in my throat, leaving me unable to repeat the name out loud.

Daniel squeezes my shoulder. "My guess is that those are his initials. It's not some teenage crush with a heart though. So I'm curious what the number seven stands for. A pointer." He laughs and waggles his brow. "To buried treasure and it's located seven paces from the tree?"

"Could be." I finally clear my throat. "Since there's nowhere else to look but down. Maybe we'll find another hint on the ground. The issue is, would it still exist after all these years? Wind. Rain. Storms. Floods three years ago. Snow and ice. The landscape changes with nature. If my dad carved this, it's been too long to find other clues he might have left." I don't know why I feel like I lost something I never had. It's probably nothing. But why does my gut tell me otherwise? "I don't know what it means."

Daniel's eagle-eyeing the surrounding trees when his hand slips away from me. The absence of his touch bothers me more than not knowing what this carving means. I step over some brush and bump up against him. "Yeah. It meant something to someone."

I'm not sure we'll ever know, so I leave the mystery for another day.

We walk back to the house holding hands after the

adventure. I'm not ready to return to reality after having sex like the cottage was ours. I need a shower, and I know he wants one, too. "We could shower together?"

"You? Naked? Count me in."

"Dad?"

Daniel's eyes shoot to mine as his smile falters, but it brightens his cheeks again. "Duty calls. Rain check?"

"I'll hold you to it."

He kisses me. "I'll make it up to you two times over." Stealing another kiss, he says, "I'll see you later, baby."

I feel so grateful and live with a smile on my face. When did life get so good? I might owe those pipes an apology for bringing Daniel into my life. If they hadn't broken, I don't know if we would have seen each other again, much less fallen madly in love.

*Luckiest girl ever.*

# CHAPTER 27

## SUMMER

*TEN DAYS LATER . . .*

Starting my day drinking coffee on a patio in the Hamptons is another pinch-me moment. I've only had these moments because of the sleepyhead still in bed. I glance back at him. The covers are half off his body, and the slumbering sounds aren't loud, but I like to hear them.

Daniel brings me a solace I didn't know I needed.

I slow down with him and smell the roses. I care for him without having to worry about the details. He handles his life without me. I've been given the luxury of loving him without strings attached.

As nice as it is to enjoy a leisurely morning coffee in such a beautiful place, I don't know why I'm not in bed with him. He's all I want, and the need to make the most of every moment together is strong.

I tiptoe back inside, setting my mug on the coffee tray and shutting the door behind me. It's quieter without the ocean breaking against the rocks nearby, but I prefer the sound of him. I climb into bed and scoot back against my big spoon.

His arm comes around me, though his breathing pace never changes. The man's sense of me is quite astounding.

Closing my eyes, I ease into a dreamworld that will never be as enchanting as the one I'm living in with him .

"ARE YOU NERVOUS?" I ask, straightening the color of his crisp navy-blue shirt.

"No. Not much makes me nervous. You did." He smirks. "Before we were dating."

"Lies. You never once acted less than arrogant around me before we were dating. There." I'm pleased with my work, though the contribution is minor to the overall outfit he pulled together. The man knows how to dress. I'll give him that. "Looking sharp. Handsome as always."

I check my matte red lipstick once more to make sure I didn't mess it up. It's not supposed to smear, but my trust issues go way back to the eighth-grade dance, when I walked around with bright pink on my teeth all night. No one told me until my dad picked me up afterward. I got an ice cream out of it to make me feel better. Surprisingly, it worked. I did feel better with two scoops of Rocky Road and Cherry Chocolate Chunk in my belly.

I'm impressed. This lipstick is still exactly where I put it. I tuck it into the pocket of my white eyelet summer dress and make sure the ribbons around my ankles are still tied so my wedges stay on. A Fourth of July party on the lawn of a mansion in the Hamptons had me shopping for days, trying to figure out what to wear. I'm happy with the results.

Peeking out the bed-and-breakfast's window at the water view, I can't help but compare it to the Cove. They're similar. The water is a little bluer here, more emerald during the summer than at home. "I've never been to the Hamptons before."

"It's nice, but I prefer the Cove," he says, rolling up his sleeves. I grin, hearing his heart grow fonder of my small town. A large silver watch wrapped around his wrist is exposed, those veins causing an ache to forget the party to stay in and make love all night. Grasping me by the waist, he grins as he takes me in. "You look beautiful." Tilting his head, he looks at me eye level. "Are *you* nervous?"

"I don't know what to expect. This isn't my world." I flip the lipstick in my pocket over a few times before I ask, "Did I pick the right dress and shoes? Am I the girl from the red carpet or a quieter supporter of yours? Do I tell them where I'm from, or is that embarrassing to you? It is to some people. Jerks, but it's true."

"Yes to the dress. Yes to the shoes. You be whoever you want to be. I'm happy with who you are. That's who I've fallen in love with." He sighs when he angles his head back up. "You're never an embarrassment, Summer. I tell you you're beautiful because I still can't believe I'm the guy who gets to be with you. But that's not *why* I'm with you."

Caressing under my jaw, he lifts me enough to make sure eye contact is secured, and says, "You're driven and so smart that I feel like a dummy around you sometimes. You read a lot and even journal because you have so much going on in your head. But it's how you care for everyone around you—Roman and me—that did me in. Being loved by you is unlike anything I've ever experienced and a highlight of my day."

He kisses my cheek and slides the tips of his fingers

down my arm, adding, "And you're so fucking funny. You make me smile like an idiot and laugh more than I knew possible. You keep me on my toes, Sunshine." He shrugs. "That's naming only a few reasons I like having you around. So no, don't lie about who you are or where you're from. Those are the reasons I fell in love with you. They will, too."

"You keep that up, and you're going to have a fangirl situation on your hands."

Tapping my nose, he chuckles. "A guy can dream. Are you ready?"

"I'm good to go." Before he turns, I grab his arm. "Are there going to be fireworks?"

He scoffs. "Let's hope not."

It's safe to assume we're talking about two different things, but his version has me wondering what we're about to walk into. It's good Mia wanted to take Roman with her to her boyfriend's family reunion, after all. Just in case there are fireworks of the fighting kind.

On the drive over, we talk about the red-carpet event that didn't exactly improve things. Sure, he was seen with someone, but we failed to soften his image and managed to harden mine. He says they'll know I won't take their shit. But I'm more worried that if we don't fix things at this party, he'll be off the team. Or worse, forced to retire.

He isn't nervous, but my nerves have multiplied exponentially in the past fifteen minutes. "Last-minute advice needed. Who should I talk to, and who do I avoid?"

"Players are safe to talk to, though there won't be many. Only a few were invited. I've never spent much time with their dates—wives and girlfriends—"

"WAGS. I don't like that term. Feels icky, like we're one mass not worth an individual mention."

"I never thought it was that deep, just easier to say."

"I can see that." It's not something I thought too deeply into either. I also was never confronted with the possibility of being lumped into that group before now. When he pulls onto their driveway, I scramble. "Any last-minute tips?"

"Sports are cutthroat. Everyone here will play nice, but don't think they won't stab me in the back the first chance they get. Hockey is fun for me, but they're in it to make money. Period." I don't know how to process this information. Should I be on guard? "Don't overthink, Summer. Enjoy the day but also remember I wasn't invited for my sparkling personality." He shifts the car in Park and comes around to the other side to open my door. When I'm on my feet in front of him, he says, "Ready for some fun?"

Other than being with him, none of this sounds fun. "I sure am."

After the valet drives the car away, we walk down a brick-laid path around the house. Holding his arm, I say, "Remember, family-friendly, no swear words. Keep it light and fun. Love fest."

"Sounds awful," he says, his eyes focused forward as we come around the corner.

"Did you notice you never asked me to say or not say anything, to act a certain way, or to wait off to the side while you were on the red carpet? Even tonight, there was no prep for me." I suck in a shuddering breath. "Any words of wisdom, topics to steer clear of, or—"

"No." He smirks. "You hold your own just fine." He stops to face me and takes my hand. "You're the last person I worry about betraying me. And you only help my image." He brings my hand to his mouth and kisses it. "Say whatever is on your mind. We don't play by the rules. We break them."

I'm not sure if I should feel relieved or brace myself. Either way, it's going to be an eventful night.

We come around the corner of the house to an expansive lawn. Clothed tables and formal chairs dot the grass—white against green. White beach balls float in a pool with clean lines, making me think of Old Hollywood. I say, "It looks more like a wedding than a Fourth of July party."

"I've never had to wear business casual to a backyard barbecue."

"Maverick's here!"

"Hey Sutton, come over here."

I feel such pride being with Daniel, so happy for him when I see the grins and excitement on others' faces when they see him.

"Heeyyy," Daniel says, grasping hands with guys I assume are other players based on size and build, and sticking out from a lot of the other guests. Daniel introduces me, confirming my hunch.

I hate it when the two groups split off, leaving me without him by my side and stuck in a circle of minor gossip and a few judgy comments.

I meet their dates—Lori, Katrina, and Lindy—and make small talk. Wife, date, girlfriend. They're really into titles. From the constant mentions of who they are with and their role in that player's life, it seems there's a hierarchy they identify with and respect. And where you are on that pyramid determines everything, from when you speak to your seats at the arena during games.

Lori finishes her champagne and sets it on the tray of a passing server. She leans in like I'm a close friend, and says, "Don't worry. You'll sit with me. Maverick is at the top of the food chain, so you eat first. I got your back."

Being from a small town doesn't make me dumb. We

don't like fake people or opportunists. Ten red flags are flapping like a halo circling the flashing sign above her head that she's achieved ultimate puck bunny status by marrying a player. And she loves to use it to her advantage with others. I have no interest in playing their games. "My back is just fine, but thank you."

Katrina steps between us like she's passing through, and whispers, "You're too pretty to be from a small town."

I don't know what that means, so I won't address it directly. What would I say anyway to a backhanded compliment? Turning away from her, I lift on my toes to see if I can find Daniel. We haven't been apart long, but he's managed to leave me in a pit of vipers. "If you'll excuse me."

I'm not far enough to miss Lori snark, "She's not that pretty."

So much for a good time. I walk around the pool, searching for Daniel. He's tall enough not to miss, but I still can't seem to find him.

My spirits lift when I see him across the lawn talking to a man and his wife. I'm guessing the owners by how so many flock around them. She's the epitome of old money and the consummate host in her silk charmeuse dress that has her standing out in this red, white, and blue crowd. Champagne in one hand with her attention on Daniel while still managing to keep an eye on the party. I head in his direction.

He catches me approaching out of the corner of his eye and smiles. Even in a crowded party, he manages to make me feel like the only one he sees and that matters. Holding his arm out, he brings me in for a soft landing against his side, kissing my temple and giving a quick introduction before they continue their conversation.

The woman takes me by the wrist and leads me to the

bar. "Hockey talk," she starts like we're sharing secrets. "Sometimes I zone out."

"I'm still learning so much, so it's interesting."

She smiles, patting my wrist. "Give it a few years. My husband never even played, and look at him surrounded by his idols and favorite players."

"Silby," a high-pitched squeal startles me from behind. "I didn't know if you'd make it."

I shift so they can talk without me being in the middle. They come together, digging right into stories I have no idea about. I get a glass of champagne and wander to the edge of the ocean. I sip but then look around for Daniel. This is too pretty to admire alone.

He's not where I left him fifteen minutes prior, and I don't see him with any other group. I walk to the house, needing to use the bathroom. My head is swiveling as I do one last search for my man with no luck. When I enter the house, groups of people are scattered around the living room, and there's a short line for the bathroom. I wait for a while, still keeping my eyes peeled just in case I spot Daniel.

I leave the bathroom, looking both ways to see how I exit this hallway when a familiar voice drifts to reach my ears. I listen again and then follow the sound around the corner. The tense tones of the two men tell me I'm not supposed to be here. I can't say anything, or I'll be interrupting.

Daniel says, "You let that retirement story run and run it did. Rampant. Every sportscaster was talking about it." I come to a standstill, so my shoes don't make any noise on the marble floors. "Every paper. Page Six, of all fucking things. I thought we were closer than that, Coach."

"I'm not in marketing or PR, Sutton. I had no idea until I read it online. Like you."

"The difference is you didn't care—"

"I care. I've put twelve years into this team. Ten into you. I called to give you the only heads-up I was given." The silence has me wondering if I should slip away before I'm discovered or if he'd want me in there. Daniel can fight his own battles, but would he want the support?

His Coach finally says, "I think you have some years left in this sport. It doesn't sound like you want to be a part of the evolution of the league."

"I want to play hockey," Daniel says. His voice is almost small, unlike his stature. Or ego, for that matter.

"Then you know what you need to do. The program will soften the image and—"

"I give up Summer and get to keep my spot on the team. Oh, and we can't forget doing time—"

My hand flies to the nearest wall, hoping I can stabilize myself before I fall. Give me up? My stomach convulses. I'm a detriment to his career now? The walls start to cave in as my head spins. I run, rushing through a group in the living room blocking the exit. "I'm sorry," I plead when I spill a lady's drink. I turn back, focused on the door. *Just get out of here, Summer*. I throw my arms out for balance as I run down the front steps and land on the driveway.

Looking both ways, I groan, "Now what?"

The fresh air feels good in my lungs as my hurried breaths rush in and out of my mouth. I start the way we came. Although I know it's a long walk to a neighbor's house, but I have crappy cell service and no other choice. I walk through the open gates and almost run into Lindy smoking a cigarette.

She hides it reflexively behind her back, but then breathes an audible sigh of relief. "I'm so glad it's only you."

"Yeah, *only* me."

"What are you doing out here?"

Holding my phone, I say, "Spotty cell service."

"Ah."

"You?"

She takes another long drag and laughs. "I don't smoke much anymore, but those women are toxic."

"Katrina and Lori?"

"Mm-hmm." She hides the cigarette again when a car pulls onto the driveway and heads through the gates. "They're driving me to drink and smoke to take the edge off." Shifting closer, she says, "Word of advice. Steer clear. If you can't do that, ignore anything they say. I need a shower after I spend time with them." Lindy looks at me again like she sees something she missed before. "Why aren't you with Maverick?"

*I give up Summer.* Tears don't threaten. The pain is already transforming into anger. I could feed off that anger to get me home, which is hours too far from where I am now. "It's complicated."

She takes one more long drag and then offers it to me.

"Thanks. I don't smoke."

"You're too nice. I can tell. Dating a hockey player will ruin you if you're not careful. Cheating on the road, dealing with the puck bunnies always trying to steal your man. And one day, you'll wake up caring about who goes first in the buffet line out of the WAGS at the arena." Dropping the cigarette, she squashes it with the toe of her cute shoes. "As someone who rides the line as a pro hockey player's girlfriend and having my own damn life in the city, I love giving unsolicited advice because I can tell you're a good person. Talk to Maverick. It's rarely 'complicated' if you can talk to each other." She passes, starting the hike back to the house but doesn't get too far when she says, "Maybe I'll see you around, Summer."

I'm left with nothing to say again. My thoughts are muddied from the toxicity of the hierarchy of women, that there even is one, and Daniel sacrificing me without a second thought. I start walking. If nothing else, I'll get to clear my head. Hopefully.

*Why would they even ask that of him?*

*Is Daniel not allowed a life after all he's done for them?*

*Was I embarrassing, and the Coach is protecting his star player?*

I don't know. I sigh, wondering if I acted too rash and should go back to talk to him like Lindy said. Stopping, I look down at the phone, hoping the map can give me an idea of how far I am from . . . from anything.

The sound of a car pulls my gaze into the distance. Vintage black sports car and that dang license plate on the front: **HATTRICK.**

Daniel slows down and then pulls up in front of me with the top down. Sunglasses, perfect flow to his hair, handsome as ever. Some of the anger begins to null just being close to him again.

"Need a ride?"

"No." I look back at the direction I was heading. "I think there's a . . . um. Something up here where I can get a ride back to the bed-and-breakfast."

He shifts into Park and slips off his seat belt before climbing out, so suave like a movie star. So annoying.

Coming around the front, he gets close but leaves me some room to vent if I need to. Lifting the sunglasses to the top of his head, he shoves his hands in his pockets and leans on the passenger door in front of me. "Why are you leaving me, Sunshine?"

*Cutting right to the chase.*

I think this is what Lindy meant by communicating. This would be my turn. "I overheard you and the coach talking."

"And needed fresh air?" I kind of hate that he already knows this about me. I also love it to pieces. "I understand why you're upset. I'm upset, but I'm also not ready to give up the sport."

I cross my arms over my chest. "No. You'll just give me up instead." The words summon him to stand, and the confusion wrinkling the corners of his eyes has me rolling mine. "You didn't even have to think about it. You just gave me up like I'm bad for your health and you need a lifestyle change."

"What?" Stepping closer, he reaches for me. "What are you talking about, Summer?" I step out of his reach, keeping my arms securely fastened over me like chain-link armor. "Bad for my health? You're the best thing to happen to me in years. I'm not giving you up."

"You said it, Daniel," I shout, my temper flaring flames through my chest. Does he think I'm stupid? Taking a breath, I lower my voice. "I heard you. I heard you tell him. "I give up Summer and keep my spot on the team." I *heard* you."

His head drops back on his neck, and he scrubs a hand over his face and chuckles.

That laugh is salt in my broken heart's wound. "There's no point talking to you." I start walking, my anger too much to keep from blowing if I stay put. I fist my hand around my phone, each step getting me closer to losing my shit.

*Dang it.* He even has me cussing now.

The road is too smooth and fancy to give a girl a warning

of when a car approaches, so when the front of his car hits my periphery, I say, "Don't follow me."

"I'm not. I'm next to you."

"Well, don't drive next to me either."

"Fine," he states like his patience has worn off. He has some nerve turning this around on me.

He drives ahead and then angles right to cut off my path. Hopping out of the car again, he comes to stand in front of it. Wide stance. Arms crossed. I don't have to be that close to know his jaw is ticking.

I stop where I am, leaving a good fifteen feet between us. "What are you doing?"

Daniel smirks.

Breathing through the insult of that cocky jerk's smirk, I try not to stoop to his level. And fail. "You listen to me, Daniel Stanley Sutton." I rush forward, pointer finger leading the charge. "I didn't have to let you into my life. I was doing just fine without you bringing this weird hierarchy of women in this sports league to my front door."

Not fazed, the wall of his torso is staying put even when I poke him. *Hard.*

"You're right. You didn't have to let me into your life. You lost me on the women chart, but I don't regret staying with you when the bathroom broke or showing you off at that party we went to. I love the time we've spent under the stars and listening to the birds sing at sunrise. I don't want that to end. I don't want us to end. You misheard what I said." He grumbles, "*Shit.* You didn't mishear. You misunderstood. I have to give up summer, not you, Summer."

"Wait . . ." My mind spins through the conversation I heard, my chest deflating when I realize he could have meant something else. It's in the realm of possibilities, yet I jumped to conclusions without giving him a chance.

Without communicating . . . I like Lindy. I could see us being friends.

He says, "The summer months, the rest of July and the week I had booked in August. They want me to get back to skating and bond with the new guys. They want me to run a mentoring program. Sort like an easy out for them to find talent by making me scout them out."

That he was still trying to honor the rental schedule, as if he were still staying at the cottage, was sweet. My chest inflates like a balloon full of hope for our future together, knowing he would be with me if he could. "A mentoring program?" My heart flutters to life again. "I actually love that for you."

Taking one tentative step and then another, he takes hold of my upper arms. "I kind of do, too. I think it will be a good way for me to do something outside of playing."

"You bring so much to the game, your experience. Your drive. Your three times voted *People's* "Sexiest Man Alive." I crack a smile, breathing so much easier now.

"I'm sure that will go over real well with the new guys." He chuckles. "But Summer, I need you to know that I wouldn't have given you up. Not even for hockey. July and August . . ." He shrugs. "Okay. I don't love giving up those months I'd get to spend with you, or with Roman this summer at the Cove, but I think it's best if I do this training program."

Relief washes through me, wondering if I've just been waiting for a shoe to drop, and when it did, I fell with it the first chance I got. If this is the worst of it, we can overcome it. I need to trust him, and myself, but more so, I need to hold onto the trust we've built together. I push into his arms, embracing this man with my whole heart. "You're leaving Mountain Laurel Cove."

"Yes. But I'm not leaving you."

I look up. "*Technically*, you are." Smirking, I can't contain it. "Sooner than I hoped. But this is life, and we'll face it together."

"We're a few hours apart. I'll do everything I can to make this work. Do you want that, too?"

I know the answer, feeling it in my soul. "I do."

# CHAPTER 28

DANIEL

*THREE WEEKS LATER . . .*

"What the fuck are you doing out there?" I punch the air, imagining it's his face. Cupping my hand to the side of my mouth, I shout, "What the fuck kind of play was that, Landers?"

Shredding ice, he skids to a stop in front of me. "It's called hockey, old man." He pounds his fist twice on top of the wall, tempting me to jump over that wall and show him how the pros play. "Guess that's why you're on the bench, and I'm out here."

"Listen up, fucker. Hockey requires you actually make contact with the puck, not skate by it like you're still in PeeWee league."

"It's not 1985, Maverick. You need to get yourself some glasses."

I'm yanked backward before I lunge over that small wall he thinks is protecting him. Two players pull me back as I shout, "Say that to my fucking face."

"I just did." He laughs, skating off.

A slow clap echoing from the tunnel has me looking over to see what shit is about to be thrown my way. I pull my arms free and sit on the goalie's seat because I'm sure as shit not going to greet whoever it is after that entrance. "Old man? Ha! Good one." Coach rounds the corner into our bench. "It's rough out there, Sutton."

He's not wrong. This next generation of players is something else, the little fuckers. If I'd had the talent of some of these guys, my early years would have gone a lot smoother. "Coming to check on us, Coach?"

"Nope. But looks like I should have before now." He cuts down the back of the bench to stand next to me. Arms crossed, looking all business, he keeps his indifference on his face as he watches the players on the ice. He's always been hard to read unless you anger him. "Any talent?"

"As much as it hurts my hockey soul to say this . . ." I shake my head, but I won't keep real talent down. "Landers is a good fucking player. He's also a shit human."

He chuckles. "Takes one to know one, huh?"

"Funny." I chuckle. He's not entirely wrong, though. I was a bastard before I met Summer, and with our schedules keeping us busy and apart, the role fits like a glove again.

Coach has never been much of a conversationalist unless he's drinking, and then you can't get him to shut up. His gaze is too distant, his mind not on the players on the ice or the bench. So I take a guess, "What did you really come down here to talk about?"

Pointing up at the second-level seats in the barn, he wags his finger. "I've spent quite a bit of time up there watching you this past week."

"I didn't know I was being spied on."

"I like to see players in their natural habitat."

Snapping, I point at the rink. "My habitat is out there, not here on the bench."

He nods, looking down at his shoes like they've changed feet. "But I will say . . ." He looks at me again. "You're not terrible. Your delivery needs some work, but the guys respect you, Landers excluded—"

"Fuck him."

Laughing, he says, "I've seen some of their games improve."

Crossing my arms over my chest, I stand like a proud papa, mentally patting my own back. "I only made some suggestions and tweaked a few things. Landers is hard-headed, so not much progress there, but . . ." I shrug. "I was just making suggestions to do it, not that he needs my opinion."

"Sure, he does. He's listening. I've seen adjustments he's making when you're not looking. The coaches have been watching playbacks."

"If you're trying to woo me into coaching, I'm not done on the ice yet."

He pats me on the shoulder. It's nice not having to be the one to do it all the time. "When you are, let's talk."

I've never thought about coaching. I didn't have to because I was playing well. Am I still playing my best? Fuck yes, I am. But it's been interesting to be included in the development of other players.

As the players take the ice, Coach takes the spot where he stands during games and watches. The players swap without me having to direct their every move. Nice change from me telling them to pay attention, learn how the pros play, and learn the cues. They have a coach, not a babysitter.

His eyes stay on the play ahead when he asks, "How's the relationship, Sutton?"

It's a loaded question, not for him to ask, but for me, since a war has been waging in my chest. I was doing okay the first week; calls and videos were working. It's gotten worse over the past two weeks. Hanging up feels bittersweet —glad I heard her voice or saw her face, but the loneliness after is consuming my nights.

"Good." Generic is best.

Looking me over, he asks, "Good?"

"Yeah." I shrug like he's not seeing right through me. "Good."

His eyes return to the ice. "Where is she located again? Ashford?"

"Mountain Laurel Cove," I reply, following Crosby toward the goal. "Ah, fuck." I clap. "Good play."

He claps. "That's right," he says, picking up where he left off. "Mary and I went there once."

"Mary's the one who found the rental for me."

"My wife was sad we didn't get to meet her at the party."

Telling that story isn't going to land like it did that day, so I don't bother. "Next time."

"You know." Here we go . . . "Mary has gotten into some new age stuff, manifestations, and that kind of thing. She fully believes she helped us make the playoffs last time." He chuckles to himself, peering at me out of the corner of his eye.

"Are you going somewhere specific with this, Coach?"

"I've seen a change in you. When you get on the ice to show the guys a skill, you're keeping the aggression on the move and the puck, focused on scoring, not on the other players on your team." I'm not going to give him the satisfaction of smiling, but it has been fun. "Can you admit that maybe spending time with young talent isn't so bad?"

"It's not so bad." I've poured my energy into this scouting

program. The nights suck without Summer, but the days keep my mind occupied and off what she might be doing.

"Let's remember this talk when preseason kicks off in September, and there are new guys on the team." His eyes swerve with the players on the ice. "Come on, Landers. What the hell are you doing out there?" He looks back at me. "You're right. He's good. But like you, he needs to learn that it's a team game. Not a solo sport. We're pulling him up from the minors and offering him a contract next week."

"His life is about to change forever." I don't know if that's a good or bad thing anymore. Having all the money I could dream of didn't fix my past, but it changed my future. That sky-blue dress and matching eyes, white sneakers, tanned legs, and a smile that knocked me on my ass. My future comes into focus from the mere mention of it.

"It is. Speaking of, are you ready for your meeting tomorrow?"

"I know what I want, and I know what I'm worth. I'm bringing my attorney to make sure they're ready to meet the demands."

Shaking his head, he looks down. "I'll put in a good word. You've done a good job helping me build the next championship team. Good luck, man." When he glances at me again, I can see the approval in his eyes. He can make jokes about me being a shit human only because we share a level of respect between us.

Waving two fingers, I say, "Thanks."

He slips out when I'm talking to Crosby about not letting Landers cut him out of his position. I glance at the tunnel, then up at the seats where he was watching, and scoff with a grin on my face.

~

"I GOT THE MONEY," Summer says.

"That's good." I'm left in an awkward state of trying to sound happy for her benefit while hoping not to fall apart for mine.

She didn't want to video, claiming she looked terrible and that's not how she wants me to see her. But I hear the sadness in her tone even when she should be excited about tomorrow.

If I ask about it, she just says she misses me is all.

*Same.*

How did meeting her and one month flip my world inside out and upside down? I miss her so fucking much that I swear I can still feel her in my bed next to me, only to reach over and find it empty. Her laughter follows me down the hallway. When I turn back, ready to pull her into my arms, she's not there. And sometimes I sit out on the patio just because I know we're sharing the same fresh air.

I drop my head and wrap my arms over it.

"Daniel?" she says, a wisp of a voice calling my name. "Thank you."

I fall back on the couch and stare at the TV with playbacks of the week on the large screen. "Tomorrow at this time, you'll have everything you ever wanted, Sunshine."

"Everything I ever wanted." The giggle I expect doesn't come, not talking a million miles an hour about nothing and everything that crosses her mind. No smile is heard in her words.

Melancholy is choking this relationship to death, and the distance is harder to manage than I thought. There's no draw to other women. There's no draw to anything. Even hockey isn't as entertaining when we're apart, and it's not something we did together.

"Are you ready to take on big money corporations tomorrow?"

That earned me the lightest of laughs. "As ready as I can be. These past few weeks, I've done a ton of research. I'm hoping the extra mile of protecting our town, and that land, stewarding it for growth in the right way, will win her over. Did I tell you it's a blind bid?"

"What does that mean? You have to submit without knowing what the other guy's offer is?"

"Yep. She claims it makes you put in your best offer. So maybe preserving the history of the area will tip the bid in my direction if I'm under."

"She's a fool if she doesn't sell it to you. *Fuck.*" I sit up, too anxious watching these players to kick back.

"What?"

"Playbacks for the training."

"*Oh* . . . I should let you go so you can watch without interruption."

"Hey Summer, you're not interrupting. I don't have much going on or to say when we talk at night lately because I'm not doing anything you'd find interesting."

"I find everything you do interesting, but you don't seem to want to share anymore."

She knows how to make a guy feel good. "Hearing your voice gets me through the night and another day knowing I get to hear you again the next."

"I feel the same way. I'm a ghost in my life haunting where I kiss you or we made love, when you smacked my ass, or fed me hot dogs on the big deck. Everything is a memory instead of living life like we used to. I hate it."

Her pout at the end leaves me smiling. "I hate it too." Rubbing the bridge of my nose, I try to ease into the next conversation, knowing it won't be getting better anytime soon. "We need to figure this out. Once I'm on the road . . ."

"I know we need to talk about it, but can we do that when we're together instead of however many hours we're apart?"

I can't fully follow her line of reasoning, but I'd do anything for her, including saying yes if it will make her feel better. "We can talk about it another time. Together."

"Daniel?" Her voice is barely above a whisper. "I hope you also get everything you want. Good luck tomorrow."

Nodding to an apartment that doesn't have her scent on the sheets anymore or her dress on the floor of the entry, only her absence from my arms, I swallow. "Good luck tomorrow. I love you, Summer."

*Summer is with me.*

The signs are everywhere this morning as I make my way to The Breakaways' franchise offices. Blue in the sky and on a dress displayed in a store window. Golden sunshine strikes my eyes when I round the corner. A sign above a swimsuit shop that reads "Are you ready for Summer Season?"

*So fucking ready.*

I meet the attorneys in the lobby, and we ride the elevators up together. We're led down the hall to the large conference room. The assistant opens the door, and announces, "Mr. Sutton is here for the meeting."

As soon as I'm seated, the door is closed, and we begin the negotiations.

## CHAPTER 29

SUMMER

"*Breatheeee*, Summer." I exhale long and slowly, manifesting my way into winning today. "You *will* win this bid. You *will* own a cottage. All your work *will* pay off."

*"The Maverick of Hockey scores!" . . . "He just locked down league MVP, Josh." . . .*

"*Ohmmmm*," I hum with pinched fingers, meditating to the sound of Daniel winning four years ago blaring from my computer.

"You're *still* watching his old games?"

"Cheez-Its on a cracker." Opening my eyes, I grab my chest but then slam my laptop closed like I was caught watching porn. "You scared me, Fall. Announce yourself."

"Do you prefer I go with 'I, Lady Autumn of the Seasons of Mountain Laurel Cove'?" She cracks herself up. "Or does shouting 'I'm coming in' work better for you?" She sits in the chair at the desk, crossing her legs and looking bored.

I drop my hands beside me on the bed, and I roll my head to the side to see her. "A knock will suffice."

"The door was wide open. Isn't that the universal signal for come on in?" She turns toward the mirror and takes a green bauble necklace down to try on. "Still blue over your beau?"

"I half watch just to see him or hear his voice in interviews. It relaxes me." My arms fall wide beside me. I don't tell her that I fall asleep with his games playing and have been spending time learning about hockey. "I'm hopeless."

"You're not. You've just lost some of your spark. You'll get it back, and you don't need a man for that."

"What about a cottage? Think that would help?"

Getting up, she comes and flops on the bed next to me. "A cottage should do it." Rolling over, she says, "Will you fasten this for me?"

"It's not helped that I've worked so much at the Honey Hive this month." I sit up again and take the clasp of the necklace and hook it together. "Fall, I've been putting in forty- and fifty-hour shifts to help get the shop off the ground."

"July is peak tourist season, Sum. I even picked up a Honey Hive shift after a twelve-hour shift at the hospital." She rubs my arm. "I know Winter appreciates our help."

I know she's right and that Winter does appreciate it. But even if she didn't, I think I'd probably find myself doing the same thing, anyway. I can't fill every minute of my day with old hockey videos.

"I keep thinking maybe it's a godsend to keep me occupied. The other cottage has had a lot of turnovers, too. A new renter every week. Cleaning, prepping, shopping. My spark is exhausted."

*And ... sad.*

I catch my sister's kind eyes and the sympathy she has for me. I've tried desperately to keep myself busy and moving, filling every moment so I don't have time to think too much about him. It's kept me from having a total meltdown because I don't have time for it. But seeing my sadness reflected hits hard, and when she places her hand on top of mine, my bottom lip begins to quiver.

"I miss him," I whisper, the words freed in the room for the first time. *Will I ever be able to catch them to hide in the back of the closet and ignore again?* I'll have to. They're too heavy to carry around and weigh my shoulders down. "I'm afraid of how terrible it's going to be when I'm not so busy that I have to sit with my feelings."

Taking my hand between both of hers, she says, "He's an athlete who travels a lot for his job. This isn't a one-off. This is how it's going to be more often than not. You, sweet sister, need to figure out if this is the life you want, if it's one you can live with or not."

"That's what I was trying to do with the meditation. Figure out life's path for me."

She grins. "Have you tried a shorter, deeper *ohm*?" She slides off the bed to admire the necklace on her neck in the mirror, her gaze latching to mine in the reflection.

"I can't tell you anything." I know I can trust my sisters to take our secrets to the grave, but it's fun to still tease her.

"You can. Always, and it will stay between us." Walking to the door, she waves her arm in the air. "Put the hockey game back on." She laughs. "If it works, it works, and I'm sure there's some peer-reviewed study to back the science behind seeing a partner succeed as encouraging and motivating ... or something like that. Can I borrow this necklace?"

I don't need an obscure study to tell me that seeing and hearing the love of my life puts me in a better mood. I feel it as strongly as his love for me. "Yes. It looks good on you. Where are you going?"

She grabs the doorframe and balances her weight with a smile that feels like she's up to no good. "Lunch date. I'm off for the next two days, so I said yes. He came in with a broken arm last night." She giggles. "As you know, it's hard to find a guy in the Cove when they aren't spontaneously dropped into your lap or renting the house next door. Lucky you. What a score." Her giggles turn into all-out laughter. "Good luck today. You got this!"

"Thanks, and good lay to you. *Oh my God.* I mean, good day. Have fun." I fall back on the mattress again. "Oh, forget it."

I hear her laughing as she trots down the stairs.

Opening my laptop, I push play and close my eyes to absorb the positivity of Daniel winning the Chalice a few years ago. His voice is a balm to my aching heart, even if it's a post-game interview and I have no idea what they're talking about.

His laughter and the cadence of his words—*I miss him.* Not just his presence. I miss his soul caressing mine, waking up with his eyes on me, and the sweetest smile already on his face. I miss the way *I love you* never came forced but flowed like a river from his heart to mine.

I squeeze my eyes closed, so tired of crying all the time and this constant hole in the middle of my chest that food or even a phone call won't soothe. *I need him.* I need to be held in his arms again, to see the way he looks when he's touched heaven, deep inside me. I miss how he calls it like he sees it, and those eight ab muscles of his. *I miss him.* And I miss Roman and the way that kid livened up our house and Dolly again. I miss both of their sweet hugs. And Daniel's kiss on my head.

Touching my forehead, and it's just me with no traces of him anymore.

The tire no longer spins, and the swing has been empty since they left. I've found myself running to the cottage when the loneliness gets to be too much, searching for any sign—a morsel left behind—that he was real. That *we* were real. That he really existed in my world and not just on my laptop or a voice on the other end of a phone call.

Curling onto my side, I let the next video play as I wrap myself up in my own arms to keep from falling apart again. It won't work. It never does, but I'm all I have left of what we once were.

~

*Buzz.*

*Buzz.*

*Buzz.*

Sportscasters arguing about the greatest of all time weaves into my periphery. I open my eyes, seeing the video sideways. "Daniel Sutton," I reply, as if I'm part of the conversation.

*Buzz.*

*Oh no!*

"The cottage," I gasp.

Popping up, I grab my phone and turn off the alarm. I push out of bed, scrambling to change into the clothes I planned to wear to the meeting. Rushing through a quick freshen-up, I slip on a pair of flats and grab my laptop before stopping and looking out the window. A storm is coming. *This better not be an omen.*

I run down the stairs, and each old creak squeaks when I land on it. "Slow down before you fall, honey." Dolly is waiting in the entry with a glass of orange juice and two sausage links. "Thought you could use the energy and protein."

I kiss her cheek. "You're the best." Taking the juice in my free hand, I say, "Shove them in."

She pokes the sausages into my mouth and then hands me my keys on the way out. "You can do it, Summer. Proud of you for chasing your dreams."

I waffle my head since I can't speak with a mouth full of breakfast meat. Still chewing, I don't make it to my car before I hear, "And tell that old bag to do the right thing or she'll be dealing with me." I want to laugh, but I'll choke if I do. And I'm not entirely sure she doesn't mean it.

Shoving my laptop in the car, I finally swallow and wash the food down with the juice. Cocking an eyebrow, I turn back. "I won't be telling her that, but I appreciate you having my back."

"Rain is coming this way. Slow down so you don't get in an accident."

"I want to get there before it pours." Probably not the answer she wants to hear. "Bye, Dolly."

The speed limit is way too slow when I have to be somewhere important. Driving behind a row of tourists sightseeing makes it worse. "What are we taking a Sunday drive here? No. We're not."

The sky splits in two, sending a downpour to take over the town. A blanket of heavy rain won't keep me from winning the cottage. I lay on my horn out of pure frustration and consider breaking the law by going around the three slowpoke cars.

"I'm starting to sound like a certain hockey player with a penchant for rule breaking," I say softly, my heart clenching as his voice echoes through my head. *"Rules are made for breaking."* The voice of the devil plays on repeat in my head. Do I? Should I?

The time on the dashboard urges me to drive the defense down the line. I don't know what sport that's from, but that's what I'm going to do. It's the only way to put in a bid on time. I slam the pedal to the floorboard and drive like a speed demon down the two-lane road, cutting over into the other lane to pass the slower drivers.

The headlights hit me first. A horn blares straight at me. I swerve back into my lane at the last minute to avoid being run over by a semi-truck. I check my rearview mirror for the other cars. "I did it. Daniel would be so proud of—"

Wheels spinning.

Tires skidding.

I turn into the skid with rain shielding me from seeing my life flash before my eyes. My laptop becomes a flying guillotine, slicing through the interior, hitting the far window, and dropping like a barbell as the car skids into a barbed wire fence.

My mouth is agape, but no sound comes out. It happens in the slowest yet fastest motion, making it hard to compute in real time.

I'm white-knuckled, eyes the size of dinner plates as I catch a quick breath—heart pounding so hard I'm dizzy. Through the streaks of the wiper blades, I spot Bessie on the other side of the mangled fence, judging me.

"Oh my gosh," I groan, releasing my grip on the wheel.

I drop back in the seat and fill my lungs with air, so grateful to be alive. Gingerly, I touch my head and face, before running my hand down my chest and kicking my legs. *I think I'm okay.* I unfasten the seat belt, letting it snap back against the car.

My train of thought is a little foggy as I try to get a grip on reality. *What do I do now? Call the paramedics? Where is my phone? Is anyone else hurt?*

Blood soars by my ears as my heart pounds even harder. "Don't panic," I say, searching for my phone with shaky hands as tears stream down my cheeks.

The sound of metal clanging together from behind me makes me jump. "Are you okay?"

I look over my shoulder and find a man giving me a quick once-over. "I think so." My voice wavers as I try to stay calm.

"You shouldn't speed in the rain." He starts back to his car. "Sit tight. I'll call the police."

Grabbing hold of the steering wheel again, I flex my fingers around it and stare ahead. I'm freezing cold and starting to tremble. I just want Daniel.

I turn again to look for my phone when a notebook catches my attention from the floorboard.

*The cottage!*

"MOST LIKELY, you're going to live." Brandon holds the ice pack to my head.

Propped behind the large steering wheel of the fire truck, I laugh, taking over for him with the ice pack. "You need to work on your bedside manner. It's not very comforting." I lift a brow. "Most likely?"

Hanging onto the rail, he searches my eyes for the fifth time, smiling this time when he hops down. "I'm a fireman, not a doctor."

"You're also a paramedic. Trust me, I know this. There must be a little extra training to work on patients who almost died."

Running his thumbs along the underside of his red suspenders, he chuckles again. "You didn't almost die, Summer. You got close to taking out Bessie, though. Mrs. Dover wouldn't have been happy if you had."

"She's not really happy anyway," I say, sounding more like Dolly than myself.

"I need to get downtown to check out an alarm going off at the pottery store. Security said it was a cat who'd gotten in, so duty calls." He helps me to solid ground. Eyeing my head, he says, "Hold that on for a few minutes. I called your sister to pick you up since your car had to be towed. She should be here in five minutes."

"Autumn?" I ask, grinning. It's Brandon. Of course, he called Autumn. "You didn't."

"I did." He smirks, reminding me of a certain other smirker I know.

"She was on a date, you know?"

A wry grin works its way up to his eyes where it settles. "I know." He shuts the door. Quite the mic drop. Make big moves and get big rewards.

The rain has stopped, and the sun is attempting a daring reappearance before it sets for the night. The sky shows off in beautiful pinks, vivid oranges, and striking purples. It's a beautiful ending to a terrible day.

Most of the witnesses to the accident have already left. There are a few bystanders still hanging out by the fire truck, probably whispering that I was out joyriding. Dolly will love hearing about that gossip. They don't understand, or care, that I was trying to get to a very important meeting.

*One that I missed.*

My heart sinks in my chest as I fight back another bout of tears.

"Well, Bessie," I say, turning toward the fence. "Looks like it's me and you, old girl."

She moos in response. I reach over and pet her, feeling my heart slowly splinter into pieces. I'm losing Daniel, and now I've lost the cottage, too.

"You're a good girl," I tell her.

"So are you," someone says behind me.

Deep, dulcet tones take aim with an arrow. A clear voice, firm and insinuating so much more than I meant, strikes my heart like his own personal bull's-eye.

My hand freezes on Bessie's nose.

I lower my head, clenching my eyes closed. I must have hit my head because I'm imagining things.

Daniel is real, but he's not here. He's in New York. Somehow, he manages to have me smiling even in his absence. A balm to my bruises, even from far away.

The warmth of his hand splays across my shoulder blades, causing me to gasp. When he slides both hands around my waist, he presses his chest to the back of me, and nuzzles his face into my hair.

"I love you. I'm sorry I wasn't here for you, Sunshine," Daniel whispers.

I turn so fast that my nose scrapes across his chest, embracing him so hard that even the ghost of him couldn't escape. I dare to look up, hoping my imagination didn't totally run away from me, and this is a figment of my imagination, too.

The soulful brown eyes that I could spend hours staring into, and have, peer down at me. The soft wave of his hair that's always a little messy from tugging looks especially unkempt. I run my fingers over the scruff of his jaw as if he wanted to get to me so fast that he didn't have time to shave.

His strong arms refuse to let me fall for anything besides him.

"You're real," I say, a smile slipping across my face.

"I'm real." Cupping my cheek, he kisses my head and then lingers on my lips, filling the parts of me that have been empty since he left. "I've been looking for you."

A tear falls as I find his hand, folding my fingers with his. "I've been right here all along."

## CHAPTER 30

DANIEL

"We need to preserve the natural beauty of our land by keeping it in the hands of someone who plans to have generations come after them. *Me.* I want my kids and grandkids to play hide-and-seek in the woods and swim in the water off the shoreline, not have a mega resort built where my parents got married or where they're now buried."

*She's sold me.*

But I'm not the critic between Mrs. Dover and me.

I don't think Mrs. Dover knows I'm out here. Summer set me on the front porch in a rocking chair to wait it out, saying it would be more comfortable than in the car. I don't think so, but I do think she wanted me close, so I'm happy to be outside this screen door. I figure it's no great secret that I'm here since I drove her after she insisted that she still had to shoot her shot even though she missed the deadline.

*My determined, strong girl.*

With the door wide open for Bessie and me to overhear the conversation, I listened to Summer tackle this presentation and nail it after she'd been in an accident, and I surprised her out of nowhere. I'm proud of her. Prepared with bullet points and heartfelt stories, she has me convinced. I'll buy the whole damn town for her if she asks.

There aren't any indicators of where Mrs. Dover stands on the topic, though. She's not spoken much, letting Summer say what she needs to ... even when it takes her a little longer to get to her destination.

The mention of "generations coming after" her doesn't twist me up like it would have in the past. Roman squashed any fears I had about having kids. *But marriage?* After watching my parents, I've never felt the need to walk down the aisle. If anything, I've felt the pull *not* to do it.

Summer, on the other hand . . . There are holes in my heart that only she can fill. And that has me reconsidering my stance on many things these days.

"Summer," Mrs. Dover sighs heavily from her chest. "It's too late to convince me. I've already made my decision."

*What?*

The sudden scrape of chair legs across the hard floor is followed by rapid footsteps. "Please, Mrs. Dover, I know I was late. The roads were wet and—"

"The contract has already been drawn up."

I don't know Mrs. Dover, but I don't like the short tone she's using with Summer. My jaw clenches as I continue listening—promising myself that I'll do what I promised and stay on the porch. Not that Summer needs me to handle this for her. My girl is brilliant. But I can't help that it gets under my skin to hear anyone be unkind to her.

*Doesn't she know what she's gone through today? Damn.* She could be more understanding.

"Our families should get to experience Mountain Laurel Cove like we've had the blessing to do," Summer says. "I have the mon—"

"I've heard enough." The click of Mrs. Dover's shoes crossing the room is easily deciphered from the softer soles of Summer's. They're louder with every step. "Come with me, Summer."

The screen door flies open. I stand, dragging my hands down the front of my pants, meeting Mrs. Dover's eyes for the first time. She looks me over as she comes outside, leaving the door to swing for Summer to catch.

*Lady, you're skating on thin ice with me.*

"You're my tenant?" she asks. Her hard stare would be intimidating if I didn't face guys on the ice who want to end me every game. She thumbs over her shoulder. "You're Summer's gentleman?"

No final answer has been given to Summer. Mrs. Dover might have contracts drawn up, and she could have even taken a deposit. But even if those things are true, they aren't final if they aren't executed. As much as I want to rip into this woman—as much as my conscience will let me rip into an older woman, I need to think about what's best for Summer.

A little charm never hurt anyone, and it's definitely closed a few deals for me over the years. Maybe, just maybe, it can close one for my girl, too.

"Yes," I say, reducing the gap between us. I shake her hand. "I'm Daniel Sutton. It's nice to meet you, Mrs. Dover."

She searches me with wary eyes, as if she hasn't made up her mind about me.

"I refunded your rental fees this morning after hearing how extensive the damage at that cottage is," Mrs. Dover says. "I want to personally apologize for the hassle it caused."

The sinking of Summer's shoulders behind Mrs. Dover pulls my gaze to her. *She lost the bonus.* It was the only reason

I didn't bother requesting a refund. I knew it would roll down to Summer losing money when she needs it more than ever.

I glance at Mrs. Dover. "Things happen." My gaze returns to Summer again, and a soft smile graces my lips. "It worked out in my favor."

Emotion fills the deep breath Summer inhales, her dream slipping from her grip and hope draining from her eyes. She clings to my gaze as if it's a life preserver and the only thing keeping her from breaking down.

I want to bring her to my arms, hold her, and whisper, *"We'll get through this. Together, we can get through anything."* Selfishly, that's for me. She wouldn't want that in front of her employer, though. I get it. I wouldn't either.

Mrs. Dover lifts her chin. "I was just telling Summer the decision has been made and the contracts drawn." It's unclear why she's telling me. I'm not involved in their business dealings. But the way she says it gives me an opening, and I'm taking it.

"I'm sorry to hear that," I say carefully. "Is there anything either of us can do to change your mind?"

"No. I'm stubborn in my ways." She walks to the door again and pulls it open. "Would either of you like a glass of lemonade before we get started?"

Summer's eyebrows shoot to the pale-blue painted ceiling as she latches onto the door and pulls it wide open. "When you say get started—"

"It means get your caboose in here and let's finalize the deal."

Glancing at me for reassurance, like she might be misinterpreting, Summer turns back to Mrs. Dover. "Are you serious?"

"I'd say as serious as a heart attack," Mrs. Dover says.

"But at my age, heart attacks aren't something anyone should joke about."

I bite my lip to hide a grin. My opinion of Mrs. Dover is already changing, but I'm squarely Team Summer until the ink is dry.

"But we haven't even discussed money," Summer stammers.

Mrs. Dover leaves us at the door, calling to us over her shoulder. "We don't need to. You're like family, better than most of mine." She stops and looks back. "Look, Summer ..." She glances at me and then back at Summer under a tight-lipped smile. "I listened to the proposal. I saw the dollar signs that came along with it as well. It's not easy to pass up that kind of money. I joke that I'm an old woman, but I'm only seventy this year. I could live for another forty years in Mountain Laurel Cove."

*Forty years?* She's being generous, but I'm not correcting her. Especially when this sounds like my Sunshine is about to get everything she wants. I move behind Summer, holding the door for her.

Mrs. Dover sighs as if a long battle is finally over. "They had a parking lot across from the docks, and they plan to tear down our historic downtown and replace it with what they call a 'more efficient way to shop.' I call it a generic strip center you can find anywhere but here currently." She shrugs. "They sucked the personality away from our little town. That's when I realized, I don't need the money. Bessie and I are doing just fine. But I do want someone who cares as much as you to own it. So you are the only person I'm willing to sell that property to, but I'll do ya one better and give it to you. Seems right with your property bumping up to it and the family history." For the first time, a smile touches her lips. "It's yours, if you want it."

Summer gasps, holding it in her lungs. She's in shock. Her hands tremble at her sides while she watches Mrs. Dover with wide eyes.

I lean down with her head blocking my mouth from view, and whisper, "Breathe, Summer." I rub small circles against her back. "Breathe."

Her breath is harsh as she sucks air into her lungs. Flipping her gaze to me, she asks, "Am . . . Am I hearing things?"

"I think your hearing is just fine." Giving her the slightest encouragement forward, I say, "Go get your cottage."

A burst of happiness wiggles her shoulders as it sets into her expression. "I want it."

Mrs. Dover laughs. "Well, get in here and let's get this done before *Wheel of Fortune* comes on."

Summer stays, troubling her lip at the threshold of her past and future. I've always known her heart's rightful direction. At this moment, that's forward. But when she takes that first step and then both feet land solidly on Mrs. Dover's hardwood floors, I worry about being left behind.

I signed a multi-year contract with The Breakaways this morning for more money than any player in the league. I have a guaranteed payout built in, even if I get injured or fired. Regretting signing my own contract pumps through my veins as she walks away from me. "Summer?"

She stops and looks back with a smile worthy of her nickname shining on her face. Holding her hand out, she says, "Are you coming?"

It's the happiness in her features, the steadiness in her eyes that washes any doubt, any fear, away from me. Yes, things might just have gotten more complicated. But complicated doesn't mean impossible. And when it comes to us and our love, nothing will stand between us.

I take her hand, lacing our fingers together. "Yeah. I'm coming."

Mrs. Dover is mid-conversation, like we'd been in her kitchen the whole time listening. ". . . we'd be having a different conversation if you had harmed Bessie with your vehicle."

"If it helps, she seemed her usual self when I was petting her," Summer says.

Picking up a file, she stills her hand as she stares at Summer. "You pet her?" The astonishment is unmistakable, though I can tell by the twist on Summer's face she's thinking the same thing—*what's the big deal?* "You pet Bessie?"

"Yes. She's a gentle girl."

Mrs. Dover drops into a chair on the other side of the table. "But no one pets her. She won't even let me. I coax her with carrots, but she's a moody girl if I try to pet her." Handing us the file, she says, "If Bessie trusts ya, I do, too. The notary is on the way. She and your gentleman friend can be witnesses to validate the sale."

When we sit down, Summer slips her hand into mine on top of my lap. I catch her excitement in a glance and smile with a squeeze of my hand.

And when the notary arrives, we get started.

As the t's are crossed and the i's are dotted, my mind has a moment to catch up. I think through everything, starting with the moment I met Summer.

My life hasn't been the same since that ray of sunshine came into my life. I've known it for a while. *But that gutted feeling that I had on the porch?* That's the tell. That's the truth —truer than anything in the world.

I've wanted many things in my life. My sights have been set on contracts and Stanley Cups, stats and titles. Everything I've wanted for myself has had something to do with ice. Ironically, everything I want now has everything to do with Sunshine.

*I want Summer.*

Hell, I might even need her.

There's not a signing, milestone, or performance bonus that comes anywhere close to being as attractive to me as her. Being in her orbit is like winning the Stanley Cup times a hundred, and holding her hand is far better than lifting the Cup over my head.

She's it for me. But I won't be responsible for dimming her dreams.

My life is on the road and in the city where my son lives. Hers is here in Mountain Laurel Cove.

I don't know how we're going to make this work, but we will.

*We have to.*

## CHAPTER 31
### SUMMER

"Summer?" Daniel grumbles, lowering my arm from his chin. He's so gentle, as if the bruises on my body from the crash are much worse than they really are. "It's a little tight around the neck." His bobbing Adam's apple tickles the inside of my elbow as he clears his throat. "Any reason you're squeezing so hard?"

"I want you to stay," I say, jutting my bottom lip out. The idea isn't revolutionary—I've said it a million times in the past few hours. He just likes to hear me say it.

Hooking his fingers through a small opening under my arms that I left unguarded, he manages to loosen my hold on him and take a deep breath like I'd cut off his air circulation. *And people call me dramatic.*

"I don't want to leave either, but think of all the things you can accomplish at the cottage without me bugging you."

"You never bug me."

"You'll be so busy, you'll barely notice I'm gone."

"Impossible." I steal every opportunity I get. Diving into the exposed nook of his shoulder, I drape myself over him, hoping I can keep him from leaving. It will never work, and

I know it *can't* work. He must go back to the city. But lying this close to him gives me comfort, like there's a chance one day that things will be different ... and he can stay. "Can't you stay one more day?" I ask, the words slightly more of a beg than I care to admit.

Rubbing my back gently, he slows his hand.

He might like me to ask him to stay, but it only makes it harder to actually leave. We both know that our time together is up. The deed must be done, whether we hate it or not.

Each visit we manage to squeeze in makes it that much harder to part. I thought, or maybe hoped, that it would become natural to see him here and there. That I would be able to go about my life without his presence, as if half of my heart wasn't missing.

I was wrong.

His touch lightens even more as he drags his calloused fingers along my spine. My lashes drift closed as I listen to his heart beating steadily in his chest. Breathing him in, I could fall asleep without much effort. When he yawns, I know he could, too.

It was a late night. We stayed up much longer than we should've because sleeping when we only have precious hours together feels like a waste. He tended to my wounds—a slight cut to my arm, a big bruise on my leg, and a knot on my forehead. I, in turn, tried to kiss away the pain from the bruise on his ribs he received from the end of a hockey stick. It was a tender, sweet night that flowed at a slower pace, allowing us time to appreciate the small details like a tiny birthmark on his back and the thin scar that remains on the front side of my hip from a rope swing accident when I was twelve. So different from our usual nights together. But I wouldn't change it for the world.

"I wish I could stay another day," he finally replies, his voice low. "Three weeks of intensives with the new players start in about . . ." He glances at the clock on the nightstand. "Four hours."

*Ouch.*

My heart sinks as guilt riddles me. Complaining won't help, but it will make him feel guilty as he makes the long drive back to the city. He'd stay if he could. He just ... *can't.*

Tracing a figure eight on his shoulder, I sigh. "There's enough time for a quick nap before you head back."

I love the span of his hands when he holds onto me, covering my entire rib cage effortlessly. Sliding them over my hips, he clamps down on the cushion of my backside and gives it a good squeeze. "Yeah, we could nap," he says playfully. "Or . . ." He palms me until his fingertips bite into my ass.

With my cheek against his chest, I smile. "Yeah. Let's do that instead."

## CHAPTER 32

SUMMER

*SIX WEEKS LATER . . .*

My stomach tightens as the ache reaches my heart before I can stop it. I should be used to being without him by now, but another passing day doesn't dull the pain. It worsens it. And right now, the loneliness hurts so much that it's hard to breathe.

I gaze out the window at the water and feel my spirits sink.

When we promised each other that we'd meet up as often as possible, I had no idea that it wouldn't be all that possible. Daniel's preseason training is intense, and his schedule isn't nearly as forgiving as it was this summer. The couple of days he did get free, he spent with Roman on back-to-school outings. And the tourist season in Mountain Laurel Cove was the busiest that I can remember. It took all hands on deck to keep things going, but we did it. The Honey Hive has been wildly successful, and Dolly's new front porch is proof.

"I hope you picked out the tiles," a voice seeps into my spiraling thoughts, making me jump.

I look up, happy not to be met with a plumber's crack today. "Huh?"

"If you want this project finished on time, we're going to need the new tiles," Willie says, standing next to where the tub basin used to sit.

*Tiles?* Right. "Oh yeah. Those were ordered last week, but I thought you had a lot more to do."

"Once I got beneath this floor, the pipes to the kitchen looked in better condition than I thought. I replaced a few O-rings and sealed a few places, but the PVC for the drain lines isn't cracking like it is in here, and the copper looks solid."

"What does that mean?"

He grins. "It means less money you'll have to spend."

"Music to my ears, Willie."

Kneeling again, he pulls a wrench from his toolbelt and looks at me like I'm intruding. "I should have this bathroom put back together in a few days. You can bring in your reno guys to repair the floors and walls."

"Thanks for the update. Keep up the good work," I reply, taking a wide berth around the beige couch in the living room when I rush past it to exit. I still can't look at it without the memory of Daniel making me tingly.

I shut the front door behind me, my gaze catching on the waterline in the distance. Instead of rushing back to the house, I walk across the deck and down to where Daniel set up the Adirondack chairs for us. I never moved them back. It felt weird, like I was erasing pieces of our time together.

They look good there. *So did he.*

I take the seat he loved most and run my hands lightly over the painted wood. A breeze blows through this muggier

September afternoon, providing a bit of relief that my heart refuses to give me.

My brain starts calculating the time until I might see Daniel again. For someone who hates math, I spend an awful lot of time with numbers these days. I'll do anything to make this work between us, but how do we bridge the distance? It's the missing piece of the puzzle, one I'm finding myself wondering more and more if it was ever included in the box at all.

"I hate this," I groan softly, the words swept away on the breeze.

Rocking back, I sling my arms over my knees as I pull them to my chest. I take a deep breath, resting my head against the chair and letting my gaze sweep over the property. At least the cottage is coming along faster than I anticipated. That's one silver lining to this dreary situation.

"Stop it." I sigh, dropping my knees down. "You're not going to sit here and sulk. It's not going to fix anything."

I drag the Adirondack chair back to the deck and angle it like it should be—perfectly placed with the feet between the lines on solid wood planks. The devil is in the details.

*Devil . . .* Grinning, a warmth spreads through my veins. I have my own personal bad influence. The Maverick himself.

But just as the grin appeared, so did a host of unshed tears.

A swell of emotions rises in my chest, and I fight hard not to succumb to them.

*How can I finally have everything I've ever wanted and still feel ... sad? Overwhelmed? Alone?*

I wrap my arms around my stomach and gaze across the water. The sun warms my cheeks. My eyes close as peace settles across my soul.

*"You're strong in mind and resilient . . . doesn't mean you have*

*to walk life's path alone . . . You'll know when you meet them. They'll be the ones there when you need someone most."*

A solitary tear drips down my face as my mother's voice echoes through my head. Her words are so perfect, so desperately needed. It was like she knew all those years ago that I would be in this place at this time and need to hear them. From her.

"What do I do?" I whisper, opening my eyes again.

*"You don't have to be strong all the time."* Daniel showed up when I needed him most. *"You don't have to travel life's path alone."*

My heart clenches, but I laugh as more tears fall down my face and wonder if I'm losing my mind. My head was caught in a future I thought I wanted. But the fog has lifted. The sadness brightened. The overwhelming sensation of fighting a losing battle has vanished. And my true path has never been clearer in my life.

The puzzle piece that I worried was missing is right in front of my face.

*"A missed opportunity can turn into regret."* Dolly's words strike like a lightning bolt. *"Go have the kind of fun that leaves the town gossiping."*

I refuse to live with regrets. I know what I need to do. "It's time I break some rules," I say, laughing and wiping the tears from my cheeks.

My heart pounds as I race back to the pink house and head straight for my bedroom like a woman on a mission. I sit at my desk, grab a pen and a piece of paper, and let the words flow.

*Dear Daniel,*

I hate to begin this note by inflating your ego, but here we are.

You were right.

I'll give you a minute to enjoy that before I move on.

I've grown up feeling like I must care for everyone around me and that accepting help from others makes me weak. I must be strong. I must stand tall and take the hits to protect others from feeling their effects. But what I've realized lately is that isn't the case. I just needed the right person to walk into my life and allow me to set down my shield.

The way you love me is breathtaking. You make me feel safe and supported, cared for and worthy. You love me when it's inconvenient and messy while loving you makes me feel strong and capable of anything—even being vulnerable.

I've been so busy with the renovation that I lost sight of the goal. It wasn't about making it pretty. It was about making it a home. I picked out the tiles and the faucets with renters in mind, so they would be comfortable. And feel at home. But that's not what I want.

Well, I want it to be a home. Our home.

It will be our place together, where we can raise Roman and maybe our own children.

Writing that makes me panic a little. Not because I don't mean it, but because I hope it's not too forward. But I've been a rule follower my whole life. It's time to break a few for you.

But laws will still be enforced because I learned my lesson with the accident.

I love you, Daniel Sutton. And I want you to know that my heart is yours and my life is with you. I looked around today and realized I have everything I ever wanted, and none of it makes me happy because you're not here.

You are my home. You are my everything.

XOXO,

Summer

## CHAPTER 33
DANIEL

"You want me to show you how to put the biscuit in the basket, Maverick—*Oof*."

The words are barely out of my mouth before I'm sliding backward on my ass after being blindsided. *What the actual fuck?*

"Landers!" Coach yells. "Out. Now."

Skating away, Landers throws his arms up like he didn't just body check one of his own teammates. "Come on, Coach. It's not my fault he can't take a hit."

Kovlov circles me once before skidding to a stop. He watches me warily as I get to my feet, as if he's trying to decide how to handle a pissed-off me.

"He's a goon on the ice, Mav," Kovlov says.

I stare at him. "No fucking shit." Adjusting a glove, I skate toward the bench. "Well, that *goon* is about to get his teeth knocked the fuck out."

Today started out so well with a FaceTime call with Sunshine. I got to practice early, felt like a million bucks, and then it all went to shit with these new twentysomething kids the franchise picked up in the offseason. I won't take their shit. That was Landers's free hit. He'll pay a price the next time. They'll learn that I'm not the one to fuck with. I only wish the learning curve wasn't so steep.

Slamming my skates into the wall, I glare at Coach. "You going to handle your boy?"

"Working on it." He moves down the bench, standing in front of me. "Stop antagonizing him."

"Tell me you're kidding."

"I didn't stutter, Sutton."

My jaw dusts the ground. "It's *my fault*? I've done a lot of shit, for sure, but I've never taken out *a teammate*."

Coach dips his chin, glaring at me. "Oh, that's rich, coming from you."

"I stand corrected," I say, unflinching. "I've never taken out a teammate who didn't deserve it."

"Neither has Landers." He turns away from me, clapping his hands to gather the team's attention. "Get back out there, Landers. Try to remember you're on the same team as Sutton."

Landers skates by me, pointedly not looking my way. He's skating a little stiffer than usual. It's the posture of someone who knows they now have a mark on their forehead.

*Good.*

"Don't fuck with the big dogs, little puppy, or you're going to find out who's boss in this barn," I yell at him.

He keeps skating, giving no indication that he heard me. But he did. We both know it.

I take a breath and give myself a second to recenter.

There's so much work to be done before the season starts, and by the looks of things, I'm not sure the preseason is enough time to get our shit together. There's a lot of talent on the ice, and we're fortunate to have veterans back for another year. But we're just not gelling as a team. We're not coming together. And if these new guys don't step up and get their heads on straight, we never will.

I glance at Coach. "You sure you can pull this team together in two weeks before preseason starts?"

He takes off his hat, scratching between the few hairs hanging on for dear life. His gaze sweeps across the arena. With every inch it moves, his frown deepens.

"This is what we have to work with," he says, putting his hat back on. "We have the best players in the league. If we can stop the rookie's bad habits and the veteran's egos, we might have a chance."

I feel his sigh in my hockey soul.

"Whatever happens," I say. "It's going to be a hell of a season."

"It sure is." He motions for me to get back on the ice. "Now let's get to work."

The next few hours go by quickly—thankfully, with no additional blindsides or bullshit. Everyone puts their heads down and does their job. By the end of practice, I'm slightly more hopeful that we can create some semblance of an actual team before we take the ice against an opponent.

I hang around the bench until everyone else has gone to the locker room, then grab my stick and a puck. It's my favorite time of the workday. With the arena quiet and my body calm after a blistering practice, I have the place to myself. I missed having the warm-up before practice because I had to run a few errands. Important, but it stole the time I like to put in prior to dealing with others.

This is where champions are made. It's where you get

ahead. Working on the basics, creating muscle memory—putting in time when everyone else is relaxing. This is the time that matters.

I work on a few shots that gave me a bit of trouble today and kill another hour. It's one hour less I'll have at home, missing Summer.

*Fuck, I miss her.*

I miss the way she laughs at the most random things and the way her smile lights up my insides. I crave her touch, kisses, the taste of her tongue first thing in the morning. Every day without her feels off. Unbalanced. Incomplete. Less in every way.

I just . . . *I love her.*

"Screw this," I mutter, heading for the tunnel. I need to hear her voice. In reality, I need to see her, to touch her, but hearing her voice will have to suffice.

But just as I turn toward the exit, it's not the mouth of the tunnel that catches my eye. It's the woman in the stands just to the right of it.

Ten rows up.

Summer stands.

My speed slows and a smile stretches across my face. *She's here?* As if she sensed the desperation I've been feeling.

She comes running down the steps to the edge of the tunnel and leans over. "Can I have your autograph, Maverick?" she teases.

Setting my stick against the wall, I chuckle. "I can do you one better." I pull off my gloves, dropping them on the floor and dumping my helmet right after.

I missed that smile shining for me like I'm the only one in the world deserving of its light.

"Oh yeah?" she asks, grinning. "What's that?"

"I'll show you."

Planting that fine ass of hers on the ledge, she swings her legs over. "You got me?"

"I got you." *I'll always have you, Sunshine.* She hops into my arms, and I turn, heading back onto the ice. "Hold on." Wrapping her legs around my center, she loops her arms around my neck.

Her giggle melts me. Having her in my arms knocks a weight that I've been carrying across my shoulders onto the rink. For a few moments, at least, my world is righted on its axis. *Complete.*

"What are we doing, babe?" she asks.

"Babe? I like that." I grin at her, still not believing my own eyes. "Just thought I'd take you for a spin."

She caresses my face, her thumb running under my eye where a bruise is healing. She places a kiss there. "I don't like this."

"Part of the game."

"I still don't like it." She looks at me, her eyes soft at the edges. "I missed you. A lot." In a heated crush, her lips find mine.

The lights in the arena seem to fade, and the sound of my skates cutting through the ice grows distant. It's just my girl and me together like it should always be.

Far too soon, she pulls away. "I needed that."

"I need much more than that." I kiss her again. "Let me get changed, and I'll show you all you've missed."

Her smile falters. "I can't."

I flinch, pulling away to see more of her face. *What does she mean she can't?* She drove all this way. "Surely, you're coming home with me, right?"

"I have about ten minutes before my car gets towed," she says, then catches herself. "Fall's car, actually. If it hasn't already."

"What are you talking about?"

She sighs. "My car is still out of commission, so I borrowed Fall's. But she has an overnight shift at the hospital, so I promised her that I would be back before then. But I couldn't find parking since the arena garage is closed. So I parked in a loading and unloading zone at the end of the block. Her eyes widen. "I probably need to go."

"You came here for a kiss?" I ask, confused. Not that I'm mad about it, but it seems like a little wild decision . . . even for Summer.

"No. I came here to give you something."

I skate back to the tunnel and set her back on her feet. "They have delivery companies these days, you know."

She laughs. "I know. But this needed to be hand-delivered. With a kiss."

I pop my skate guards on the blades and step off the ice just in time for her to hand me an envelope with my name on it.

"What's this?" I ask, starting to open it.

She places her hand on mine. "Wait. Don't open it in front of me."

"Why?" *Shit.* My stomach drops. Is this a break—

"It'll be embarrassing."

"For whom?" I ask, holding it on my palm like it's a hot potato.

She grins. "Me."

My hackles lower. My curiosity is piqued, but I would never want to embarrass her—even if I'm dying to know what was so important that she drove all this way to hand deliver an envelope just to turn right back around to drive back again.

"I really gotta go," she says, frowning. "It was so . . ." She sighs, but this time, a smile spreads like it's staying put. "It was good to see you. You look great. Sexy on that ice."

"You're beautiful, as always." Her hair is pulled back, and she's wearing a T-shirt and jeans that fit just right. Damn, she looks good. "You sure you can't stay? I can be outta here in five minutes if I skip the shower."

She reaches up on her tiptoes and presses a kiss against my lips. "I can't. I love you, though."

"I love you, too, so much."

Her cheeks flush before she kisses me again. Then she turns to leave, picking up pace the further she gets away from me.

"Summer?" I call out.

"I'm really probably getting towed," she says over her shoulder. "Call me when you get into your car. I have a long drive, and we can chat on my way back to the Cove." She turns a corner and is gone.

*What the hell just happened here?*

I get to the empty locker room to remove my skates and stretch. My muscles are tight, but the envelope Summer gave me is too enticing to ignore.

*Dear Daniel,*

*You were right.*

*You make me feel safe*

*. . . Our home.*

*It will be our place together, where we can raise Roman and maybe our own children.*

*. . . You're not here.*

*You are my home. You are my everything.*

*XOXO,*

*Summer*

My heart pounds as my eyes bounce through her words once more before they settle inside my brain. *This means . . .*

"Fuck!"

# CHAPTER 34

SUMMER

"Oh, thank God," I say, panting as Fall's car comes into view. *It's still there.*

I stop, planting my hands on my knees to catch my breath. I'm no runner, but I did my best running impersonation all the way from the arena for fear that the car would be gone before I made it back. It didn't hurt anything that running got me farther away from Daniel, making it that much harder to turn around.

The sky is dark too soon for the hour, with gray clouds hovering above, threatening rain. At least I'm in my sneakers if it starts to pour. I shove off my knees and start down the sidewalk again as a bolt of thunder strikes in the distance.

I pick up my pace as even darker clouds roll in. A woman walks toward me with a concerned look on her face. I give her a small smile as I grow closer, wondering if I should say hello or nod kindly as I pass. I don't know the etiquette in New York.

"You should run," she says as the distance between us diminishes.

*Huh?* "It's not raining yet."

"A man is chasing you. Run!"

*What? A man chasing me?* My heart leaps as my feet falter, and I look over my shoulder and find Daniel blasting toward me still in his Breakaways uniform.

"Summer!" he shouts.

"Daniel? What are you doing?" I ask, coming to a full stop. I glance back at the car to make sure it hasn't been towed.

The lady marches by, muttering something under her breath.

He covers the distance twice as fast as I did. At least he has the decency to gasp for breath as he takes me in his arms. "You can't leave—"

"I have to," I say, taking in the way his eyes scrunch at the sides as he peers down at me. "I don't want to. But Fall needs her car for—"

"No. I mean, you can't leave before I tell you . . ."

"Tell me what, Daniel?"

He licks his lips as rain begins to sprinkle from the sky like glitter. He searches my eyes, looking for something that I can't exactly name. I stare back at him, trying not to lose myself in his beautiful browns like I usually do.

I snuggle in closer. "Not that I mind being in your arms this long, but what do you want to tell me?"

He takes a deep breath and closes his eyes. The wind picks up, and so does the rain. It pelts the top of our heads and splashes into little puddles at our feet. We should be running for cover. *No, I should be in the car and driving away.* But he ran after me for a reason, and rain and deadlines aren't keeping me from finding out why.

"Daniel?" I prompt again.

He takes a breath as his eyes open. This time, they're steady. Like he knows exactly why he just raced down the sidewalk to find me in a rainstorm. "I needed to tell you that I love you."

Cupping his cheek, I kiss the other. "I know. I love you, too."

The statement sounds more like a question than anything because, while it's true—I love him with my whole heart—I don't think that's what he really wanted to say.

My mouth goes dry as I consider all the ways this could go. "You can tell me anything, you know."

A big raindrop lands on the tip of his nose. It doesn't faze him.

"I was planning to do it this weekend, but you're here now. And I read your letter, and yeah, I want that with you, too. The home, a place for Roman, and . . ." He stares into my eyes, and a smile slips out. "And kids. *With you.* I want it all with you, Sunshine."

*Oh, my gosh.* Chills break out across my skin as his words sink into my brain.

Slowly, he releases me. Then he drops to one knee in the middle of Brooklyn.

I gasp, my right hand covering my gaping mouth as he stares up at me like I'm the only girl in the world.

"I got this for you," he says, smiling softly.

My heart is too big to fit in my chest, the beats so loud they drown out the rain that's falling harder.

A black velvet box is tucked safely in his hands. "My apartment hasn't felt the same since you left. You gave it soul with your sweet smile and brought it to life with your laughter. You brought it—brought *me* to life, Summer. You are my home. My heart. My love. My everything." He chuckles. "Those were some good lines."

I laugh as tears flow down my cheeks.

"But it's how I feel," he says earnestly. "I don't want this life without you in it. My career, the penthouse, the contracts. Nothing makes me whole the way you do."

Carefully, he takes a ring out of the box, then drops the box into his jersey.

My hand falls to my heart as I watch him hold the physical representation of the biggest promise a man can make between his fingers. A platinum band and a gorgeous diamond? It's too much. *He's too much.*

He's ... mine.

"Daniel ..." I say, my voice cracking from emotion. "I would've said yes with a Ring Pop."

He grins. "I'd already fallen in love with you. But seeing you with my son and watching how quickly you cared for him like he was your own, and how you two bonded, I knew you were the perfect partner for me. You'll also be an amazing mother to our children like you are with Roman. Summer Season—"

"Yes?" I reply too fast for him to finish.

He chuckles. "Will you marry me?"

I crash my mouth into his, and my arms hook around him as we come together. Our tongues touch and caress, slowing the frenzy as his hands hold me to him. We're left breathless and still grinning when we part again.

Sitting on his knee, I say, "Yes, Daniel. I'd love to marry you more than anything."

I look down to watch him slide the ring on my finger when we hear, "Hey man, sorry to interrupt. Are you The Maverick of Hockey?" When Daniel looks up, the guy says, "Shit, it is you. Can I get a picture—"

Daniel's eyes narrow at the intruder, losing his smile. "I'm kind of busy. I'll give you a photo if you can give me a minute here."

"Sure. Sure. I'll just wait over—"

"Yeah, you do that," Daniel says. When his eyes return to mine, he kisses me gently. "Sorry."

"It doesn't matter. We're engaged, babe." Nothing could ruin this for me . . . Lightning cracks, startling me as the sky opens with torrential rain. *Except for that.*

"What color is your sister's car?"

"Blue. Why?" *And the car getting towed . . .*

Daniel lifts me to my feet and runs with the speed of, well, a professional athlete, catching up to the truck that's backing up to Fall's car.

I slip between two other parked cars to catch up to Daniel, who's already talking to the driver by the time I reach them. I stop with my hands on my hips, huffing to catch my breath.

"This her?" the guy asks, eyeing me. I'm sure I'm quite the sight, soaking wet with my makeup running down my face.

"It is. This is my fiancée." I didn't expect to be called that so quickly after it happened. But, man, do I like it.

He tries to be a hard-ass, but eventually breaks. I get a smidge of a smile. "Congrats. Lucky woman."

"I am."

Daniel says, "Trust me, man. I'm the lucky one." He glances at the car before looking at the driver again. "Think you can release the car? There might be box seats in it for you."

The man grins this time. "What car?"

They shake hands as my shoulders sag in relief.

"Thank you. Thank you. Thank you," I say, sighing. "I appreciate this so much."

We wait on the sidewalk as he unhooks Fall's car.

As much as I want to be celebrating, I still must leave. Getting engaged is amazing, but it doesn't change the logistics or erase the promise I made to my sister to return her vehicle.

Daniel wraps his arm around me, not caring one bit that we're wet and running into one catastrophe after another. But, really, I don't care about that, either. It doesn't matter. I have everything I ever dreamed about. I have Daniel. I found my true home.

I lean my head on his shoulder, looking down. "You ran after me in socks?"

With a quick shrug, he laughs. "We only get one shot at this life. I had to go for it."

I turn, wrapping my arms around him just as the rain gives up. "I'm so glad you did." I kiss him, and this time, there's no rush. Until I remember I must get back . . . "I wish I could stay with you and celebrate."

"There's no one who can take Fall to work?"

A thought crosses my mind. *Why didn't I think of this earlier?*

I smirk. "You know what? There might just be." I dig my phone out of my pocket. "Hang on. I need to make a call."

I walk away as he supervises the car situation, and call the one person I know who will be more than happy to help. "Brandon?"

## EPILOGUE 1

DANIEL

*"Landers is taking a pounding by Beauchamp on his left. Deacon coming for the assist . . . Oh! That's rough. Deacon's gonna be feeling that tomorrow. Beauchamp's still in control."*

*"Landers isn't in the minors anymore. He can't freeze the puck for long. There's no way out. He shoots or turns it over."*

*"There's no way to make that shot from the boards, Dan. That puck is as good as gold for the Boston Rebels if he tries."*

*"Dallas is finally making it out of the block to help Beauchamp!"*

"Hey, Carston," I say, sweat dripping into my eyes. "Are you gonna take me out to dinner after humping me all night? Get off my fucking stick, dick."

Shoulder checking him, I finally break free from the asshole and dig my blades into the ice, charging to save Landers.

Damn rookies.

"What the fuck is going on?" I grumble, skidding into Dallas as he stumbles into the mess against the boards. Beauchamp knocks the puck from Landers when I get my stick in the mix of a board battle.

Time slows, the noise disappears, the crowds are gone. It's me and the puck.

This is my game. My arena. My goal.

I take possession, turning so fast that my opponent catches his stick on my skate and flips to the ice as I break away.

My blades scraping through the ice.

The blood rushing past my ears.

My father shouting at me when I was ten, "Don't fuck it up, Danny Boy," has always played on repeat in my head.

I close my eyes, no longer giving him power over me.

I own every one of my goals, trophies, and successes. I only play for me now. And my son.

My muscles push me forward, the stick an extension of my body. I open my eyes and shift my arms back, putting the puck in flight over the ice, cutting through the air over the goalie's shoulder.

Cutting behind the goal, I turn to watch it bounce against the net. "Yes!"

*"Maverick puts it away!"*

*"Goal! The Breakaways win!*

*"The Maverick of Hockey showing why he earned the title."*

*"Sutton is still going strong, Dan. Put the rumors to bed. I think we're going to be seeing him for years to come."*

*"Top of his game."*

Kovlov slams into me. "Fucking amazing, Mav!"

It was fucking amazing. My body vibrates with adrenaline as the moment washes over me. The energy from the fans is electric. The bench clears as my teammates rush to find me. Before they can do that, my gaze shifts to a set of the prettiest blue eyes staring down at me.

"I love you," she mouths, her hands clamped together at her chest. I lift a glove her way just before my team drives me into the boards in celebration. Their cheers ringing in my ears, I laugh to myself. Damn, it feels good to be a part of something great.

But it feels even better to have my son and fiancée here to witness a legend in the making.

"Good job, old man," Landers says, shoving my shoulder. "I knew you still had it in you."

"Fuck off, Landers."

"Got to keep you on your toes," He grins, skating away as the crowd grows louder.

"Mav-rick! Mav-rick!" The chants echo around the arena. "Mav-rick! Mav-rick!"

Kovlov moves out of the way, smiling brightly. "Get out there so your fans can see you."

Slowly, I skate toward center ice and bask in the moment. It's a victory on the scoreboard, for sure. But it's also a victory in other ways. I made it another year when not everyone thought I would, I've created a warm, stable home for Roman, and I'm marrying the best woman in the world.

It's good to be me.

I spot Roman and Summer at the glass and skate to them. My son's wide eyes are filled with admiration, something I hope he never loses for me. I push my forehead against his.

"Love you, kid," I say.

"Love you, Dad."

I pull away, my gaze traveling to Summer. She watches me with pride, but also with something that's way more important. With love.

Her hands touch the plexiglass. "So proud of you."

I take my gloves, drop them onto the ice, and press my palms to hers on the other side of the clear wall. "Marry me."

Holding up her left hand, she points at the ring. "I am marrying you."

"This weekend. Marry me, Sunshine. I don't want to wait any longer."

Her smile softens, and she nods. "This weekend." Nodding toward the ice, she says, "Go celebrate with your team. Enjoy it." She lowers her hands to Roman's shoulders. "We'll see you at the apartment."

I grab my gloves and join my team as they head toward the tunnel. Slipping my guards on, I look back to see Summer and Roman watching. My whole fucking world waves at me. I raise my hand, committing the moment to memory, then head to the locker room.

Celebrating with the guys used to be fun. Now, I want to see my family. I don't need loud cheers or bottles of whiskey passed around. I want to listen to Roman give a rundown of his favorite parts of the game, like he loves to do. He slips in a little advice to which I always reply, "I'll incorporate that next time." And then when he goes to bed, I'll hold my girl on a lounger on the patio, taking in the crisp fall air, and talking about all the things we want to do next summer in the offseason.

*It's my favorite season, after all.*

# EPILOGUE 2

## SUMMER

I hold no regrets for falling for Daniel—love at first sight or whatever someone says to make it feel less. Time wouldn't have given more than we have now. I regret not recognizing sooner that we're allowed to change and evolve—our priorities, goals, and even the rules we live by. They didn't allow for growth or for seeing what was right in front of my eyes. At least for a bit.

Once I knew how much I loved him, I fought for us. *And won.* Daniel and I won at love. But seeing him parked where he's supposed to park, away from the cottage, has me falling for him all over again.

Fall shifts into park and whips her gaze toward me. "Why is Brandon here?"

I pivot my eyes to see him and Spring setting up the chairs on the big deck. "He's a friend and offered to help." I study her green eyes, looking for any sign that gives her real feelings away because surely it can't be hate toward him. "He's the nicest guy."

"He's just . . ." She looks back at him again. "Too nice."

I open the door and get out when I can tell this conversation isn't going anywhere. Dipping back in, I say, "There's no such thing as too nice."

I shut the door and pull my dress from the back seat. Pulling a ceremony and reception together in three days hasn't been as fun as it should have been, but Dolly made it a potluck. Now I'm worried the entire town is going to turn out. Mountain Laurel Cove loves two things: a wedding and a potluck. You give them both, and they show up.

Fall whisks my dress from me and hurries into the cottage. "Hide your eyes. Bride incoming!"

I laugh, which feels so good after the craze of the past few days. Stopping just shy of the front door, I ask, "Safe to come in?"

"It's safe," Fall says, and then hustles me inside and drags me to the primary bedroom.

With a hard shut of the door, I turn startled. "Geez, Fall, what the heck?"

"Don't want the groom to see you, do you?"

I peek out the window but can't see the setup from this part of the house. "He's seen me plenty. That's how we got here." Seeing the water is calming, but I don't like the look of the gray clouds gathering for the ceremony. "Do you think it's going to rain?"

"Forecast says 100 percent."

"Lovely," I deadpan.

"At least your white dress isn't see-through. You wouldn't want to look like you're in a wet T-shirt contest."

Staring at her, I blink. And then again. "Guess that's a silver lining."

She drops onto the edge of the bed, and her gaze falls to the floor. "Wish Mom were here." When her eyes find mine again, she wrangles a smile, but the effort is obvious.

I sit next to her, wrapping my arm around her back. "I thought I was supposed to be the emotional one today."

With a laugh, a tear falls from her eyes. "Your to-do list was already too long." Her smile is genuine, and she shakes her shoulders. "I took it off your plate."

A knock has us both looking up. Fall wipes her eyes just as Winter walks in, shutting the door behind her. A quick smile to me gives way to her sitting on the other side of Fall. Tucking Fall's hair behind her ear, her lower lip juts out. "What's wrong?"

"I'm happy," she replies. "I'm just a sucker for a wedding."

Winter rubs her back and smiles. "Me too." Getting up, she comes around by me to sit. "How are you doing, big sis?"

"I'm good, really good." I take inventory of my emotions. For the past few days, I've been expecting to be hit with a blast of nerves or cold feet—but neither has happened. I'm just so incredibly happy. It feels so . . . right. "Is it weird that I'm just excited? I can't wait to marry Daniel and celebrate with everyone."

Winter says, "I think that means this is the right decision."

Fall leans forward with another swipe under her eyes. "Mom and Dad would have really liked Daniel."

Thinking about my parents has brought me immense sadness and comfort. As much as I wish they were here, I still carry them with me. I see them in my sisters, and in the bouquet Winter picked for me from their little haven.

When everyone was busy with their own emotions, I used to think I was never given the same courtesy to grieve. Things needed to get done. Kids needed caring for. Dolly needed support when becoming the guardian of four girls.

Finding my own happiness and sitting in that joy gives

me a new perspective. I was grieving all along. It just looked different. Now, I can rest from the weariness and set the sadness aside, carrying them in my heart down the aisle instead.

The door opens, and Spring peeks inside. "Are we getting dressed?"

"We're talking," I say, falling back on the mattress.

She comes next to me and lies back, with Winter and Fall following the lead.

"Sisters?" I whisper, feeling the love. I'm so dang proud of each of them and how far we've come. "I love you."

We roll together, hugging in awkward limbs and laughter. "Love you," each says before Fall says, "We need to get ready."

"It won't take long. Look," Spring says, pointing out the window. "It's raining."

Sitting up, I move to look for myself. "Saves time doing our hair."

Winter jumps up. "Wait, you're going to walk in that?"

I nod. "I am. Nothing will keep me from marrying him."

"Well," Fall starts, "we can move it indoors?"

"No. It's okay. Rain has been a part of every other major event that brought us together." I walk to my dress, running my fingers over the soft fabric of the tulle. "For everyone else, it's bad luck. For us, it's a good sign."

"Really?" Winter asks. "We're not doing our hair?"

We probably shouldn't be laughing as hard as we are, but it feels good to let it out, and the joy begins.

White umbrellas arch over the small crowd gathered on the

deck, sprinkles of rain tapping on the tops set the stage as pretty as a painting.

The front row holds a collection of my favorite color in dresses of varying styles to suit my sisters' tastes. They could have chosen any shade of blue they wanted, but they all showed up matching the sky on a sunny day. I'm in awe of how similar we all are in unexpected ways.

With swollen eyes from all the "happy tears" as she calls them, Dolly kisses my cheek and gives my hand a little squeeze under a large canopy where my future husband waits for me. "I'm so proud of you, sweet girl," she says with a sniffle and tap of tissue to the inside corners of her eyes. "You're going to have the most beautiful life together."

We are. I know it in my gut and heart. This process, while a little stressful just because we put it together quickly, has been so easy. And when we came up with the idea to get married before the start of the season—to stop wasting time and just do it—I felt peace.

I've only felt loved.

I hug her, the gravity of the occasion kicking in like the storm above did. Dolly joins Fall under her umbrella as I turn to face Daniel. *My love.*

Bucking traditions, a.k.a. breaking the ceremonial rules, the warmth of his embrace welcomes me into the fold of his arms. A kiss is placed on my head, and the gentle pressure of his lingering lips stirs my heart to beat faster. When he lifts, I pull back to catch his eyes still closed as he inhales me into his lungs, a small smile appearing right after. Slowly, he opens his eyes to see me as if he might be dreaming. His smile spreads so wide that I can't contain my own.

Happiness gets the better of me, and I laugh lightly. "It's raining on our wedding day."

"Doesn't matter." With our hands joined, he says, "No

storm nor any other circumstance can stop our love." He kisses my hand before admiring me. "You are so beautiful."

My hair is not how I would have ideally chosen, but it doesn't bother me that it's flatter to endure the changing weather. "We make our own luck, handsome."

"We don't need luck. We have each other."

I have never doubted how much we love each other and never will as I fall deeper into it with him.

The minister rolls through the ceremony and directs Daniel to say his vows. He shakes his head. "My girl will come first."

*Why does that sound like a promise for later as much as a statement for now?* I gulp, my cheeks coated in blushing heat.

Tightening my hold of his hands, I take a breath and look up into the assurance of his brown eyes. The rush of tears flows along my waterline. I close my eyes to try to keep them from falling, but one manages to break free, slipping down my cheek. Daniel catches it and brings it to his lip to kiss. "It's okay, Sunshine."

I nod and take a deep breath. "I didn't expect to meet the love of my life right next door, but there you were in swim trunks and a smirk, and I was a goner." A little stroke of the ego to kick off the festivities. "But it was the heart you wore on your sleeve for me that I was pulled so strongly toward that I couldn't stop long enough to talk myself out of it. And I couldn't be more grateful or blessed that I broke my rules for you."

I pour my heart out to him, wanting to share what the beauty of his love means to me.

And when it's his turn, his smile just about does me in. He fixes his gaze, so steady and strong on me, making me swoon through promises and sweet memories we've made, the connection we have, and how he feels fortunate to have found me for him and his son. "I vow to love you with all my heart, to follow your rules . . ." He smirks. "And to make your favorite breakfast food at least once a week for you."

He has me smiling, a laugh tickling my chest, and my heart in his hands. As he professes how we will always be a team and work for each other and together. And when it's time to seal our commitment with a kiss, his hands slide around my waist and wrap around my lower back.

Holding me close, he looks deep in my eyes, a ribbon of our hearts tying together. And when our lips meet, the pressure is confident, and the weight of balancing everything on my shoulders my whole life lifts as he lessens the load. A partner willing to walk life's path with me, like my parents always wanted for me. Like I hoped and dreamed that I'd find someday. Daniel is a dream come true, and every day I get with him will be the blessing I prayed for.

Daniel never had anyone worrying about him, though. He not only wants to take care of me, but I will also show him how much it means to me to be able to love him fully. Every flaw, perfect ab, and broken rule. I will always make him feel the love he has always deserved.

The sun sneaks through the clouds, shining bright above the canopy as our lips part, but my breath hasn't been caught quite yet as he looks at me. "I love you, Sunshine."

The cheers of our family and friends, even his mom making the trip, makes the moment even more wonderful.

We're given a beautiful afternoon for our reception. Roman has been attached to me as we mingle. He's been all smiles and chocolate cupcakes from the potluck table, and his happiness over the wedding has been so fun to watch.

I bend down and look into his brown eyes that match his daddy's. "I'm so happy you're my family."

Throwing his arms around my neck, he says, "I love you, Summer."

I hug him so tight, the sweet boy. "Love you too, Roman."

Then he runs off to spend time with his grandmother and Dolly.

Daniel's arms wrap around me from behind, and I find myself melting into him. He kisses my neck. "Do you know how much I love you?"

"Enough to marry me?"

He chuckles. "More than that."

"I heard about the carving in the tree," Winter says, walking up to us just before I was about to kiss my husband utterly inappropriately for public viewing.

Spring asks, "What are we talking about?"

Daniel replies, "There's a tree with a carving in it. CS #7."

"What does CS #7 mean?" Fall asks, handing me a glass of champagne.

I shrug. "We don't know." I sip, watching Brandon join the group with a bottle of beer with a ripped label.

His eyes on Fall, he smirks and says, "I know."

*Yours Truly, Fall is coming this August. Preorder now!*

## YOU MIGHT ALSO ENJOY

**Recommendations** - Looking for something to read after *XOXO, Summer* while waiting for *Yours Truly, Fall* to release? *I got you!*

***Read in Kindle Unlimited and Listen in Audio***

*Long Time Coming* - This brother's best friend, Single Dad story will have swooning, smiling until it hurts, and choosing a cowboy all day every day over a horse. *winks* **Turn the page to read Chapter 1.**

***Read in Kindle Unlimited and Listen in Audio***

*Never Got Over You* - Is third time a charm? Meeting on vacation leads to encounters that will change their lives in the most fun, sexy, and charming ways. You will fall along with them.

***Read in Kindle Unlimited and Listen in Audio***

*Along Came Charlie - Weddings, funerals, and New York City - these two Charlies have fate on their sides in this friends to forever (?) modern day When Harry Met Sally romance.*

# Long Time Coming

 Published in the United States of America. ISBN: 978-1-962626-39-2

# CHAPTER 1

**Christine "Pris" Greene**

FRIDAYS ARE the best day of the week.

I practically shoulder the door open to Peaches' Sundries & More in my rush to get inside. If I'm even five minutes late, I'll end up empty-handed. The smell of fresh bread escapes through the door as the bell chimes above my head.

Coming from the bright outdoors, I take a quick second for my eyes to adjust to the indoor lighting. And when they do, I'm not disappointed. One remains. One glorious cheddar biscuit sits inside the bakery display.

"Lauralee?" I call, walking toward the glass-and-brass-trimmed display. I'm used to my best friend greeting me when I walk in. When she doesn't, I peer above the counter and toward the ice cream on the right side of the register. "Lauralee?"

"In the back with some cookies," she says, her voice slipping through the crack of the swinging door to the back. "I'll be right out."

"I'm getting the last biscuit, okay?"

"It's all yours."

I lean over the counter to slide the case open from the back, but I can't wedge it open far enough. My stubborn side sends me toward choosing the more difficult route in everything I do, and since I have no intention of climbing over the counter, I prop my knees on a stool and try again. I just about have the buttery, cheesy bread of the heavens in my hand when someone says, "Pris?"

Startled, I slip forward, sending my ass into the air as I slide toward a face-plant on the linoleum floor. Big hands catch me, grabbing my hips as the strength of fingers dig into the plush of my lower waist.

*The voice . . .*

*The nickname . . .*

*The butterflies awakened from the dead now fluttering in my stomach . . .*

I'm brought to safety on the stool again and swirl around to come face-to-face with the same man I just dreamed about rather recently. Though I'll keep that tidbit to myself instead of giving him the pleasure. I smirk. "I haven't been called that in a long time."

His smile just about knocks me right off this stool again. I'd forgotten how potent it was. Although, judging by my heart's rapid pace, it didn't. I'm right back to that sweet sixteen little girl who righteously earned the nickname. "It's been a long time all around."

I can't help but notice his hands haven't left the curve of my hips, and it seems he notices at the same time. I'm released against my silent protests, leaving a chill where his warm palms once were. Regretfully, my brother's best friend never held me like that before. He didn't take the chance. The threat of death from the middle Greene sibling, my brother Baylor, might have played a part as well.

I set one foot down and then not so gracefully scuttle down until I'm solid on both, coming toe-to-toe with my childhood crush after eight years. A lot has changed.

His hair isn't as wild, though I wouldn't call those strands on top tame. The Pass's winds probably whipped through them when he arrived in town. A day or two worth of stubble only adds to the rugged good looks he was bestowed at birth. I have imagined a clean-shaven face from the last time I saw him. My memory didn't serve as well as the real thing does. I think he's even taller, if that's possible. *Damn him.*

"It sure has. Tagger Grange," I say, smiling like I still have a crush on the guy. I might. *Fine. I do.* The rolled-up sleeves and tailored pants aren't deterrents to scrambling my chemistry all over again for him. "What brings you back to Peachtree Pass?" Straightening the skirt of my dress after revealing a lot of leg in my almost tumble from the stool, I fuss about it. But when the hem anchors on the top of my boot, I leave it, not wanting to come off as nervous. This dress is the least of my concerns since the man in front of me is busy stealing my full attention.

A smile hasn't left his face, but it's not pure sunshine. The devil lies inside as he looks me over like my brothers wouldn't kick his ass if they caught him. Licking his lips, he takes a breath and slowly exhales. "It was time."

The way his green eyes hold my gaze, I start taking inventory of all the ways I could have made more effort today—a swipe of mascara and a coat of lip balm are all that I'm wearing on my face while I chose a dress I reserve when it's laundry day for everything else in my wardrobe. My cowgirl boots are scuffed and worn, broken in, and the most comfortable pair of shoes I own. I can't say I'd be wearing anything else other than these, but maybe something more feminine would have given me the confidence to stare into his eyes a little longer.

"Can I have these, Daddy?"

*Daddy?* I look down at the boy tugging on Tagger's hand. His eyes are green like his dad's, and his smile so sweet as he looks up at Tag like he's his hero.

Tagger squats down, getting eye level with him, and then eyes the bag of candy. "I think that's okay. Are you still wanting ice cream?"

But I'm still stuck on the daddy part. Seems Baylor has left a few details out of our conversations over the years. Still in a bit of shock by this news, I watch the interaction, utterly fascinated that Tag's a dad.

The blond-headed boy nods as his smile spans his face. "Yes, please."

Looking up at me, Tagger says, "This is my friend Pris—" Shaking his head, he blinks long and hard as if the habit was just too hard to break. "Miss Christine." He takes hold of his son's hand as he glances at his son and then at me again when he stands to his full height. "This is my son, Beckett Grange. Beck."

As if I wasn't already charmed by the past standing before me, my heart melts for this little cutie at his side. I kneel to shake his hand. "It's nice to meet you, Beck."

"You too, Miss Christine. How old are you?"

"Oh." My chin juts back in surprise. I start to laugh at Beck's bluntness. "I'm twenty-six. How old are you?"

"Six." His eyes flick up to his dad, and then back to me.

"I turn seven soon. Dad said I can ride a horse while I'm here."

"How fun. I love horses. Have you ridden one before?" I can't imagine raising a kid without the wide-open spaces I grew up with. The animals, and farm, the striking sunsets, and diving into the river on hot days. It was fun to visit Baylor in New York once, but I was a fish out of water. Austin isn't too far of a drive from here, but it's not the same culture shock to my hill country system.

"No. We're not allowed to go near them at the park."

"The horse carriages at Central Park," Tag slips in.

"Ah." I nod. "Yeah, they're doing a job. It's probably best not to disturb them. I have lots of horses if you'd like to come out to our ranch and see them."

His face clenches in excitement. "Yes, please."

"Great. We'll make sure it happens while you're visiting."

The squeak of the door swinging open alerts us to Lauralee entering from the back. Stunned, she stops, and the door practically hits her in the face. "Um." As she wipes her hands down the apron, her eyes volley between the two of us, then dips to Beck. "This is unexpected."

"Hey there, Lauralee. How are you?" Tagger's voice is smoother than I remember as if he's grown into more of himself over the years. He was always confident, but now there's an ease to his words that makes me think he's more at peace.

With his eyes set on her, he smiles, causing my sweet friend's cheeks pink. *Girl, I know the feeling firsthand.* When she pushes her hair back from her face, flour dusts her dark brown bangs, which she's been growing out for a year and are too stubborn to stay in the elastic at the back of her head. She moves to the counter, resting her palms on the hard surface. "I'm good, Tag. How are you?"

"Fine and dandy," he replies, which has my gaze racing to meet Lauralee's. We silently agree that, yes, he is, indeed, very fine. "Are you running the store these days?"

"Yeah, but my mom still comes in to work a few hours most days. Keeps her and my dad from getting on each other's nerves since they retired early. Also takes some of the load off my shoulders."

"Tell Peaches hello from me."

A tug on my skirt draws my attention down to Beck, who asks, "How do you know my daddy?"

"Oh, um." Another one of his little blindside questions causes me to laugh. I glance up at Tagger. "I've known your daddy all my life. He's best friends with my brother Baylor."

Tag's hand shags through his son's hair. "You know Baylor, buddy. That's Miss Christine's brother."

"He's my uncle," Beck replies proudly.

The sentiment warms my heart for many reasons, but maybe even more that my brother has family in the form of friends since he lives so far from Peachtree Pass, Texas. I stand again. "How's my brother doing?"

"He's . . . I don't think he'll ever change."

Smiling like we're both in on the joke, I reply, "I doubt it. It would take a miracle and the right woman to get that wild card back home."

He nods, seeming to know exactly what I mean. Baylor was never subtle in his pursuits, whether wrangling the cattle, pursuing his career in New York City, or catching women. They all fell into his golden boy hands without much effort.

I could say the same about the man standing here in Peaches, but it's best if I don't travel down unfamiliar roads. The four years that separated our birthdays felt like ten when we were young. Not so much now that we've grown up.

Tag encourages his son forward. "Go pick out your ice cream, and Miss Lauralee will get you what you want."

Lauralee grins. "Come on over. I have the best peach ice cream in the state, or if you like bubblegum, my personal favorite, you're in luck."

He runs toward her, dropping the bag of gummies on the counter, then presses his nose against the glass.

A tension that wasn't there sweeps between as if neither of us knows what to say or where to go from here. I don't let it build. "I—"

"I was thinking—"

We both laugh, letting the awkwardness fade. I ask, "You were thinking?"

He runs his fingers through his hair, something I watched him do a million times when we were younger. A shyness I don't recognize takes over his expression, and he lowers his gaze. "My parents sold the stables." He looks at me, this time with an intensity that makes me wish I had something to hold on to to steady me.

"I heard. A few years back, right?"

"Yes. It was a lot to handle without me or my brother being around. They always preferred a slower pace of the small farm to feed a family over housing the toys of ranchers who only visited every six months. They hated seeing them treated like prized possessions instead of animals that deserve care and respect." He shifts. "Anyway, I was going to pay Rollingwood Ranch a visit in hopes of introducing my son to one of your horses." The question isn't obvious in the words but is clear in his eyes.

"The invitation stands. Come out anytime."

"Thanks."

I find myself shifting in a way that makes me feel embarrassed. Am I flirting? Am I flirting with Tagger Grange? I smile. I sure am. "Maybe we'll even get you in some jeans and cowboy boots again, like old times."

"I might have left The Pass, but it never left me." He starts walking toward the counter, stopping even with me. With his hand brushed against mine, he lowers his head, and whispers, "It was good seeing you, Pris."

My breath stops in my chest, and before I have a chance to reply, he's already gone. I take a moment to myself and catch my breath again but fail to calm my racing heart before I turn around.

Lauralee hands him back his credit card and then shrugs. That's when I discover what the traitor has done to me. I clasp my lips closed because what am I going to do? Rip the last cheddar biscuit from Beck's sticky hands?

I'm supposed to be the grown-up here, but I'm feeling ready to stamp my foot in dismay and snatch it anyway. I won't, of course, but it's tempting, just like that biscuit.

Heading for the door, Tagger says, "Bye, ladies."

"Bye," we say in unison with a swoony sigh tainting our tone.

"Lordy, we're weak," I say to Lauralee as soon as the door closes behind them.

"Listen, we don't get much action in the middle of nowhere Texas. That it was *the* Tagger Grange . . . well, it's not the first time he's heard a woman swoon over him."

"True." Anchoring my elbows on the bakery display, I drop my head into my hands. "But why does seeing him make me feel like an insecure teen again?"

She rubs my shoulder. "Because we were when he lived here. Once he was gone, though, you flourished. You don't have to shrink just because your all-time crush is back in town. You could do the opposite and get him out of your system once and for all."

I pop back up, ideas filling my head . . . ideas I shouldn't even consider but suddenly am. "And by once and for all, you mean jump him?"

Laughing, she replies, "Or something a little more subtle like making love in the back of the Chevy."

Now I'm laughing. "Thank you for indulging me, but I think it's safest if we just stick to the platonic relationship we've always had as the younger sister of his best friend. No need to muddy the waters when he's only visiting for a few days." I push off and head toward the soda fountain. "I'm sure a week tops."

"Guess we'll see when he visits you out at the ranch."

"Guess so." I get a cola with light ice and two dashes of cherry cola and then cap it with a lid. Pushing the straw in, I return to the stool that had me almost meeting the floor in pursuit of warm bread and spin around once. "But I still need to keep my thoughts and intentions clean when it comes to him. His life is fifteen hundred miles away while I'm settled here like the previous seven-plus generations of Greenes." My chest deflates. "God, now I'm depressed."

"Don't be. You're a good daughter for coming home when you did. You've made a life for yourself." Smiling, she adds, "And you always have me. We can grow old together rocking on the front porch."

I pull a dollar from my pocket and lay it on the counter. "As appealing as that is, don't you miss having a guy look at you like you're prettier than a sunset could ever be?"

"I miss guys. Period." She rings up the soda and slides the money into the register. "You know you don't have to pay."

"But I always will," I singsong, walking backward toward

the door. "I'll take you up on that front-porch-rocking-chairs offer when we're old and gray, though."

She laughs. "Deal."

"In the meantime, keep me posted if any hotties come to town."

Throwing her arm out to the side, she says, "One just did, and you already friend zoned him."

"Tagger Grange can never be more than a friend. First, my brother would kill me." Holding out two fingers, I continue, "Second, I'm not sure I ever got the details of where things stand with his son's mother."

"They're not together."

My feet come to an abrupt halt. "How do you know that?"

"Peaches. She knows everything, and she's on the Peach Festival committee with his mother. She gets all the gossip at meetings."

My mom used to be on that committee before she passed. Hearing about it so suddenly has my chest tightening, though I know Lauralee would never mention something to hurt me. But not all wounds heal. "Then how did we not know he had a son?"

"We did know. I told you back when you—" She looks down and then says, "It was around the time of your return. A lot was going on back then."

More doesn't have to be shared, and I'd prefer if we didn't. Hoping to move past this, I reply, "Yeah." Refocusing on the man who was just at hand, I feel a little lighter again—mind and soul. "That still doesn't mean he's single, my friend." I start backing toward the door until my back rests against the handlebar. "So third, I'm sure he has a stable of women waiting for him back in New York City. La de dah and fancy pants. I'm just a small-town girl with dirt under my nails. I think I'm safe from falling under his spell."

"Again."

"You don't let anything slide, do you?"

"That's what friends are for."

"So are enemies." I laugh as the bell chimes when I exit. "You also owe me a biscuit."

"Next Friday," she calls out before the door closes.

I head to the truck, still laughing, until I notice my nails while reaching for the door. Shaking my head, I try not to feel embarrassed. It's not a competition for Tagger Grange's attention. I have too much on my plate to worry about being perfect for a man who's basically passing through town.

It still might be time to have a girls' night again to get my nails done and a haircut. I might be a whiz at cutting split ends, but my nails need outside help.

I start the truck and back out, creating a plume of dust behind me. Needing to get back to the ranch, I shift into drive and leave my encounter with Tagger right where it should be—in the rearview mirror.

But why am I still thinking about him when I cross onto Rollingwood Ranch property fifteen minutes later? I know. I just hate to admit it.

*It sure was good to see him again . . .*

~

Continue reading on Amazon, **Audible, Kindle Unlimited, Paperback, or in Audiobook.**

***The Peachtree Pass Series is now complete. Read the full series now.***

***Long Time Coming***

***Lead Me Knot***

***Small Town Frenzy***

# ACKNOWLEDGMENTS

*Thank you so much to this incredible team:*

Kenna Rey, Content Editor

Jenny Sims, Copy Editing, Editing4Indies

Kristen Johnson, Proofreader

Andrea Johnston, Beta Reading

From Cover Art: Khrystyna Bzovska

Back Cover Design: Mr. Scott

Formatting Design: Serendipity Formatting

*I also want to send Adriana Locke a big thank you and hug for all the support and love!*

*Thank you for taking this journey with me.*

*Sending my love always to my sweet husband and amazing sons, and Ollie, my little fuzzy co-worker for keeping me company. I love you all more than the universe! Thank you for your support and love. Love you always. XOXO, Me*

## ABOUT THE AUTHOR

Suzie loves a great view of the ocean, spicy margaritas, and spending her free time with her family and sweet dog, Ollie.

*New York Times* and *USA Today* Bestselling Author, S.L. Scott, writes character driven, heart-racing, and swoony romances that will leave you glued to the page. With stories ranging from witty beach reads to heart wrenching and heart healing, her stories are highly regarded as emotional, relatable, and captivating.

Her books are more than escapes for the voracious readers of today. They are journeys of the heart that always come with a happily ever after reward at the end.

Find her at: www.slscottauthor.com

www.ingramcontent.com/pod-product-compliance
Lightning Source LLC
La Vergne TN
LVHW041101080826
845145LV00007B/1654

* 9 7 8 1 9 6 2 6 2 6 6 2 0 *